The Galactic Mage Series

Book 1: The Galactic Mage
Book 2: Rift in the Races
Book 3: Hostiles
Book 4: (in progress)

John Daulton
www.DaultonBooks.com

HOSTILES

Book Three: The Galactic Mage Series

John Daulton

To Michael,

You rock.

[signature]

This is a work of fiction. All characters and events portrayed in this book are fictitious. Any resemblance to real people or events is purely coincidental.

HOSTILES
Book 3: The Galactic Mage Series

The phrase "The Galactic Mage" is the trademark of John Daulton.

Cover art by Cris Ortega

Interior layout by Fernando Soria

DEDICATION

For Mom, who believed in me long before I did.

MAP

Pros

Duador

String

N.

☼

Chapter 1

Gromf crouched behind a stalagmite, binding a long cut on his forearm with a strip of deerskin. He thought about healing it, but his last glimpse into the mana pool showed the stuff of magic waning. He didn't want to waste any of it repairing this minor wound. If he were going to win, he'd need that mana later. Besides, healing was a cowardly thing for an orc to do, an act of last measure, of desperation. Gromf was hardly in a position for that.

He tied off the wrap with his free hand and his teeth, his thick green fingers nimble and efficient at the work. When it was done, he risked a look back down into the arena, a vast expanse of empty aquifer, though filling rapidly with the dark blood of so many dead and dying orcs. Thousands lay strewn about, twisting and moaning, their bodies like a bed of fallen leaves that have found the lungs for agony. A pile of them had formed at the center of the cavern, an enormous heap, at least a thousand corpses, mounded high and surmounted by the current holder of the yellow stone: Drango-Kal, a shaman of the sand orcs.

Gromf saw him and shook his head. It was a mistake for Warlord to bring that clan to this holy event. Sand orcs would never hold to Discipline.

None of that mattered now. Drango-Kal had the stone, and somehow he had made it work for him. He stood atop the mountain of dead competitors and roared defiantly.

Gromf wished he could cast an ice lance. It was a favorite spell of the humans for good reason. Low mana, reasonably quick to cast. But he dared not do it. If he sent one, Drango-Kal would know where he was, would trace the line of its flight back to Gromf. And so would any number of the stupid hundreds down below.

He let his yellow eyes slide up the dark face of the opposite wall, far off, where the golden light of torches flickered and shaped a long rectangular balcony high above the embattled cavern floor. Warlord watched from up there, he and his high shaman, Kazuk-Hal-Mandik, a detestable withered old husk. Gromf would let them know what he thought of this when the time came. And he would get his due. But first he must win.

He watched as a knot of twenty gray orcs from the western tribes moved in to wipe out six idiots from his own clan, one of his whelp mates among the doomed. They should have known better than to get themselves cornered. Stupid. Undisciplined.

The grays fell upon the six with howls of victory echoing up at him. Gromf shook his head at the stupidity of his race. Then he began his ice storm spell.

The icicles fell like a rain of spears, hurtling down amongst the flailing motions of the gray orcs with their fists and their clubs and their rods of coarse iron beating upon the green flesh of the local tribe. The meaty mash of their blows stopped suddenly as the first, then the second, and a third gray cried out in pain and alarm. Some looked up to see what fell upon them, and the rough shafts of ice slipped through the soft balls of their eyes like fork tines into salmon eggs. Mouths wedged open and jaws broke.

Skulls gave way to the force of gravity and icy element, and in moments, Gromf had his own small mountain to stand upon.

Twenty-six down, he thought. So easy. But not with the yellow stone. It had to be *with* the stone, or the victory wouldn't count. That was the only rule, the entire contest: master the stone and take a place at the high table when all the others were dead.

Right now, it was Drango-Kal holding it. And the mounded corpses upon which he stood suggested he'd found something like mastery.

Gromf climbed down from his perch and took up an iron rod from one of the fallen grays. He looked at it in the dim light of ten thousand torches running at even intervals around the vast arena, God's Cauldron, his people called it. The metal was rough, almost like stone, and black as an old woman's teeth. The heft was good, but he was embarrassed for his people anyway, even if it was a weapon of the grays. No wonder the humans owned the open places beneath the sun. No wonder they ate the fat meat of the mammoth and the wooly rhino while his people ate wolf and wolverine. "We deserve the scraps," he spat as he flung the crude iron aside. He would not stoop to using it. If he could not have steel, he would rely on magic and teeth.

Drango-Kal upon his mountain of gore was being rushed by a group of thirty orcs, several green-fleshed northern orcs, a handful of grays and three of the sandy-skinned southerners from Drango-Kal's own clan. They came from all sides, clamoring over the bodies, their big hands groping for handholds, their feet driving into the soft purchase of fallen comrades and enemies alike. The bodies rolled and shifted beneath the powerful press of their growling ascent, slowing them, giving Drango-Kal time.

3

He laughed at them, cried down a boast in the secret cave language of his people, and then, with not enough time to chant, at least not by Gromf's measure, filled the air with lightning of a kind Gromf had never seen. A ring of it. A cylinder of it, a great barrier of floor-to-ceiling electricity that sparked and danced and hissed in the air. This arcing, sparking formation perfectly encircled the mound of bodies upon which Drango-Kal stood and then began to rise, to constrict, a choking grip of blue-white lightning growing tighter, moving slowly inward, upward, in pursuit of the attackers climbing to the top.

The curving wall of electricity came upon the clambering orcs in an instant, closing in on them and popping them like kettle corn. Gromf could hear it from where he was, the hissy *pifff* as they burst from the inside out, turned to breezy gusts of blood and steam. *Pifff. Pifff. Pifff.* Thirty of them, just like that. They were gone before he could really fathom what he had just seen, before he could put some kind of context on a magic spell like that. And before he had, he found himself blinking into the blackness, the lightning stain on his retinas blinding him even after the spell was done.

Drango-Kal's laughter came to him across the expanse of darkness. Gromf blinked and covered his eyes, hoping to speed them back to sight.

"Do you see me, Warlord? Do you see me, old shaman hiding in his wing? I am Drango-Kal of South Rock. I am the master of the yellow stone. Prepare my feast and wash a fat woman for me, for I come tonight to sit at the table of Discipline and respect."

Gromf shook his head and grinned as he listened to the taunts of the sand orc. *You have no concept of Discipline, you fool.*

He muttered a brief spell of darkness, an illusion to hide him, making himself invisible, then snuck his way along the rock face that was the eastern wall. He wanted to understand what he could of the yellow rock before he took it from Drango-Kal. He wanted to observe. Its power was obvious. And not only by the nature of that impossible lightning wall, or even by the monstrous fireballs and hideous transmutations that he had seen during the last two days of this combat. No, the real demonstration of its power was the fact that Kazuk-Hal-Mandik wasn't using it himself. Gromf had the advantage of being a clansmate of the dried-out old warlock. He knew the elder would never have given such a treasure over for the purpose of sport, not even one meant to find a successor, as he claimed. No, Gromf was not so stupid as that. Gromf was a new orc, an orc of Discipline. He would think first if he could. And his thought was that Kazuk-Hal-Mandik was afraid of it, afraid of the yellow stone.

Another of Drango-Kal's clansmates ran up the mound at him. "Drango-Kal, the great one. I will stand by you," called the dusky orc as he stumbled and crawled toward the ruler of the heap.

Gromf shook his head, once more ashamed of what passed for guile amongst his people. He was glad that Drango-Kal was not stupid enough to fall for his clansmate's ploy.

"A harpy's tongue won't save you, Lod," said Drango-Kal. "Save it for God." Gromf watched as Drango-Kal mouthed two short words. A blinding stroke of lightning came, huge, thick as the orc's head, and drew the jagged line in the darkness that burst Lod into yet another puff of steam.

Gromf was not a conjurer of lightning, so he had to think very hard about what he knew. Lightning was common enough magic. Easy for some, if not for him. But he'd seen it before and it was never like that. Not thick like that. The bolts should be slender, narrow streaks of light, drawn flat upon the air like the cracks in breaking ice. He'd never seen them wide and fat before, not thick bands of glare like Drango-Kal had cast.

So this was the effect of the yellow stone. It had to be. And only two words. The stone made magic fast. And big. That had to be what it did, and that made it very powerful.

So why would Kazuk-Hal-Mandik be afraid? What orc should fear power? That was not in keeping with reason, much less in keeping with Discipline. He knew there was something he was missing.

The sound of breathing came behind him, disrupting his thoughts. He turned and saw an orc of his own clan coming toward him along the wall. Another of his whelp mates, the one with the tattered ear. Gromf would not speak his name, would not think it. This was a mate stealer, a *doh-ruek*. That ear was the price of his shame. Gromf would be glad to see him die at the hands of Drango-Kal's lightning.

Gromf pressed himself into a crevice, buying himself just enough space for the tatty-eared orc to pass. He saw there was a dagger in the mangled orc's hand, gripped with the blade angled downward. The *doh-ruek* paused as he came even with Gromf, turning to stare into the space, his nostrils flaring as he sniffed the air. Gromf prepared to fight, prepared to die. For a span of three heartbeats, he thought he might be caught. He hadn't woven an odor-mask into his illusion. A human would have done so. He cursed himself inwardly for such a lack of Discipline. He deserved to die. Even by the hand of a *doh-ruek*, a creeper into the rugs of higher shaman.

But the mate-thief kept going, moved away, making his way from stalagmite to boulder, boulder to pile of broken rock, creeping toward the center section of the wall, keeping to the shadows as best he could, and, for a *doh-ruek*, doing a fair job of it. At length he came to where the distance between hiding spots was too long, the torchlight too revealing. There were twenty-five paces from where he stood to the bottom of the pile. Gromf grinned, happy to watch him try. To watch him hiss away in the flash of light and a wisp of vapor. *Go*, he thought, silently cheering the *doh-ruek* to his doom. *Go. I will watch your empty death and learn.*

The dagger-wielding orc didn't go, however. Instead he crouched down and muttered to himself, casting something. And then he was gone. He appeared an instant later behind Drango-Kal, the dagger already buried to the hilt by the time the sand orc knew what had come of him.

Drango-Kal's eyes opened wide, the bloody veins that crept out from the secret places in his skull revealed by the expansive orbs of his surprise. He let out one short gasp, the least portion of a shout, and slid off the *doh-ruek's* knife like a sack of dead fish. The *doh-ruek* kicked him as he fell, and the one-time lord of the pile tumbled down the slope, coming to rest amongst the still smoking remnants of his own recent victories.

Gromf shook his head again as he watched, continuing to marvel at the stupidity of his people, continuing to curse them as a race that doomed itself to such displays. He sighed as he did, found himself shamed by one who should be beneath him and unable to cause shame. Shame even in thought. He waited to see how long it would take the rug-creeper to realize his mistake.

Not long.

The *doh-ruek's* eyes suddenly shot wide, almost as wide as Drango-Kal's had in the moment of his demise, and he practically threw himself down the pile to where his victim's body lay, still bleeding into the base of the mound.

He desperately rolled the dead sand orc over and took up the limp left arm. He opened Drango-Kal's hand there and found nothing. He looked frightened. He flung down the left arm and grabbed the right one by the wrist, opened the dead fist. Relief came upon his face.

He took out the yellow stone and studied it for a moment. Relief turned to a toothy gape of glee. His eyes narrowed then, and his grin became thin and calculating. He turned his head toward the shadows, looking straight through the darkness into the nook where Gromf lay in wait. The *doh-ruek* flipped his dagger in his hand, the bloody point downward again, dripping into the grit and filth of the heap. He closed his eyes and muttered three words, enough for the teleport.

Gromf only had enough time to realize he'd been caught when he heard the breath in his ear, felt it right behind him. No time to even turn, no time to duck. By the time he understood what happened, the *doh-ruek* was there, at his back, with his knife and his yellow stone.

Gromf cringed as he waited for the blow, for the bite of the knife into his stupid, undisciplined flesh, and, even as he did, his mind welcomed death. It was only right for the stupid and weak to die. He should have shrouded himself in odorlessness. He was stupid and lazy and cast his illusion like a fool. He would spend eternity in the cowards' place with the idiots and weaklings.

When the blow did not come as quickly as the thought, he spun and prepared to defend himself. Perhaps God wanted him to have a chance. He was young. The young could learn. He did not expect to see what he found.

The *doh-ruek* stuck out from the rock in places as if the stone were giving birth to him. A portion of his face pushed through the wall just far enough to clear his mismatched ears, but the rest of his head was engulfed in solid stone. The knife, still poised for the killing blow, was held in the grip of a hand and arm that stuck out from the wall like a branch, but that, traced back to its origins, ended at the elbow, the rest somewhere in the stone, out of sight. All of him was. His whole body but for his face, his right arm and his left hand, and only barely that last, half the hand, the fleshy pads and fingers, and no more. All the rest was completely encased in stone.

A few moments had to pass before Gromf could process what he saw. He couldn't fathom it, once more this magic made no sense. But slowly the shock wore off and his mind went back to work. He shuddered at the vision before him. The *doh-ruek* was somehow inside the cavern wall. But how?

Thoughts felt as if they came to Gromf through a lake of sap, but they came. It was the stone. The *doh-ruek* was a teleporter, that had been obvious right away. And yet somehow he'd done it wrong. Or done it too far. Which had to be the yellow stone.

That was when Gromf realized the stone was there. Right there. And he was nearly as lack-witted as the *doh-ruek*. He opened the fingers that jutted like a lumpy green shelf from the wall. It was there. The yellow stone. The stone that made skull-thick lightning and buried teleporters in walls. It was there, but it was stuck, partially sunk into the rock, half its width, lengthwise, in there like the foolish orc was.

Gromf spun, looking to see if there were hordes of his fellow competitors coming for him.

There were not.

He forced himself to calm, controlled his breathing. Think and Discipline. Of course there weren't any coming. He'd been hidden all along, invisible no less, and nobody could know where the teleporter had gone, not here in the shadows, not there in the wall. Some observing him on the mount might have thought he disappeared. He had looked this way though, so Gromf knew that perhaps a few thinkers would figure it out. They might come investigate. He had to be quick.

He tried to pry the stone out of the rock face with his fingers but it was in too deep. He knew he would have to chip it out.

He reached up and took the dagger from the *doh-ruek's* hand. At least the mate-stealer had been of some value to his clan in the end. He raised the knife and prepared to make the first blow, then stopped.

"Idiot!" he cursed, a silent hiss to himself. *Discipline*! he thought. He calmed himself in yet a deeper wave. Willing himself to patience. He closed his eyes and cast a new illusion, this time on the knife. Silence.

Now the work could begin.

Chapter 2

Altin staggered as he released the spell, stumbling backwards and nearly tripping over the plush crimson and gold of the stool just behind him. The backs of his knees hit it, which spun him and forced him to catch himself with one hand braced against the rich velvet cushion lest he fall. He blinked a few times, then looked to Her Majesty seated in the concert hall's front row. He nodded to her, saying, "It is done."

"It is," she beamed. "And I see you and our new friend, Blue Fire, were successful." She managed to make a common magician's seat look regal simply by sitting there, her golden plate armor gleaming in the bright light that radiated from nearly everywhere in the room, seemingly without source, but brilliant just the same.

There were only a few gathered in *Citadel*'s great concert hall for the cast that sent the Earth fleet home: Her Majesty, her assassin, the marchioness—who had only recently arrived on *Citadel*, and uninvited no less—Altin, Aderbury, the seers and teleporters guildmasters, and, of course, Conduit Huzzledorf. Beyond that, the vast chamber was empty, a cascade of empty, crimson seats forming the audience hall that served as the heart of the first great royal space fortress.

The Queen, as did the rest in the room, looked up into the space above the conduit's place in the center of the room. As one, they gazed into the illusion that the one-eyed seers guildmaster, Master Alfonde, maintained through the images relayed to him by a seer-telepath from atop *Citadel*. The image portrayed the view of the space, the empty space, beyond *Citadel* where the Earth ships had just been. The vacancy so displayed confirmed that, in fact, the fleet ships were now gone. "Nicely done, Sir Altin," continued the Queen. "Please tell Blue Fire that we appreciate her assistance in sending those people home."

"She knows," said Altin as he blinked away the awe that still hung upon him. He was not sure he could ever grow accustomed to the magnitude of Blue Fire's power. She was so vast, her reach so far, her abilities so completely outstripping anything the wizards of Prosperion knew. In helping her send the Earth ships home, Altin felt like a barnacle on a whale's belly, shouting directions to it for how it might swim across the sea but otherwise just along for the ride. He'd guided her magic to the seeing stone Conduit Huzzledorf and his team had cast in place in the space above planet Earth in what had been only a matter of hours before, but beyond that, he'd done little more. Still, it was done, and regardless of how small he felt by comparison, the spell had worked. The fleet folks were home. They would be angry, Captain Asad for sure, but they were home. That's what their people wanted, and, well, more importantly, that's what the War Queen required. And he couldn't blame her. The order to knock Altin out and lock him up in an anti-magic cell was not a smart move on the part of the fleet, at least not as far as Her Majesty was concerned. While he could understand it from their perspective, well, he could see it from the perspective of the Queen even more clearly—especially since he'd been the one in the cell, not to mention the one with the lump on the back of his head.

"Show me Earth. Show me where they went," demanded the Queen. "I want to see what they are doing now." She gazed down at the wrinkled figure of Master Alfonde, who sat on one of the eight stools ringing the conduit at the center of *Citadel*'s crimson-clad concert hall, two seats from where Altin stood. "Get me to the conduit's seeing stone, or get me on one of their ships ... what is taking you so long!"

After a few moments' exchange between Master Alfonde and the conduit, the image in the air above the conduit shifted to one depicting planet Earth, a huge round vision of it that filled the chamber with a gentle blue light. For most in the room, this was the first time they had ever seen it. Altin had seen it recently, guided to it by the conduit's seeing stone, and of course there was the conduit himself. He and his team of teleporters had actually been there once, in orbit anyway, if briefly, gone on the orders of the Queen and helped with the distance by High Priestess Maul. Those few had seen this new and inhabited world, but for all the rest, this was a first, a unique experience that quite deserved the gasps and murmurs of appreciation the blue-marbled beauty inspired.

"It's lovely," said Aderbury staring up at it, his mouth slightly agape. "I don't suppose I will ever get tired of seeing new worlds like that. It is truly a great time to be alive."

"It might be lovely if it weren't entirely infested with blanks," said the marchioness.

"Indeed," said the Queen, ignoring the main thrust of the comment in favor of its lesser but just as true implications. "They are rather limited by their reliance on machines."

"I don't know about that," Altin said, staring up at the globe like the rest. He thought of Orli being there and hoped she was happy that she was home. He hoped she had recovered from her injuries, the mysterious injuries of spirit that he blamed himself for. Maybe now she could find peace. He knew it wouldn't be easy for her, but he knew she would. Their love had been poisoned by Thadius, and he knew he would never get it back, especially not after she found that it was Altin who had guided the cast that sent her people home, thrown them back to Earth as it were, and without so much as a homing lizard note to tell them what was about to come.

He would find her and explain, of course. He would try. He could only hope that somehow they could recover the love that they had lost. But he knew it would never be. He had for consolation only the knowledge that at least now she was safe. That was what mattered most.

"What are all those bright flashes?" Aderbury asked. "Over there, on the right side."

Sure enough, looking more closely at the vast glowing ball filling the center of the room, there was a distinct pattern of light play. Altin had noticed and dismissed it as lightning at first. He'd seen lightning in the clouds above Prosperion a few times from a vantage upon Luria, Prosperion's bright red moon. But this seemed different. "Run out to it," he demanded, preempting even the Queen in his urgency.

Master Alfonde, a brilliant U-ranked seer, sent the image careening toward the area where the lights flashed, and soon the audience in the concert hall found themselves spectators of a most horrifying scene.

A huge battle was being waged in the space above Earth. There were spaceships everywhere, some of the design the Prosperions were familiar with and others that looked nothing like the ships that had just been teleported back, though all were clearly the product of Earth technology. All in all, there were far more ships than they'd ever seen before, far more than they'd ever suspected might have been created by such unmagical means. There were thousands upon thousands of them, some of them absolutely enormous, dwarfing the ships that were like those they knew, while others, most of the others actually, were far smaller, some seeming tiny by comparison, like aphids moving around a meadow amongst the lumbering bulks of mastodons. But all of them sent out beams of light, the "laser" light they called it, some red, some blue, some violet. The scene was thick with the striping motion of missiles shooting outwards into space as well, each of them directed at the most horrifying revelation of all, the recognition of which brought gasps of horror from everyone in the room: there were Hostiles everywhere. Far more Hostiles than there were Earth ships.

A huge expanse of space above the embattled planet was absolutely filled with Hostile orbs. Tens of thousands of them at least, hundreds of thousands perhaps. It was impossible to count. In places, they hung so closely together, in such numbers, that at first, as the seer's vision was moving toward the fight, it began to look as if a haze of smoke was covering huge areas of the globe.

The nearer the seeing spell got, however, the more and more clear it became. Earth was under attack by an incredible number of Hostiles, an invading force so much larger than anything anyone in the concert hall had ever considered possible that it took a full two minutes before anyone spoke. When someone did, when Her Majesty finally turned to Altin, as did everyone else in the room, there was only one thought in every mind: *What have we done?*

"Sir Altin," demanded the Queen, and the quality of

her voice made it clear she was passing the blame on to him, "how did you not know this Blue Fire of yours intended such treachery. Could you not see it when you were joined with her in casting the spell?"

"I .... I ...."

"Yes, I–I, indeed. What have you gotten us into, Sir Altin? Have we all been duped so seriously as this?"

There was nothing Altin could say. He was stunned beyond speech. There had never been anything in Blue Fire's manner that had suggested she was capable of such utter betrayal. She was the one who could hardly even grapple with the concept of "truth that was not truth." And yet, here they were now, all of them, witnessing the grandest act of betrayal in all of history.

And worse, he'd just sent Orli into that.

He stepped quickly to Madame Kenouvier, the teleporters guildmaster, and held out his hand. "Give me your fast-cast amulet," he demanded.

She huffed in her surprise. "What?"

"Give it to me, now. Aderbury, I need yours too."

Aderbury pulled his off immediately and handed it over, questions in his yes, but no hesitation in the delivery. Altin put it over his head as he swung back to the guildmaster and reached for her amulet again. "I said, *now*!"

"Sir Altin," began the Queen as the fleshy guildmaster continued to stammer with indignity over Altin's dictatorial tone. Altin reached down and grasped the sapphire pendant from where it nestled in the woman's corpulent bosom and snatched it off with a jerk. Then, without the least utterance or gesture, he was gone, leaving Her Majesty to stare into the empty space of his departure, her mouth slightly agape. "Not even so much as a by-your-leave. We shall see about that."

"He will have gone off to save the girl again," remarked

Madame Kenouvier, looking up at her monarch while she fingered the stinging area at the back of her neck where the chain had snapped.

"Indeed," said the Queen. She said nothing else, however, instead staring into the image and looking, at least for the span of a hundred heartbeats or more, completely at a loss. They all did, all stared, all completely bewildered by what they saw. It was some time before anyone had the nerve to speak. When it came, it could hardly be said to help.

"It appears Her Royal Majesty has rather grossly underestimated our enemies," said the marchioness. "And her own influence. Again."

Glaciers have formed in warmer climates than the one that came upon the concert hall just then. Had the Queen not been so out of sorts by the unraveling events, she might have done something dire, but, perhaps for the marchioness' sake, it was better that the Queen's mind was awhirl with other thoughts. Just the same, the admonition had more than venom in its tone. "You forget by whose whim you keep those lands your father once held, Marchioness. Now is not the time to press me."

"You forget whose conscripts will be needed when Captain Andru's hundred thousand orcs arrive. Another symptom of your fine rule, My Queen." Contempt sprayed like cobra spit from the smirking slits of her eyes. "I press what others think silently."

"Take the crown if you think you can. I invite it. Join with them if you like. Join the orcs and Hostiles and come against me all together. See what it gets you. But speak one more seditious word in my presence, and you'll lie bleeding at my feet in the span of my next breath. Test my influence in that." No doubt could be held about the truth of it. It gleamed like the bright edge of a newly sharpened blade upon the teeth made visible by her snarl.

The smug defiance did not leave the marchioness' expression, but she curtsied her compliance with a glance at the elf standing nearby. Everyone present knew this exchange could never be undone.

"For now," said the Queen, "I think that Sir Altin's inclination is the one we must emulate. It seems we've sent our Earth friends into a nasty strait, and, guilty as we are, unfortunate as that guilt is, we must now at least go and try to help."

"They will fire upon us the moment we arrive," remarked Aderbury. "We'll be fighting two enemies at once."

"They are not our enemies," corrected the Queen, her voice stern and her countenance severe, "and even if they were, what kind of people would we be to leave them to a fate like that?" She pointed up at the mass of flashing lights, streaking lasers and dive-bombing Hostile orbs. "We are obligated by honor to help them. And, as you may recall, Blue Fire's peop—the Hostiles take no prisoners. If we don't help them, this will be the end of the Earth people for good. All of them, and by our mistake."

The taut quality of the marchioness' face made it clear she wanted to point out that they were obligated by *her* mistake, the errors of the Queen, but she knew better than to speak it now. But apart from her, nods from around the room confirmed that most agreed with the need to lend a hand.

"All right then," said the Queen. "Master Aderbury, in the absence of Sir Altin, it is your charge to get it done." She turned to the conduit. "See to it, Master Conduit. It is up to the two of you to fix this thing."

"Yes, My Queen," they replied in unison, though Aderbury found himself looking to the conduit with more than a little trepidation and surprise.

The conduit sent him back a rather wicked looking

grin, his teeth shining bright and his wild ring of wispy white hair giving him an aspect of insanity. "This will be fun. It's what we've been training for!"

"Well, get on with it," said the Queen. "I've got a war at home to fight, but I'll expect regular reports." With that and a glance at Madame Kenouvier that conveyed an unspoken command, the Queen, the elf and the marchioness were sent back to Prosperion, leaving the rest of those aboard *Citadel* to figure out how to save planet Earth from what appeared to be the high probability of its demise.

Chapter 3

"Holy shit," said Roberto as he rolled the shuttle onto its side and only barely avoided a long shaft of stone sent like a missile from one of the Hostile orbs swooping past. He wasn't sure which orb the shaft had come from, and in fact, he wasn't even sure it had been aimed at him at all, given that he had just come off a swing around the starboard side of one of the Northern Trade Alliance's new Juggernaut-class star cruisers. The ship was a monstrosity that dwarfed the *Aspect* on the same scale that Roberto himself might dwarf a slice of sandwich meat. And meat was what they—Roberto, Captain Asad and Orli, the latter drugged unconscious and strapped to a gurney in the back—were going to be if he let another one of those rocky shafts get that close again. Worse, he also had to hope that in dodging Hostile projectiles, he didn't fly into a laser beam, which was a real and significant threat, and one that had him convinced that half the idiots on Earth had been assigned to weapons posts on some of these ships in lieu of actual trained officers. "Why are these morons shooting at them?" he asked, though mainly rhetorically. He knew the smaller ships didn't have the power for a gravitational pulse big enough to crush the orbs.

"Save it for when we land," Captain Asad replied. The captain's hands moved across the controls with familiar ease as he worked the navigator's panel, helping guide the shuttle on its way down toward Earth's atmosphere. "Let's just get there."

"What could the director possibly need Orli for that was bad enough to fly through this?" countered Roberto. "This is insane." He rolled the ship back the other way as a Hostile orb flew by, missing the shuttle by eight and a quarter inches.

"We have orders, Commander. Just fly."

"Flying, sir." Roberto's mouth stretched and gaped in turns as he did so. He winced and leaned from side to side in his chair, his body contorting as if he were physically dodging each incoming attack, the arch of his back, the expanse of his teeth somehow in keeping with his ability to pilot them through the chaos of so many thousands of combatants. No amount of training could have prepped him for this, and friendly fire was as much a problem as the enemy's. After a few more close calls from both, he was not entirely convinced that actually trying to avoid the crisscrossing mayhem was any better than just closing his eyes, hitting the throttle and hoping.

"Fuck me," he called out as a stripe of violet light cut through the back third of the shuttle's starboard landing skid. The length of it tumbled away, heading toward the upper deck of one of the Juggernauts. This expletive was followed by two more repetitions of like profanity as he barely escaped another shot from the same ship only to steer almost directly into the path of a rushing Hostile, which, fortunately—sort of—was on its way to attack another, larger ship. What followed was an endless string of swearing and more than a few utterances of "Holy God, save us" before they finally made it through the swarming melee. But ultimately they did, somehow—miraculously he felt—and he straightened the small ship and brought it into Earth's lower atmosphere with sweat running down his brow.

He breathed a long sigh, glancing at Captain Asad, who also made no effort to hide his relief. The captain shook his head and let go a short breath of his own, blowing out tension as he punched up the coordinates for the NTA headquarters at Fort Minot.

"Fort Minot traffic control," he said, "this is *Aspect Shuttle Six* inbound with the director's security package, requesting lock and dock. Over."

A brief silence followed before the reply came. *"Aspect Shuttle Six*, permission granted. Transmit docking code to zero-four-seven-one, lock for pad alpha one-one-seven northwest. Security detail en route. Over."

"Roger, Minot traffic control." He looked to Roberto who tapped in the code that would release control of the ship to the Minot spaceport computer. Roberto nodded when it was done. "Code sent. Over."

"Received and verified, *Aspect Shuttle Six*. Enjoy the ride." There was a moment of silence, followed by a less official, "And welcome home, *Aspect*. Over."

Captain Asad did not respond, and instead he rose from his seat and went back to where Orli lay. He hawked over her with an expression that suggested she were an axe murderer, a threat at any moment to burst her bindings and mutilate the both of them. He checked the small console at the foot of the gurney, making sure the readings being relayed from the monitors attached to her in various places still showed the figures the nurse had told him to watch for. They did. She was still completely out. He pressed the button that delivered a few more drops of the potent sedative anyway. Despite the nurse's assurances that she was dosed well enough to get down to the base, he wasn't taking any chances.

"Holy shit. Captain, look at this," said Roberto. The exclamation turned the captain around. "They're everywhere."

The shuttle was just making its way past Winnipeg, west of it and moving very fast but still low and slow enough, given the distance, that Roberto could see a small swarm of Hostiles flitting about the city's airspace. He zoomed in a video feed and discovered that not only was the air abuzz with them, there were many Hostiles draping themselves over the buildings like wet blankets. He watched one orb fly down and smash into the corner of a tall building, sending a spray of broken glass and busted concrete flying everywhere. Then the orb settled in, at first looking like a scoop of ice cream that had begun to melt down the sides of the structure, but quickly spreading, abandoning its spherical form in favor of stretching over the surface of the glass and concrete more completely. He had no idea what the Hostiles had in mind, but he was sure he wasn't going to like it when he finally found out.

"They're different," observed the captain, his eyes moving back and forth from the image on the screen to the distant view now fading out of sight through the window.

"What are?" asked Roberto.

"These Hostiles. They're red. And they're smaller."

"These must be the ground assault version."

"I expect they carry the disease."

"If they do, then NTA better have been cranking out vaccines for a while already. If not, those people back there are screwed." Roberto wrinkled up his face as a shudder ran down his spine, the memory of the ravaging disease on the *Aspect* still all too fresh, the shouts of madness and screams of agony, people he'd known and cared for, friends now gone forever.

He tried to bring up a local satellite news feed, but there wasn't one. After a moment of searching, he discovered that well over a hundred of the major entertainment and news satellites were not responding to his queries. He finally found one he could connect to, and he put it on a secondary display.

... Coast cities are overrun, and the West Coast isn't doing any better. Mexican President Domingo Rios-Muñoz reports major urban areas in his country are seeing twenty percent infection rates from as far south as Mexico City to as far north as Portland ....

"Guess that answers that," said Roberto as both watched the gaunt-faced woman on the screen. The reporter stood before the easily recognizable Manhattan skyline, the familiar scene of the gondolas moving through the canals giving a false sense of serenity to the obviously besieged city. A closer look showed that the boats were all empty behind her. There were no tourists lounging in the lazy comfort of the automated craft, no one enjoying a day on the water as they floated down Broadway or Fifth Avenue taking in the sights. Not while the same scene Roberto and the captain had witnessed in Winnipeg played out in the skies above.

Director Nakamura announced this morning that only NTA associates with health care access ratings over five hundred will be given vaccination codes. All others are advised to stay indoors until further notice. All travel is prohibited and NTA security forces have been authorized to prevent the spread of disease with "all necessary rigor." So, stay at home, folks.

The feed went to commercials right after that, which brought another round of profanity from Roberto, who could hardly believe they would break for advertising at a time like that. He looked through several other channels, and in the ten minutes it took them to get to the Fort

Minot spaceport, they had confirmed that most of the major cities around the globe were under Hostile attack, and that the Hostile disease had been detected in all of them. One anchorman proclaimed, "It seems they're like insects, attracted to the lights."

Roberto didn't know if Hostiles could see light, but the map graphics being shown by the various stations all confirmed general bad news for the largest population centers everywhere. He stared at the most recent graphic and shook his head. "The Hostiles sure did all that fast," he said. "And the disease thing, how did that happen? It didn't set in that fast on the ship. It took several days before anyone showed symptoms before. How can it be manifesting so quickly now? It hasn't even been a day."

"They've been studying us all along, Commander, of course they have improved it. And the Hostiles arrived fifteen hours before we did. This is why I have been summoned to speak to Director Nakamura in person. And why we were ordered to bring your pal Pewter along."

Roberto couldn't ignore the real sense of fear that settled in his gut as he flipped off the television feed. It was hard to believe how wrong everyone had been about the Prosperions. Especially him. He'd been sucked in almost as bad as Orli had. It made him feel gullible, and stupid, and worse, it made him feel responsible for what was happening now, almost as responsible as everyone thought Orli was.

The shuttle came up on Fort Minot then. He stared out over the massive hundred-foot walls as they approached, marveling at how so much concrete could be stacked so high. The walls, as thick as they were tall, marked off a massive space covering seventy square miles, and passing over the wall seemed to bring them into another universe, a universe of severity, a place where strict dedication to function was not only the rule, but the absolute totality of all things. Other population centers they'd been flying over as they came in, or looking at on television during the flight, were largely vertical settings, vast land-locked islands of mirrored monoliths, majestic feats of engineering where buildings thrust skyward like great fingers of delicate-seeming glass, bejeweled by lights and shimmering architectural artistry reaching proudly toward the stars. But not Fort Minot. By comparison, Fort Minot seemed squat and surly, a seventy-mile expanse of low buildings, few more than ten stories high, and almost entirely covered in the same black solar paneling. While these too gave a glassy effect, the uniformity of it all seemed to smother any chance the place had at beauty. Not even the play of sunlight upon the surfaces could change the numbing devotion to function there. It was as if the panels themselves knew they weren't pretty, weren't even all that important in the scheme of things, given that these surface structures, the buildings, the massive hangars, all of them were built over a bunker so enormous, dug so deep into the Earth, that the solar panels were counted as merely an ancillary power source. Even still, there was a brute magnificence to it that Roberto couldn't help admire, if for no other reason than for its role in history. Had it not been for Fort Minot, the lion's share of Earth's technology would have been lost in the three centuries of chaos that followed the third world war.

Only a few minutes passed before an octagonal section in what seemed a veritable plain of solar paneling opened like the iris of some great fortified eye, and the shuttle was drawn inside. The small ship settled to the ground, and shortly after, the sound of the roof panels locking back into place vibrated through its frame. They were officially back on Earth.

"I wish I could say I'm glad to be home," said Roberto, "but I think we got here in time for it all to go to shit."

"We'll see about that, Commander." He got up and went to the shuttle hatch, throwing a scowling glance Orli's way. As he waited for the hatch to open and descend, he added, "Commander, do not be late for the court martial, and when you arrive, remember that while that foul mouth of yours is arguably acceptable on a ship, it has no place down here. Nor do we have time for any ill-conceived debauchery that might land you in court as well. Until this war is over, you are still a member of my crew, do you understand?"

"Yes, sir," Roberto said.

When the ramp was down, a pair of Marines saluted the captain, who directed them inside to the gurney upon which Orli lay. "You are to stay with her every second until she is in a cell. I don't care if there are six hundred Minot doctors, nurses and interrogators with her, do you understand? You walk her into that cell, check the lock and make damn sure the cameras are on. That cell security needs to be armed and ready to go off at all times. Make it certain. And if they decide to move her, keep her drugged. If they need her awake, put a gag on her."

"Yes, sir," the two men replied.

"And listen close. If Meade or any other Prosperion shows up, you shoot them on the spot. To kill, do you understand that? No questions. No 'hold it, mister,' no, 'freeze,' just right through the heart, and a second through the head just in case. You have not seen what these people can do, or how fast they can do it. Especially Meade. Do not hesitate. Do you have that?"

"Yes, sir."

Captain Asad turned to look over his shoulder, toward the front of the shuttle where Roberto was finishing up the shutdown of the ship. "Commander, let's go."

Roberto set the ship into sleep mode and joined the captain at the hatch. At another time, he might have felt insulted by the captain's comments regarding his behavior, like a chastened child, but not this time. Not while standing there looking down at his friend like she was, still and seemingly lifeless, strapped there helpless and likely to be set upon the whims of the great military bureaucracy. A sinking feeling came upon him as he looked into her face. It was eerily empty, vacant, like somehow they'd killed her already, and now she was just waiting to die. The captain had been cryptic in his answers about why they'd brought her down here from the start. They obviously thought she was a threat. They'd drugged her nearly to coma for fear that she might try something, might make an attempt to escape or use some secret magic whatnot that Altin had made for her and that she'd hidden on her person somewhere. Roberto shook his head ruefully. It had been a rough twelve years for her, most of it not her fault. She made some dumb choices there at the end, but he couldn't really blame her, all things considered. And he'd liked Altin too.

He caught himself looking around the hangar then, thoughts of Altin sending his gaze darting into the shadowy corners, searching for movement behind the stacked crates and parked gravity-lifts. A flutter near a pile of boxes caught his eye, looked like the billow of gray robes, but he saw that it was only a tarp thrown over the boxes, one corner of it blown about by air coming from massive ventilation ducts high above. He shook his head and followed the captain out.

Altin wouldn't come down here anyway. He couldn't. He didn't even know where "here" was. Roberto knew how that magic worked, at least a little bit. He was pretty sure that was the main reason they'd been ordered to bring Orli down off the ship: to get her away from Altin's all-seeing magic eyes. Roberto felt a little better about that. His experience with Prosperion spell casting told him that was a real risk, Altin finding her. He knew the Prosperion would try. So it made sense to get her away from the ship, which was a thing, a place, Altin was familiar with. Teleporters couldn't go somewhere they'd never been before, or at least that they hadn't seen with their magic sight. Roberto had worked with enough teleporters to understand that fact very well. But thinking about it still made him shudder. What if Altin had already found her? He was the most powerful sorcerer they had. What if he was watching right now, spying on him, planning ... whatever he had next in mind, the next move in the great betrayal?

Suddenly he could feel Altin's eyes crawling on him like a thousand tiny insects, the small hairs on his arms prickled with the sense of it. He turned back and looked around again, searching everywhere, even up into the rafters high above. Altin could easily be up there.

There was nothing to see, but still the feeling clung to him. He shook his head as he peered up into the vacant space. "Fuck you, Altin. I thought you were my friend."

Chapter 4

Altin had exactly enough discipline to do two things before going to the *Aspect* in search of Orli. The first was to teleport himself to his old friend Doctor Leopold and insist the doctor remove the tracking device the Earth people had implanted in his arm. He had no intention of letting that thing be his downfall this time as it had been on the *Aspect* the day he got caught visiting Orli. The second thing he did was cast a version of Combat Hop on himself that would keep him out of danger from both the laser beams and the projectiles that the fleet weapons discharged. He accomplished both in just under an hour.

From there his plan was simple: get Orli out, and not get shot. If he could talk to them and try to explain things, he would, but even then, he would slip Orli the fast-cast amulet the moment he arrived, just in case something went wrong. That way, no matter what happened, she could get out of there. He hoped it wouldn't come to that.

He cast a seeing spell directly into the sick bay of Orli's ship, right where he knew her bed had been. It occurred to him as he did it that he might be able to simply send her the amulet secretly. That could make things very easy for them both. Unless her hands were bound.

In the end it didn't matter because Orli was not there. And not only was she not there, the bed was not there. No one was there.

He pushed his sight into the next room and found Doctor Singh sitting before a monitor, staring into it, at the battle taking place outside his ship, and slowly shaking his head. Altin spared a moment to watch the activity in the monitor as well before shoving his sight through the rows of beds looking for Orli. She wasn't anywhere he could find.

He pushed the seeing spell right through decks, bulkheads and machinery, darting furtively into chambers and bays, hangars and loading docks, spaces set up for work about which he had no inkling. He looked everywhere, up and down as he made his way through the ship. He didn't know his way around it very well, but he knew he was moving toward the bridge. She might be up there. They might have put her back to work. She was not. He pushed his way down through the floor, through several more decks, speeding his way down in search of the *Aspect*'s brig. That's where she had to be. But there was still no sign of her when he got there. For several more minutes, he chased his fear down the lift tube and through a few random corridors before realizing he'd never find her that way. He let go of the spell.

"Minotaur's horns," he growled, stuffing Orli's amulet into a pocket of his robes. "I don't have time to divine."

He cast another seeing spell, this one to Aderbury's house in Crown City. He knew it was an invasion of privacy, but he didn't have time to worry about such things. Fortunately, Aderbury's wife, Hether, was home and not in a state that would make her indisposed toward company. He quickly searched out an empty room and with a thought that barely allowed him time to release the seeing spell, teleported himself into their home.

"Hether," he called out in a voice loud enough to be heard but not startle. "It's Altin. I'm sorry to intrude."

"Altin?" she called back as the sound of footsteps on the wooden floor came nearer with each passing heartbeat.

"Yes, Hether, it's me," he replied and pushed open the bedroom door. "It's really something of an emergency—and yes, Aderbury is fine, it's my emergency. I need a homing lizard."

Her surprise at seeing him transformed to curiosity at the abrupt nature of his request. She stammered for a moment, thinking to ask, but seeing in his eyes that haste was in order, she moved immediately to oblige. "Why yes, of course. What's happened? Why not telepathy?"

"You mustn't say anything to anyone. You truly mustn't. But it's all gone horribly wrong." He quickly rattled off a truncated version of what had happened as they made their way to Aderbury's cluttered study and the small cage where the couple kept their homing lizards. He told her of his capture, the Queen's outrage, the rescue led by the royal assassin, and his subsequent work with Blue Fire to send the fleet home to Earth. Altin brushed past Hether the moment they entered the room and threw open the lid to the homing lizard cage, reaching in and grabbing the first one that came within reach.

Without a backwards glance at the confounded and increasingly frightened woman standing behind him, he went to Aderbury's desk and scribbled out a note. *Where are you? I will come for you.*

He hastily wound the scrap of parchment around the lizard's slender abdomen, its soft white throat calmly pulsing with each breath, no more excited by such treatment than it might have been by the touch of the wind upon its black and yellow speckled skin. Altin tied the note in place with string, a bit roughly, and almost tossed the lizard down. He realized that, wherever she was, she might not have anything to write with, so he took a bit of drafting charcoal from Aderbury's desk, snapped off a quarter of it, and stuffed that under the string atop the note, which gave the lizard quite a squeeze. He tossed the lizard down, nearly barking Orli's name as he did it. In the time it took for the lizard's little feet to touch the ground, it was gone.

He turned back to Hether. "I'm sorry for the rush, and I promise I'll explain in more detail at another time. Aderbury is fine, though I know not what the Queen has in mind for him after what has happened. And remember, you must not speak a word of this to anyone. The Queen may not want this news out just yet. I fear it doesn't make her, or any of us, look very good."

Hether could only nod and bat her long lashes over a still-bewildered pair of bright blue eyes. A smile creased her pretty round face as she nodded the promise of her silence. "Be careful," she said, but he was already gone—once again causing her to marvel at another unanticipated event. Never before had she seen anyone do magic without so much as a single uttered word.

Altin appeared in sick bay on the *Aspect* again, near where Orli's bed had been. The room was still empty. His bare feet allowed him to move silently across the floor, and he peered through the open doorway to where he'd seen Doctor Singh not all that long before.

The doctor had moved from the desk and was treating a man whose skin was blackened and crisp looking all across his upper arm, shoulder and part of his neck. Altin reflexively cringed upon seeing it, the jagged black edges and the shine of fluids glazing the angry red wounds. Fortunately the man appeared to be unconscious, which was a good thing, for such an injury could be nothing but unbearable.

Altin watched for several minutes as the doctor worked,

the nurses in assistance moving in perfect synchronization with the skilled physician as his treatment progressed, their gloved hands darting in and out methodically, slapping tools precisely into his waiting grip, barely a word uttered in between. Eventually, it was done, and the patient was rolled away by one of the nurses, and Altin couldn't help but wonder if he were going to be put into one of the pink-fluid tanks like the one in which his arm had been regrown. The injury certainly would require something on that order if it were ever going to heal.

Altin waited until the other nurses left, a matter of several minutes, before he entered the ward. His hands were held out, open, clearly unarmed. "Doctor Singh, please don't call the guards. I don't want to hurt anyone. I just want to find Orli."

The doctor spun on him, and for the first time in Altin's memory, there was anger there, a deep, simmering anger, controlled but reflective of the great sense of betrayal that the gentle doctor felt. "She's probably dead, Altin. They took her down to the planet, or at least they are trying to, and when she gets there, she is going to be tried for treason and executed, just like in the good old days."

"They what?"

"Don't you dare act surprised now, Altin. Don't you do it." He moved to a nearby nurse's station and picked up a tablet. He tapped it to life with a finger, and called up a video feed from outside the ship. He spun it around to where Altin could see the chaos of activity. The explosions, the streaking laser light, the broken husks of ships and the oozing orange strands of ruptured Hostile innards. "She's flying through that, Altin. Right now. And if she somehow happens to make it down alive, she'll be dead in a few days at best. And it's because of you."

"I know how it appears just now," Altin said. "But I assure you, things are not as they appear. We were manipulated too."

Doctor Singh stepped toward him, thrusting the tablet forward at Altin, his large brown eyes glistening with the tears of impotent rage, held barely in check by the kind fibers that made him the man he was and prevented him from the violence he so desperately wanted to act out. "You said you loved her, Altin. That's what you said. And she believed you. She trusted you. We all did. So congratulations. You win. Yours is the greatest deception of them all, and you can stop the game now. Victory is at hand, just look and revel in what you have done."

At first Altin wanted to defend himself again, to try to explain it, to make the doctor see. But he knew it would be pointless; he could tell by the severity of the doctor's gaze. So instead, he went back to his original query. "So where is she? You don't have to trust me. You don't have to believe me about the Hostiles—and I can hardly blame you for that—but you must believe I love Orli. I love her more than anything. Than everything. Tell me where she is, and I can get her out."

Anger swelled inside the doctor again, a pulse of it that had his lungs expanding with the breath that might have unleashed another wave of his truest sentiments, his fury, his frustration, his grief. But instead he let it go wordlessly. His head fell, his chin to his chest, resting on the white coat, now marred by the browning smears of the burned man's blood. "I have no idea where she is. She's in there somewhere." He handed Altin the tablet and then went to the nurse's station where he took a chair. He buried his face in his hands and Altin thought he might be crying, though it might just as easily have been simple weariness and frustration that left him so.

Altin lifted the tablet and watched the battle playing out upon its glowing screen. Earth, bright and blue, dressed in the same livery as Prosperion, the wisp of clouds and the armor of hard brown and green continents. These were the colors of humanity, serving as the backdrop for what was a seething mass of motion, bright lights moving like dust motes beaten out of an old couch near a sunlit window, the frenzy and random violence of their movements making no apparent difference to the movements of the next nearby. Randomness in action. No pattern and no recourse. A dance with no choreography, only the whirling step-stepping toward death.

Orli was in that somewhere.

He turned to the doctor, who looked to have recovered a bit. "I'm sorry," Altin said. "It never should have come to this."

Doctor Singh only shook his head.

"I have to find her," Altin pressed again. "Show me how." He stepped over to where the doctor sat and presented the tablet to him. "Show me how to find her in this. With the chip in her arm, like the one I had." He pulled up the sleeve of his robe and showed the bright pink line where his chip had been removed, a fading mark that might have been gone all together had he allowed Doctor Leopold time to finish the work.

"I can't, Altin," Doctor Singh replied. He looked completely worn out, like a man who hasn't slept perhaps ever in the course of an entire life. Dark brown circles shadowed his face beneath his eyes, so dark he looked as if he'd lost a fight a few days before. The whites of his eyes were brown around the edges, with lines of bloodshot visible. He pushed his fingers through his hair in an exhausted way and repeated it. "I just can't."

"Yes, you can," Altin insisted. "I know you can. Colonel Pewter found her at Northfork Manor using that chip when we were flying in. I can use it too." He pushed the tablet forward, practically right into Doctor Singh's face. "Do it. Show me. You don't have to like me. But if you care for her, then you will show me. She has a chance for a life back on Prosperion. You said she is dead if she stays here, if she goes with them. What is there to lose?"

But still the doctor shook his head, though for a moment appearing as if he might change his mind, as if he wanted to. But he didn't. He stared into the small screen of the tablet and watched. Watched and shook his head. "You must think I'm a fool," he said. "And I suppose it's true. In the end I am, aren't I? But even I am not that much a fool."

Altin nearly gasped in his impatience. "Just tell me how, damn it." He thrust the tablet against the doctor's hand, trying to jam it into his grip, but he would not take it. "Mercy's sake, Doctor, I'm not here to fight with you. My people aren't your enemy. It was a gods-be-damned mistake. Blue Fire has betrayed us all. She betrayed Orli. She betrayed me. She even betrayed Her Majesty and the priests of Anvilwrath. It was her. Can't you see? If we'd wanted to do this, we would have just done it and had it on."

The doctor took the tablet from him. Altin could see in his tired face that he wanted to believe, but that he'd just run out of faith. His ability to trust was gone.

"For her. Show me. Let me save her. Let me get her out, then I will go find Blue Fire and make her stop. I'll make her call off the attack. If she won't, I will carry one of your weapons to her heart chamber and stop it myself."

That made the doctor look up.

"I'm serious. I know how this looks, but you are wrong. And I do love Orli. Help me find her. What possible deception could I have for your people in wanting to get one woman out of here? Think about it."

That was true, and the doctor's head slowly began to nod. It was possible. But then, the Prosperion mage could simply be finishing the act, just as Captain Asad had said. This could be the last thing, the last bit of information. A way to follow her, and Captain Asad, into the heart of the NTA. Perhaps even in possession of a nuclear missile. But he wanted to believe it wasn't so. He wanted to believe that Orli might still have a chance, that they might all still have a chance, especially as he stared into that vast cloud of death revealed in the tablet's glowing screen.

Altin leaned forward, hoping, trying not to seem so eager that Doctor Singh changed his mind. That's when Doctor Singh let out a short portion of a laugh, the least part of it, the part that breaks when it discovers there is no humor there.

"Really, Altin?" He sounded disgusted. He looked up at the practically panting mage and shook his head in a sad, resigned sort of way, as if he'd just discovered some essential missing detail. "You almost had me."

"What?" Altin gasped. "What now?"

Doctor Singh handed the tablet back to him, rising from his seat. He said nothing more and simply walked away.

Altin frowned at his back and then looked down into the image on the tablet screen. At *Citadel*. Which had just seconds before appeared.

Chapter 5

"Call them off," Altin shouted into the green clump of stones, the patch of them glowing dimly, surrounded by the yellow crystals that filled the rest of the narrow chamber that was the heart of Blue Fire. He shouted straight into them, his red-flushed face leaning near, for he'd gone himself, straight there in his rage. Not just thoughts, but physicality for this confrontation. "Call them back right now, or I will see that you are destroyed, just like you should have been." He was nearly breathless with the rush of his anger as he sent every last ounce of his emotions out in the wake of his words. All the rage, the terror—both for Orli and for what amounted to just about everyone—and, most of all, the sense of gullibility and guilt. "How could you?" he roared at her. "*You* were the one who went on and on and on about betrayal. About truth that is not truth. And now look at you. Look what you have done. All of that was emptiness and lies."

She sent back the sense of absolute bewilderment. Terror of her own. Terror of him. Her incredulity at how Orli Love had become so suddenly filled with hate. Hate for Blue Fire.

"Don't spread that offal on my plate," he snarled in

41

response. He pushed images of the combat taking place in the space around planet Earth up at her through his memories. He shoved them at her as if they were mud and he was smearing it, jamming it into her loathsome, lying face. "What are you?" he shouted. "What kind of duplicitous monster could do such a thing? You used our love against us, against everyone. That is the very soul of evil!"

He forced himself to calm. Closed his eyes, regulated his breathing.

More calmly, he repeated his earlier threat. "I will kill you if you do not call them back. Call off the attack."

Not mine, she sent. It came upon a sense of otherness.

"Just do it. No more vagaries. No excuses. Call them off, and do it now."

Not mine, she repeated in his thoughts.

"What do you mean, 'not mine?' How stupid do you think I am?"

Not mine. Other.

"There are no others. You are the others. There is only you. You told us so yourself. No others. Just poor sad Blue Fire floating out here all alone with the memories of a dead star to comfort her in between bouts of genocide."

Not mine. Other. Truth.

"You don't know what truth is."

Love is truth. Altin Love truth of love. Orli Love hate hate of Altin Love.

"I don't have time for riddles anymore. They are going to kill Orli because you lied. Now call them off, or planet Earth will not be the only planet with no life on it when this is done. You have my Truth on that."

He filled then with a sense of her fear. Not fear of him. Not even fear of death. Simply fear. It was as if he could feel her trembling in a way that, for some reason, struck him in the same way Pernie had trembled in his arms when he'd rescued her from the orcs. It was a childlike terror, a helpless, lonely, inconsolable sense of dread in the face of something out of one's control.

The rational part of Altin's mind tried to fight it off. He knew now that she could convince him that any emotion was real. That was her best weapon. Making truth out of lies. She did it in a way that made falsehood feel in a whole-bodied way to be true.

"I don't believe you," he said.

"Then I must die."

That startled him. It was real. Actual sound. The sound came as an approximation of a voice, barely discernible as one, but one all the same. And it was loud. Cavernously so. It was as if thunder tried to shape words through the echo of itself, a great grating coming out of a deep and enormous cave. It was so enormous it threw Altin to the ground, the vibrations coming in the form of an earthquake, a violent rumble that tossed him against the wall and jabbed him full of shallow puncture wounds, his back and arms stuck first by the tips of the many crystals jutting from the wall, and then his palms and knees when he hit the ground.

What in nine hells?

"Then I must die," rumbled the mighty voice again, the words more articulate this time, as if once was enough practice for that.

"No," he said, scrambling to his feet, his mind awhirl. When did she learn to speak? Had she always known? More of the ruse, the lie? "You don't need to die. No one has to die. Just call them back. I beg of you. There is no reason to kill them all."

"Not. Mine." Once again Altin was thrown to the floor by the shaking. The resonance of the consonant sounds moved the ground half a span vertically. Blood dripped from Altin's hands, and he could feel it running in several hot rivulets down his shins.

"Then whose? Tell me that, and explain. Make me believe." He didn't want to hear it. He knew it would be a lie.

"Not mine." This time he caught himself against the wall, though his hands were minced more just the same. Her voice came from everywhere. It was terrifying, but not more so than Altin's fear for Orli.

"That's not good enough."

"Not mine." This time it barely rumbled beneath his feet. It came once more after that, only in his mind, gently, like a thing settling back into place. Then Blue Fire fell silent.

Altin slumped against the wall. Exhausted. He looked at his palms, which gleamed wetly in the golden light coming from the walls around him. He could see, just visible as a faint line around the edge of his ring, the green pulse of the stone embedded in the silver. The stone she had given him. Blue Fire's gift of heart stone, a bit of herself, a bit of the father's gift, which was the dark green stone.

Maybe he was wrong.

He thought about the look on Doctor Singh's face only a few moments before. The hate and sorrow. The total lack of trust.

Maybe he was doing it too.

Truth. The thought came into his mind on a wave of sadness.

"Then who?" he repeated yet again. "Is there another one? Another Blue Fire?"

No other Blue Fire.

"Then it has to be you."

Not mine.

Altin exhaled so long and so deeply it made him see stars. Or perhaps those were on account of utter fatigue.

The emotions coming off Blue Fire had been so intense, they sapped his strength just as water takes the heat out of newly forged steel. It had to be her. There was no one else. She was either lying or there was something wrong with her and she didn't realize what she was doing. Either way, it had to stop.

"I wish I could believe you," he said. "I want to. But I can't. If you can stop them, if this is some game, or some feeding mechanism for you ... just stop."

Not mine.

"If Orli dies, so do you. Or I will die trying to finish you. That's a promise."

Orli Love live. Blue Fire die. The thought was demure. A pleading surrender. A willing sacrifice.

Altin shook his head trying to block her from his thoughts. He needed her out of his head long enough for him to think.

He stooped and picked up Doctor Singh's tablet from where it had fallen when he was first knocked to the ground. He stared at his reflection in the blank space of its glassy surface. His dumb face looking haggard and helpless. He had no idea how to make it work. He had no idea how to find her. The homing lizard hadn't come back. For all his power, he could do nothing right now. Orli was flying toward certain death, certain death that would claim her if the certain death of the flight didn't get her first. If it hadn't gotten her already. And there was not one thing Altin could do about it but pray. And prayer was not his way.

Thinking was.

With a thought, he teleported himself back to Prosperion. There was one other possibility.

Chapter 6

Kazuk-Hal-Mandik leaned out over the edge of the stone wall, peering down into the cavernous arena, down the face of the rock into the shadows below and around to the left. He'd seen where Drango-Kal's killer had looked before he disappeared, before he'd vanished from the base of the mound of dead orcs. But now the teleporter was nowhere to be found, the light from the torches around the ancient shaman was too bright, spoiling his vision for the dark edges of the vast death pit below.

He reached into a rabbit-skin pouch and pulled out a small fold of vellum. He opened it and extracted a silver ring, a thing of the humans. Small and fragile like they were. But smart like them too. He slipped the ring over the little finger of his left hand. It barely fit at the tip, squeezing tightly to the green flesh only midway down his yellowed fingernail. It was good enough.

His vision shifted then, from his eyes to his hand, and in that instant it seemed as if he held his vision at the tip of his finger. This was the sight. Kazuk-Hal-Mandik had no magic sight, not by nature, not by the gift of God. But the ring gave it to him, the ring itself a gift of God, the one God who had appeared to them, the conqueror of the old gods, the God who brought them Discipline, the God that would lift them from the shadows and give them a rightful place among the races of Prosperion. Respect from Discipline. That was God's promise.

He pushed his vision down into the vast dark arena, slipping over the edge and sliding down the wall like a winged thing swooping for its prey. He descended and slipped into the shadows along the edge of the cavern, wending his way around boulders and stalagmites, seeking the new leader of the contest. Where had the teleporter gone?

He ran his vision all the way down to the far end of the chamber where it began to arc around and head back on the other side. But there was no sign of the teleporting shaman with the stone. Kazuk-Hal-Mandik thought he must have missed him, Drango-Kal's killer, crouched in the shadows somewhere. He had not seen any movement across the open center of the empty aquifer, the bloody grounds of this great contest. He lifted his vision some, gave himself a higher angle, this time two spans above the ground. He drifted slowly back along the wall, watching, listening. He had almost come back beneath Warlord's suite where he'd started this search when he heard a sound, something faint, very small. He stopped. He stared down into the darkness, scanned every nook and crevice of the area nearby. He could see nothing. There was no one there.

He heard it again. Something falling. A pebble perhaps.

He turned back and let his vision drift once more toward the back of the cavern. A whelpling could crawl faster than he moved. He dropped back down to a span's height off the floor. He heard it again. Behind him.

He spun back. Still nothing. So he waited.

He began noticing a pulse. Not so much a pulse of light,

but a pulse of less darkness. Not steady, no rhythm, but visible motion in the darkness, something pale, and small, very small.

He moved to it. There was the stone. The yellow stone, the purpose of the contest, embedded in the face of the cavern wall. Half in, half out, and perched atop a leaking oblong expanse. Dark fluid ran down the rock. The stone flashed, or more accurately, vanished for a moment and became visible again. This happened twice more.

He noticed then the face above. An orc's face protruding from the rock, the rest of its head buried in the cavern wall. He saw a hand above that, poised as if about to hammer down a blow, though the fist was loose and open now.

The yellow stone vanished and reappeared, as if it were blinking, followed by the sound of a stone chip hitting the floor. This time Kazuk-Hal-Mandik heard a hiss to go with it. A curse. He followed the sound to the piece of rock that had fallen. He watched it skitter to a stop. Then it vanished.

High above, back up in Warlord's suite, in the well-lit room with Warlord's food-laden tables and the soft strum of a lute, the old warlock laughed, his body laughed while his vision watched far below, beyond his open, laughing mouth.

He watched the progress of the invisible contestant for a while as whoever it was worked at chipping out the yellow stone. He raised his vision up and surveyed the area around them. Three sand orcs were tearing up a lone shaman from the northern tribe, Kazuk-Hal-Mandik's tribe. There were two others making their way along the wall from the opposite end, though they were moving slowly, cautiously. He could not tell from this location whether they were hunting or hiding.

He lowered his sight down to the work of the invisible

orc again. The stone vanished completely for a time. Two more rock chips fell to the cavern floor.

Kazuk-Hal-Mandik pulled off the ring, returning his vision to the well-lit suite. He turned to Warlord, who had moved from observing the contest to lean over the book from which a captive human read. The human's words were a jumble of nothing in Warlord's ears. He raised his hand to smite the bedraggled creature, but the ancient warlock stopped him, calling, "Warlord, no."

Warlord spun on him and glared a yellow-eyed stain of warning at him. Warlord could break Kazuk-Hal-Mandik before he could cast a spell. No one in the room doubted that.

"Warlord, we need that human's knowledge of the sounds they keep in those symbols drawn there."

"In days gone we beat these things from them. Not this weakness you call for."

"In days gone we were chased into these hills and kept here for centuries, Warlord. We must smear ourselves in the excrement of our enemies in order to creep into their camp."

"Spoken like a coward," Warlord said, but he did move away from the reader. He snarled at the orc woman strumming the lute. "You make our women weak with this excrement as well."

"The lute compels him to read, Warlord."

"And what will you do when he is done? That woman will have your human knowledge in her head. She will summon the demons into your bed, and you will cry out for me to come and save you from them. I will not come."

"Yes, Warlord." Kazuk-Hal-Mandik had no desire to win the argument. He already had what he needed when the massive leader of the All Clans did not mash the human into unconsciousness again. "Their eyes swell shut, Warlord," he'd told him the first time. "And then they can't read."

Kazuk-Hal-Mandik allowed himself to listen to the human reading from the book for a while, droning on in the common tongue of the humans intermingled with long passages in a foreign language he believed belonged to the elves. He glanced up at the woman playing the instrument, a thick-thighed and broad-shouldered young thing he'd sired eighty seasons ago. She was a smart one. She would learn the song and teach him to sing it. And then, he would have a new power, the power promised him by God.

Still smiling, he went back to stand behind Warlord, the hulking figure's massive hands wrapped around the steaming foreleg of a moose. The great warrior snapped it in half, and the sounds of him sucking the marrow from it filled the chamber for a while, blocking out in places the tuneless notes of the lute and the tired muttering of the human bent over the book.

The whole of the cavern suddenly flashed with light. Bright and orange, and for a moment Kazuk-Hal-Mandik thought a fissure must have opened and the whole mountain was going to erupt.

The vast flare of light was gone as quickly as it came, leaving behind instead a field of smaller fires where the bodies strewn across the cavern floor now burned like the cook fires of an army encamped down there.

He heard laughter then. Deep and resonant, rising from below like a dark thing climbing up the walls to mock them. He, like Warlord beside him, leaned out through the opening, peering down the face of the rock to see if they could find the source. There was nothing to see. He looked left, then right. The two orcs who had been creeping along while he was using the seeing ring had come close enough to be observed clearly now. The flash of light had stopped them, however, and they looked about furtively, and obviously considered going back.

"Cowards," said Warlord as he watched. He yelled down at them. "Cowards. Go find it and kill it. You stand there like old women. You shame your clan." He spun back to his ancient companion. "Your powers make you weak. All of you." He turned away with a contemptuous sound rumbling in his throat, leaning back out to watch, hoping the two orcs would make some courageous move or be slain before they further polluted the air with their enfeebled breath.

A wall of fire surrounded them as Warlord watched. It rose up and crashed over them like a circular splash, a bright ring of brilliant orange, five spans high, and then, *whoosh*, it fell in on itself and smoldered in a pool of flame for a while. When it was gone, there was no sign of the two cowards anymore.

More laughter from below.

Waves of fire then began to wash out from the area beneath the two observing orc leaders. Enormous waves, five spans high, twice that thick, spreading in expanding arcs that blasted out and swept across the arena for a hundred spans before dying down. Every time a wave faded away, another appeared back at the point of origin.

The source of the waves began to move away from the wall, and the arcs became rings that radiated out from a central point and washed across the broken bodies, the writhing wounded and the screaming contestants that got caught in them as they passed. And so it went for some time. Wave after wave after wave.

The unseen source continued to move. It moved around the edges of the arena in a careful sweep. Always blasting out its fiery waves, steady and meticulous. It pushed to one end of the cavern, and then came back through the middle. The rings of fire turned to long straight waves that ran wall-to-wall across the chamber, larger and hotter now, filling it floor to ceiling.

"What is this?" demanded Warlord.

"I suggest you move away from the window," the old shaman said.

Sure enough, the fire wall eventually came across the opening through which they looked. It did not enter the room, flattening itself as if pressed against an invisible barrier as it passed, but it burned with a monstrous heat that did make its way into the room. Then it was gone, moving steadily toward the other end of the arena, meticulous in its fury, consuming everything in its path.

The mountain of dead bodies burned brightly as the fire passed over it, a massive pyre of failure, thought Kazuk-Hal-Mandik as he watched. His smile showed all his teeth, or all of them that remained. This would be his legacy. They would chant songs of his glory for centuries. He would be the one who unlocked the secrets of the yellow stone, God's stone.

Soon, anyway.

He reached down into his rabbit-skin pouch and fingered another fold of vellum, different than the one that had held his ring. This one held his piece of the yellow stone. Together, he and the orc making the spectacular show below would bring a new era of glory to the All Clans. He could hardly wait to find out who it was.

Chapter 7

Citadel arrived far enough away from the Earth ships that its Combat Hop abilities would not bring it anywhere near the ships, in part for safety should they be attacked, but mainly for fear the Earth people might see their arrival as an aggressive act. Aderbury commanded the fortress from the tower high above the battlements upon which rested the two hundred and twenty-five redoubts, small towers, made as blocky replicas of Altin's original space-traveling vehicle, a tower which had been plucked from the corner of distant Calico Castle back on Prosperion. From his lofty perch, Aderbury could see *Citadel*'s wizards scurrying into position still, the colorful robes of the redoubt pilots making their arrivals from the stairwells seem like little birds emerging from burrows at the edges of a huge square meadow, flitting out and swooping about perhaps in search of something to eat. And they would eat, in a manner of speaking. They would dine on Hostiles if they got the opportunity.

The redoubt mages ran to their respective towers, many hopping through the sections of the vast grid-work of low stone walls like gymnasts vaulting their way through a human steeplechase. Eventually, the leaping and scurrying slowed, and the fluttering chaos of robed magicians became an even spread of manned redoubts, each tower holding at least three mages, two teleporters and a conjurer for most, or two teleporters and a transmuter for others, although there were a few four-man teams where healers and illusionists seemed optimal.

Aderbury turned away from the assembling mages and looked out into the space he could see around planet Earth. From his vantage, the battle above the blue world seemed an impossible swarm of activity, and even trying to contemplate so much motion made the muscles that moved his eyes grow warm.

He sent a telepathic message to the concert hall relay, an old woman by the name of Cebelle. She'd been chosen by Conduit Huzzledorf for her stalwart sense of calm. "Cebelle, is the illusion up?"

"Yes. We can see what's going on out there." For all the urgency in her reply, she might as easily have been reporting on the progress of a teamster hitching up his mules.

Aderbury picked out two Hostiles at random from the churn of battle and followed them pointedly with his eyes, marking them in his mind. "See them?"

"Yes."

"Send it to Huzzledorf."

"He sees them," she replied.

"Try a merge."

A moment later one of the distant Hostiles vanished and the second bloated and ruptured like a crushed grapefruit, its side splitting open in great rents and spewing glowing orange gore out into the night.

"It works," he said unnecessarily.

"It does," she agreed.

"Tell him to start taking them down. My people will handle our defenses from up here for now—at least until I figure out what else we need to do. I may send a few of the boys out, so make sure you don't merge anything with straight edges out there."

"Of course."

They might have been talking about sending a few school kids down to play beside a creek, such was the calm she maintained, even as they thrust themselves into war. Aderbury was glad she would be the voice in his head this day. He'd been trained for war, but never one like this.

The ships from Earth were much more numerous and varied in shape than he had anticipated, even based on the view they'd seen shortly after the fleet had been sent home. But after a short study, he was confident there weren't any that might be mistaken for Hostiles.

He turned back and looked down into the field of redoubts again. He saw that more than a few of his wizards were looking up at him, their faces expectant, the altitude of their eyebrows asking, "When do we go?" But he did not know when. And he damn sure wasn't going to send them out just for the sake of seeing what might happen if he did.

He'd been given two tasks: save the Earth ships if possible, and find their leader—and he'd been expressly directed to go through someone other than Captain Asad if assistance was required on that front—and from there, his task was to explain what had happened as best he could. He was absolutely convinced he was the worst possible person for the second part, though he was more than willing to do his best on the first. *Citadel*'s diviners were working on the leader problem as quickly as they could, but the assistant guildmaster had already told him not to expect an answer right away. No surprises there.

He sent a telepathic message to the X-ranked teleporter Envette, who shortly after appeared standing at his side.

She stood prepared to receive his orders for several

moments, but when none came right away, she turned and looked out into the glare of the bright blue planet beyond, watching the flicker of lights, the explosions, the streaks of laser beams, the whorls of orange Hostile goo. "A lot going on out there," she said after a time. "Seems like a lot for one space fortress to fix."

"It does," he said. "A million mosquitoes swarming above a pond, and we have a rapier."

She nodded. "We've got a little more than that, but still, hardly enough. We could swat them all day and it wouldn't change much." She watched for a while, then added, "We've got to drain the pond."

"That's the problem, isn't it," he replied grimly. "High Priestess Maul is going to try to talk to Blue Fire, but Her Majesty isn't expecting much to come of it. I just hope that's where Altin went, though I have my doubts about that. At least not while Orli is out there somewhere."

She nodded again. Everyone knew about Altin and the comely young Earth fleet officer.

A huge gout of orange Hostile innards suddenly erupted in a wide sheet, a bright spew smoldering in the black sky for a moment before its rotation began to tear it apart into smaller pieces, all of which drifted away and slowly began to dim. Aderbury gauged by the lumpy mass from which that gout had sprayed that at least ten Hostiles had been merged, probably more. That was good. He wondered how long it would take the enigmatic alien spheres to figure out what the conduit and his concert hall mages were doing to them.

That answer came immediately as a large group of orbs quickly coalesced and streaked toward *Citadel*.

Aderbury snatched the brass cone from its hook on the wall behind him and shouted into its narrow end. "Incoming," he cried. The sound of his voice, enhanced by the enchantments on the cone, carried clearly to everyone across the vast assembly of battlements. "Watch your sections, keep to your team sequences, and ring your bells if you get behind."

"I need to get back to my team," Envette said.

"Isn't Mason an M?"

"He is."

"He'll be fine for now. I need you to do something scarier anyway."

She looked at him, one eyebrow sliding up, creating slight lines in the smooth, youthful flesh of her brow. "Such as?"

"I think I need you to go looking for someone to talk to. We have to find their leader, or at least someone high enough up the chain of command to get us there, and it obviously can't be Captain Asad. I don't think we have time to wait on the diviners."

"What about the old woman?"

"What old woman?"

"The one with the spectacles."

"Captain Eugene," said Aderbury. "I think her name is Eugene."

"Yes, that's it."

Aderbury rubbed his chin for a moment, the stubble of two days' growth making a scratching noise that he could hear. "You think that's a good idea? She may have been the least hostile of the fleet captains, but I doubt she's going to be any happier to see us after what happened than Asad would be. None of the captains that know us are going to want to talk to us at all."

"She struck me as someone who would listen," countered Envette. She looked out over the balcony railing and gestured at a giant spaceship moving across their view, a vessel far larger than anything either of them had ever seen before. "Trying beats sending every seer on *Citadel* running around the decks of that thing hoping to find

JOHN DAULTON

someone in ermine or wearing a crown, or whatever else, which is essentially what you are asking me to do."

Aderbury harrumphed. "True." He looked at her. "This thing I ask of you is as dangerous as all nine levels of hell at once."

"I know."

"You have your fast-cast?"

She gave him a sideways look, tilting her head and making a ticking sound with her tongue that suggested the question wasn't particularly well thought out. She pulled out one of the several amulets that hung around her neck, disentangling it from the rest before stuffing the others back down into the collar of her robe. She held it up for him. The gem in the small silver eagle's talon mount was almost as red as her hair.

"Right. I'll get you a few bodyguards from downstairs."

"No," she said. "I think I'll be better off alone. I'll just keep this ready to strike if it looks like Captain Eugene isn't as friendly as I think she is." She made a point of fingering the stone she held as she spoke.

"Get a seer to make sure it's clear. And I want Combat Hop on you in case they start shooting those light beams at you."

"Duh," she said, and then, with the confidence and enthusiasm of her youth, she teleported herself to the enchanters' offices on the fourth floor.

He hoped he hadn't just sent her to her death. Giving the order made him feel a little sick inside. It wasn't that he was uncomfortable with command, he'd been doing that since the *Citadel* project began, before that even, over the course of many construction projects these last several years. Even death was not something he'd never dealt with before. He'd suffered the loss of two crew members on one of those construction jobs, an accident, and entirely the fault of the young man on the transmutation team

60

whose mistake had gotten them both killed—what kind of an idiot puts a liquefaction inflection in a hardening spell? No first-year transmutation student would get that wrong on a construction site; the cadences were as different as black and white. But still the deaths had hung upon him for a long time after.

And of course, there was Master Spadebreaker. The kind old mine foreman, Ilbei. That loss still had the bite of recency. And guilt. Aderbury had been so glib, joking with the old miner about working with anti-magic as if it was just the easiest thing. He'd teased the man about his reluctance and his fear while trying to hide behind a door. Sure, it was a joke, well intended, but what made that particular action seem like the funny one? The truth, that's what. Anti-magic was new, unknown, dangerous, and he had ordered Ilbei to face it. Laughing. He knew he was going to wish he could take those jabs back for a long time to come.

Just then an explosive spew of orange marked where the first of the incoming orbs had been merged with another. That was quickly followed by another just like it. He saw one of the huge crystal spikes hidden in the surface of *Citadel* light up suddenly and streak off as well, if streak was the right word: it glowed, it blurred and then it reappeared, embedded in one of the smaller Hostiles like a massive icicle. The impact sent a plug of the orange lava substance spinning off like a gob of spit mucus.

And so it went for a span of perhaps a hundred and a half heartbeats. In came the twenty or so Hostiles, and then, they were dead. Merged, severed, pierced, or turned to solid blocks of ice or stone depending on the mood and aptitude of the transmuter that had made the cast. And just like that, it was done, leaving Aderbury once more contemplating what he might do next.

From the increasingly huge globs of Hostile guts he

could see, the concert hall mages were gathering Hostiles up in clumps of fifty and even approaching a hundred at a time. It was a spectacular display of power, but even that didn't seem to make any discernible dent in the threat. At this rate, it would be at least another day or two before they could clear enough of them out to call it hopeful, much less a victory. It was like trying to bail out the reflecting pond at the Palace with a teacup. Meanwhile the Earth ships were being steadily destroyed. Especially the smaller ones.

It was obvious from the volume of rupturing Hostiles that could not be attributed to the wizards on *Citadel* that the Earth people had mastered the strategies Captain Asad and Commander Levi had devised. Their ships wrung the glowing orb blood from their attackers with frightening efficiency. Unfortunately, it was also obvious that this was a numbers game.

Aderbury didn't want to think about how many people were dying out there. How many fathers, mothers and sons, sisters and cousins and wives, lovers, all for whom others would weep and wear the emptiness forever in their hearts. Empty chairs at dinner tables, images on mantles and hearths. Sad tributes and misty prayers come each passing holiday. And for what? So that the infernal Blue Fire could cleanse their world? To what end? So she could claim that it was back to natural? That it was pure? Pure of what? Pure of joy? Love? Friendship?

What kind of end was that?

Whatever kind it was, it wasn't one he was going to let happen, even if the Earth people never spoke to them again, which he thought was a pretty likely scenario. That brought his thoughts back to the task he had. He was the one who was supposed to make sure that didn't happen. And that began by helping clear out all these orbs.

As if resenting his thought, a new pack of Hostiles

separated itself from the haze of all the rest around the planet. He couldn't count them, but if he'd had to guess, he would have said about a thousand or more.

"Cebelle," he sent to the telepath down in the concert hall. "Are you seeing this?"

"We are," she replied.

"So, you may want to help us out on that."

"We will," she said.

The knot of Hostiles flew up at them at breathtaking speed. One moment they were distant forms and the next they loomed like an inbound stampede.

Then they were one giant ball, a massive clump of lumpiness, like a tiny moon that had died of a hideous case of smallpox, the boils of the disease spraying out thick streams of glowing guts, many of which slopped against the diamond surface of *Citadel* and clung to it like flung paint.

"Get that off," Aderbury ordered, yelling through his brass megaphone to the magicians below him. "Do it now."

Soon the "windows were clean" again, as that process would eventually become known, and with about as much effort as it would take to swat away an insect, the Hostile threat to *Citadel* was, again, gone.

"Nicely done," Aderbury sent to Cebelle as he watched his redoubt mages jumping about and whooping with glee.

"Conduit says, 'Indeed,'" reported the concert hall telepath.

Aderbury turned back to watch for an even larger incoming attack, but none readily shaped itself. This allowed the concert magicians to get back to work crushing clumps of Hostiles in the main body of the fray, if such a thing could be said to exist. They focused their efforts around the edges of the fight nearest to the largest of the Earth ships, the one Aderbury and Envette had so recently watched moving in the distance. Aderbury felt those largest ships must hold the greatest numbers of people, not to mention the greatest defensive power for Earth, so by those two reasons, those ships were deemed the most essential to protect.

The fight went on for some time after that. He watched and tried to keep count of casualties amongst the Earth ships, but there was little he could do. The small impact their efforts had on the overall numbers was frustrating. He was about to order half the redoubts out to help on the offensive, convinced that the Hostiles had learned better than to mess with *Citadel*, when a formation of Earth ships could be seen heading their way.

At first Aderbury felt a rush of hope as it occurred to him that Envette must have already met with luck, but then he realized she probably hadn't even got off the fortress yet, and if so, barely so.

Then came the first of the missiles. Eighteen of them. And forty-six beams of laser light. Fortunately, the energy coming from the Earth ships was easily diverted through and out the back side of *Citadel*'s armor. Though no one would ever say it aloud, that particular enchantment was a direct order of the Queen, and Aderbury for one was, at that particular moment, quite happy that he had so willingly complied. The missiles were another matter, however. *Citadel* did have a variety of Altin's original Combat Hop spell, the one he'd adapted for his tower, but it had been devised for the Hostile weapons, the long battering rams of stone, not the Earth weaponry. There was no description woven into the spell to trigger it to leap away from the explosive missiles the fleet ships used. And from what Aderbury had been made to understand, it was not just the impact of these weapons that was cause for concern: close was bad too.

"Conduit wants to know what you want to do with

those missiles," Cebelle said, her thoughts and those of Conduit Huzzledorf clearly in echo of his own. Fortunately, the woman's constitutional calm remained in place, though there was an edge to the telepathic request that let Aderbury know he didn't have much time to decide. "Will it be you or us?"

"You," he said. "Ice walls. Time it so they don't have time to dodge. And make them thick. Forty spans."

She didn't answer, but he felt her leave his mind. He turned and, through his megaphone, called down to his men. "Illusionists' marks by sector on those missiles in case the ice walls fail. Get them up now. Teleporters grab them if they get through and send them out behind us as far as you can. Keep sending them away if you have to, until we can coordinate merges and transmutes."

He saw the movements indicating his people were setting that plan into motion, and he turned back to watch as the blue auras of light that glowed from the back ends of the missiles grew in size with their approach. He waited, his fingers tapping the stone ledge of the balcony in anticipation of the first ice wall. The Earth weapons were still too far away for him to see the conjured ice walls very well in that darkness, but form they did, and, one by one, the missile fires flashed in one manner or another, then either snuffed out immediately or went spinning off wildly before burning out. None of them made the enormous blinding flashes Altin and the teleporters who had fought alongside the fleet had spoken of. He wondered if these were different kinds of missiles, less powerful than those he'd heard of. Or perhaps hitting the ice walls had simply broken them before they could go off. Either way, it didn't seem to matter. At least the threat was past. For now.

It might be called bad timing that the particular

moment of Envette's arrival on the *NTA II*'s bridge coincided with the complete obliteration of the first salvo of missiles the fleet sent at *Citadel*. It certainly did not set the conversation off on very good footing. It did, however, give her a chance to see what had happened, for when she arrived—carefully placed at the back of the bridge out of danger of merging with anyone—she was able to watch as the ship's lasers, like those of its squadron mates, skewed and fanned out harmlessly, shooting off into the vacancy of space after being diverted through *Citadel*. While none of the crew seemed overly surprised by that, they were all made instantly furious by the appearance of the ice barriers, into which the missiles collided like goats charging into a castle wall that had suddenly appeared before them. Even though the *NTA II* herself had no missiles to add to that barrage—a condition that they would say came thanks to the Prosperion deception that had disarmed them during the attack on the Hostile world—everyone aboard felt the letdown when those weapons were all so easily destroyed. In that moment, it became clear that lasers and missiles all meant nothing against *Citadel*.

"Well, that's it," said a lean fellow sitting at the controls near the large monitor on the wall. "We're screwed. There's no way we're going to beat them with anything we've got."

"Stay focused, Ensign," replied Captain Eugene, a sturdy woman with a mound of gray hair bound tightly upon her head and old fashioned spectacles riding low upon her nose. "We're not going to win the fight with the first punch is all."

"They might," replied the nervous crewman. "One punch from that thing and it's over. Everyone knows it."

"Ensign, be still. We'll figure something out."

The ensign didn't seem mollified by this reply, but he

fell still.

"If you don't mind," said Envette in her most mild-mannered voice, "we'd like to help you figure that something out."

Everyone turned to see who was speaking, and no one seemed too startled, at least not at first. But in the next moment, four blasters were trained on her.

She raised her hands high above her head, her right hand opened, but the left, perhaps conspicuously, curled into a fist. "This was all an accident," she said. "We had no idea Blue Fire was planning this."

"Right," sneered the ensign at the controls.

"Ensign!" snapped the captain. She pressed a button on her chair. "Security, I need a detail up here. We've got a Prosperion aboard. Bring a gag."

"Please, Captain," said the young teleporter. "I'm begging you. Just listen to me. Just for a moment. Then I will go."

"You have until security gets here. If you move, I will shoot you. Please do not make me do that." She pushed her wire-rimmed spectacles high up to the bridge of her nose as she aimed the weapon pointedly at Envette's heart.

"I won't. I promise," Envette replied. She couldn't help the hard swallow that followed. She sure hoped that damn enchanter got the Combat Hop spell right, or she was about to have one really short career as a space mage.

"Go on," said the captain.

"We've been betrayed. All of us. Blue Fire lied. She deceived both our worlds. If you could see how badly that went with Her Majesty, with all of us, you'd understand. Everyone is completely stupefied. Her Majesty is right now working out how to force Blue Fire to recall the attack."

"She wouldn't have needed to work that out if she hadn't turned on us the first time," pointed out Captain

Eugene. But at least she was still listening.

"Please, just let us explain. I am under orders to find someone in a position to make the decision to speak with us again. To speak to Master Aderbury on *Citadel*, or to Her Majesty. We understand why your people will be reluctant to do that. We know how it must look. But I swear to you on the soul of my departed mother I am telling you the truth."

Captain Eugene shook her head, her mouth and eyes drawing parallel lines of doubt across her face. "I don't think anyone is going to listen to you people anymore," she said at length. "I want to believe you. I do. In fact, I am convinced you believe what you are saying right now is true." Some of the severity left her face then. She even smiled. "You are young. Look at you. Strong, hopeful, maybe even smart. But easily manipulated."

"No," Envette began, her hands coming down reflexively, reaching out into the air in front of her defensively as if she might hold back those words, as if she might stop them before they became reality. Three beams of red light streaked from weapons held in nervous hands. Only the captain didn't shoot.

The crew all stared into the vacant space where Envette had stood, their brows in rows of consternation, the bulkhead blackened and smoking where the lasers had hit. They looked around warily, knowing the wizard didn't melt that thoroughly or that fast.

"I'm over here," said Envette, once again in her least threatening voice and with her hands held high.

Three more beams of energy cut across the bridge, and the ship's weather station burst into sparks that sprayed brightly for a moment then dimmed to a low yellow flame.

"You can't hit me," Envette said, this time from a place near the lift at the back of the bridge. "And I'm not going to fight back. I only want to arrange talks. Please, ask your king, or your emperor, even a duke ... anyone with the authority to rethink this thing. Please, just tell them that we need to talk. It's a mistake. All of it."

The lift doors opened then, and with the exquisite reflexes of their craft, the two Marines saw her standing there and knew immediately that she was why they had been called. One grabbed her around the neck, his arm darting out quick as a shooting star, while the other snatched her right arm back and twisted it into a brutal lever of pain that prompted her to yelp.

"Gag her," ordered the captain to her men. "Get those necklaces off of her and whatever is in her left hand." To Envette she could only add, "I'm sorry, kid. I know this was never about you."

"I'm sorry, too," replied the young mage. With her free hand she struck the fast-cast amulet she'd been holding since leaving *Citadel* against the edge of the lift's door frame, leaving the Marines groping at thin air.

When Envette returned to the balcony upon which Aderbury stood, Aderbury was staring open mouthed into a section of *Citadel*'s inner dome. He'd activated a magnification spell in a two-pace area of its surface, calling up images within it of the space that would, for all practical descriptions, be considered behind them. "We've got incoming from somewhere out there," he said, pointing over his shoulder with a thumb, but still looking up into the portion of the dome showing the expanded view. "Another fifty or so ships, and two of them are those giant ones."

"Where'd they come from?" asked Envette, seeing no need to force the explanation of her failure into the moment. Her return surely spoke clearly enough of how that enterprise had gone. "Were they summoned from somewhere else?"

"I have no way to know," he said. "But look." He pointed

out in the direction from which Envette had just returned. "There's at least a hundred more coming out to join the rest."

"They won't be coming to talk," Envette said. "Even the patient Captain Eugene is not inclined to help put together talks. I just spoke to her."

"Then it's tea time on Duador for sure," Aderbury spat.

Aderbury had been given access to the secret whispers of the Palace telepaths, and in a matter of moments, he'd explained the situation they were in to a messenger of the Queen: the Earth ships, roughly two hundred of them, were spreading out around them, despite the assistance they'd already given in the fight against the Hostiles. Surely the commanders of those ships did not think the massive clumps of rupturing Hostiles were the work of their own weaponry. And yet, on came the ships anyway, peeling out of the defense of their own besieged world long enough to make war on *Citadel*.

"Do not engage them," was the order he finally received. "Get out of there for now. Let's not make things any worse."

Aderbury could hardly believe they were retreating after only a few short minutes and nothing but victory after victory in the fight, but he knew well enough what Her Majesty's orders meant, and it was the only thing they could do. For now. So, with a shrug, he sent down to Cebelle and told her to have the conduit take them home.

The collective groans of over seven hundred redoubt pilots greeted the great blue ball of Prosperion the moment it replaced the one of Earth. They all knew this wasn't going to help anyone.

Chapter 8

Altin fumed as he left the Temple of Anvilwrath. High Priestess Maul wouldn't even speak to him. He'd been brushed off, sent away by her assistant, Klovis, as if he were some foolish child seeking a healing spell for an injured cat. He hadn't even been given time to explain what he was there to ask of them. They'd simply dismissed him. But such was the vanity of the Church sometimes, with its answers already in hand, its diviners full sure of themselves and often when curiosity would serve them best. But Klovis had told him they were working on the Hostile problem, which he supposed was hopeful. And she had healed his hands and knees, which he was grateful for.

While he was glad to know that the Maul was responsive to the request of the Queen and that she was working to get Blue Fire to call off the Hostiles, he knew it wasn't going to happen. He knew it better than the Maul ever could, for he was certain Blue Fire would not open her heart to the priests any deeper than she had to him. Far less so, he surmised, and he'd been there physically. They'd never get that close. The love of Worship was not the same as the love of Love, and he knew with more than mere instinct that Blue Fire could sense the difference and would never allow the calculating nature of power, even in the background wisps of the Maul's mind, into her private places, the deepest chambers of her heart, the vulnerable place where her life force was. And if the Maul didn't have that kind of access, she wasn't going to change Blue Fire's mind and get her to call off the attack. Altin couldn't prove it, but he knew it in the way one knows that rain has come by the petrichor.

However, his mission remained. The dismissal by Anvilwrath's priests in Leekant merely meant he needed another diviner. He'd been confident that the combined power of the Maul's circle of twenty-five could find anything for him, but that was no longer an option. They were busy. So his next best option, being that his own lowly level of divination was not worth the time it would take to try, not to mention the fact that he was already in Leekant, was Doctor Leopold. He made his way straight to the Guilds Quarter part of town.

He burst into the doctor's office twenty minutes later, panting for having jogged the entire way. A few months ago, he might have risked teleporting into a back alley to expedite the trip despite such things being expressly against the law. But not now, not with the Orc Wars ratcheted back up. There were wards up and watchers monitoring the mana flow. The last thing he needed was conflict with the city guard, running was only slow, a delay with the guards could be catastrophic.

"Why hello, Sir Altin," greeted the buxom and nearly-ever-cheerful Lena Foxglove. "I'm glad to see your arm has recovered so nicely, even though you didn't let the doctor finish healing the incision." Her smile was wide and white, her eyes sparkling, but he was glad to see she didn't go to the great lengths she'd used to in displaying her cleavage to him every time he came by. He had Roberto to thank for that.

"Thank you," he said. "It's fine. I need to see Doctor Leopold immediately."

"Oh, you always need to see him 'immediately,'" she teased. "I don't suppose you have another mangled mouse for him, do you?"

He shook his head, impatiently. "Lena, I really need to see him right away. It's a matter of life and death."

"For you or for Taot? You know the doctor had nightmares for a month after spending that much time with the dragon that day. You really should make a point of acknowledging what he did for you. He still gets requests for veterinary services because of it, and he's lost two good patients because he refused their pets."

"Lena, please. It's Orli. She is going to die if I don't speak to him right now."

"Oh," replied the comely receptionist then, a thin film of ice forming over the lake of her loquaciousness. "Wouldn't that be a shame?" She made a show of looking through some papers on her desk. "Let me see," she mumbled as she rifled through them.

Altin went to the door leading back into the doctor's office and examination rooms and tried to open it. It was locked.

"Your choice," Altin warned. "You can open it, or I can blow it down. I don't care which."

"He's with a patient," she said then. "And if you break it down, I'll have the constable on you."

Altin rolled his eyes and was about to argue when he heard the doctor's voice coming down the hall. The door opened a moment later, revealing the tremendous bulk of Leekant's top physician and the well-dressed figure of Lady Falfox, the self-proclaimed nobility of Leekant, though in truth merely the wife of one of its more prosperous citizens, Bucky Falfox, proprietor of the

Patient Peacock Inn.

"And so, Madame, I'll have the alchemist mix you up some tom-tom and willow powder and bring it by this afternoon. Mix it in tea twice a day, and you'll be as good as gold by the end of the week," the doctor was saying as they emerged.

"Oh thank you, Doctor," she exclaimed. "You have no idea how much your work means to me. You cannot imagine how I do suffer, and my husband could not care less about all my agonies. He'd rather write another campaign speech than spend the tiniest bit of energy on sympathy for me."

"Yes, I'm quite sure," agreed the doctor as he opened the front door and gently guided the woman outside.

She dabbed a soft palm up to the long feathers projecting from her sparkling turban as she stepped out into the breeze. "Oh yes, it's quite true," she began, but the doctor, smiling, politely cut her off.

"Goodbye. Don't forget to take your medicine."

He turned to Altin once the door was shut and exasperation flared his features for a heartbeat or two. "If I were Bucky, I would have hung myself years ago."

Altin didn't have time to empathize. "I need a divination," he said in lieu of greeting. "Orli is going to be executed if I don't find her. She's being taken somewhere on planet Earth, and I have to get to her. Her execution is certain after what has happened now."

"Whoa, slow down," demanded the ponderous physician. "What are you talking about? What has happened?"

The frustration that gasped from him was nearly as loud as a gorgon's rasp, but he knew he'd have to explain it all in detail before the doctor could divine. Divination was about what the caster knew as much or more than it was about what they might find out.

Altin grabbed the doctor by the upper arm, his hand not even wrapping around half of the doughy girth, and nearly dragged him back to his office. The doctor was wheezing by the time he made it to the creaking chair at his desk.

"The Earth people tried to attack the Hostile world. I found out, or Orli did and then I did, that the planet is alive. It has a name, Blue Fire, and apparently it is female. The extermination of the people on the Andalian world was a terrible mistake. Blue Fire, through Orli, tried to explain, to apologize, but the fleet wouldn't listen. They've lost too many ships and too many people. So, I, with permission from the Queen, helped her to thwart the attack from Earth, in hopes of getting it all sorted out. But, well, they took me captive, and then Her Majesty took that as an affront—you know how she is—and, so words were exchanged, the fleet was getting ready to fire on us, so, well, Blue Fire and I used a seeing stone Conduit Huzzledorf's people sent to Earth the day before to locate the planet for ourselves, and then we, Blue Fire and I, sent the whole fleet home. Which didn't seem like a bad idea at the time, but then, it turns out Blue Fire sent a bunch of her minions—eggs she calls them, but orbs in the eyes of the fleet—and, well, it seems she is bent on taking out Earth in the same way she took out Andalia, although she denies it entirely, which I know, because I went to her and asked." By the time he was done speaking, he was nearly as out of breath as the doctor had been from the effort of hustling through the hallways.

The doctor stared, his mouth open, his mind still processing Altin's hasty summary a full half minute after Altin's tale was told. His brows furrowed, then un-furrowed, then furrowed again. "So, you're saying ...," he began, but stopped, and there followed another few sequences of wrinkles forming upon his brow.

"They're blaming Orli for it," Altin said as he watched the doctor trying to work it out. "Or at least for part of it, and after all that's happened between us, they think she is a traitor and that I, that all of us, everyone on Prosperion, have been in league with Blue Fire all along."

That much the doctor could grasp easily enough. "I can't say as I blame them," he said. "From where they stand, that's surely how it appears."

Altin nodded. "But it's not true, and Orli must not die for their misapprehension."

"No, she must not," the doctor agreed. "But what about this Blue Fire? That seems a larger problem, don't you think?"

"I'm working on it. But I can't do anything until Orli is safe."

"Ah, the priorities of youth," cooed the older man. He nodded to himself as he said it, which made the folds of the many chins cascading down his neck spread outward like smiles intent on strangling him.

"She doesn't have time for a lecture on priorities. I need you to find her. My divination is too weak, and there isn't time."

"Surely they'll have a trial and that sort of thing first. The Earth people are not orcs."

"Their entire world is surrounded by an uncountable number of Blue Fire's legions. They will know I am coming for her, and they'll cut her down as quickly as Her Majesty would were she in their shoes. Her Majesty is not an orc either, and you know how it would go if things were reversed."

"Hmmm. You're probably right. Then let's not waste any more time."

Altin could not have looked more relieved. "Please, hurry."

"I think speed is the last thing you need, my boy. You're

asking me to find someone on a planet I've never even seen and as it relates to a tumult of events caused by another planet I've not only never seen but never had a chat with, as you seem to have, and much less a thousand other intricate details about which I have no knowledge at all."

"I can fix that. Some of it anyway."

The doctor looked intrigued and terrified in turns by the way Altin's eyes were narrowing. "Then do so," he said, but his expression made it look as if he were admitting that having his head removed was the best remedy for a headache.

Altin wasted not another moment, and by the time the doctor had finished speaking, the two of them were at Calico Castle. Altin had teleported them directly to the clean room, a space reserved for teleportation in the tall tower that had been occupied for centuries by Calico Castle's recently murdered keeper, the great mage Tytamon.

"That was fast," commented the doctor. "I didn't see you cast."

"I've gotten better," was all Altin said. He closed his eyes for a few moments after that, then stepped out of the chamber, beckoning the doctor to follow.

Altin went straight to an arched window on the far side of the cluttered room, stepping over the tumble of Tytamon's collected artifacts and magical curiosities as he went. "There," he said, pointing through the window. "That's Blue Fire."

The doctor nearly stumbled twice trying to navigate his prodigious bulk across the room, squeezing between tables that were set at random angles and which created pathways never meant to accommodate such commodiousness. Muttering and cursing his way through them, stepping over and around the stacks of books and the odd antiquities, and doing so with far less grace than Altin had, he finally approached the window where Altin stood. Upon looking out, his mouth fell open and stayed that way for quite some time.

This was a man who had never been to space. Despite Altin's several invitations in those first few months after the fleet had arrived on Prosperion, the doctor had always found a reason to decline. Not even a trip to the pink moon Luria had tempted him past his fear. And now, here he stood, gazing down upon another world in its immensity, a massive brown and gray globe with vast seas around both its poles as if it wore a mantle and an immodest skirt of matching blue.

Altin gave him exactly long enough to adjust to the suddenness of the teleport and the equally sudden discovery of his whereabouts—which came with no small degree of awe—and then he did it a second time. In the span of a blink, at least as the doctor saw it, the planet he observed changed clothes, so to speak, and was, in that seeming instant, transformed to a bright ball of blue, painted in places with wisps of white clouds, beneath which stretched large expanses of land similar in hue to those he'd just seen, though not nearly in equal measure to its seas. This world was wrapped mainly in blue.

"And that," said Altin impatiently, "is Earth."

Doctor Leopold simply had nothing he could say for a time, and he leaned against the stone of the windowsill staring at the world, his breath whistling audibly through his nose as he slowly pieced things together, eventually realizing what the movement and flashing lights were, and how all of what he'd seen related to Altin's tale.

Altin waited as long as he could stand to do so and then called the doctor out of his reverie. "Doctor, we have to work fast or Orli will die somewhere down there."

The doctor blinked free of his amazement and turned

to face his longtime friend and patient. "You hop around the universe like a rabbit on hot rocks," he said.

"Yes, I do," said Altin. "You get used to it. Now, please, we have to get her out of there."

"Look at them all," the doctor intoned, his voice sounding as if his lips had gone numb. "I take it the little reddish balls are the Blue Fire planet's eggs, and the bright fortresses are the fleet ships?"

"Yes, Doctor, but please, you of all people appreciate the value of her life."

He shook himself, a great wiggling of jowls and folds of breast and belly beneath his clothes, waves of movement that made it seem as if he were scarcely more than a bag of buttermilk below the neck. "You are right," he said. "I will marvel at it more when we are done. Let me see what I can do. Have you got anything that belongs to her?"

Altin's mind raced, but he couldn't think of a single thing. He briefly considered going to the evacuated mining base on the Naotatican moon Tinpoa to search for something. But he wasn't sure if there would be air to breathe. He knew the fleet had taken many of their machines when they left to attack Blue Fire. He then thought about going to her ship, snatching something from her quarters and then coming right back, but that seemed too risky as well. Even if they didn't have some energy trap or poison gas waiting for his arrival, he might appear just in time for a Hostile to destroy the ship. He was tempted to do it anyway, but he knew he wouldn't be any good to Orli dead.

He realized in that moment that he didn't have anything of hers at all. He had nothing. No trinkets. No gifts. The daisy chains and crowns of laurels she'd made for him on their outings together had all been lost when his tower was destroyed, now several months back. He had nothing of her now. If she was lost, her absence would be in totality.

He felt panic begin to rise.

The doctor saw it, sensed it in that way that people whose entire lives have been spent in comforting others can. He reached a hand out and placed it on the small of Altin's back. "I know her well enough," he said. "I did heal her leg, you'll recall."

"That's true," Altin breathed with relief.

"All right, clear me out some space to work. I can't do anything in all this clutter."

Altin rushed to the table at which Tytamon had sat in work for so many centuries and, with a sweep of his arm, pushed everything onto the floor. He pulled out the chair and indicated the doctor should take a seat.

Doctor Leopold looked at the heap Altin had made upon the rug, the dust cloud of its manufacture churning thickly in the air, but held back any disparaging expression or remark. He waved his hand before his face as he walked through the dust storm and took his place upon the chair. From the ticks and creaks it made, Altin feared it might not be up to the task of supporting the doctor, but it didn't give out. He wished he had a strengthening enchantment memorized to cast upon the wood, but he let the thought go, resigned to hoping that the chair would make it through the duration of the spell. If it broke, the doctor would have to start again. Altin didn't think Orli had that kind of time.

Chapter 9

Orli came out of the drug-induced haze slowly. The rigidity of the surface upon which she lay suggested she was back in her quarters, although she couldn't remember leaving sick bay. The memories of Captain Asad coming into the room with two Marines and a nurse slowly coalesced as images in her mind. There had been a syringe and Doctor Singh's voice shouting something as one of the Marines dragged him bodily away. That was all she could recall.

She sat up, blinking into the brightness. She was weak and had to use her hands to push herself upright. Even blurred as her surroundings were, she knew she wasn't in her quarters. Her quarters weren't this small, this stark or this white. To her right was a door with a small square window in it, covered from the outside. To her left, a stainless steel toilet and a tiny matching sink jutted from the wall. Beneath her was this bunk. That was it.

Someone had dressed her, for she was no longer in the hospital gown. She felt for her communicator, but it was gone. So were the emblems of her rank. She wore only the plain black bodysuit of a first-year cadet, this one completely unadorned, not even an NTA patch. That was odd.

She looked under the bunk but knew before she did so that there wouldn't be anything beneath it.

She lay back down and stared at the ceiling. Light came through all of it, a diffusion screen scattering it all evenly, the whole of it glowing so that the light came from everywhere above all at once. It was too bright.

She was in prison again. Why, she did not know. She couldn't remember what she'd done this time, at least not clearly, though her thoughts were still reassembling themselves. She tried to focus, to think and speed the process along.

She vaguely remembered seeing something on a computer. There had been an orderly talking about Hostiles at Earth. Or that they were at Earth, the *Aspect* and the rest of the fleet. Yes, that was it. She could remember feeling shocked. And Orli was strapped to the bed. She remembered that too, prompting her to look to her forearms where the straps had been and to make a reflexive movement of her legs, both confirming that she was no longer bound.

Why had she been strapped to the bed? And what did the Hostiles have to do with Earth?

She looked around the cell again as her mind cleared. It slowly came to her that this room was not on any ship. The door was a conventional one, not the sort one finds on a spaceship. She was back on Earth.

Memories came rushing in. Suddenly she knew why she'd been bound to the bed. She'd tried to rescue Altin. She remembered the fight in the hallway outside his cell. The Marines and the canisters of gas. Shadesbreath, the Queen's assassin, had come with a few other Prosperions. They must have gotten him out. Please, she begged silently, they must have gotten him out. The thought filled her so fully it almost burned. She sat up with the urgency of it.

He had to have escaped. She could vaguely recall the empty cell, the last thing she'd seen through the fog. Surely he had.

And then something must have happened. The Prosperions had somehow sent the fleet home. That had to be it. And good for them. The best thing for everyone. Especially Blue Fire.

Thinking of her helped calm the rising tension that had begun to fill Orli, the torrent of emotions stirred to life by the recollection of recent events.

But how recent? She had no sense of time. She stared up at the bright white luminescence of the ceiling. No help there. It could have been days. Or hours. Or months. How long had she been asleep? What had they done to her?

She looked back at her arms, where the straps had been. There were faint red marks there from where she'd struggled trying to get out. So it couldn't have been too long. And there were needle marks. Several of them. She wondered what they'd put into her. And why.

She lay back and tried to calm herself, tried to make sense of what she could recall, but in the end, she couldn't. She had only a sequence of events, but somehow they lacked cohesion. Visions of things that had happened as if viewed through that gas cloud outside Altin's cell.

At least he had gotten away. That was something to cling to. He was safe. They were all safe. The rest could be worked out in time.

Time was an odd commodity for her, however, for she had no gauge of it beyond the red marks on her arms. But more of it passed after. Her only measure of it was the fact that two meals were brought to her, pushed through a narrow slot in the door. She knew the meals must mark the passing of some set number of hours. The empty plate of the second had been taken away for what had to be another hour before she saw her first human face since awakening. Two faces, actually, both Fort Minot Security by the patches on their sleeves, which proved that the return to Earth was not some drug-induced dream. She wondered if the Hostiles' arrival, if their presence in orbit around Earth, was also real. She feared it must be.

The two security personnel cuffed her and, unforeseeably, gagged her, shoving a black rubber ball in her mouth and binding it tightly in place with a series of straps over and around her head. The question in her eyes, sent to each of her captors in turn, prompted only, "Your captain's orders," from one of them.

They brought her out of the cell and led her through a brief series of hallways and onto an elevator. They kept her facing the back wall when they selected the destination floor, so she had no idea how far they'd gone when the doors opened again. She could tell by the sense of vertigo that hit her when she stepped off that they'd climbed very far and very fast, indicating that her cell was deep below the surface, well into the bowels of the Earth. The ball gag was uncomfortable. It spread her mouth too wide, hurting her jaw and making it hard to breathe.

They guided her down another series of corridors and finally into a small room where they sat her down in a small plastic chair at a small plastic table. An empty chair sat across from her. One of the guards removed the gag, and she couldn't decide if she should thank him or tell him to fuck off. She chose neither, and both men immediately exited the room, leaving her once again alone.

She looked around. Again there was nothing in the room but white walls, too-bright light coming from above and a single door. Were it not for the absent toilet and sink, it might have easily passed for the very same room she'd just been taken from. She didn't know what she was waiting for, but she waited for it anyway.

She sat for so long her backside began to hurt, so she rose and stalked the edges of the room, all the while her mind running through events. Running through reasons why she might be here. She knew it had to be mainly because of Captain Asad. But why? And why the gag?

Finally, frustration building to a near frenzy that she thought might make her burst, a gentle knock sounded upon the door. Immediately after, a smallish, squinting young woman came into the room. She wore a conservative skirt in fleet black and a white blouse beneath a jacket cut in the military style. Orli thought she might still be in her teens. "Ensign Pewter," said the woman upon entering. "My name is Angela Hayworth, and I'm here as counsel for your defense."

"My defense?"

"Yes. General court martial. Charged with conspiracy to commit genocide, conspiracy to commit mass murder ...," she paused and activated her tablet, pulling up the list before continuing, "attempted murder, espionage, aiding and abetting the enemy, dereliction of duty and conduct unbecoming of an officer." She looked up from the tablet with a medicine-taste face and added, "Those are the most important ones anyway. There are several more."

Orli's first instinct was to argue, but she skipped it. This was obviously the work of Captain Asad. She calmed herself and studied her defense counsel for a moment, the young woman standing straight and silent as she did. "How old are you?" Orli asked, not bothering to pretend she wasn't skeptical of the woman's youth.

"Twenty," Orli's attorney replied in a tone that suggested she was used to the question and simply wanted to get it out of the way. "I graduated high school three years early and was ahead of the curve all the way through law school, which I finished almost a year ago. And if you want the truth, you're lucky you got me, because I don't think we'd have had a snowball's chance in hell even if I'd been at this for the last fifty years."

Orli laughed. Sort of. But she did relax some. "I don't think you're supposed to say that kind of thing out loud. At least not in front of me."

"I'm not. But, while I may be young, I'm not stupid. My only hope is to delay the execution long enough to get real justice in here. This is the worst railroad job I've ever heard of. It's as if all safeguards for your rights have been thrown off. And from what I understand, they didn't even get anything from the chemical interrogation to justify doing this."

That was a lot to process. Orli didn't doubt that the young lawyer was sharp, and she even decided she liked her well enough. At least she had a smart attorney, if not an experienced one. She sat back down, trying to work through the rest. "Justify what? What is 'this'?"

"Your execution."

That set Orli back. She blinked up at Angela a few times, trying to figure out what missing memory she hadn't reclaimed earlier. Nothing came. "Executed? When? What do they think I did? They have me on video trying to get Altin out of the cell. That's hardly a death penalty offense, much less one requiring validation through a chemical interrogation. They already had the evidence."

"That's just one of the charges. I read you the list. In fact, that one is way down toward the bottom. It's all the rest. The conspiracy to commit mass murder is the big one, that and the aiding and abetting the enemy, there are several counts of that. They'd have charged you with one count for every one of the hundred-thousand-plus Hostiles in orbit if they'd thought they needed to."

"Hundred thousand Hostiles in orbit?" Orli's mouth

gaped. Then she knew; the missing memories came flooding back. It was real. She could vaguely see the image on the screen in sick bay in her memory. It was true. The Hostiles had come to Earth.

"Yes. Well, they don't know exactly how many, but those are the newest estimates. More are coming all the time. They blame you for it. They had at you in that chemical session for over an hour trying to discover whatever secrets and covert plans you had or knew of regarding Altin Meade and the Prosperion monarch in that regard."

"Well, then I didn't tell them much."

"No, you didn't. Apparently either you never knew of any plans, or you did but the Prosperions buried them too deep in your mind to find. That or they erased them before you were taken away. Not that anyone down here cares which, by the way."

That didn't seem right, much less fair. Orli studied the woman's face, wondering for a moment if maybe she had been chosen because she was so smart, and so young. Maybe they picked her to come in here and try to trick information out of her. But Angela sat there so patiently yet clearly indignant about what she thought was going on. Her eyes had seemed so wide and honest as she spoke, her passion rising with each word, so much so that Orli had a hard time believing all that was fake. And, as she looked about the room, in the end it wasn't like she was in a position to do anything about it anyway. She had no choice but to trust her. "So when will they ... you know, come for me, to do it? What do we do?"

"Well, for the most part, you just sit there," said the young attorney, a softening of her aspect making it appear as if she understood what had just passed through Orli's mind. "They haven't technically convicted you yet, but if what I think is going to happen happens, it's not going to matter what either of us has to say. I'm convinced what's really happened is that they've decided you are far too risky to keep alive at this point, even as a bargaining chip. They believe you are a magnet for Altin Meade. Or a beacon. Something like that. I mean, think about it: they actually flew you down here, through that nightmare up there. It's insane the risk they took."

That made Orli cringe as she once more recalled the image on the nurse's station monitor.

The attorney nodded when she saw the look in Orli's eyes. "Yes, exactly. They're so worried about what you know or have learned from the Prosperions that they actually think you might be capable of doing magic yourself."

That made Orli laugh, although short lived, fueled mainly by incredulity and nerves. "That's ridiculous. They know all about the Prosperion brain thing. The mythothalamus. They know perfectly well I can't cast spells."

"That doesn't change the fact they put you in that gag, does it?"

She nodded. That explained a lot. "What's to keep me from doing magic now?"

"The room is electrified. They're watching us. If you do anything that looks like magic, zap. Both of us. So please don't even pretend."

"Wow," was all that Orli could say. She looked up and around the room again. It didn't seem much different, but she supposed the floor had sounded a little different beneath her feet than the hallways had. So had her cell. What a bunch of bastards.

"Yes, exactly. So as you can see, reason is mostly out the window and anything like justice is long gone. This is all being pushed through for the show, which means it has to come from the very top, surely the director himself."

Orli had sense enough to be frightened now as reality began to settle in. "Then why are you here at all?"

"Like I said, the show."

"They'll have this conversation recorded. What's the point?"

"No, they won't. This is your confidential time." She looked disgusted as she said it, as if all the high ideals she'd gotten as she gobbled up all that coursework in school were lies, as if she'd consumed the principles of justice and equality and trusted the value of the system in which it all worked so seamlessly, processed and locked it all down in her facile, eidetic mind only to discover that it was rancid and poisonous. It was as if she'd been eating from some rotten carcass found lying on the side of the road and yet never known, the whole time thinking it something else, something held up throughout her childhood as some great feast for the mind. Orli's treatment by the system sickened her, and it was obvious.

Orli saw it in the woman's eyes, and the dawning sense of her plight grew. Somehow, without ever having thought about it, she'd always assumed that her people, the people of Earth, had a polished and refined sense of justice. Especially back here on Earth, on the actual home world. Earth was supposed to have something on the order of mechanized justice, a system of automated right, or at least something as close to it as humans were capable of. Not this. Not something where one man could just type in an access code and override the work of centuries trying to master the concept of human decency. How was this any better than the wave of the War Queen's scepter, or even the whim of Lord Thadius and his desire to own her as if it were his noble right?

And to think people in the fleet called the Prosperions primitives.

Orli repeated her question of moments before. "So what

do we do?"

Angela pursed her lips, shaking off whatever lament she'd entertained. Back to business. "The main thing is not to do anything that gives them reason to carry out the sentence any more immediately than I think they're going to. They never execute anyone earlier than forty-eight hours after sentencing, although that's not actually written in the NTA rules anywhere. What we don't want to do is give them justification to deviate from that convention, given that they've already thrown out the rest of the rule book. I hope you understand, because I need time."

Orli nodded. She wasn't going to be able to do much anyway, not with her hands bound, her mouth gagged and while buried God-only-knew how many miles beneath the Earth's surface in a base for which she had no door codes or chip recognition. And if they put her on the stand, she'd tell them what she knew, which, according to her fledgling defense counsel, had already been dismissed as lies and Prosperion propaganda. She nodded. "I understand."

"I will do everything I can in the courtroom, but my cousin works in the JAG office, and he said he heard Commander Adair, that's the prosecutor, talking with the judge on the com, talking about how this is all going to go down. That's how I found out what I ... what we were in for. Our only hope lies in the fact that my uncle is the ranking judge advocate at Fort Reno, and I'm going to him for help the moment this trial is through. You're not even getting a hearing first. It's completely wrong in every way."

"I have to tell you, as my attorney, you're not making me feel very confident at all."

Orli's attempt at levity didn't work for either of them. "I know. I'm sorry," Angela said. "I wish I could tell you something different, but I was taught that dealing in the truth is the fastest way to justice. I have to believe that is true, despite how it seems otherwise right now."

Orli harrumphed at that, every cell in her body filling with the irony. "Well, we'll see how that works out. But let's not be above lying if it seems like it might help. If what you're saying is correct, I'm not sure a perjury charge is going to hurt me much. If we have to throw out a few ideals to save me, I'm fine with it."

Angela ruffled at that, shaking her head and looking as if she were about to make an argument. A knock on the door prevented her from doing so. Two guards came into the room, the taller of the two with his assault rifle drawn. He pointed it at Orli as soon as his partner was out of the line of fire. "It's time," the shorter one announced.

"Time for what?"

"Your trial," both the guard and Angela said at once.

"Wow, you weren't kidding," Orli remarked. "That's how much time they gave you to prepare with me?"

"I hope you don't think I made up any of what I just said, Ensign. You are in serious trouble here. Try not to make it worse. Give me time to help."

The young woman's sudden formality stung a little, but she relented immediately and reached down a hand to help pull Orli to her feet. Orli swallowed hard as Angela looked deeply into her eyes, sending in that heavy glance all the weight of dreadful certainty. Orli drew back from it, from that severity, and the cavalier impulses of an instant ago were completely gone.

Orli stared out into the small courtroom from her seat on the witness stand. There were Marines all around the edges of the room, three of them with rifles raised and trained on her, prepared for her slightest incantation, the least hint of her invoking her magical powers. If she weren't in such deep shit, she could have been amused by it all, but she was, so she wasn't.

She had to avoid looking at Roberto sitting in the back row because every time she saw him, she felt like she might come unhinged a little. He just kept staring at her, like his heart was breaking, and she knew that for the burly Spaniard, it probably was. She tried to send him back a reassuring glance, to let him know she would figure something out, but there was a brokenness in his expression that scared her.

It was easier to look at Captain Asad. He was the center of this whole nightmare. He always had been. From the very start he sought conflict. He'd never wanted to trust the Prosperions no matter what they did. It was his absolute dedication to finding hostility in everything that got her here. And when he'd taken the stand, she'd watched him give his testimony so methodically, so systematically, and so incorrectly that she'd wished she really could cast magic. She'd read once in one of Altin's spellbooks that Prosperion transmuters could actually unbind the energy in living cells. Unmake them. She couldn't think of anything she'd like to do more than unmake him as she'd watched him drone on and on. She hated him.

But there was no hate in his relating of the story. The man was as efficient in giving his version of events as he was brutal in his interpretation of the facts. And worse, young Angela couldn't even put a dent in his version of how the whole Prosperion-Hostile debacle came about. How could she? Everything he'd said was true. The Prosperions, and Altin, had helped save Blue Fire from fleet attack. Blue Fire was the party responsible for the annihilation of the Andalians. Blue Fire was responsible for the death of most of the *Aspect*'s crew. Blue Fire was responsible for the destruction of more than half of the ships that had been sent out those twelve long years ago.

All the Hostiles in the air above Earth that very moment had appeared during the heated exchange following the Prosperion intervention that had saved Blue Fire's world, and right after Altin Meade had been taken out of the *Aspect*'s brig. With Orli's help.

There was nothing in any of that that wasn't spot-on true.

Captain Asad now sat next to a JAG officer of roughly the same age, Commander Adair. From the familiar way they whispered back and forth, she was pretty sure they'd known each other for years. The jury had been dismissed. Orli's young attorney had requested it when Orli pointed out that Captain Metumbe and Captain Putin, two of the three jurors present when they'd come in, were confidants of Captain Asad. So she'd waived her right to a jury. Which meant it was up to the judge. Based on what Angela had told her, she was pretty sure she already knew how that was going to go.

Asad's crony finally rose after Orli swore to tell the truth and came to stand before her. "Ensign Pewter, thank you for being here today and cooperating with this investigation." He did not wait for a reply. "I'd like to cut to the quick if possible, so let me start by asking simply: how much did you know about the intended attack on planet Earth?"

"I thought you guys already picked my brain while I was under?"

He repeated the question in a patient, patronizing voice.

"Nothing. There was never a plan to attack Earth. Ever."

"It seems that's not quite true, Ensign. I believe you are familiar with what is happening above our planet right now, are you not?"

She nodded.

"So, I'll ask you again. What did you know about this attack?"

She repeated her answer. "Nothing."

He turned to the judge seated nearby. "You can see how this is going to go." The judge motioned for him to continue.

"Ensign Pewter, were you or were you not in a romantic relationship with the Prosperion called Altin Meade?"

"I was."

"Do you still have feelings for him now?"

"I do."

"And it was Altin Meade that you were attempting to help escape from the *Aspect*'s brig, was it not? And remember, we have sworn affidavits from three Marines on duty at the time, not to mention the testimony of the Prosperion, Annison, and, of course, video."

"Yes. I was trying to get him out." Orli's attorney cringed visibly.

"Records indicate that Mr. Meade was taken from the *Aspect* at sixteen hundred twenty-eight hours on the day of October nineteenth, less than three days ago. The first of the Hostiles arrived exactly seven minutes and nineteen seconds afterward. Don't you think that seems a remarkable bit of timing, Ensign Pewter?"

"Objection," Angela said from her place at the defendant's table. "Ensign Pewter's opinion of the timing is irrelevant."

"Withdrawn," said the JAG officer before the judge even spoke. He put his hands on the railing at the front of the witness stand. "Ensign Pewter, you are reported to have also had some form of relationship with the leader of the Hostile world, an entity described in the reports as Blue Fire. Is this correct?"

"Yes."

"What form of relationship would you say you had

with her?"

"An honest one," Orli replied.

"Ah, well that is always a good thing, isn't it?"

Orli made a "no shit" face at him, which he ignored.

"So, Ensign Pewter, being honest, as we all want to be here, what can you tell us regarding this Blue Fire's relationship with Mr. Meade."

"I was unaware that he had a relationship with her."

"But surely you were in communication with him, and with her. At some point one of them must have mentioned the other."

"The last time I spoke to Altin about her, he didn't believe she existed. I told him I could only speak to her in dreams, and he didn't believe it."

"And what about Blue Fire? Did she ... did she believe in Altin?"

"Yes."

"And you have never once had any communication about either from the other, no conversations about plans or cooperation between them?"

"No. Never."

"And you expect we should simply trust you on that, Ensign?"

"Objection," came the call from Angela.

"Sustained," said the judge.

"Have you been in communication with Blue Fire since returning to Earth?"

"No."

"She hasn't contacted you to ask you for information about our defenses, looking for any aid or advice?"

"No."

"How about Mr. Meade? Have you been in contact with him?"

"No."

"Are you certain?"

"Yes. I have no way to contact him."

"What about him. Does he have a way of contacting you?"

"No. He doesn't know where I am. He has to know where I am to communicate with me."

"And would you tell us if he did have a way of doing so, Ensign?"

"Objection."

"Overruled. Answer the question."

"Probably not," Orli said. "But he doesn't, so it doesn't matter."

"Oh, I think he does," said the prosecutor.

He went to a long table against the far wall and lifted a pair of sealed plastic bags, which he brought back and presented first to the judge, then to the court in general, and last to Orli. He brought them near enough for her to see, raising one up nearly to the level of her face. Orli's intake of breath was audible for everyone to hear.

"I see you recognize this creature," he said, referencing the spotted lizard in the bag. Its body was flattened near the head, and its front limbs were broken and bent akimbo from when it had obviously been crushed. "Can you explain to the court what it is?"

"It's ...," she looked to Angela who sighed visibly, if not audibly, and nodded to indicate Orli had to answer. But still Orli couldn't speak. Her eyes flicked to Roberto, whose response nearly mirrored Angela's. She felt trapped and manipulated, anger burning in the pit of her stomach. She'd forgotten about the homing lizards. And why had they killed it? What was wrong with these barbarians? That poor wonderful thing of Prosperion, ruined by the boot of some brute. Seeing it there, so mangled in that bag, nearly set her off. She looked back to Roberto again, and he could see it in her face, the way her body tensed. He shook his head, his wide brown eyes silently pleading with her to keep her cool.

"Answer the question, Ensign," said the judge sternly, obviously misreading her reluctance as a sign of guilt.

The smug look on Captain Asad's face helped her find herself again, if only barely. She drew composure from her unwillingness to be beaten by that man. She gritted her teeth and answered. "It's called a homing lizard. It's a Prosperion communication device. Like a carrier pigeon that jumps across space."

"Thank you, Ensign," said Commander Adair. "That is an excellent analogy. So it will not surprise you then if I tell you that this note was tied to the animal?"

She didn't look at the note. "No, it will not surprise me. That is what they do."

"So who sent you this note, Ensign?"

That made her look. "I didn't know the note was sent to me. What does it say?"

"It says: *Where are you? I will come for you.* That is translated into English of course. So who sent it?"

Orli started to answer, but her attorney cut her off once again. "Objection," Angela called. "Conjecture. Ensign Pewter's guess as to its origin is no more relevant than anyone else's."

"Your honor, Ensign Pewter may well be able to recognize the handwriting."

"Your honor, my client has no training in the forensic analysis of documents," countered the young defense attorney.

"Surely her opinion, were this handwriting to belong to her lover, would have some value in these proceedings," said Commander Adair to that.

"I'll allow it," said the judge, "seeing as I'm deciding this thing anyway." He looked impatient, though, or perhaps made a show of it for the cameras.

Asad's old friend brought the second plastic envelope

close enough for Orli to see the strip of parchment in it. She recognized the handwriting immediately and had to force herself not to show any expression that might make that recognition obvious.

"So, Ensign, do you recognize the handwriting on this note?" Commander Adair asked.

She glanced down at her lap for a moment. She didn't want to look at her attorney, because her attorney was going give her that faith-in-truth face that Orli didn't want to deal with right then. In her heart she knew this was a great place for perjury. She looked up at the JAG officer and gave her best vacant look, shaking her head. "No clue whose handwriting that is," she said.

"Ensign Pewter, please. You have already tried to tell us that Altin Meade had no way to contact you without knowing where you are, and in the next breath you admit to us that the Prosperions have these creatures called homing lizards. Surely you don't expect us to believe this message came to you randomly from any other Prosperion than your lover, Altin Meade."

"Objection."

"The witness will answer the question."

"I said I don't recognize it."

There followed a long silence as the prosecutor glared at her. He turned back to the judge. "Clearly the witness has no intention of being honest with us here today, your honor."

"Objection," put in Angela again.

"That will be for me to decide," agreed the judge.

"I can prove that this is the handwriting of Altin Meade," went on the commander.

"Please do," said the judge.

The commander went back to the evidence table and brought forth several more plastic bags. In each of them was a strip of parchment, and upon all of them were written notes. "We found these in Ensign Pewter's quarters, stored with her private things." Once again he showed them to the court and to the judge and then to Orli. "Do you recognize these?" he asked her after she'd looked at them.

The way she winced when she saw them was obvious to everyone in the courtroom.

"Yes," she said reluctantly. There was no way she could lie her way out of that. They were notes she'd exchanged with Altin during his convalescence two years ago, their romantic exchanges made via homing lizard while the *Aspect* and the other ships were first making their way to Prosperion.

"Can you tell the court what they are?"

"They are notes."

"Yes, we can see that, Ensign. Notes exchanged between who and whom?"

She looked up at Angela who was shaking her head. Roberto clearly sighed again by the way his broad shoulders moved. "Between Altin and myself."

He handed her the note they'd taken off the smashed homing lizard. "Now do you recognize the handwriting on this more recent note?"

"Objection," tried Angela again.

"Overruled. Answer the question, Ensign."

"No. I don't recognize it."

Commander Adair turned, rolling his head in an annoyed way, overly dramatic, and appealed to the judge impatiently. "Your honor. The defendant clearly has no interest in cooperating. I move that we end this now and carry out the sentencing before the Prosperion magicians have time to locate her and effect her escape or, worse, send some sort of device to her location that will further compromise this fort and the security of planet Earth."

"Objection," barked Angela, leaping from her seat. "I

repeat that my client is not a handwriting specialist, and her inability to match two documents is in no way proof that my client is unwilling to cooperate, much less reason to convict."

The judge looked past her, Orli couldn't be sure if at the clock on the wall above the door or at the camera above the clock. "Sustained." He set an irritated gaze down upon Commander Adair.

"I have a handwriting expert," the commander said. "You have his sworn affidavit there in your files. He ran the file comparisons, and they came back a perfect match. Perfect."

The judge thumbed through a few screens on a tablet set before him on his desk. He found the affidavit and saw that it was in order. He turned to Orli and shook his head. "Ensign Pewter, playing games with this court is not in your best interest."

"Then what is in my best interest, your honor?" Anger smoldered in her icy blue eyes as she glared up at him. What had she ever done that hadn't been in the best interest of planet Earth? "Is it in my best interest to sit here while these people, while you, all play games and do your stupid meticulous questioning, claiming the intent of finding truth, but not showing any real interest in it? If you want the truth, I'll give it to you. The truth is that Blue Fire didn't do it. None of it. Not the way you think. Not the way it sounds. Neither did the Prosperions. You have the facts but not the context. Without the context you won't find truth."

The judge slammed his gavel down repeatedly as she spoke. "Silence, Ensign. Outbursts like this will not be tolerated."

"I don't give a shit what will be tolerated. You are listening to that idiot over there," she said, standing and pointing at Asad, "and you are ignoring everything that matters. You don't have to tolerate me. What you have to do is stop letting the facts get in the way of the truth. The Prosperions aren't the enemy. You need to look and think. This whole thing is stupid."

"Ensign Pewter, I understand you are under a great deal of stress right now, but you will sit down and come to order, or I will leave your defense to your attorney in your absence, and you will have no say at all."

"As if you're going to listen anyway." But she sat down. She at least had to try.

The judge looked back to Commander Adair. "Carry on."

"I have nothing else, Your Honor. Further questioning would be pointless. She is obviously hostile and protecting the enemy. I move for verdict and sentencing. Every moment she breathes brings us closer to an inside attack by Altin Meade and the Prosperion War Queen. Possibly right here in this courtroom. Meade can strike at any moment."

"That's right, he can," spat Orli. "But he's not going to. If you'd stop trying to fucking railroad me here, I could explain why he is not your enemy."

"Ensign, this is your last warning."

"No. Fuck you and your warning. You need to listen. Stop this goddamn circus and listen. This is all a mistake. And you are going to make it worse."

Commander Adair made a big showman's sigh and looked impatiently to the judge. The judge for a moment looked relieved, as if he'd finally gotten an anticipated opportunity, but then he put his stern judge face back on.

"Take her away," he said to the Marines stationed nearest the doors. Two of them came forward and grabbed her by the arms, dragging her up over the railing and yanking her out of the witness stand.

"Just listen to me, goddamn it," she shouted at them as

they dragged her toward the doors. She twisted and tried to yank herself free. "Let me go, you morons. I'm trying to save your lives too."

Orli was still shouting as they dragged her out of the courtroom, her cries and profanities echoing down the corridor beyond the doors, heard dully through them by everyone in the room for a long, awkward half minute before the proceedings could finally carry on.

Angela did her best to defend Orli after that, trying to prove Orli's innocence through various legal technicalities, but the result was inevitable. The best she could do was buy Orli time. All told, she went on for just over an hour, padding her closing arguments as best she could, but that was it, an hour and a few minutes more. And within moments after she closed her statements, Orli was pronounced guilty on all charges and sentenced to death by lethal injection, a sentence to be carried out "immediately," which in legal parlance meant that there be no delays and that the reports and processing be expedited. When the judge gave the verdict and sentence, so clearly prepared in advance as it had been, so clearly in absence of consideration for anything Angela had said, all the young attorney could do was shake her head and leave. Her efforts had bought Orli nothing, though it came as no surprise.

When she returned to Orli's cell, she was allowed only five minutes with her client. The guards wouldn't even leave the room. One of them, a thick-necked fellow built like a six-foot stack of steel plates unfastened the ball gag and pulled it roughly out of her mouth. "Five minutes," he repeated. "And if she says one word of magic, anything that might work to contact the enemy, she's done." He stepped back and watched, like his partner, gun level and trained on the prisoner.

Angela could not hide her frustration for what Orli had

done. "Congratulations," she said in her irritation. "You managed to get your time, *our* time, nearly cut in half. You just cussed away half your life." Her jaw worked back and forth visibly as she paced the tiny room. "I don't even know what I'm supposed to do now, not with so little time."

"Don't worry about it," Orli said trying to keep fear at bay. "Altin will come for me."

Apparently that was enough to get the ball gag jammed back into her mouth, for the moment she spoke Altin's name, the burly Marine stepped into her and shoved it manfully back in place. He cinched the straps down so tightly they dug into her skin at the hinge of her jaw, and the buckles cut into the back of her head. When it was done, he turned back to the diminutive attorney who was staring wide-eyed at the rough treatment her client had just received.

"You need to leave now," the Marine demanded.

"I'll have you up on charges for this," she said. "My client still has rights, you know."

"Well, she won't be needing them for long. Now get out, or you'll get the same."

The Marine pushed Angela out with the muzzle of his weapon, and the door closed on Orli's protests, muffling them to nearly nothing in the lawyer's ears. She listened anyway as the guards escorted her down the hall, trying to make out the words, reaching for them as one might reach for the hand of someone who has slipped and is falling forever away. She wished she could at least do Orli the last courtesy of listening to her, that one final bit of humanity, to hear what she had to say, even if most of it sounded like threats and profanity. She would have liked to have at least done that.

Chapter 10

Gromf watched the dark figures leaping and stomping before the fire and did not hide the curl of his upper lip. Let Warlord see the length of his tooth at this. These were the old ways, the ways taught by the old gods who had led the clans to shame. It was the old renewal dance, and they believed it a hopeful thing, hope for new beginnings. Youngling warriors reached for a first fistful of female flesh, the women all twice as old as the stupid youths, with their rigid eagerness jutting and apparent for all to see. The women mocked them, kicked dirt at them, leapt wildly about the fire in gleaming nudity, tormenting the younglings with the power of their jumps, the motion of their soft tissues with each cavort, jiggling taunts above golden light that glinted from skin stretched taut over powerful abdomens, broad backs and exquisitely muscled limbs. The light playing on such sumptuousness burned across the shadow spaces of the dance and sent fits of quivering into young and untried loins. And so the younglings groped and growled, spoke words of carnal intent and prowess that were laughable and naive. The ritual was primitive and old, and it made Gromf feel ashamed, for it seemed to him a ceremony of nothing but the lack of Discipline.

But there was no chance that Warlord would gauge the nature of Gromf's thoughts, for Warlord watched with a great snaggle of teeth. He threw the gnawed-clean rib of a wolf at one of the dancers, striking the youngling in the back of the head. The youngling paid no more attention to the blow than he had any of the others, the rain of bones and soggy greens that fell upon the dance, no more concern than he had for the smoke rising from the fire into the night.

Kazuk-Hal-Mandik, sitting beside Gromf, however, did notice the disgust on the face of his newly chosen apprentice, the victor of the contest for the yellow stone. The old shaman nodded privately to himself, glad that Gromf understood the new ways well enough to despise the old. There were still those who did not. And Gromf was a northern orc. That was good too. An omen, perhaps, of God's favor.

"I see you find no joy in the ceremony," he said. "It is a tribute to your glory."

"There is no glory in the shame of seasons too numerous to count."

Kazuk-Hal-Mandik nodded, revealing the gaps in his own natural weaponry, the emptiness. He had spent his life in service of the old gods, but it was he who the new god had found and first spoken to. "I am pleased it was you, Gromf," he said after a time. "The winner needed to be someone like you."

A youngling fell for the tricks of a woman crawling upon her hands and knees, gnashing her teeth temptingly as she waggled her tattooed buttocks at him. He ran to her, shoving two others down, and made to mount her. When she spun and threw him into the fire, he screamed and howled, and Gromf had to wait for him to roll out of the flames and extinguish himself in the dirt, his cries making it impossible to speak to the elder shaman for a time. The woman's coarse laughter echoed from the surrounding cliffs, rising on the tide of laughter coming from everyone else around. Gromf had to wait for the wave of that to pass as well.

"Why do you fear it, old one?" he finally asked.

Kazuk-Hal-Mandik leaned back and studied Gromf, his lined green face seeming faded in the firelight. Dancers passed in front of the fire, throwing darkness, fleeting shadows, across the severity of his broad countenance, like the blinking of time. He considered hiding the truth, what little he knew, from today's victor, but decided he would not. He would trust in God's judgment in this.

"It is not fear," he said after a time. "It is caution, which is a thing of Discipline. We do not know how it works. It is God Stone. It will help us take our rightful place on Prosperion. God has said it will be so."

"Does Warlord know you speak such things?"

"He does."

"Then he is weak. He should have pulled out your tongue."

"He should have. But he did not. For he has, at least for now, faith in Discipline. Why else would he hold back an army that is over a hundred thousand strong? How could he have grown such a force?"

Gromf nodded across the heaped food at the scene that continued to unfold around the fire, the dance of beginning. "But he does not believe in the one God. His Discipline will fail. It will fail when we need it most."

"It is possible," admitted Kazuk-Hal-Mandik.

"The enemy's spear is thrown," insisted Gromf. "Warlord must dodge, duck or lift his shield. He must choose, or we will all be struck the death of his indecision."

"Your Discipline must include faith in your leaders, Gromf. Warlord did not get his seat by stupidity."

Gromf nodded. This was true.

Laughter rose again, a guttural rush like the sound of several hundred boars startled all at once. The burned youngling was crabbing backwards on hands and feet, moving away from the approach of the woman who had thrown him into the fire. She slapped at him, punched the flaccidity that pain had brought upon him, as she mocked his impotence. "I see you do not want me anymore," she taunted over the laughter of the crowd.

"Would you like to speak to God?" Kazuk-Hal-Mandik asked after a time.

Gromf turned to face him, his eyes narrowing as he fixed the ancient shaman with a doubtful stare. "It is not so easy as that."

"It is," said the warlock, sipping water from the bowl of an abalone shell. "But there is one thing you must tell me first."

"And that is?" said Gromf, knowing well what was coming next.

"You must tell me what you learned of the God Stone."

"And if I don't?"

"Then God will choose another."

"And what of you? You will simply watch me take the stone away? Leave its power to me? There is no Discipline in that."

"You underestimate God, Gromf, because you have only seen him in your heart. I have seen him with my eyes. As you might if you choose to walk this path with me. As you will tonight. That is up to you. But do not believe he has no power to get what is his from us. He sees us and knows what we do. You do not take the stone from me. You do not take it from Warlord. You take the stone from him. And that is your choice. I cannot tell you what is right."

Gromf watched as one of the younglings pinned a

woman over a rock. The burly youth wrenched her arms behind her back, her wrists crushed together in one huge, powerful hand. His free hand pressed her head against the rock as he took his victory, his thrusts accompanied by triumphant barks which were echoed by the crowd. Even the subdued woman joined, though the sound was muted by the pressure of his hand upon her jaw and the angle of her face jammed against the rock.

Gromf let his gaze move from the first of the evening's victors to the assemblage watching, the open mouths, the hoisted fists, the shouts and grunts of primal revelry. How could they ever beat the humans like this? It seemed unachievable. Humans were organized and patient. They thought and thought and thought. They hid their desires carefully. Somehow they all did. Or at least most of them. Enough of them to take and hold everything. Meanwhile, his people were still doing this. The things they had always done. The ways of strength without mind. No Discipline. They would never defeat the humans in this way. If they were going to win, they would need something else. Something like the favor of a god.

"I will tell you what I know," Gromf said at last. He lifted a leg over the log upon which he sat, riding it in the way humans rode on horses, the way even a few of his people did now—when they could be made not to eat the beasts the moment they were caught. "I will tell you everything. And then you will take me to see God."

Kazuk-Hal-Mandik nodded. "It is agreed."

Gromf did not need much time to explain what he knew of the God Stone to Kazuk-Hal-Mandik because, in truth, he knew very little. He explained how the mana became thin and moved easily, like water rather than like honey. That is what Gromf knew. He also knew, or at least gauged by what he had seen from the *doh-ruek* who had teleported himself into a wall, and from the numbers of orcs who had briefly ascended to the top of the mountain of dead bodies only to explode or vanish or simply fall down dead for reasons that could not be explained, that magic could go very wrong with the stone. These things Kazuk-Hal-Mandik had also seen.

But Gromf's description was enough. It filled in the missing bits of information the old shaman had gleaned while using the lamp he had stolen from the old human fortress at the base of the great mountain, the fortress with the towers of mismatched stone. The water effect is the changing of mana to a thing more powerful. It was the thing God had hinted of when he told Kazuk-Hal-Mandik of the stones.

Now, Kazuk-Hal-Mandik led Gromf down into the deep and sacred caves of the clan, the dying places where the honored warriors went to the last season. This was the place where the warlords and heroes came never to be seen again. The old ways said the gods came to claim them and take them to a new place where they were reborn in greater bodies, a land of beasts many times larger than those that roamed the vast plains of Kurr, the greatest beasts. There were no humans there. No dwarves. No elves. Only orcs. Orcs and the greatest beasts endlessly seeking to devour one another for all of time.

Gromf no longer believed that this was true. The new God promised other things. He promised a land where there *were* humans. And elves. There was justice in this land. Eternal justice and the enslavement of hated humanity. The squeaks and squawking of birds during the day, the howling of wolves at night, all of these were replaced by the weeping sounds of broken men and their sobbing pleas for mercy and forgiveness. Gromf thought those stories seemed too good to be true, but he hoped that they were. He allowed himself to believe in the one God, had faith in his promises, for had not everything he had told them worked thus far? And it was with that faith and hope that he followed Kazuk-Hal-Mandik into the chamber where God was said to speak.

"You are the only orc alive besides me to see this place," said the ancient warlock as they entered the sacred chamber. "It was here that God found me."

"Where is he?" Gromf asked. He was in no mood for long histories now. Enough talking had been done. "Call him forth."

"One does not call forth God," Kazuk-Hal-Mandik began, but he did not continue for suddenly the chamber filled with light as the pool itself appeared to come to life.

The water filled first with the light of a bright blue sky, so bright Gromf felt as if he stood in broad daylight, and in a way, he did. Into that nearly blinding azure grew hazy shapes which solidified into a formation of rocks and gnarled trees. The trees were low-elbowed things that looked as if growth for them was the pursuit of obsequiousness. They seemed to bow and scrape across the uneven terrain, snaking over the jagged stone and only daring to put the barest spread of greenery up into the air, feeble tufts like trees in miniature, and even those too fretful to be green, favoring instead a groveling yellowed hue.

In the midst of the jumble of stones sat a figure that might once have been an orc, though upon closer examination, even that similarity seemed farfetched beyond merely the count of its head and limbs.

Its head was a vast, craggy thing, colored and textured so as to nearly match the stones upon which it sat, red and brown and black, no pattern, and covered with lichens and the white and gray smears left by the droppings of passing birds. Despite this head, its location relative to the rest of the form, it could not be said to be head-shaped, though it did sit upon a chunky foundation that shaped in its fissures and angles a set of shoulders and a torso. From this grew a pair of arms and legs, though none of them of equal size, and at the ends of each, three of them at least, were things that moved in the way of hands and feet. The left arm of the figure was far longer than the right, longer than the body as a whole, so long its terminal end could not be seen. What served for legs were a bramble of twisted joints, too many joints to be needed, four on one leg, six on another, and none of an orientation that seemed to complement the rest. Gromf couldn't imagine what it must look like when it moved.

To Gromf's eyes, it was a thing of unrivaled deformity sitting there, an abortion to be cast off a cliff the moment it arrived. Such misshapenness would never have been allowed to live amongst the clans. It was an abomination to be rid of, nothing more.

"He has come," muttered Kazuk-Hal-Mandik in a low voice as he threw himself to the ground. "It is the one God."

Gromf did not fall so easily to the ground. He stood staring into the pool at the hideous thing sitting there. He studied it even as he suspected it studied him. Gromf noticed that the rocks it sat upon were covered with crystals, stones like the yellow stone, hundreds of them, thousands even. The more he scoured the image in the pool, the more of them he saw. It was everywhere. God Stone. A heap of it, a whole place of it. What power must this one God wield?

"You do not fear me," said the figure in the water. A crack in the craggy rock-heap of its head moved as it spoke. Gromf thought the voice was in his head, not his ears, though its timing matched the motions of its mouth. The pond remained still.

Kazuk-Hal-Mandik was groveling at the edge of the

pool, hissing at Gromf to get down before he got them both killed.

"No, I do not fear you," Gromf said. "Are you a god, or do you have the power of so much yellow stone to pretend it?"

The figure in the pool laughed, and there was fluidity to the movement that convinced Gromf it could not be a creature of solid stone. It had a body like an orc beneath all that, or in spite of it.

"There is no difference," said the one God. "I am God. Your God. I have vanquished the others, and now have come to help you destroy the children of those gods that I have slain."

"What children?"

"The humans and the elves. Just as I destroyed the dwarves before them. When it is done, I will set an orc upon the throne of humanity and another in the elven vale."

"Why?"

"Because it is just."

Gromf stared into the pool, tried once more to count the bits and pieces of all that yellow stone. He knew little of the dwarves or the elves. But he knew enough of power to recognize the promise of what he saw.

"What must we do?"

"You begin," said the one God, "by killing that one. He is weak. Break his neck, and you may take his stone as well."

Gromf glowered down at the horrified expression that briefly crossed Kazuk-Hal-Mandik's face. In that instant the old shaman knew fear, but he put it quickly away. He was as ashamed by it as Gromf was at having seen it. He recovered in an instant, then nodded, solemn and calm. "It is true," he said. "My part has been done."

Gromf felt better then, and forgave the old warlock for

his fear, though he would not break his neck. He turned back to the one God. "I am not done with him," he said. "He will die when he is no longer of use to the All Clans. That is the way of Discipline. You demand waste."

The one God laughed, the sound of stones rolling down into a hole. He turned away then and spoke to someone Gromf could not see. "There is hope after all," he said. "Finally." There came from behind him, somewhere far below, a great caterwauling, raucousness formed in throats that Gromf could not picture the creatures for. Nothing he'd seen in his life made such sounds.

Gromf looked down at Kazuk-Hal-Mandik still on his hands and knees. "Get up," he said. "The time for groveling is done."

Chapter 11

Doctor Leopold came out of the divination spell seven hours after he began. As unspectacular as it was to watch, him sitting there mumbling with his eyes closed and doing nothing else to entertain the eye, his masterful inquiry into the location of Ensign Orli Pewter was high-level magic coming from a diviner of his rank. He leaned back, causing a ruckus of protests from the rickety chair in which he sat, and pulled a handkerchief from his waistcoat pocket. He dabbed at the beads of sweat that had formed on the expanse of his hairless brow and then did the same across his thick forearms which also showed a sheen of sweat by the light of the candles burning low nearby.

"Well, my boy," he said at length, "you are correct in assuming she is on that planet. I need parchment."

Altin rifled through the heap of items he'd dumped on the floor and found a basket in which had once been stacked a pile of blank parchment sheets. He fished around until he found a piece that wasn't too wrinkled and then sought for a quill and the inkpot he knew had to be down there as well. Fortunately, there was still enough ink in the ink pot for the doctor's use.

The doctor set to work making a sketch of planet Earth, upon which he drew the shape of one of its significant landmasses, and upon that he drew a small circle to which he pointed as he handed his map to Altin. "She is in that area somewhere."

Altin took the parchment to the window and looked out, the vantage he had on the distant planet good enough that he could just make out the landform described by the doctor's picture. The continent he'd drawn occupied the upper portion of the globe from the angle of Altin's view, though with some portion of it out of sight around the left side. He spent a few moments looking back and forth between parchment version and the actual landmass, then turned back to the doctor with a frown. "Surely you have more than this. If this world is remotely similar in size to Prosperion, that is at least two or three hundred measures you've marked there." He poked at the map as he spoke. "You can't expect me to find her in time in all of that."

"If it helps," said the doctor, "I get the feeling she's in a fortress of some kind. Possibly in the dungeon."

Altin's eyes bulged and the doctor knew immediately that Altin only barely kept his temper in check. "Are you telling me we just wasted seven hours to narrow it down to ... to *that*?"

"Well, I'm not sure it's entirely a waste," the doctor replied, his cheeks billowing with his indignity. "That is a large and completely foreign world, you know. I've gotten you quite close."

Altin spun and stared back down into the bright light of planet Earth, his jaw working as furiously as his mind.

He turned back and strode to the table where the doctor sat, taking a chair from nearby and setting it across from him. He fished into his robes and pulled out the tablet he'd taken from the *Aspect*'s sick bay. He stared at it for a moment, could see his reflection in the shiny black surface of its rectangular face. He wished it worked like the mirror he'd made for her, even though he knew that, in some ways, it could.

He pressed the small button on one edge of it as he had seen Orli and Doctor Singh do with this type of device, and as expected, it lit up when he did. He pushed the symbols on it randomly, but none of it made any sense. He could not read the language printed there. The translation spells on his amulet required the person speaking or writing to intend that he might understand. Nothing on this tablet was written for a Prosperion.

He poked at it anyway, stared into the bright bluish light of its window hoping somehow to find something that looked like the map Doctor Leopold had drawn and that somehow he could then add Orli's name to it. He knew how to make her name in Earth letters. She'd drawn it in the sand for him once while they were chasing sunsets. And he'd seen it on the monitor in the troop carrier he'd been on with Colonel Pewter the day they'd gone to rescue her from Thadius. If he could find that map, he could bring up the symbols chart on this machine—he'd seen Orli and Doctor Singh do that much as well. But no matter how many times he tried, no matter how many icons he poked, he could not find the map.

He did find what appeared to be a scrying spell in progress, and there was a woman wearing strange clothing, much different than the familiar uniforms of the fleet, standing in front of a scene depicting Hostiles flying amongst huge shimmering monoliths. The structures were familiar to him, at least in a general sense, for he recognized their type from pictures Orli had shown him before, images of Earth cities made of magnificent mirrored towers with lamps that burned but never flickered and could be made any color of the rainbow.

These great structures were besieged by Hostiles, and he could see that many of the mirrored monoliths had Hostiles draped over them like sheets of dripping red-hued clay. Several of the structures appeared to have eroded beneath the blanket of whatever the Hostiles did, and it was apparent from the slump and missing angles at the tops of several of the structures that whatever the orbs were doing, it was dissolving the material. Altin could not help but wonder if this is what they had done to the world of Andalia. From the pictures Orli had shown him, on a tablet very much like this one, there had once been structures like these on that world too, or at least close enough that they seemed alike to Altin's Prosperion-born eyes. When Orli's people arrived on Andalia, however, there were no such structures to be found. The entire world had been wiped clean. And it appeared that Blue Fire was at it again.

He had to find Orli fast.

He pressed the button that shut off the images and the meaningless drone of the woman's voice. The tablet was no use. Doctor Leopold was only marginally useful, and High Priestess Maul, who had Altin's lost Liquefying Stone, refused to speak to him. Which meant he needed to find another, better, diviner.

Magic ranks worked by halves and doubles. If Doctor Leopold was a Y-class diviner, then a Z-class diviner would be twice as powerful. And given that the best the Y-class healer could do was draw a three-hundred-measure-wide circle on a map, Altin definitely needed a Z. With that kind of power, he might be able to narrow that circle down to something more manageable, even if only by half—and he hoped for much better. He needed much better. But there was only one Z on Kurr that Altin knew of: the crazy Ocelot, a wild witch-woman living in the depths of Great Forest, rumored to be over a thousand years old and completely mad. The answers provided by divination were ambiguous at the best of times. He could not imagine how unintelligible hers would be. Assuming he could find her at all. But he resolved to do it anyway. He had no other choice.

"I'm going to Ocelot," he announced as he stuffed the tablet back into a fold of his robes. "And you are coming with me."

"I'm what?"

"You're coming with me to talk to her. You can tell her what you saw. We can bring her out here, and the three of us will figure it out."

"I doubt she'll be of any use. I suspect all this sort of thing is quite beyond her grasp." He waved a thick-fingered hand toward the window and planet Earth beyond. "Ocelot is barely more than an animal."

"When was the last time you spoke to her?" Altin already knew the doctor never had.

"I read my Diviners Guild newsletters. She comes up as a topic every fifty years or so."

"I need your help," Altin said. "Orli needs it. We have to try."

"Listen here, young man, I'm not going to be dragged into the dark reaches of Great Forest in quest of a psychotic. You have almost no chance of finding her, likely less than none, and there is nothing I can do to help you with it. Furthermore, I am hardly in the kind of shape to be tromping up and down hills and clambering over fallen trees and under rocks. Not to mention the fact that my death in the pointed mandibles of some monstrous spider will not serve anyone here in town."

"You're coming," Altin said. "I won't let Orli die because you are fat and afraid of bugs."

"I hardly count spiders in the forty-stone weight class as simply 'bugs.'"

"Did you know the Earth people have candies that make you thin?"

The change in tactics took the doctor aback. He huffed and flustered for a moment, blowing out his cheeks. "That has nothing to do with anything, young man."

Seeing his shot land a telling blow, Altin was relentless in following up. "Yes, it's true. Orli remarked once about how we have a preponderance of big fat fellows just like you trundling around Kurr. She thought it interesting that we didn't have magic to fix that sort of thing. At the time, I only shrugged, pointing out that only in the larger cities was that sort of thing common anyway, but she laughed and told me about these candies her people make. Little things, barely bigger than the tip of your finger. They do something to some sort of mechanism in your body and you simply can't be fat anymore."

"I am sure that being eaten by wood ticks, titan spiders or dire wolves would constitute a form of weight loss as well," countered the doctor.

"Imagine how good you would look. How long ago was it that your dear wife passed?"

"How dare you!" the doctor said, and he looked shocked that Altin would stoop to such a thing.

Altin merely shrugged at that, tilting his head a little and letting his expression suggest the doctor hadn't finished thinking the question through. "Seventy-one years," he said, answering for him. "A shame, and Mercy bless her soul. But here you are, still a young enough man. And imagine what powers you in particular must have, as familiar as you are with the functions of anatomy, both male and female." Altin blushed as he spoke it, knowing he was seriously transgressing, but desperate needs need desperate acts sometimes.

For a moment Altin worried that he had overplayed his hand. Doctor Leopold was clearly as embarrassed by the inappropriate suggestions as Altin was, perhaps more so, for he had not had the time with Orli that Altin had, Orli who was constantly teasing in the most audaciously sexual ways, which had toughened Altin up a bit on that particular front. But finally, biology being what it is, and the doctor being a doctor after all, he relented with a sly smile. "Lose the weight, you say? And but a bit of candy to get it done?"

"Yes. Just that. And you can eat all you like after. The pounds fall away like pushing goats off a roof."

"Goats climb back again."

"Not if you keep eating the candies. I give you my word; Orli will make sure you have a lifetime supply."

The doctor's gaze flickered toward the window for a moment, then back. "Well, we do need to save the girl."

Altin smiled. Briefly. And then they were gone.

Chapter 12

Blue Fire came to Orli in her dreams again. The fullness of a planetary-sized friendship washed over Orli with familiar warmth, a richness of love and joy that the young woman hadn't felt in what seemed forever now, not since Thadius Thoroughgood had poisoned her with siren's blood, a love elixir of magic made on Prosperion. When Thadius had corrupted Orli's love for Altin, stolen it for himself, Blue Fire had mistaken it as betrayal, assumed Orli had been fickle and treated Altin's love as something of inconsequence. Such was an unacceptable thing for the bereaved Blue Fire, whose own lover, a love that had spanned thousands upon thousands of years, perhaps even millions, had been lost in the flare of a sun. That flare had left her in silence for eons. For her, the thought of such reckless treatment of love, a precious thing beyond all else, was unconscionable, and had Orli been within her reach, Blue Fire might have squashed her for it, for having believed Orli could waste such a gift. But now Blue Fire knew the truth, and she once more sought her first friend, the first kind voice she'd heard in the span of all those lonely millennia. She understood now, and she knew that Orli had never betrayed Altin. Blue Fire was slowly coming to understand the nature of deceit, of lies, of truth that was not truth. She thought of it as a disease. Orli had been infected, but now the toxin was gone. All was forgiven. And more than forgiven, for Blue Fire was glad to have her friend back. And so was Orli, particularly in this place where injustice once more ran amok and her life was, again, out of her control. In fact, Orli was so overjoyed to feel the vast presence of Blue Fire flow into her dreams that at first she didn't realize it wasn't simply that, just a dream. So frustrated and frightened was she by her situation that she didn't believe Blue Fire was real, which made Blue Fire have to repeat herself.

Orli Love hate Blue Fire, came the thought a second time, this time with even greater urgency. The thought pressed down like a heavy, frenzied weight upon Orli's dreaming consciousness. *Altin Love give truth Orli Love.*

Struggling to stay in the dream and not wake up out of sheer joy, Orli had to grapple with the frantic nature of Blue Fire's thoughts. Something about Altin. "I don't understand," she said to Blue Fire in her dream, a technique she'd learned and practiced plenty in recent months.

Orli Love hate Blue Fire. Altin Love speak truth for Blue Fire. Altin Love give truth Orli Love. Blue Fire not truth that is not truth.

Orli could see herself and Altin in the dream that Blue Fire directed at her. She was talking to Altin. Blue Fire's reckoning of human speech made for overly animated movements of her mouth, but the meaning was obvious. There came with it a tremendous sense of urgency and fear. It was a colossal dread of loneliness that filled Blue Fire most.

Clearly Orli was supposed to tell Altin something. Something about the truth.

Truth, came the echo of that thought right back at her, Blue Fire having picked up Orli's nascent comprehension.

"What truth?" Orli asked, and bitterness backfilled the thought as she sent it away. It bubbled up from her own situation, her own reality where truth seemed to hold so little sway. "I don't understand. And I can't tell him anything. I'm in a prison cell on Earth." She followed it with an unspoken "as usual," but she didn't need to say it, as thoughts and words were all the same. Speech in dreams was a convenience more than a necessity. "And besides, they're going to kill me soon."

Blue Fire did not seem to recognize the importance of that. *Orli Love hate Blue Fire. Blue Fire hate Orli Love hate Blue Fire.*

Blue Fire was so afraid as she conveyed it that the sense of her dread spread inside Orli like icy water surging in and flooding her. Orli could not help but be caught up in Blue Fire's terrible stress. "What do you mean Alti—Orli Love hates you," she said. "He could never hate you."

Hate spilled into Orli's dream for a moment, but it was shaped into something more like blame. Condemnation. She saw an image of Altin pointing at a blue star. Blame. Definitely blame.

Orli Love blame, concurred the thought in Orli's head as she felt the emotions of it. Blue Fire pulled the idea from Orli's mind like an epiphany and sent it back. *Orli Love blame Blue Fire kill Altin Love world.*

Orli had to wrestle with that idea, as was so often the case with this strange and magnificent planetary creature, working to extract meaning from the convolution of Blue Fire's largely visual language. She had so little of words, though she seemed to be seeking more of them. She now knew they existed, but they remained foreign to the enigmatic being, clumsy and unnatural. Still she tried, and eventually Orli figured it out.

"Altin blames you for killing my world?" her dream self said, then amended, "Orli Love blames you, is that what you mean?" Keeping track of the abstractions was difficult, even with practice. Blue Fire knew them not as themselves but by who loved them. Orli thought it was beautiful, a better measure of the being. Humans default to the sense of self, which seemed so small by comparison. Still it was puzzle-like in nature, and navigating conversations in such a way was difficult, especially while trying to hold on to a dream that was not just a dream, but a dream the dreamer was aware of. Doing so required a certain agility of consciousness, which sometimes didn't work so well, especially when trying to decipher cryptic emotional thoughts. "That doesn't make sense," she said.

Orli Love blame Blue Fire. Blue Fire kill Altin Love world truth that is not truth. This thought was followed by images of large black and brown orbs swooping down on an alien city, melting away its parts, injecting diseases into its atmosphere that would wipe out every last human that lived there. Orli recognized the city as Persepiece. It was a city on Andalia, a city that Blue Fire *did* destroy, on a world she'd destroyed, or at least rid of its human populace. *Blue Fire kill world. Truth.* Orli's dream filled with sorrow then, a torrent of it pouring into her heart and mind, followed by unfathomable regret. Shame. It dissolved after a time and was gone. It was an admission. But Orli already knew that much. She had known it for a while. It was why she had worked so hard to stop the allied attack on Blue Fire's world. The frenzied urgency returned. *Blue Fire kill Altin Love world truth that is not truth.*

Orli filled with the honesty of it all. The shame of the first part and the fear in the second. Frustration, even. But still, she wasn't sure what Blue Fire was trying to tell her. "I don't understand," she said in her dream.

The frustration swelled nearly to the point of becoming

painful. Orli felt it twofold. From her distant, enormous friend, and from her own recent experience, the feeling bouncing back and forth in her mind like light between two mirrors. She conveyed that back to Blue Fire, told her she was trying to understand, urged her to keep trying to explain.

Then came an image of Orli standing on the Earth, balanced upon it, not in triumph, not godlike, but clearly in possession of it. Earth was hers. *Altin Love world*, came the thoughts. *Blue Fire not kill. Truth.*

"Are you trying to tell me it isn't you attacking Earth?" Orli asked.

Not mine. Orli saw images of the orbs flying around Andalia, followed by a return to the image of Orli standing on the Earth. There were no orbs flying around her or the world upon which she stood. *Truth.*

"Then whose?"

Not mine.

"I believe you," Orli said. She made a point of filling her dream with an appreciation of truth, of trust and love. "I believe you," she said again.

Truth, repeated Blue Fire. *Orli Love hate.* Orli got the sense of a flash flood crashing down a ravine, washing away strange trees, spindly and straight, growing so tightly together they looked like bundled toothpicks. Total disaster. And all the while the sense of Blue Fire's dread of loneliness.

Then she knew. She understood, finally, recognizing the flood was Altin's trust and love being washed away, the broken trees the fragile bit of happiness she'd found since meeting him. Orli realized in that moment that Blue Fire was stricken nearly senseless with fear that Altin would take his friendship away from her and that she might again be alone in the endless night. She needed the presence of a male mind, even one as small by comparison to Blue Fire's as any human mind was. In fact, the disparity was tragic in its inadequacy. Blue Fire knew this as well. The whole of it, the despair, the pathetic nature of it all, she understood it perfectly, and that too became so clear to Orli that she began to cry for Blue Fire's misery, the sobs in her dreams convulsing her body as she lay upon the hard prison bunk, just as helpless in her own way. Blue Fire continued to send that sorrow in great and growing waves, layering the weight of fear and grief on her until it had gone on so long that Orli finally remembered she could push it away.

"No," she said, forcing away the misery that crashed into her dreams, denying the premise that sent it from far across the galaxy. "Orli Love will never abandon you." The thoughts she put behind it were ferocious in their certainty. "He won't. Just as he never abandoned me. He *is* truth that is truth." She sent with that idea feelings of constancy, of solidity, of eternity.

Blue Fire repeated the sequence of images that conveyed Altin's belief that Blue Fire was attacking Orli's world. She showed Altin shouting at her from within her very heart. He really did blame her. He'd made it perfectly clear. *Not Blue Fire*, was all that she could say. If thoughts could be whimpers, that one was.

"Then we have to find out who it is," Orli sent back. "If it is not you, then it is another world like you. Another Blue Fire."

No other Blue Fire.

"There has to be another."

I am Blue Fire.

"Yes, but you had a mate once. There were two of you."

Yellow Fire.

"Yes, Yellow Fire. So there must be another one. Another *Fire*." She did her best to convey the sense of another sun, a colorless sun, simply a star. She tried to

128

construct an image of Blue Fire as she was in dreams, vast blackness with a pink lining that softly glowed, but she changed it, made the aura around its edge colorless. It was her best attempt at creating the idea of Blue Fire as part of a species. She wasn't sure how well it worked.

Then came another sense of epiphany from Blue Fire, and Orli's mind was once more flooded by Blue Fire's images, this time a torrent of dark textures and temperatures, of stones and weeds, creatures and vacancies. A gush of ideas and concepts from the microscopic to the vast blasted through Orli's brain for what felt like hours, a speeding meteor storm of ideas and visions that ended at last with a small round patch of dark green crystals pulsing in a field of yellow ones. *This*, came the sense at the end of it. *Blue Fire. Yellow Fire. This.* Orli saw dandelion seeds blowing across a pond. She'd seen that before, but this time the pond was filled with stars.

Orli could never know what all that she had witnessed added up to precisely, but she knew well enough what it meant. Blue Fire had tried to convey the essence of what her species, her race, was. Everything she'd just seen blasting through her dream was Blue Fire's idea of self and of others like her, whatever they were. "I understand," Orli said then. "You are that, as I am this." She traced her own figure with her hands as she stood upon the endless black plane of her dream. "We are dandelions across the pond of space."

Truth.

"Well, then we must find the other one of ... all of that you showed me just now." She did her best to send back some distilled version of all that Blue Fire had sent, the swarm of images. "Another living world, like you. Do you know where there is another?"

She got the sense that Blue Fire did not. A feeling of vacancy.

"But there must be one somewhere close," Orli insisted. "How else could it have found Earth?"

Orli saw a pink ocean appear before her, great swells of it rising and falling, but its surface smooth and glimmering. A tone sounded, brief, like the plucking of a bass string on some enormous cosmic cello. A dent appeared in the surface of the pink ocean, as if someone pressed upon a tightly stretched span of pink plastic tarp. Then ripples came, as if a rock had been thrown into water, spreading away from the source, expanding until finally the energy was spent, diffused in time to nothingness. *See*, came the sense from Blue Fire. *See. Use. Come.*

"I don't know what that means." The words left Orli's mind on a wave of utter confusion. She dreaded starting this process again. Working through Blue Fire's puzzles was mind-bending.

A flare of frustration washed back over her, suggesting that Blue Fire felt the same way about trying to be understood. But then planet Prosperion appeared in the pink ocean, half submerged, as if it were a fishing bobble. Again came the cello string sound. Ripples spread outward from the planet, traveling across the smooth pink sea. Again came the sound. More ripples. Orli followed the ripples as they moved away, her vision guided by Blue Fire's compelling dream-speak. She followed as if surfing upon the wave of them until there, in the distance, was Blue Fire, the planet that was Blue Fire with its vast landmass and polar seas. *Blue Fire see*, repeated Blue Fire. *Orli Love world use. Blue Fire see.* Orli's view was quickly sent back to Prosperion floating in the pink ocean, and once more, after the sound came again, she watched the ripples flow out toward Blue Fire's world far away.

Orli was stricken by the thought, the revelation of what she'd just seen. Several of them, actually. "You know where Altin's world is? You know about Prosperion? You always have."

Sorrow filled her then. A great sadness and mourning, though different than any she'd felt from Blue Fire before. Maternal mourning. She saw Prosperion again, and this time there was a large black orb streaking toward it like a meteor. The orb, black as coal, flew into the planet's atmosphere and crashed into a patch of desert in the south of Kurr. The impact punched a perfect hole into the planet's crust as if the orb were a cookie cutter and the planetary mantle but a stretch of dough. Orli recognized the spot immediately. It was the Great Sandfalls. Altin had taken her there one time, a time that now seemed so very long ago.

Make new, came the thought then. She saw Blue Fire's yellow sun next to the blue star at the center of the system that had been her mate, Fruitfall as Orli knew it now. Once again came the long, long gush of textures and temperatures and all the things that represented whatever it was that Blue Fire and her mate were. Planetary beings, centered around a patch of pulsing crystals at the heart, which humanity only knew as Hostiles. She saw the orb again, striking the desert sand. This was followed by a cloud of dandelion seeds blowing across a lake. She saw birds' nests filled with eggs. Tiny round balls of spider web, like marbles made of thread. Other things she didn't recognize, globes and globules, pods, even strange obelisks, alien things nestled in dens and burrows or deep down at the bottoms of lakes and streams. *Make new. Death,* Blue Fire sent. There came a flash of light, then darkness, sorrow, and Orli knew Blue Fire's mate was gone. Once again Prosperion appeared in Orli's mind. *Now Orli Love world*. Again came a wave of grief, this time maternal. The grief that can only come with the loss of a child.

The power of Blue Fire's grief was so intense this time,

it so overwhelmed Orli, that the sobs broke the dream. She woke up choking and gagging in turns, unable to breathe for the fluid now clogging her sinuses and with her mouth plugged with the ball gag still strapped in place. She coughed and choked, blowing mucous out of her nose and saliva out from around the hard rubber of the gag. The tears pouring now were caused by pain, and her nose and cheeks burned with the pressure of each cough, the back pressure swelling her sinuses and making her fear that she might drown in her own spit. Panic threatened as she frantically clutched the ball gag in her teeth, pushing it outward with her tongue as she pulled a breath around it. She took several long breaths as she waited for her heart to stop racing, pushing back the panic of near suffocation. She breathed until she could think again. She thought of Blue Fire.

"You lost your baby on Prosperion?" Orli spoke aloud, her words, of course, muted by circumstance. And, of course, Blue Fire could not hear or answer now. "I'm so sorry," Orli said anyway.

She threw herself back into her pillow and willed herself to sleep so she could speak to her again, but sleep would not come. Nearly choking had shocked her system wide awake.

She stared at the ceiling, the ridiculously bright diffusion panel filling her with hate. What if she'd choked to death just then? Would anyone have even come? For a moment she thought at least someone might have gotten in trouble for that, maybe even get a real court martial for incompetence. A small victory in that at least. Fucking bastards. Somehow she would show them. Make them pay.

But how? She was lying there helpless, watery-eyed and trapped, as pathetic as that poor unicorn in Thadius' menagerie. Which got her thinking again about all that had happened to her, the kidnapping and all that had transpired since. She thought about Tytamon too. Poor Tytamon. She wished he were here. He'd know what to do. Tytamon had told her she was supposed to be the one hope for everyone. Like somehow she could help save them all. How the hell was she going to save anyone if she choked to death in her sleep? Or if she died tomorrow filled with chemicals.

She lay there for some time stewing on that, gnawing on the gag in her mouth with her front teeth. She couldn't help marvel at how stupid they all were, gagging her as if she'd somehow become a sorcerer like Tytamon. Like Altin. What idiots.

She thought about Altin. Imagined his sweet face. She hoped he was okay. She knew he was. The fact that he'd accused Blue Fire was oddly comforting in that. At least he was alive, a fact confirmed. She could understand Blue Fire's feelings on that front. Altin did make her feel safe. There was safety in the constancy of his love. She realized how much she'd taken it for granted the more she thought about it, the more she allowed herself to feel the emptiness of Blue Fire's last million years. One lover in all of time, torn from her in the hot blast of a sun. And worse even in that she'd lost a child as well. Questions and imagination mixed with the images Blue Fire had put into her mind, becoming a sequence of empathetic daydreams too horrifying to be the precursor of sleep. She couldn't even bear to imagine it.

Blue Fire's life was an awful tale of misery, endless loneliness and loss. Orli could not remotely conceive how torturous such an existence would be. She marveled that Blue Fire hadn't found a way to kill herself. At some point, wouldn't eternity like that become unbearable? If the sorrow never ends, never heals, how long could anyone be expected to endure? And yet, she had endured, and she hadn't killed herself. Perhaps Blue Fire couldn't even do that, couldn't take that much of fate into her own control. Or maybe she just wouldn't. Either way, what a cruel, cruel plight to live through. What unspeakable, unremitting agony.

And worse, the poor thing thought Altin was going to abandon her now too. She had Altin blaming her for the attack on Earth. Somehow he had cut her off based on misunderstanding, on truth that was not truth. The very thing that had cost billions of Andalian lives, and now the very thing that was going to cost more lives, lives everywhere it seemed. The scale of the injustice was truly cosmic.

Orli had to get back into her dream. She rolled onto her back and tried counting backwards from a thousand. She counted it all out, down to zero. Twice. She couldn't stop her mind from wandering to thoughts of her impending execution. If they really did kill her, if somehow Altin didn't find her, she wouldn't be able to help Blue Fire at all. She couldn't help anyone. Whatever planet was attacking Earth, whatever Hostile world—she hated to use that term, even mentally, but what else fit so well, so familiarly?— whatever and wherever it was, it was going to keep going until all humanity on Earth was destroyed, just as it had been on Andalia. Total obliteration. Erasure even.

Or if not that, if somehow the fleet managed to hold off the invading orbs, then Blue Fire would die in the counter attack. She would be gone, perhaps mercifully for her— and still the Earth would be in jeopardy, for the real assailant would remain. Somewhere.

If there was a god or gods out there, she wondered if they were laughing. She could imagine them wringing their vicious hands in delight, capering about their god houses giddy and pleased with how clever they'd made their little cosmic show. All of this seemed too cruel to be an accident.

She had to tell someone, had to let someone know before ... in case she didn't make it through. She had to tell the guards at least. She had to explain what was happening, that it wasn't Blue Fire for sure. It was another Hostile world. Somehow it must have found them.

But how? How had it found them? And why now?

Something about ripples on a pink ocean. Coming from Prosperion. Which made no sense. Unless, maybe, life made ripples. But even if that was the case, if somehow another Hostile had ... had felt the ripples from Earth, the timing was difficult to believe. If the ripples were some kind of life waves, why hadn't the nameless Hostile world come before? Long before.

So it couldn't be life.

But if not life, what then? What else was there? Oxygen? Water? There was plenty of that all over the universe, and even if that was it, it left the same question of timing anyway. It had to be something else. There was technology. That was what had gotten the Andalians killed. Blue Fire had told her as much months ago, shortly after they'd begun speaking through her dreams. But was that how she'd *found* Andalia? It was definitely why she'd killed them; that much Orli knew. Blue Fire saw all their digging and the harnessing of the materials stripped from their world as an act of cruelty, the symptoms of a disease ravaging the planet. She'd wiped them out to save it. She thought she was being kind. She didn't know the Andalians were sentient, that they were human, the same species as those found on Earth and Prosperion. She hadn't known because she'd never found one of them to share dreams with, never learned that they had intelligence and, most importantly, that they had love. She hadn't known until she found Orli in a dream.

For a time, Orli tried to convince herself that it must be technology that somehow caught her attention, some particular discovery on the part of the Andalians that sent the ripples out for Blue Fire to see, but then she realized it couldn't be that either. Altin's world had no technology, at least nothing to speak of beyond an enchanted windmill or some other simple, ancient-seeming device. Whatever bit of technology might have served as a signal did not exist on Prosperion. And even if they had somehow discovered it, that hole had been punched into the desert long before his people had even invented the wheel. Altin said the origin of the Great Sandfalls was beyond history, a mystery relegated to myths alone. It might have happened hundreds of thousands of years before humans had evolved, millions even. She had no way of knowing. But whenever it was, that was the time Blue Fire had discovered Prosperion. So technology wasn't it either.

That left magic. Perhaps magic was how the Hostile worlds found life. It made sense. In fact, Orli even recalled Altin's having mentioned that he perceived "mana," whatever it was, as being a thing of pink and purple currents, whorls and vortices. It would make sense for that to be true, as Blue Fire obviously had magic powers to spare. Perhaps she could detect a world when someone or something on it used magic. The problem was Earth had no magic, so whatever world was attacking Earth, it didn't find it by ripples in the mana either.

Leaving Orli with nothing to hold on to. Certainly not enough to make a case to fleet command. Hell, she couldn't even shout it to her guards, assuming there were any outside. Not only would they have no idea what she was talking about, she had a goddamn gag in her mouth. They'd taken away her only way to warn them. The fools. Which meant all she could do was wait. Wait for fate or God or random chance to do whatever it had in mind for her in this sick game it played with everybody's lives.

Chapter 13

Roberto marched in handcuffs alongside Captain Asad into the hangar, a pair of Marines behind them looking almost as stern as the captain did. The captain went up the ramp first and once inside the ship leaned out the hatch and motioned for Roberto. One of the guards shoved him up after the captain by jamming the butt of his rifle into the Spaniard's back.

"We have orders to shoot him if he even turns back to look, Captain."

"He won't."

Roberto knew better than to tempt them. He could still feel tingling in his feet and fingers from where the electricity had jolted him to unconsciousness, and his whole body was sore. He'd almost made it to the same floor Orli was being held on before they caught him. Almost. He didn't remember much from there. He'd "just been going to say goodbye." At least that's what he told them when he woke up. Everyone knew that was bullshit because he'd jump-wired two sets of elevator controls and knocked out the staff sergeant at the receiving desk on the floor above the level where Orli was. That was how close he'd gotten. Only Captain Asad's connections—and the fleet's desperate need for pilots of Roberto's skill—had managed to get him out of the predicament. Otherwise, he might have been in that cell with Orli now, and not in a rescuing way.

Roberto took his seat in the pilot's chair mechanically. He couldn't shake the malaise that lay upon him, the frustration and sense of futility, and the outright grieving that had begun. That trial had been a farce. The child of an attorney they gave Orli had never had a chance to get her out of it, and he knew it now. He wished he'd lied on the stand, but he hadn't realized what was happening until too late.

He hadn't told them anything they didn't already know, though. And he had tried to put things in context as best he could. So much so that Commander Adair had accused him of being a "hostile witness," but Roberto still felt like everything he had said was a nail in Orli's coffin. A coffin he wasn't even going to get to stand beside. There would be no NTA flag draped over it, no honors for what she had done to save all the survivors of the *Aspect*'s crew. No nothing. Her only monument would be in memory. His memories. His recollections of her struggle to stay sane during all those years in space followed by a few glimmers of happiness on Prosperion—even those stolen from her at the end—and then a ramrod trial that would end it all. He wondered if Colonel Pewter even knew. His absence at the court martial suggested he did not. And the more Roberto thought about how it had played out, the more he was sure there was no way the colonel had been told. The fleet had to be unbelievably paranoid to do what they had done, to simply throw out the rule of law. Intellectually, he understood that the Hostile invasion gave them reason, but how much of a threat could Orli really be? Or even Altin for that matter. What more could Altin do if he did come? How much worse could it get? There were Hostiles literally everywhere. One more magician one way or another wasn't going to make a difference now.

Roberto considered trying to get word to Colonel Pewter, but he couldn't help wondering if that would be a terrible idea. What brand of recklessness would that initiate? Probably recklessness of the variety Roberto himself had just tried. Or worse. And the colonel was not in favor with the upper echelons of the fleet like Roberto was, not after he snuck off ship just as the fleet was about to attack Blue Fire, abandoning his post to assist Altin in searching for Orli right at the moment the battle began. No, the colonel had burned down any mercy he was going to get with that maneuver. And likely Roberto had burned down all the mercy he had coming for himself as well. And since the fleet was not interested in fair hearings at this moment in history, he knew exactly what would happen if he got caught leaking Orli's plight to the colonel, just as he knew what would happen to the colonel if he got caught doing whatever he might do to try to stop it. They'd all three of them, Orli, Roberto and the colonel, be lying on the executioner's table with poison running into their veins. The whole thing was so infuriating he could hardly concentrate.

Captain Asad removed the handcuffs once the hatch was locked. Neither Roberto nor the captain spoke as they left Earth's atmosphere and headed back through the melee that seemed to be everywhere in orbit at once. Roberto flew as if he were the autopilot function of the ship, emotionless and detached, his movements automatic, his evasions of the incoming Hostile shafts reflex. He avoided death without interest, his ability to care parched to nothingness by electricity and the realization of the kind of world he lived in. He was simply part of the machine making its way back toward the *Aspect*, back toward the fight, unsure what it was they were fighting for anymore. But he did. That was who he was.

The shuttle's lasers were far less powerful than the *Aspect*'s, and the missiles it carried only a fraction of the capacity of those that the starships deployed, but he was compelled to use them as they wove and dodged their way up through the cosmic clash going on above the Earth. Fortunately, the Hostiles were of a smaller variety than he was used to as well, and it was with some luck and some natural proficiency that, when a Hostile swept in at them, this one perhaps twice as large as the shuttle itself, Roberto was able to swat aside its plunging stone shaft with the push of laser energy while launching a pair of small tactical nukes. This was the same old strategy he'd used during the earliest combats with these orbs, the technique he'd used prior to having devised the gravity-pulse strategy that had ultimately proved far more effective and deadly to the enemy. The shuttle didn't have the power for a gravity pulse anyway, nor did he have another ship flying with him to make the strategy work even if it had been so equipped, so it was all learned reflex and instinct that kept them from being pulverized, certainly no great interest on the part of the pilot.

And so it was, at first disinterestedly, that he noticed his most recent missile had struck a speeding Hostile dead on and exploded with full force. The explosion blew out the back portion of the orb, which then stretched like a thing made of rubber. This was the Hostile shifting its composition from solid to something more elastic in an attempt to absorb and disperse the force. The orb elongated for a time, and both Roberto and the captain assumed it would snap back eventually, changing forms at will and intent on coming after them again. They'd seen this elasticity before. But it did not snap back. Instead, the extended length of its back portions seemed to reach a point of no return and snapped off, a large section tearing away at the thinnest point like chewing gum breaking as a child stretches it out of his mouth. For a time the end that remained attached to the main body blew out the orange goo of its innards as if its guts were being pumped out through a length of culvert pipe. The broken end seemed entirely dead.

The orb wobbled as it flew past the shuttle, and it looked to Roberto like a teardrop made of clay. The shuttle's aft cameras showed that it was slowly retracting the broken portion of itself even as it shot off in pursuit of its battering ram, which still streaked away from the shuttle, growing smaller with distance as seconds passed.

For whatever reason, seeing the orb wounded but not quite dead lit the fuse of Roberto's anger, and without asking permission, he swung the shuttle in a wide arc and went after it.

"Commander," barked the captain, "let it go."

"It's almost down, sir," Roberto said through clenched teeth, doing his best to pretend he cared what Captain Asad had to say. "I can finish it."

"Commander!" yelled the captain.

"Just wait," Roberto yelled back. He spun and faced the captain with all the fury and helplessness of a man whose twelve years in space has just culminated in the loss of his best friend at the hands of what amounted to an Inquisition-style tribunal and a death sentence. The heat of his emotions burned in his eyes like reactor cores. "I'm going to kill it."

Captain Asad glared back at him, his own reflexive anger as hot as Roberto's was. But Captain Asad was not a fool, nor was he entirely inhumane, especially not for an officer he valued as much as he did Roberto. And beyond all that, his anger had its largest root in the Hostiles too. His frustration ran as far back in time as Roberto's did. Farther perhaps. And seeing the determination in his best officer's face, he decided to relent this time.

"Very well, Commander. We will finish *this one* off." To prove he was in earnest, he tapped up a chemical-fuel burn, a thrust that spat the shuttle forward, bringing them right up behind the Hostile's still protruding "tail." Roberto unleashed two more missiles and the small ship's laser cannon in response.

The Hostile made a weak dodge of the laser fire, but seemed not to see the missiles, and therefore both missiles hit it, blowing through it like the first one had.

Its mass spread out from the blasts like paint thrown on a wall, and for a time it looked like a big rust-colored chemical spill cart-wheeling across the stars. Two great gobs of glowing ichor squeezed out of rents in the Hostile's surface and drifted away.

"That's got it," said the captain with more than a hint of satisfaction in his voice.

Roberto was about to agree, but then he shook his head. "Nope. Look." The orb, still flat and wobbly, though slowly retracting itself, picked up speed and shot off toward the western edge of the planet, apparently abandoning the thick shaft it had been chasing in favor of saving itself. "Oh, no you don't," Roberto said as he reached over and mashed the thrust controls still lit on the panel before Captain Asad.

"Commander," the captain began again but Roberto's response was already on its way.

"Captain, you said we would finish it. I've never known you to run from a fight."

Captain Asad actually laughed at that, if only briefly. Commander Levi hadn't earned his promotions for being a poor tactician. With a flick of his finger upon the back of Roberto's hand, he said, "I've got it, Commander."

Roberto let him take the thruster controls back and, with a degree of satisfaction, watched the Captain move the slider up to a rate that would burn through their chemical fuel in a very short time, a commitment to speed.

Soon they were right behind the fleeing Hostile again, which was back to its fully round state and still accelerating. Roberto sent a laser shot at it, but the orb appeared to pulse and then jumped ahead, a feat made possible by magic, Roberto knew. That's how the Hostiles could defy physics like they did.

The Hostile completed its reformation as they watched, or at least it did so as best as possible, for they could see that it had huge crevices in it and some jagged-edged fissures that hadn't been visible before. Still, battered looking as it might have become, it was clearly not interested in dying yet. Now spherical, it continued to transform, hardening itself to the point where its surface became shiny and reflective, similar to the volcanic glass the two *Aspect* officers were familiar with from previous encounters with the orbs. The color was different, though. This orb turned dark red, like a drop of blood, not the deep black they'd seen in battles past.

"That's weird," Roberto commented.

"Well it won't be weird for long if we let it get away," said the captain.

And indeed it was pulling away from them again. Fully reshaped, it was now free to focus on its flight, leaping away in what Roberto had come to think of as "impossible motion," short jumps across space that were quick as a blink, but not so far in distance as to be obvious it had disappeared. It was like watching a video where the recording skipped a half second every now and again. This effect increased in frequency and the fleeing orb began to blur in the direction of its retreat. It would pulse forward in jumps of a quarter mile, and then a half. Soon it was three and four miles at a time, little jumps that both men recognized as something akin to a Prosperion teleport.

"We can't keep up with that," Roberto said, his fury cooling some over the course of the pursuit, "and we'll lose it if we jump."

"So now you're going to quit, Commander? That's disappointing."

"What are we supposed to do? It's jumping through time or whatever the hell that crap is. And it's getting faster."

"We can warp space time too." Captain Asad was furiously tapping in commands on his controls as he spoke, his dark eyes narrow and his mouth the very shape of focus, pursed and pressing forth aggressively.

Roberto leaned over and looked into the settings Captain Asad had underway. A moment later he leaned back and grinned. "That's fucking genius."

Soon the shuttle was echoing the movements of the Hostile, matching its magical hops with fluttering pulses of warped space. To an onlooker, of which there were none, it would have seemed as if the pair of objects were alternately blinking eyes racing through the solar system at a quarter the speed of light.

They continued the pursuit in that fashion for several minutes, but despite the rough portions of the orb, the lasers couldn't cut into it deeply enough to finish it off. Missiles were obviously of no use, and soon it seemed that they might have obligated themselves to a futile chase that could take them farther than either of their respective needs would allow.

"Can't hit them," Roberto announced pointlessly as another streak of red laser fire vanished into the galaxy. "And I damn sure don't want to risk trying to get ahead of it."

"That would be reckless," agreed the captain. "And now

we're getting too close to the sun."

Roberto could tell Captain Asad didn't want to order a halt to the pursuit. He was showing Roberto unheard-of respect in that, but he was also not going to wait much longer for Roberto to come to the same conclusion himself, for legitimate reasons this time, not simply frustration. Its legitimate reasons for running was a curiosity that suddenly gave Roberto an idea. "Do you think that's its plan? To suck us into chasing it into the sun, like a suicide run meant to take us out?"

"I wouldn't put it past them. We saw enough of them using their own sun to destroy missiles when we fought them at Goldilocks." The captain tapped in a query to the computer and spent a moment reading the calculations it returned. "Except it's going to fly past the sun on its current heading. It looks like it's going to just miss Mercury too."

"Well, it's definitely not trying to lead us to its home world so that Blue Fire can finish us off—or if it is, it's going the wrong way. Which means it's either damaged or stupid or, maybe, even more likely, it's just trying to drag us out of the fight since it can't beat us outright. In which case, mission accomplished." Roberto leaned closer to his monitor and made a face at the fleeing Hostile, but the force of his emotions had finally come under his control. For the most part. "I guess I should give up now, shouldn't I?"

Captain Asad made a point of staring into his monitor. Another rare courtesy.

They chased it for a few long moments more, both men silent.

"It's fucking bullshit, Captain," Roberto said when he finally began to slow the ship, realizing as he spoke that this confrontation was probably the only reason the captain had indulged him at all. Might as well not do this in front of the rest of the crew, Roberto realized. He suddenly felt foolish. Young. Gullible. Captain Asad rarely missed a trick. If it was one. Whether it was or wasn't, it ratcheted Roberto's feelings back up a notch. "You know that trial was a goddamn joke. And worse, it was a betrayal. No matter what you think of her, she was part of your crew. And you helped set her up."

"She set herself up, Commander. She betrayed *us*, all of us. And I had orders to bring her in."

"Those orders only came because of what you said about her in your report."

"What bit of evidence in that court martial wasn't true, Commander? What tiny spec of it? Give me one fact that was not absolutely spot-on accurate?"

Roberto glared, and his mind raced for one, for anything, any comment made by anyone. But there wasn't one. It was all factual. It just wasn't accurate.

He mashed the laser controls and sent seven beams in a series striping harmlessly into the space already vacated by the Hostile they no longer pursued. "Fuck," was all he said as he slumped and stared vacantly into his controls.

Captain Asad punched in the command to begin swinging them around, steering them wide of Mercury. The shuttle's shields could withstand temperatures near the sun to a point, but beyond that it wouldn't last long. They were very close to arriving at that point. It was time to go back.

The shuttle had slowed nearly to a stop, and the Hostile they'd been chasing was only a flickering dot on the sensor screen now. In the sensor grid, its image had almost merged with the bright disc of Mercury as it flew over the planet's northern pole, and Roberto sighed. He couldn't even kill one goddamn Hostile as retribution for Orli's life. He stared down into his console and felt the tears burning in his eyes. He'd let her down again, even in this.

"Hmmm," hummed the captain with concern rising in his voice.

Roberto didn't care what the captain had to say just then.

"Commander, we have to go." That was stern urgency. A creeping dread apparent in the way he said it, which this time caused Roberto to blink and looked up at the man. Roberto's gaze darted briefly to his monitor, but he saw that Captain Asad was staring out the starboard window instead. He followed the line of the Captain's gaze.

Just visible around the western rim of Mercury was a great red orb, several hundred miles in diameter by Roberto's estimate and looking every bit like Mercury had grown itself a moon.

At first Roberto tried to tell himself it was a trick of light, that what he was seeing was the Hostile they'd been chasing coming back at them and looking odd due to the nearness of the sun. But the tiny speck of red that had been their quarry could still be seen, separate and slightly above, as it approached the giant round mass. Soon after, it got too close and could only be tracked on sensors, and in moments after that, it disappeared entirely, vanishing into the surface, the little orb absorbed by the giant one as easily as the sun might absorb the Earth. Roberto's hopes for strange light play or odd perspectives vanished. There really was a monstrously huge Hostile out there.

"Holy shit," Roberto said, his words nearly choked in the grasp of bewilderment. In the span of seconds, the shuttle was streaking back toward the *Aspect*, both men anxiously working their controls for speed.

Chapter 14

The branch snapped so loudly it startled Altin, spinning him around, prepared to hurl the hissing shaft of ice he'd conjured and had kept hovering near his shoulder since arriving deep in Great Forest. The corpulent Doctor Leopold, trailing in Altin's wake, sent him a sheepish look, directing Altin's gaze with his own down to the dried-out old tree branch his heavy foot had trod upon. The limb, half as thick as Altin's wrist, might have easily endured the weight of the young magician's tread, but the prodigious mass of Doctor Leopold counted two men at least—assuming they were hardy fellows and fond of fatty meats and ale—and so, where Altin might have snapped a twig here or there, the doctor had been snapping branches often over the duration of their hike, usually with enough volume to alert any creature that might be listening for a full measure round.

"Tidalwrath's fits, Doctor, you'll have every last wolf, spider and troll in the woods down upon us with that racket. Watch where you put your feet. I can't fend off every predator in Great Forest, you know."

The doctor's face was blotchy and red, and his breath came in a panting wheeze that began as a rattle in his chest and emerged in a high whistle through his nose. He clutched a dripping handkerchief in one hand, mopping at his throat and face in a futile attempt to stem the flow of sweat that ran from his pores as if he were some great sweat-filled wineskin and a legion of tiny archers had shot him through.

"You're the one who suggested this wretched business," sniped the doctor as he approached a fallen oak that Altin had just scurried over easily. The portly physician stared at the waist high obstacle as if it were a cliff rising a thousand spans above, shaking his head and letting go a long, exasperated breath. "I came to help save the girl, but who will save *me*?"

"You also came so that the next time you are out here, you will be able to get over that tree," corrected Altin. "Now come. We don't have time for this. And watch where you are walking."

"How am I supposed to get over that? I am not a squirrel, you know."

Altin dismissed the ice lance and, with a thought, teleported the doctor to the other side of the obstacle, bringing him beside him in the span of an instant. It was the fourth time in only an hour that he'd had to resort to such things.

"You should have just done that when you found the witch," the doctor said. "Could have saved us both a great deal of misery if I didn't have to be here until then."

Altin paid the man's complaints no mind and started back in the direction that Doctor Leopold's last divination had suggested that they go in their quest for the Z-classed diviner, Ocelot. Anything like a path had been long abandoned, and they'd been making their way through near darkness for almost half a day. Adding to their difficulties, the terrain had gotten increasingly steeper over the last hour as well, and Altin was afraid he might have to do precisely as the doctor asked if it got much worse. The man simply wasn't able to navigate the worsening incline with all its brambles and rocks. And the slippery footing of ever-damp leaves and slick needles on the slope made it hard going at times even for Altin, who had the vigor and agility of youth to aid him.

Altin recast the ice lance and started climbing again, once more heading purposefully upward. He came upon a broad stretch of rock rising from the ground like a massive single stair, high and wide, vanishing into the trees on either side. Moss covered it like dark green down, making it too slick to climb, and after giving them a rigorous pair of pulls, he determined that the scrawny vines crawling up its altitude would not hold his weight, much less the doctor's. A wide crack ran straight through it, however, and he thought he could see the slope continuing beyond on the other side. He thought about trying to squeeze through, but even if he could make it, he knew his counterpart could not. Pointing that out would only further irritate the man, so Altin moved laterally until he found a place to go around. He grumbled as he did so, aware that it cost him, and Orli, several moments in just doing that simple thing, but also aware that he couldn't just keep casting for every tiny thing, or when he needed his strength most, he might be too tired. It was a fine line of haste and conservation that he walked. Every second ticked off another moment of danger for her, for beloved Orli lost to him somewhere on distant planet Earth. Every spell ground down a bit more of his endurance, even with his ring. He'd already been awake for well over a whole day.

He waited for the doctor to catch up again, reaching out a hand to help haul him up the knee-high ledge that the blocking stone step had become. The doctor slipped on it anyway, before Altin could catch his hand, and he fell backwards, tumbling down the slope several spans before finally coming to rest, his momentum stopped by the fortuitous presence of a blackberry bush. Or at least, the marginally fortuitous presence of one.

"Sons of Hestra and the infernal rot of ten thousand harpies," swore the doctor as he wallowed and flailed in the groping bramble of the blackberry bush's entangling vines. "I'm besieged, for Mercy's sake. Ow, ow, ow." With his head downslope and his capacious posterior pointed uphill, his broad backside flashed with his thrashing, the white fabric of his pants blinking through the dimness like a signaler's flag. His stubby legs thrust into the air like the broken, twitching antennae of an insect trapped in a web, and the doctor threatened Altin with numerous forms of violence if he did not come immediately to his rescue.

On another day, Altin might have laughed, but today, he had no time for it. Irritated, he made to teleport the doctor out of his predicament, but, unfortunately, the doctor's rage and consternation precluded him from being treated so. Teleportation spells come with certain realities, and one of them is that the object being teleported not be in a frenzied emotional state. So Altin had to climb back down to where the doctor was and pull him out the old-fashioned way, by hand.

The vicious thorns of the blackberry bush did their fair share to punish Altin for his kindness, and by the time the doctor was back on his feet, both of them were bleeding profusely, though the doctor far more so than the Galactic Mage.

"I've had enough," the doctor announced with absolute finality. "I won't go a step farther." He reached into his pocket and pulled out a peach, which Altin thought he might be about to eat, but instead, the doctor peeled off a long section of its fuzzy skin. He closed his eyes and began to sing, and after a few moments, the abrasions on his face and arms were gone. He pulled off another strip of peach skin and repeated the exercise, this time for the benefit of Altin's hands and forearms. When he was done, he took a bite out of the peach as if it were an enemy and set a stubborn look upon his countenance. "Not one more step, young man. This exercise is ridiculous and barbaric. There are reasons our people tamed horses and gryphons, much less learned to weave flight into carpets and other things."

"But we're almost there."

"If we were standing on her doorstep, and she stood before us stark nude in the most buxom and comely of aspects, holding forth a platter of steaming pheasant with raspberry and mushroom sauce and promising me the bountiful joy of both food and flesh, I would still refuse to move one jot. I demand that you send me back to my office this instant. I shall bear not another moment of this torture, do you hear me? Not one!"

Altin turned away from him and looked up the slope. The doctor's divining spell had indicated that the mad Ocelot lived atop a great flat rock in a wooden hovel built for her by a woodsman whose love she had entertained some decades past. From the doctor's description of what he'd seen while casting, that rock should be at the top of this infernal hill. He'd tried to find it with a seeing spell, but it appeared that it had been hidden from such things, hence the reason for their climb.

He glanced back at the doctor, who looked quite disheveled now in his tattered and filthy clothes, his rotund torso heaving from the exertion of the blackberry fiasco and his face a portrait of misery. They definitely needed to find Ocelot soon.

With a thought, and the barest shape of the words that used to come reflexively to his mouth, he let go the ice lance once more and cast a seeing spell instead. He pushed his vision up the hill, moving around trees and over rocks, climbing up and up, the slope long and treacherous and likely to trouble the doctor even more than that which they'd already climbed. He spent several minutes in the search, knowing they had to be close. He was dimly aware of the doctor complaining, the man's voice a dull sound droning as if on the other side of a wall. Still Altin pushed upward, moving back and forth as he did, his sight snaking to and fro as he gobbled up altitude. He knew the odds were slim that he would find anything, but he was running out of both time and ideas. There must be some sign of it somewhere, some thing of hers left lying about. The doctor's divining spells were Y-class after all. They had to be close by now.

And then he saw it. At first, there was nothing but trees. But as he moved up the slope, he noticed a trail of smoke rising from nothingness, a smudge against the stars that caught his eye. It wafted up out of thin air, a plume with no source simply beginning high amongst the treetops. He knew then that they'd found her, for that smoke could not simply be. The moment he thought it, the rest of it appeared, the illusion burst and the reality revealed: a long sweep of flat ground formed a clearing in the woods, a high one, a steppe, and in the middle of it was a pool fed by a little brook. Rising out of the pool was a large formation of rock, nearly fifteen spans high and flat as a table at the top. And there, built upon it like a wooden hat, stood a modest cottage in a most dilapidated state. The thin plume of smoke poked like a crooked gray stick from its stone chimney up into the sky, moving about lazily while the pulse of yellow light coming through the wickerwork of the hovel's front shutters gave the impression that someone must be home.

Altin came out of his seeing spell in time to hear Doctor

Leopold's body land with a leafy splash back in the blackberry bush. At first he assumed the doctor had fallen into it again, but the black figure moving down the slope toward the fleshy doctor quickly dispelled that idea. A troll had thrown the doctor in!

A large figure, bipedal, mud brown with flesh rough as tree bark, waded into the bramble after the physician, reaching for him with long angular limbs that the thorns could not penetrate. It tore at the tangling vines as it pursued the doctor, who this time did not fight the thorny embrace of the blackberries but rather attempted to scramble deeper into them for protection, vain hope that it was.

The creature let go a loud, hungry roar, frustrated more by the binding ropes of the bush than any bite of its thorns, and it wasn't until the sound of that roar was reverberating through the trees that Altin recovered his wits enough to conjure the ice lance back, cursing the decision to let it go in the first place. Who knew how long its blue glowing light had kept that troll at bay?

The hissing blue spear formed instantly, and in the time it took to blink, the three-span shaft hurtled through the intervening distance and pierced the troll straight through. The power of the throw carried the monster over the blackberry patch completely and pinned it to a tree. Pinecones, pine needles and several chipmunks tumbled down like rain upon impact, the latter skittering off into the darkness, squeaking in protest to the violence that had awoken them.

The troll snapped off the end of the ice lance where it jutted out from its chest, then pulled itself free, sliding off the remainder of the spear and dropping to the ground at the base of the tree with a grunt. It came lumbering at Altin with huge, ground-eating strides, its legs nearly as long as Altin was tall.

Altin's fireball came as quickly as the thought, and it hit the troll full force, blowing it back against the tree once more, the heat of the fireball causing both troll and embedded ice lance to steam and hiss. The troll rebounded quickly, however, bouncing off the tree as if striking it were the merest inconvenience before plunging back up the slope toward Altin again.

He sent another fireball at it, this one spinning the troll off the tree to go tumbling downhill for forty paces or more. Flames leapt from its body as if it were a bonfire, and yet back up the hill it ran, oblivious to the heat. A third fireball had a similar effect, blowing it back but not stopping it. Many trees had begun to burn.

Altin watched the monster charging up at him again, this time from nearly a hundred paces off. He was going to set the whole forest on fire if he kept up like this. But the ice lance hadn't done anything either. He had never fought a troll before.

"You have to cut them up," came a diminutive voice to his right.

He looked for its source, but didn't see anyone. He scoured the area all around, searching through the trees, but the forest beyond the light of the fire was now lost in impenetrable darkness, made so by the growing glow of the mighty flames.

"Sheet ice, conjuror. Your first instinct was the better one."

Altin followed the sound to the exposed roots of a nearby pine, where two bright yellow eyes glinted in the light of the flames. Slowly his squinting gaze began to shape the feline face out of which those two yellow dots shone.

"You ought to hurry," said the animal. A slight forward thrust of its pink nose pointed to where the troll was only a few paces away.

Altin reflexively hit it with another fireball and sent it tumbling back down the hill again. The blaze of its descent was bright enough to be uncomfortable to look upon now. "My gods, but you'd think it would burn to death by now," he said, shielding his eyes from the glare with a raised forearm.

"It might in time," said the animal, stepping out from the shadows of the trunk, revealing a small creature with a soft coat of ochre fur, spotted black across the back and ribs and with a bright white chest and underbelly. It had large eyes and large tufted ears, the black fur at the tips of them nearly as long as the whiskers growing from its feline muzzle. It stood no higher than Altin's knee, and he knew right then that he'd finally found the object of this trek, the fabled diviner, Ocelot. Somehow he'd always thought that name was, well, just a name.

He watched the troll right itself and come charging back yet again. At least trolls were dumb, he thought. That helped. He opened his mind once more to the mana all around, still not quite used to the change that had come upon it since he'd been given the green marble of Blue Fire's great gift. No longer were there teeming currents of mana coursing like rivers through his mind. There was simply mana everywhere, a uniform vapor that moved not a lick.

He could shape anything he wanted in it, just as a sculptor might make anything he chose from an infinite block of stone. This time, rather than forming a spear of ice, Altin shaped a long flat sheet, just as the ocelot, Ocelot, had said. He took care to make it fine along the leading edge, adding bulk to it as he gave it size, forming in this way a plane of ice that would serve as something of a horizontal guillotine.

He sent his icy construct hurtling toward the oncoming troll and neatly cut it in half. It didn't even roar as it went down. It simply parted ways with half itself about halfway up the hill. And then it was done. The blade of ice sliced through several trees before its energy was lost, and the sound of their crashing filled the air, for a while even louder than the roar of the flames nearby.

Altin rushed down to check on Doctor Leopold. In what was a rather more elaborate and bloody reenactment of their earlier blackberry incident, once again the doctor was on his feet, though he shook with fear so terribly his whole body jiggled like a bowl of underdone pudding.

"Are you just going to let my forest burn?" came the voice from the knee-high feline, much closer than it had been before, no more than a pace away.

Altin looked to her, then to the fires burning brightly in three nearby trees—and just beginning in a fourth. Not to mention several bushes and another berry patch in between. One corner of his mouth twitched a bit. That could be a problem, he thought. "I don't have a rain spell memorized," he said. "Though I can go home and find one, I suppose." He dreaded digging through the randomness of Tytamon's library for that, and it was apparent in his tone.

The cat started to turn away. "A rude conjuror comes to my house in search of aid," she said. "This is the arrogance of man."

"I said I would go get the spell."

"But you must first know if I am the Ocelot you seek. As if it were not obvious enough. Otherwise you'd just as soon leave them burn."

"Well, now it is confirmed, isn't it? So you see, it worked," said Altin, having no inclination to pretend otherwise. He was pretty sure he wasn't going to get anything over on a Z-class diviner anyway.

She actually laughed at that, which was a strange thing coming from the throat of a cat, especially a big one like

Ocelot was. "*Tsono havora. Cosoahn na'vakalias pendinto. Mel aba menzon moson mon.* Those are the words you need but do not need." She padded cautiously up to him, and with the flick of a paw, she scratched him through the material of his robe, a short, stinging cut just below his knee. He started and stepped away from her, about to shout, considering a fireball, but then, in that moment, realized he now knew the conjuring rain spell.

That set him to blinking in bewilderment for a moment, but only that long. He supposed it made sense that she might be able to do that sort of thing. He'd heard some diviners, strong ones, could transfer spells that way, but it was mainly the sort of thing practiced by the Church. Normal people didn't go around stabbing each other when some time spent with a book would do. He might have spent more time marveling at the convenience, but then something she'd said suddenly registered. The moment it did, just when it hit him, she saw it in the widening of his eyes. He watched her recognize it—or perhaps she'd simply already known he was going to be a bit slow in catching what she'd said and that he'd be startled when he did. Altin had no idea which, but it occurred to him then that she somehow knew about the ring. And likely other things.

"Yes, I know about your world gift," she said, and as Altin stared down at her, he could see the faint green light that pulsed from beneath his ring reflecting in her eyes. He started to say something but stopped. That would have been pointless too. "Put the fire out," she said. "I'll be waiting for you and your clumsy friend. He will come when his complaints are done." With that she ran off up the hill, her paws silent upon the forest floor, the high curl of her tail suggesting she was completely at her ease.

When she was gone, Altin turned back to the doctor, who appeared to have regained some small measure of his wits, if only enough for speech. Altin verified that the doctor's injuries were, while messy, only minor, though all the while the shaken physician complained and argued and insisted that Altin take him back to Leekant at once, for surely he teetered at the brink of death. It was the matter of some time before Altin finally got the good doctor to relent in his tirade and recognize that, at least for the pain, he, the doctor himself, was the source of his own remedy if he could just calm himself enough to effect it. This recognition marked the beginning of the man's return to reason, and it was only a matter of a few minutes more before he set himself to the task of healing his wounds.

Altin, in the interim, used the spell Ocelot had imparted to him upon that scratch, and in doing so, he recognized it as being the one he'd taught himself two or so years before, the very same one he'd cast to snuff out a fire he'd ignited in the ivy climbing up his tower. Given how many variations of this sort of spell there were, he could not help but marvel at the coincidence, and he wondered if perhaps Ocelot had plucked it out of his memory, even though he himself could not. It was unnerving to think she could do such a thing, but also inspired hope, for divination worked best when the diviner knew as much as possible. What better way to know Altin's mind than to, well, know his mind? So, while in a way he suddenly felt quite exposed, it was with renewed confidence that he put out the blaze and then set to work convincing Doctor Leopold to come with him to Ocelot's humble rock-top abode. The doctor had information from his own divining spell that would serve the Z-ranked feline as much as would things that Altin knew. And, just as predicted, the good doctor eventually agreed that he would.

Chapter 15

Director Nakamura's face, even in the small shuttle monitor, looked visibly shaken when Captain Asad gave him the news of the colossal red orb orbiting Mercury, and after watching the brief video record from the shuttle's log, the director's expression only barely concealed how disquieted he was. "We can't afford to pull any of the Juggernauts out of orbit to go after it," he said. "We're not even holding them off now as it is. They're still slipping orbs through and hitting smaller and smaller cities systematically. Hell, there are ten times as many of those things in New York right now than there were six hours ago. Washington and Boston are hardly any better. None of them are. Europe is just as bad."

"But it may be the source," replied Captain Asad, as Roberto was guiding the small ship toward the *Aspect*'s shuttle bay, around which the outer lights had just turned green. "If they are coming from that thing, then we have to take it out. We're not going to win on defense. Send a Juggernaut. That's what they're for, taking down big targets, planetary assaults. I can't think of a better time to put one to its proper use."

"Until we confirm it's the source, I'm not opening us up

any more than we already are. We'll send probes to get a closer look. Maybe it's some kind of repair station, or it's the transport that brought them here. Unless it gets close enough to engage with the main body of the fleet, I'm not sending even one Juggernaut after that thing." He didn't look happy about saying it, but he was clearly not going to budge. "For God's sake, Asad, we've got cargo ships and cruise liners up there fighting alongside you guys. I move a Juggernaut, no telling how many smaller ships go down. The whole net could unravel."

"The net is unraveling. And you and I both know there's no chance it's just a repair station or a transport ship. If you won't send the Juggernauts, then take it out with smaller ships. Send twenty starships and just bombard the hell out of it."

"Captain, I don't have to tell *you* of all people how that is going to go."

The captain shook his head, frustrated. The director was right about that. The Hostiles had proven themselves extremely efficient at brushing off missile attacks, at least missile attacks where the weapons did not have the "anti-magic" enhancements put upon them by Prosperion magicians—put there for the ostensible attack of the Hostile home world, which Captain Asad was now completely convinced had been a charade and all part of the War Queen's strategy.

The director turned away from his monitor for a moment, speaking to someone off screen. When he came back, he looked even grimmer than the moment before. "Mars Station Armstrong just reported the appearance of another one of your monster orbs, Captain. We're going to contact Victoria Base to confirm, but if it's true, this new one is over six hundred miles in diameter. Makes the one you found seem small."

"We've got to stop them. You have to send some ships

to take the big ones out. This is only going to get worse if we don't act now."

"No, we need to take out the command ship. That is the most important part."

"That's what I'm telling you. I believe those big ones are the command ships."

"Wrong, Captain. We've already had visual contact with the command ship. The Prosperion vessel you sent us the files on, the one they call *Citadel*. We engaged them several hours ago, but they ran off. One of the Prosperions snuck aboard the *NTA II* and tried to convince her captain that we should let our guard down, but she got away before we could question her."

"Eugene probably let her go. That woman is an appeaser and unfit for command."

"I am well aware of your ongoing feud with Eugene, Captain, but she was not the problem. It was some kind of device the Prosperion held, a jewel or bit of glass that she struck against the bulkhead and vanished." The director looked a bit irritated at having to defend one of his officers at a time when there were larger concerns. "The point is, Asad, that Prosperion ship is the only one of these orbs that has intelligent life aboard, so we are operating on the assumption that *Citadel* is the most valuable target. Every ship has orders to fire upon it when it reappears. And given how evasive it was on our first attempt, we're not going to spread our defenses any more than they are now. If you have any suggestions on that front, I'm happy to hear them, otherwise, I need to get back to work figuring out what we *can* do about these new, giant Hostiles, particularly the one at Mars, and I need a plan that doesn't mean sacrificing the Earth to do it. But it does need to be done, I agree with you. If Victoria goes down ... I don't have to tell you how that will go." Captain Asad had a faraway look in his eyes, and when he did not reply, the director was inclined to prompt him to speak. "Captain, if that is all ...."

"Director, we do have a way to stop them. We can make them call it all off." He turned and gave Roberto a look that seemed to suggest he'd had an epiphany, the kind in which one suddenly realizes the answer has just been sitting there in the open all along. "We've had it the whole time, the key to this whole damn thing. They even gave it to us."

"Go on," urged the director.

"The harbor stones. We have the harbor stones the Prosperions made for us. All the ships that were at Goldilocks have stones just like the one the woman who showed up on the *NTA II* used to escape. If we break those stones, our ships are right back in the Prosperion system again. We can fly in and take that bitch by her royal throat and squeeze until she calls off this attack."

"You all made it very clear that using their magic for long-range travel shuts down ships' systems. Is there some reason you think that doing this won't make you all sitting ducks?"

"We will be. At least, the starships will be, but not the troop carriers. And not the handful of inter-planetary ships you are going to stuff inside our bays. Not to mention the missiles you resupply."

"I'm not following you, Captain. Your reports show total shutdown of all systems on your ships every time those people leap you across space."

"Only the ship. Not the shuttles. They call it being 'in the box.' In their arrogance, they made a point of bragging about it. That's how we restarted the ships. Our handhelds and generators all work. Everything inside the 'box' is fine. It's the 'box' that ... takes whatever the teleportation does. So let's jam every goddamn Marine and battle suit available onto all forty-nine ships, cram in a few bombers, and the moment we appear above Tinpoa, we open the bay doors and send them to Prosperion. Screw the starships. That goddamn Queen will never know what hit her. She'll call off the attack or watch us melt her cities just like she's trying to do to ours, only we'll do it a hell of a lot faster."

Director Nakamura hummed, a vibration in his throat accompanied by narrowed, thoughtful eyes. Captain Asad and Roberto could hear it over the com, watching as he mulled over the idea. They knew his answer before he spoke again, for his head began to nod. "I'll run it by the board and see what they think, but I'll be honest, that's the best idea I've heard since this whole shit storm opened up. Get Eugene and the rest of them to pull back to where the *Aspect, Sarajevo* and *Socrates* are now, get them all out at the fringe of the fight. Let's not lose any of those harbor stones." He didn't even wait for Captain Asad's "yes, sir" to cut the transmission off.

Captain Asad had no concerns with protocol or courtesy just then. His mind was already awhirl, plotting the moves that would bring Prosperion to its knees even as the shuttle came to a halt inside the *Aspect* and settled to the deck. This fight was personal, and the so-called War Queen had made a huge, huge mistake: she'd betrayed her neighbor while leaving the spare house key under her own doormat. That was going to cost her.

Roberto frowned at the look in the captain's eyes as he punched the controls that opened the shuttle hatch. The man's expression was almost maniacal.

"Get me security," the captain said, tapping the com badge on his lapel. He unbuckled himself and went to the hatch, waiting impatiently as the ramp lowered to the hangar deck below.

"Security," came the reply almost immediately.

"Round up all the Prosperion crewmen on the ship," he said. "We won't be needing them any longer."

Roberto's eyes shot wide at that. Beyond the one magician, Annison, there were a number of Prosperion blanks aboard, men and women from Altin's world who, unlike Altin and Annison, had no magical abilities. They'd all volunteered to serve in the place of the crew that had been lost over the course of fighting the Hostiles these last two years. They'd been trained, they'd signed on the dotted line, sworn the oath, even went to war with the rest of the fleet ships at Goldilocks. This measure was uncalled for.

"Captain," Roberto said. "You can't do that to them. They have served with us for quite a while, some for almost a year. They went into battle with us."

"You were just out there with me, Commander. I think you can see how trusting Prosperions pays off."

"But Captain—"

The captain cut him off. "If you haven't the stomach for command, Commander, I suggest you find another line of work when this war is won. You won't rise higher than you already have if you can't make the hard decisions. And that stunt you tried to pull with Pewter down there isn't going to help you either when it comes to it."

"But Captain—" he tried again.

"This discussion is over, Commander. Get some rest. I will need you fresh and ready to fly when we assault Prosperion. This ends now."

Chapter 16

Gromf stared into the woman's eyes, Kazuk-Hal-Mandik's singer, the spawn of the old warlock's loins. He could see the look of the ancient shaman in her face, the downward arc of her forehead where the bones of her brow curved like a crossbow pulled partway back. He did not like that Kazuk-Hal-Mandik had entrusted her with the knowledge of God's legions; he did not like entrusting the fate of the All Clans to her. She was female. This was not done.

He also knew that thought was an old thought, a learned belief rooted in the time of a thousand years of defeat. The human females fought in war. Their armies won. It was Discipline to forget his disgust at having her here, in this chamber of war. Kazuk-Hal-Mandik said the human symbols, the sound symbols written in their *book*, the things this singer had memorized, were made by the hand of a human woman. It was her power that they sought to understand. He supposed in that it was right that it should be interpreted by a woman as well. But still, seeing her before him, listening to her sing the song, made him shudder.

They sat on the floor in the Chamber of Discipline, the

center of the new mountain fortress, the first great work of Warlord. It was a vast space, two hundred paces to walk across on any side, absolutely true on its every plane, every angle equal to its opposite. It had been measured and cut that way to prove that the All Clans had mastery over stone, no longer left to dwell in the spaces of accident in the bowels of the world that the old gods had made. Straight lines could be wrought by the hands of Discipline. Warlord refused to let this chamber, this first symbol of Discipline, be furnished or covered with animal hides. It was in the stark yet grand severity of this chamber that he kept his council of war. Today the council consisted only of Warlord, Kazuk-Hal-Mandik and Gromf. Before them was this woman who sang.

Her voice rose into the darkness, rebounded off the stern walls and unseen ceiling, giving a strange cascading harmony to her voice as she ran through the stolen works of the human called Melane Montclaire, the works to which God had guided them.

The three of them listened to her sing, Warlord looking irritated by the great length of her noise, already three quarters of a day, while Gromf and Kazuk-Hal-Mandik listened intently. The woman's voice was strong and sure, and never once did her song warble or hesitate. She sang the human words and the ancient sounds, which Kazuk-Hal-Mandik attributed to the elves, as if she'd spoken the despised languages all her life, as if they came naturally. It did nothing to decrease Gromf's disgust at having her in this revered place, but he forced away the feelings every time they came.

Finally, as the unseen sun outside the mountain fortress set, the woman's song came to an end.

"This is the last book of summoning," the woman said. "This is all of it."

Warlord rose then, prepared to leave, but he stopped

when Kazuk-Hal-Mandik spoke, not to him, but to the woman. "Sing again of the hole through the center of the world."

The woman did not protest, though she'd been singing for so long. She did not ask for water to wet her throat. She did not pause or roll her eyes up into her head to think. She simply began.

> *And Tidalwrath left the fissure*
> *Through which the demons flow*
> *Brought forth never since*
> *But for those who chose to know.*
> *Cry not for the endless hordes*
> *Who fall beneath their might*
> *These are the darkest legions*
> *Come summoned to the fight.*
> *Through a world as vast as ours*
> *Tidalwrath built a passage true*
> *So summon them not lightly*
> *For unsummoning thou won't do.*

Kazuk-Hal-Mandik stopped her then, raising his hand and croaking for silence. He looked up from his place seated on the floor, up at Warlord standing tall above him. "This is the thing I told you of, Warlord. This is what happened to the dwarves. The humans say the lands of the dwarves still churn with the demons unleashed that day."

"And so it will be with the humans," said Warlord. He turned to go.

"The humans no longer go to Duador, Warlord. It is a lost land."

"That is because humans are weak." He started for the door.

"No, Warlord." The old warlock's voice was strong, insistent even, defiance that spun Warlord back around, his eyes narrow and violence shaping in the movement of the great muscles shifting beneath his skin. Kazuk-Hal-Mandik went on despite seeing it. "It is because there were too many of them to be slain, Warlord. The demons. You heard the song. 'They come like bats at twilight from a cave.'" He quoted from an earlier passage then, one that described the demons in lines that read, "A spew of blackness will arrive, swept out from summoned rift," though he could only partially recall what came next, something about "devouring thy enemies in a wave" and "thrift." He struggled to find the right human words.

Kazuk-Hal-Mandik glanced to the woman who amended for him: "A wave that knows no thrift."

"Yes, that was it." The shaman grinned at that, and the dim light of the fire glinted off his remaining teeth, making them appear as if they were broken stalactites in an old, decaying cave. "Uncounted death. Uncountable. That is the lament of the humans and the elves, for they could not take what they had conquered. We must learn from their lack of Discipline."

Warlord looked annoyed by that, his great face contorted with his scowl and his own teeth, still strong like mammoth ivory, showing in fearsome rows of opposed menace as if by that difference alone the disparity between the great warrior and the frail old warlock could be known. "We have the greatest army Prosperion has ever seen. No human king has mustered such numbers as counted in the warriors we have devouring our stores. *We* are the darkest legions. We are the spew of blackness that will bring respect to the All Clans, and we will deal with your ... demons when the time comes that I am done with them. You just make sure they appear when I call for them."

"Hush, Warlord. You must not speak such things aloud."

Warlord roared then, striding forward and leaning

down to blow the wrath that rose at such defiance directly into the ancient warlock's face. The ferocity of it sent the dried wisps of Kazuk-Hal-Mandik's hair billowing behind him like mangy tatters of fur on an old carcass lying in some lost and windy mountain pass. He was not afraid of God. "I will speak what I see," he said when the initial thunder had passed. "And I will not cower or run from your conjured things." He straightened then, took a breath. He looked down at both of them, Kazuk-Hal-Mandik and Gromf beside him, with his lip curling some. He glanced to the woman briefly before letting his yellow eyes settle back on the pair of shamans sitting there. "You got your human song, old one. And you've got your young victor of the yellow stone. Now you get three sunsets. Then we go to war."

"But Warlord, that may not be enough," protested Kazuk-Hal-Mandik.

"Silence," Warlord shouted. "You have had your time. I have done everything you asked. You asked that we take the castle of the human shaman. You asked that we help you steal his yellow stones and the words to the demon song. You said that was all God needed to promise us victory. Now you have them. I have kept my word. Now you and God keep yours. You have three days. The time has come." The wind of his passing set the small fire to dancing for a time, and Gromf contented himself with watching it while Kazuk-Hal-Mandik got up and followed Warlord out.

When they were gone, Gromf looked up at the woman, who was proper and lowered her eyes. He could not decide if Warlord's three days was Discipline or not. His decision was strong. It was action. That was good. They had been patient, and they had had an army over a hundred thousand strong waiting on the machinations of one old warlock for well over a season now, waiting only for that.

Everything else in place. That seemed like Discipline.

He wondered and wished he knew.

Eventually Kazuk-Hal-Mandik returned. He looked agitated. "I think this is not enough time."

"I think it is the time we have," said Gromf.

"Then we must learn the elf words soon, and how the human said to shape them." Gromf nodded. Kazuk-Hal-Mandik looked to the woman. "Sing us the summoning parts again. Sing them slowly."

Chapter 17

Ocelot's hovel was as disheveled and nondescript on the inside as it had appeared from without. With the nascent forest fire extinguished, Altin and Doctor Leopold found themselves the guests of the woodland denizen, sitting before her fire and waiting for her to brew tea that neither of them had any intention of drinking. Doctor Leopold sat on an upturned log, its flattened ends the work of Ocelot's long-lost woodsman lover. Altin had the pleasure of a chair, but it suffered visibly from dry rot, and for once in his life, Altin found that he had empathy for the corpulent doctor, knowing in those moments spent upon that seat what the doctor must worry about nearly everywhere he rested. The anticipation of the sharp and sudden drop that he was sure must come at any time was a distraction Altin had to struggle to set aside.

Wishing to break the silence—the only sound in the small space being the pops and crackles of the fire and Ocelot's muttering as she watched the kettle suspended above it on an iron hook—Altin finally spoke. "You're much younger than the rumors suggest," he said, hoping to start the conversation off better than it had begun with his nearly burning down what counted as her neighborhood.

He knew that her current appearance—she sat before them no longer as an ocelot but rather looking to be a girl of no more than fourteen years—was either transmuted or illusionary, but even knowing it, that was the only thing that came to mind to say. Some propitious instinct in him told him that it was best not to simply blurt out why they had come, which in a way would have been pointless, for he was absolutely certain she already knew. They were in her court, so to speak, so he would play the part of supplicant for now.

"Rumors have it you are smarter than the questions that you ask," she said, grinning over her shoulder at him. Doctor Leopold even laughed at that, which got a frown from Altin directed his way.

"Well, if we're speaking of rumors, it's not often one sits before a Z-ranked diviner rumored to be the oldest person in the land." It was the best he could do in his own defense, while trying to appear as if he had much more patience for this banter than he really did.

"You would face alien worlds alone and yet quake before one small cat that becomes a girl." She made a *tsk-tsk* sound with her teeth. "It makes more sense that I would tremble before you. You and your world gift." Her eyes, brown now, flicked in the direction of his ring. "What could I do that you could not stop anyway?"

"I do not tremble, nor did I come to fight or challenge you. But you already know that. So, if it is directness that you are looking for, you should stop wasting time."

She giggled then, a sound that seemed natural in the body of the gangly girl she had become. She took the teakettle off the fire, its handle gripped in a thick handful of large dark leaves. She moved through the dim confines of her house, the wind blowing through the places where centuries of rain had washed away the mud that had once sealed her home and kept the elements at bay. She filled three small cups, none of them matching, one with no handle, and brought them back to the fire on a tray made from a single piece of bark. She set it on an upturned log that matched the one the doctor sat upon and took the cup with no handle as a courtesy, once more employing the fistful of leaves.

"Go ahead and drink it," she said, nodding in the direction of the steaming cups. "If I wanted you dead, I wouldn't have gone to the trouble of making tea."

Altin looked to Doctor Leopold, for the man was well versed in herbal brews and their like, being a medical man and all, but the doctor, while calm enough now and curious enough normally, shook his head adamantly side to side. Definitely not.

Ocelot sighed and sat on the floor near the hearth, the chair and the two logs making for a third of the hovel's furnishings. She turned her back to the wall, leaning against the hearthstones and pulling her knees up nearly to her chin. She leaned against the stonework, and the long bones of her shins could be traced through her flesh, set to high relief by the shadows the fire made. She took a long sniff of the steam coming off of her tea then balanced the cup on the flat of a bony knee.

"So you know why we are here," Altin said after a time. "How much do I need to add to what you know before you will tell us if you are going to help?"

"I need him to drink my tea," she said simply, pointing at the doctor. "I must see the spell he cast exactly as he saw it. Otherwise, there is little you can tell me that I have not already seen."

Altin looked to the doctor, who suddenly sat bolt upright. "I won't do it," he protested. "I have not lived to my fine age by trusting every wild concoction thrust at me. If there is anything you learn as a doctor, it is that half the best medicines in the world do twice as much damage as they do good, and all the half-baked remedies are worse. I'll be having none of that brew, whatever it is. If this child is a Z, let her be a Z without poisoning me."

Ocelot shrugged and went back to watching the steam rising from her cup.

"Doctor, please," said Altin. "You can't possibly mean to come all the way out here, endure all of this, travel to other worlds, witness the attack on Orli's planet—Orli who is your patient, mind you—only to falter now at a spot of tea."

Doctor Leopold shrugged in much the same way Ocelot had.

Altin nearly panicked, horrified by the idea that everything hung upon the outcome of this childish standoff. He scowled at the doctor then swung his frenzied gaze to Ocelot. She smiled and said, "Don't worry. He drinks it."

"No, *he* does not drink it, young lady," protested the doctor, "and I'll thank you not to speak of me as if I were not in the room." Doctor Leopold tugged at his lapels, as if straightening his now filthy coat might somehow ameliorate the amount of scrutiny he was getting from Altin just then.

"I can't believe you," Altin said. He tipped forward in his chair and nearly snatched one of the teacups off the thick slab of bark. It was too hot to drink, so he conjured a small ice lance, barely the length of his middle finger, though somewhat thicker around, and stuck it into the tea, stirring with it until the cup nearly overflowed. He threw the remainder of the diminutive weapon into the fire and poured the whole cup down his throat, swallowing as infrequently as possible and trying not to taste it at all.

It was remarkably good, despite his expectations, slightly bitter but with a hint of mint. He leaned back, anticipating the worst, and waited. The left leg of his chair gave way with the tipping and resettling of his bulk. It snapped with a dry crack, and he slid off onto the floor. The suddenness of the chair leg buckling startled him more than it might have as he fell, given the tense rigidity with which he sat, expectant of some horrible effect of the tea. He cried out, one short bark of surprise, just before he hit the ground. Ocelot watched him, clearly amused.

Altin collected himself and then pushed the remnants of the chair away, settling himself there on the floor with his legs crossed beneath his robes. He would not give her the satisfaction of his indignity. He sat waiting for the impact of whatever it was he'd just drunk.

Nothing happened.

Ocelot's grin subsided as she observed him over time, the firelight glinting in her luminous, still slightly-feline eyes.

Finally Altin turned to the doctor. "There, you see? It's perfectly fine. And I doubt that log will buckle like my chair did, so let's be on with it."

"We'll see about that," the portly doctor said, his brow now glistening with the sweat of nerves. "Come here." He pointed to the area of the floor between his feet. "Sit here."

Altin scooted to where he'd been directed, and Leekant's greatest healer took the young magicians face in a pair of soft, fleshy hands. He spent the next several minutes working his way through Altin's body magically, inspecting his mouth, throat, intestines and various arteries, capillaries and veins for signs of any malignancy. There was nothing to be found. He even spent time poking through the maze of Altin's brain, feeling for currents that should not be, for pressure that grew or moved tidally, but there was none of that either. Nothing out of the ordinary at all. Finally he was forced to conclude that there was, perhaps, no poison in the cup.

"Fine," he said. "But if I die, I'll have you know I'll be

waiting for you in hell, even if I have to climb down eight levels to find you and plague you for all eternity when you finally do get there. Do you hear me?"

"I can live with that," Altin said. "Now please, Doctor, Orli doesn't have time for all of this, and a divination like we need is going to take eons as it is."

Again came the long nasal sounds of a thick and irritated exhale, but Doctor Leopold accepted the teacup Altin handed him. He would not be rushed and declined Altin's offer of a tiny ice lance with which to cool it. He blew on it and made his own reluctant time about getting it done. But eventually he drank it all.

Altin watched as he tipped the cup up and drained the last bit of it, then looked anxiously to Ocelot who still sat by the fire with her legs still pulled in to her chest like an accordion. "Well," Altin said. "Now what?"

She dipped a finger into her own tea, wincing a little at its heat, then set a drop of the liquid on her tongue. She waited only a moment or so. "The dragon must find her," she said. "He is the only one that can see."

Altin frowned, looked askance at the doctor, then back to Ocelot. "Dragon? What dragon?"

"Yours."

"Taot? Why him? What can he see?"

"Animals see in ways humans cannot. Your lover's world will be a mural of nothingness to you. A landscape of alien shapes where structures are as numerous as leaves, as grass, as snowflakes in a storm. They are a chorus of sameness that your eyes will make nothing of, a song sung upon a single note with nothing to memorize. I can show you, but you will not see. The dragon must do it for you."

"Show me then. Show me what I am looking for, and I will convey it to his mind."

"I will show you, but he already knows."

"You've already spoken to him?"

"No."

"What then?"

"Trust him. He will smell the girl when you are in the right place." She placed another drop of tea upon her tongue. "You must find her then, deep in the dungeons. She will be in the rainbow web. The web of death. You must be there before the venom reaches her heart."

"A spider has her? What spider? They don't have spiders like we have, like you have here in Great Forest. Orli told me they no longer have great creatures on her world. The great creatures of her world are all dead."

"I have seen her there. In the rainbow web. You must get her before it is too late." She looked at the doctor and frowned some. She dipped out another drop of tea. "Get to her in time, and she can help you seek the red world."

Altin groaned. "What red world? What happens on the red world?"

"It is the one you must find or everyone will die."

"Everyone who? Everyone on the red world or everyone, as in all of us?" He pointed around the room, then turned his hands over, palms up and out at his sides, his gesture encompassing Prosperion, or perhaps even the universe. He already had a pretty good idea which one she meant.

"Everyone."

"You've seen this?"

"I have seen the wind roaming two worlds looking for someone to give lyrics to the tune of its whistling. The birds know only harmony, and the stars cry in silence."

Rather than argue with ambiguities, he pressed on, growing impatient for something more concrete. "Fine. So how do I find Orli in this rainbow web? Where do I start? Surely you don't expect me to take Taot to Earth and simply fly around hoping he sniffs her out randomly in Doctor Leopold's three-hundred measure circle like some hunter's hound. You have to give me more. Give me something I can use."

"Cold is your ally. Hide in it just as you will hide in invisibility. The alien machines see the warm blood in your veins. The heat from your body glows like a beacon to their eyes."

That seemed odd, but he did not question it. "Fine, I can do that. What else?"

She took another drop of tea upon her finger, pressing it into her mouth, leaving the slender digit in there and sucking on it for a while. She looked back at the doctor, squinting. She took up the cup and drank from it directly. Twice. Then she threw the rest of it into the fire.

She rose and walked to where Altin sat, the tattered wreck of her homespun dress barely enough for modesty. Dirt smears marred the pale skin. He had just looked up at her when she became the ocelot again. Her paw flicked forward, and she opened three parallel gashes along his forearm, each about the length of half his hand. "That is where you must go."

He saw it then, as a memory, as if he'd flown over it a hundred times before. A vast and sprawling alien metropolis, an unending expanse of black- and gray-mirrored buildings, similar beyond description, just as Ocelot had said. There were measures upon measures of these buildings, broken up here and there by a flat expanse of the dark mirrored stuff or the occasional tall, spindly construct, but only to resume the endless indecipherable pattern—a pattern without pattern—again. It was such sameness, such uniformity, an indescribably massive work of man obviously, yet conceived and executed with an incalculable absence of aesthetic design. Function in its most absolute. It was hard to contemplate what kind of people would go to such lengths to avoid beauty in any way.

Orli was buried somewhere underneath all that, deep down and being preyed upon by ... by a spider of some kind. At least that he could handle. He had no fear of such things.

He shook himself out of the vision and stared down to where the spotted cat had been. The child was back, starting to move away from him, though she paused. She came back and leaned down near his ear. "Hurry," she hissed. "The venom will have her before the day is done."

Chapter 18

Twenty-four hours after the director's order came, the forty-nine remaining ships of the original Andalia mission, the ships whose crews had spent over a decade light years from home, the ones whose crews had just, finally, returned home—albeit under circumstances out of their control—found themselves restocked and outfitted to go right back where they'd so recently been, right back to the Prosperion system, and this time, intent on bringing war to the War Queen.

The sacrifice asked of these crews was beyond enormous, it was unfair, but remarkably, few among them had argued that it should be anyone else. The ships and the harbor stones the Prosperions had made were linked, and while it would have been possible to swap in new crews, those who had been on that long journey saw the attack on Earth as something personal. It wasn't simply an attack, it was an insult, a betrayal, and so they agreed to return, many seeing it as finishing the task, or the sentence, they'd already committed or been committed to. Many, like Captain Asad, wanted vengeance.

That said, there were a few new personnel going along as well: Marines. Lots of them.

The *Aspect*, like the other ships, now had aboard troop carriers loaded with Marine mech units, two hundred of them on Captain Asad's ship alone. In addition, in each of the *Aspect*'s two main cargo holds, were two small freighters carrying one planetary bomber and two inner-atmospheric fighters each. Between the forty-nine starships, they had plenty enough power to deal with the Prosperions.

As always, Captain Asad volunteered to go first, and not for the first time since meeting Altin Meade, the captain was glad to have Prosperion "magic" at hand. With Director Nakamura on screen to watch, and all the other fleet officers waiting to hear from them if the harbor stone actually worked, Asad opened the small box that contained the *Aspect*'s harbor stone.

The gem was light blue, a sapphire, and lying next to it was a small iron hammer, not even a foot long, black as space itself. The captain reached into the box and took out the mallet, showing it to the director, whose head, giant on the display, nodded.

"Patch in Commander Levi on *Transport Nine*," the captain ordered Ensign Nguyen who was seated at the main console. The dexterous fingers of the young officer pulled up the feed from Roberto's station, where the intrepid Spaniard sat in the pilot's chair of the troop carrier designated *Transport Nine*. "Are you ready, Commander?" asked the captain when Roberto came on com.

"Ready, Captain. Entanglement functioning normally." With a quick motion of his hand, he switched the video feed from one showing his own round face to one that mirrored the image on the *Aspect*'s bridge, the image of the director looking on. "See, I have the director now. I'll let him know when we get there."

Captain Asad glanced once more up at the director and

raised the iron hammer.

"Good luck, Captain," said the director.

Captain Asad struck the sapphire in the box. It shattered as easily as if it had been made of glass, and then everything went dark. Only a few months ago, such a thing would have sent a wave of tension rolling through the crew as bowels tightened and cold sweats began. But not now. Not this crew. They knew precisely what was happening. And it was with practiced calm that they set themselves to work.

Captain Asad waited until his eyes adjusted to the red glow of the emergency lights, and then made his way to the lift. He opened the doors with the manual override and quickly climbed down the shaft using rungs mounted in the wall. It took him almost ten minutes to get to the hangar bay where Roberto was, but he got there just the same, nodding solemnly as he passed through the ship at the scurrying crewmen working in a controlled frenzy to get the ship's systems back online. A glance out the small window in one of the massive hangar doors showed the bright green glow of the gas giant Naotatica, confirming they were, in fact, exactly where they thought they were.

Roberto was in his final systems check when Captain Asad arrived. Seated next to him was a lean woman in her middle years, running through a checklist of her own. The vascularity of her forearms suggested she was fit and strong, a warrior to be sure. She turned to him as he approached and smiled. "We're gonna pound them so bad," she said. "They're going to show up on horses and wave pointy sticks at us, and it's going to go like shit for them."

"You may be right, Major, but don't underestimate them. They will be more dangerous than you expect. We've seen what they can do."

"I know."

"Any word from the other ships?"

"No, sir. Not yet, but I'm sure they're here just like we are." She leaned forward and tapped the communications panel to verify. Still no signals from other landing craft.

"Systems are go," said Roberto. "We just need someone to open the damn doors and let us out."

A moment later, the main hangar lights came on. "It looks like you're about to get your wish, Commander."

"Captain, you either need to suit up or get out," Roberto advised.

"Good luck, Major. Good luck, Levi."

"Thank you, sir," said Roberto, sending the captain on his way.

With the captain and all non-mission personnel out of the hangar, the massive doors were finally set to open, the power needed to do so having been made a priority as part of the attack plan. Soon they were moving apart, and the gap between them began to fill with Naotatica's bright light. The white mist of escaping air hissed unheard out toward it as the doors opened further, and Roberto watched through the front window as someone's unsecured toolbox got sucked out into space. They'd brought several new crewmen aboard to replace the Prosperions, who had been incarcerated back on Earth, and clearly some of the new folks were as green as the big planet when it came to such things.

Roberto watched tools scatter and spin, glinting green as they tumbled slowly out of sight. He tapped the console impatiently, waiting for his chance. Eventually it came as the red lights along the hangar doors turned green. He tapped the controls to reverse gravity lock and lifted the ship off the deck. Soon after, *Transport Nine* was clear of the *Aspect* entirely.

Seeing the mother ship floating as she was, its lights out, its towers invisible against the blackness beyond, was unsettling. The *Aspect* looked like a ghost ship, a derelict, an object that might have been discarded there more than a decade ago. There was vulnerability in seeing his ship in that condition that struck Roberto as unsettling, and he forced himself to look away.

"Visual contact with *Socrates*, *Livermore* and *Pegasus*," reported Major Kincaid. "I can't tell who that is beyond *Pegasus*."

"We'll know soon enough," Roberto said, "but I'm not waiting. Where the hell is our other half?"

The com crackled to life even as Roberto said the words. "T-10 to T-9, you coming, Commander Levi?"

"Waiting on you, Jackson," he replied.

"I'm already underway," she said. "You're slow."

Sure enough, Commander Jackson's ship had only barely blinked on sensors, and then it vanished again. The signatures of transport ships T-11 and T-12 were blinking out as well. "Son of a bitch," muttered Roberto.

"Let's get moving then," remarked the major. "I got fifty Marines back there who are going to take it real bad if you make them late. Won't be safe for you to ever sleep again."

"Never happen," said Roberto, and a moment later he initiated the short hop that got them to Prosperion.

They came out of the jump and immediately found the other three troop carriers on sensors again. Commander Jackson's ship was already plunging into the planet's atmosphere, visible through the front windows as a ball of fire hurtling toward the continent of Kurr. He followed right behind, pushing the ship to its limits, not so much out of a desire to catch up or win some kind of race, but out of the need to get to the Little Earth base quickly before the wizards caught sight of them and did something terrible.

Roberto was familiar enough with what Prosperion

magic could do, and he had no interest in exploring the interior of a sun, not even for an instant.

They pushed through the furnace of entry and then streaked toward the cloud-covered northwest portion of the continent, coming in at a steep angle that would take them right to the staging point.

Roberto called up a view of Little Earth when they'd cleared the gray clouds, making sure there were no Prosperions in residence inside the fortified area. There were none.

He and the other three ships landed in neat formation at almost the exact same time, but Roberto had opened the cargo ramp while his ship was still thirty feet in the air, so battle-suited Marines had been jumping out for several moments before touchdown. Major Kincaid laughed as she watched her people landing in the mud and grass. "Hell yeah," she said. "First of the first of the first. *Oorah.*"

"Well, at least I don't have to worry about horrible shit happening to me while I sleep," he said.

"True that," she replied. She keyed in a command on the com. "*Transport Nine* reporting that A-Company is on the ground, Colonel."

"Roger that, Major. We're five minutes out. Secure perimeter."

"Roger." She looked to Roberto. "This is going to be fun."

Roberto's expression was grim. "Don't forget what Asad said. I'm telling you, we've been here. This is no bullshit. They may look like a bunch of weirdos from a Renaissance fair, but they're not. They will fuck you up and hand you back your ass if you don't watch it."

"We'll watch it," she said. She clapped him on the shoulder and said, "Thanks for the ride," before heading back to suit up herself.

Twenty minutes later, Little Earth was fortified, a hundred and fifty Marines inside and two hundred and fifty more moving out across the plains, the advanced "diplomatic" force, their destination: Crown City and the Queen.

Chapter 19

Given the dire nature of Orli's venomous predicament, Altin hated the twelve hours he'd had to spend getting prepared to go. He'd lost a lot of time learning concealment illusions and cold enchantment spells, but the largest portion of that time had been spent on *how* to enchant cold around himself and his dragon, particularly the dragon. He needed to be quick, to rush and be on his way, but he also understood that if he chose to ignore that part of Ocelot's divination, he'd likely be of no use to Orli at all. And so he'd set himself to the tasks and tried desperately not to let the incredible pressure of time distract him as he worked and researched. Unfortunately, and despite his intentions in that regard, from there events seemed to conspire against him anyway.

At first, he'd had some luck, for the hiding illusions were common military spells. He'd had enough experience with those in the past to know exactly which books held them, and so for that part of his research, the work was easy. And even for the cold spell, which he hadn't known, he'd still found one right away, for it turned out that volcanic expeditions had been enchanting the linings of their clothing with such magic for centuries. Altin simply took that spell—once he'd found it—and turned his robes inside out before enchanting them. When it was done, he turned them right-side out, and, just like that, he had what he needed ... for himself. All of that was reasonably easy to accomplish, and it had only been the work of four of the twelve hours to get it done, so at first, he thought he was making great progress.

The rest of the time, however, had been spent for things that were quite out of his control. He lost two more hours by the fact he'd fallen asleep—which he couldn't help, as he'd simply collapsed from exhaustion and didn't realize it until he fell out of the chair and landed on his face—and the other four hours had been spent in devising a means of getting the cold enchantment on the dragon, who wore no clothing and, therefore, had nothing upon which Altin could cast the spell. Oh, how it's always the unexpected and little things that vex one in the end!

With a bit more reading, Altin found that the cold enchantment could be carried and delivered using an unctuous fluid, but the only oils he had available at Calico Castle were flammable, which made using them a terrible idea, considering the intended object of it all was a fire-breathing dragon upon which he intended to sit. He'd had to spend precious time in simply seeking an oil that wouldn't have them both bursting into flames should Taot need to use his fiery breath, which seemed likely given where they were about to go. He did eventually find one that would work, but it turned out to be a very unique perfume. He'd lost more time in locating it, spent a small fortune buying it, and worst of all, lost nearly an hour getting the enchantment cast into it. This in turn became the source of a new problem, costing more time, because after all of that hasty work, Taot simply refused to be doused in the flowery smelling stuff at all. It simply went against everything the dragon understood, being that he was a creature that had evolved as a predator.

Altin had tried anyway, despite the dragon's initial refusal on the point. He'd poured a gallon of the enchanted perfume into a bucket and approached Taot with pail and mop in hand, planning to use the mop like a paintbrush and cover the dragon thoroughly. But Taot leapt away from him, giving one great flap of his wings, which threw up a rush of air and blasted the determined mage with sand and tiny bits of bone. The dragon roared as he came to rest near the cave wall, and he shot his head forward like a striking viper, blowing out a noxious cloud of acidic gas in protest.

Altin staggered back as the cloud hit him, coughing and wheezing, and he nearly tripped over a buffalo skull. He caught his balance, but dropped his mop and bucket in his haste to wipe his burning eyes. The dragon sometimes gassed him like that for fun, but the cloud he sent this time had far more toxicity. Taot wasn't joking this time.

"By the gods, villain!" Altin gasped, blinking frantically as tears poured down his face. "You'll be the death of us all."

Eventually he could see again, which revealed that he'd just dumped some twenty gold pieces worth of the perfume into a jumble of rocks and broken bones lying nearby. The area now radiated cold in an unseen, dome-shaped expanse of frigid air spanning two paces all around. Altin shook his head. He should have known this would happen.

He tried once more to convince Taot how important it was to get to Orli right away, but the dragon backed all the way up against the wall as Altin approached, working into a corner with his head drawn back, his neck arced to strike and a growl in his throat, entirely ready for combat.

Altin huffed. *Infernal creature!*

He teleported himself back to Calico Castle to see if he

could find a masking spell for the perfume, something to hide it so the dragon wouldn't know. He found one readily enough, but it cost him another half hour to learn, and by the time he got it cast on the kegs of perfume, the whole project had burned up nearly half the day.

Finally back in Taot's lair, he tried again, and while the dragon couldn't smell the perfume anymore, he still knew what it was. He growled and rumbled some more and sent another cloud of gas billowing Altin's way.

The young mage stepped out of its path this time, expecting as much now, and at that point, he had finally had enough. He filled his mind with a great surge of mana and pulsed it at the dragon like a bloating thing, a caldera of raw might pressed directly against Taot's mind. He filled it with the heat of a fireball that he'd not yet cast, the essence of the one he was about to conjure if Taot did not stop fighting with him, one big enough and hot enough to be a problem even for the dragon's fireproof hide. Doing so reminded Altin of the day he'd first tamed the beast, threatening him with his own natural weaponry. Fire. He pressed the heat of that warning across the mana into the dragon's own mythothalamus, squeezing down upon it hard enough that the dragon actually let out a yelp.

Then Altin let the mana go, the spell uncast, just a warning. But Taot knew. He was reminded who was the stronger of them if push came to shove. He snaked his head forward, low to the ground, and tilted it sideways, leaving the underside of his neck partially exposed.

"I have no need of that," Altin said, sending soothing thoughts to his longtime friend. "I just can't fight with you anymore. Orli needs us now." He sent the dragon the sense of urgency, the sense of danger for a mate, which roused the dragon's ire. He then went for the enchanted perfume and raised the mop up once again.

Taot grumbled but, in the end, let Altin do what had to

be done. Altin slathered Taot with the magic mixture, wiping him down with it as if it were whitewash and Taot a thing in need of paint, a big one that took considerable time to cover thoroughly. Altin worked as quickly as he could, but too much was at stake to be careless now.

Altin was panting by the time it was done, his breath visible in foggy clouds as he exhaled, the air made frigid now by the enchantment coming off of the dragon's hide. Altin hadn't noticed the cold on his own clothes, as the cold radiated away, but with Taot, it was different. The chill made it frightfully miserable work, but when it was through, he was confident that whatever it was that enabled the Earth people to see body heat, they wouldn't be seeing any coming off of the dragon or his rider now.

With the cold enchantments in place, he added a complex illusion that masked sight, sound and smell—for humans at least—and having finally completed their magical camouflage, it was time to go to Earth.

He sent Taot the vision Ocelot had given of where they were about to go, an image of the fortress city that was a "pattern without pattern." He showed it to him and prepared him for the impending and instantaneous change of scenery. With a pat on the neck to assure him once more that there were no hard feelings, Altin, with little more than a thought, teleported them both to planet Earth.

They arrived in the air several hundred spans above the great fortress, which appeared to be an incredible sprawl of nearly identical reflective constructions precisely as Ocelot's vision had shown that it would be. It was the first time Altin had ever teleported somewhere he hadn't been to before or hadn't at least found with seeing magic of his own. While he was awed by the scale of the fortress city, he couldn't help but also be awed by the magical gifts of the girl-creature, Ocelot. So much power resided in a diviner with a Z.

There was little time for reflection, however, for immediately upon appearing, Taot banked hard, as if he'd seen something, despite there being nothing to avoid. He let go a massive roar as he did it and even blew out a short breath of flame.

Altin was sure that only he could hear the roar, as they were both wrapped in the concealment of his hiding spells, but the fire likely shot out beyond the range of his enchantment, and Altin could only hope no one far below happened to be looking up right then, right in time to see a yellow tongue of flame suddenly appearing out of the otherwise empty stretch of bright blue sky. And that was not the only one the dragon blew.

Taot behaved as if he were afflicted with something approaching panic, and Altin sent him calming thoughts as best he could, but with little effect. Despite knowing what they were doing before they'd come, at least as well as a dragon could understand the concept of going to another world, Taot could not help reacting as he did. This place was like nothing the great reptile had ever experienced before, and the smells alone were overwhelming in the alien atmosphere. The idea of "another world" simply hadn't meant anything to him until they'd actually arrived. Now he knew, and it frightened him.

While there were familiar scents, pollens from trees and grasses that he recognized as something natural, Taot had never smelled exhaust fumes or any of the chemicals being discharged into the air. The sky was thick with an olfactory attack on everything he knew, and Taot wheeled and raged aloud, spraying the air with fire in a disoriented fit of fear.

Altin could only hold on for dear life during the first several minutes as Taot swooped and rolled and dived. He worried as he did so that Taot's tantrum would be the end of them both, which in turn would mean the end of Orli. Fortunately, however, as Taot's fit had them plunging toward the fortress in a dive of terrifying verticality, the air blasting against the dragon's face and roaring in his ears combined with Altin's pressing mellow thoughts, together helped calm the dragon down. It helped further, once Taot was more in control of himself, that Altin could now fathom the nature of the dragon's insecurities, mainly the noisome assault upon his nose.

Though never having been there before, the magician was able to persuade the dragon that the alien smells were normal for "this part of the world." He sent the dragon the sense of gasses from geysers and volcanic dust on Prosperion, strange things, awful things. He then sent memories of the acid smells coming off the cook fires of the desert nomads. He sent the smells he knew from the avenue of tanners in Leekant. He even reminded him of the perfume he'd wiped all over his scaly hide, conveying the essence of its artificiality, and yet that it was also simply a thing made by men. The dragon seemed to understand that, that men made their own foul smells. Whether ironically or inevitably, he actually understood it best by the experience with the perfume, and so Altin's argument made perfect sense to him. He understood then that they had come to a place that was filled with too much humanity. Foul, but bearable. In a way, he even recognized that the artificiality was natural in a way, normal in the way of reeking harpy caves and odious skunk dens. Just as easily as that, Taot was himself again.

Altin agreed with his assessment, mostly in conciliatory fashion, and then refreshed the purpose of their trip. With all this about odor, the point was for the dragon to find Orli's scent. He sent this idea to the dragon, along with images of her. Taot recognized her immediately and was actually grateful to have something worthwhile to search for in the cacophony of alien smells.

To help, Altin put the image from Ocelot's scratch into Taot's mind again, letting him know that the divined version matched what they saw with their own eyes. He tried to hide the fact that he couldn't even begin to direct the dragon where to go from there, for as predicted, the whole place appeared to be almost all the same beneath them. If anything even began to seem like a unique construct, like a landmark standing out from the buildings and structures around it, a few moments looking would reveal others identical to it somewhere nearby. It was like spotting weeds amongst tall grass, at first one would appear, then another not too far away, and more and more until there were lots of them dotting off into the distance in every direction with such regularity he'd wonder how he hadn't noticed them all along. It was confounding, but Taot sent back that he understood, and for the first time since appearing above Earth, the dragon's movements were sure. The sweep of his wings became strong and purposeful, and he carried them down toward the massive monotony of the fortress below.

As they flew toward the rooftops, they had to veer from time to time to avoid crossing the paths of the various aircraft flying past or that rose up out of square or hexagonal holes that slowly opened in the surface of the city. Some of the vessels were similar in appearance to the small ships Orli's people had brought to Little Earth, long boxy things, built for function more than for speed, but others looked far more sinister. There were several varieties that were all black, flat and smooth, with rigid wings sweeping back from their noses like arrowheads. These flew with bright lights that roared from their back ends and with precision to the shape of the flames that suggested something far different than dragon's fire. He thought briefly of the first time he'd encountered the long, clumsy-seeming Earth starships in space, trying to stand their ground in close combat with the slippery movements of the Hostile orbs. Out there, that fire seemed absurdly inefficient, but here, it gave these vessels frightening speed. He watched as they flitted about like enormous armored hummingbirds, their movements almost as unlikely as the Hostiles. He found himself suddenly very self-conscious about the efficacy of his enchantment spells. If one of those things spotted them, he did not think that he and Taot could get away. And he wasn't quite sure what he would do about fighting them. If they had the red-light lasers that he knew they most likely did, he doubted he'd have time to do anything about it. Should one of them see through his enchantment spells, likely that would be the end. Which meant he needed to find Orli fast.

He directed Taot down low, seeking to get out of the flight paths of so many roaring sky vessels and down into the cover of the buildings and their endless monotony. Soon they were flying between the shining structures, soaring above the avenues formed by the rows upon rows of them. From this vantage, Altin could see that upon these lanes were small vehicles, appearing not a great deal larger than wagons back home, though many were obviously immense. They moved along in endless caravans, parallel lines of them, one going in each direction, the lot of them making their way to and fro around the blocks of the black-glass buildings.

He nudged Taot closer to one of the buildings with his knees and looked inside as they flew past, peering through the dark windows of those that were lit from within to see the small figures of men and women going about their daily lives. Most appeared to be in uniform, just like the fleet officers and crew he'd come to know since his first encounter with people from planet Earth, and he couldn't help wondering if theirs was an entirely military society. He hadn't seen any other cities, so he couldn't know for sure, but from the vastness of this one, it certainly seemed so. He marveled that Orli's people were so dedicated to war. The scale of this city, this fortress, made the War Queen's city seem an amusement park, a place of fanciful magic and lovely gardens all around. Oh yes, there was a vast military complex near the Palace, massive walls all around, but nothing like this sprawling martial uniformity.

On and on they flew, sweeping and gliding around spindly towers that seemed to have no other purpose than to hold up a lone blinking light, hundreds of spans high. They flew through venting plumes of steam and down into long dark alleys between rows of buildings that were occasionally larger than the rest. All the while Taot's nostrils worked steadily, the low huffs of his sniffing sounding like steam blowing through geysers hidden at the back of some dark cave.

For hours they swept back and forth, Altin continually refreshing the image and the essence of the Orli he knew into Taot's mind, always confirmed, always sent back perfectly by the dragon, verifying that he understood. They wheeled around buildings, still dodging aircraft now and again, and Altin's began to grow panicked with the lack of progress and loss of time. He began to fear for her, began to fear the discovery that he had been too late. He saw visions of the dragon catching the scent, only to swoop down and discover her in one of the large metal bins these people kept filled with stinking refuse in the alleyways, her body rotting away, maggots crawling, burrowing in beautiful flesh turned blue and gray.

Altin Love lives.

Blue Fire's thought struck him powerfully, and he realized by the shock of it that he'd started to drift off again, like he had while researching the cold enchantment spells. He hadn't slept but those two hours in days. He was exhausted. He could imagine sleeping somewhere. Even just laying there in the garbage next to Orli's body. Her soft bosom a pillow.

No, came the thought, a mental shout like a gong. It was so abrupt it startled him. He blinked out of the sleep that had nearly taken him again. He drew in a deep breath of the chemical-heavy Earth air. *Seek. Altin Love lives. No sleep.*

He shook himself and squinted into the wind of Taot's flight. Another few moments like that and he might have slipped off and fallen to his death. He would have been the one found rotting and decayed, probably not for a week or more either, not until the illusions concealing him wore off on their own. Or until someone tripped over him, of course.

Find Altin Love. It came with such a rush of urgency, as if he were about to drown, as if he were at the edge of having to take that breath of water that would end him. He nearly panicked. Which woke him up some.

Still a little groggy, he sent back to Blue Fire, "I thought I blocked you. You lied. How are you in my head?"

Blue Fire silence.

"I should have known I couldn't keep you out."

Rainbow web. Now. Altin's mind filled then with images of Orli lying in a bed with several cords attached to her arms, similar to the wires and tubes he had seen Doctor Singh use on patients in the *Aspect*'s sick bay. He then saw a clear image of Ocelot and heard her say, "Venom," in his mind. Blue Fire had activated that memory. *Rainbow web. Now.*

Altin was fully awake then, the horror of the revelation filling him with a chill. "It's happening now?" he both spoke aloud and sent to Blue Fire across all that space.

Now. Must speed.

"Where? Where is she? Gods-be-damned, can't you show me where?"

He saw an image of Earth in his mind.

Altin's exasperation made him cry out in frustrated agony. Of course she was on Earth. To Taot he sent the sense of urgency. "Lower," he shouted. "Go down closer to the streets."

The dragon responded to the thought Altin sent, and they plunged down to only just above the movements of the rumbling vehicles. Taot rumbled in response, a growl in his throat at the fumes coming from them, the ionized quality of their exhaust and even the black material of their wheels giving off odor from simply rolling across the ground. He rumbled, but he flew. He banked sharply around corners, the speed of their flight blurring the glass panels of the buildings into one long smudge in Altin's eyes.

Finally, an agonizing span of minutes more, Taot let out a roar. He pulled up so sharply that Altin would have slid down his back and tumbled off his tail had he not grabbed hold with all his strength to one of the dragon's large scales. The dragon turned back in a steep powerful arc, twisting as he banked, nearly inverted for a time and diving down as if upon newfound prey.

He pulled up sharply again, only this time to stop, and with three powerful sweeps of his wings, brought them to the ground. Even with the braking movements of his wings, they hit the ground so hard Altin tumbled off anyway, spared injury only by having bounced once off a wing as it was folding in.

Altin wasted no time thinking of such things. He merely righted himself and sent Taot a single thought: *Where is she?*

Taot's sinewy neck snaked down, and he lay his big

head upon a metal grate set into the ground. He gave a long, audible sniff, then blew a little puff of smoke out of his nose over it. The gray wisps of it were carried instantly up and away by air currents coming through the grate.

"She's in there? Down there?"

Taot rumbled again, the sound accompanied by the mental essence of the dragon's carnal understanding of Altin and Orli's relationship.

That was good enough. With no warning for the dragon at all and only the barest glimpse of sight into his cave, Altin sent Taot home. Hardly a heartbeat passed after, and Altin's seeing spell was cast again, this time his vision plunging down into the grate and chasing hope through every twist and curve of ductwork at speeds that more than rivaled dragon flight.

Chapter 20

"I don't want your stupid meal," Orli spat at the corporal as she twisted in the grip of the two men holding her down on her bunk. "Fuck you. I hope you and your whole goddamn family die in agony from Hostile disease."

While executions were rare, the corporal charged with seeing the process through was a seasoned enough prison guard to be used to that sort of remark, so he didn't let it bother him. "You don't have to eat," he said. "It's up to you if you want something fancy or not. I'm just supposed to ask."

"Ask yourself why you're such a worthless piece of shit." She hated him as much as all the rest despite his attempts at kindness. She hated him because he didn't believe her story about Blue Fire's innocence and that there was another Hostile world. He'd only smiled politely and done his job, every time she tried to tell him, meal after meal.

"I'll put you down for whatever they've got made," he said. He nodded to the two men with him, and the biggest of the two put the gag back in Orli's mouth. She mumbled and drooled a series of unintelligible profanities at them as they left.

When they were gone, she slumped back against the wall of the cell bunk and fumed. She had to channel her panting fury through her nose, which made her eyes water and threatened to gag her by the backpressure of it. She had to mellow herself out. This wouldn't be any better than crying, she knew, and she'd done enough of that during the night, crying and all the rest, the fits of fury, defiance, terror, sorrow and regret, all going round and round. Doing most of that was miserable with the damn gag blocking everything.

She wished she knew what time it was. She had no frame of reference. Only the meals. There had been four since her court martial. And since they'd just asked her what she wanted, the one they'd just offered her would obviously be her last.

A knock on the door was followed by its opening to allow her attorney, Angela, inside. The youthful lawyer looked down at Orli with her splotchy red face and the glistening stripe of drool running down her neck and shook her head. "You look like shit," she said. She immediately stepped near and removed the headgear with the ball gag.

"What difference does it make?" Orli said after taking a long, deep breath. "They're going to kill me now. I'm pretty sure I just got offered my last meal."

"You did."

"I'm surprised they let you back in here."

"So am I. I had to make a pretty big stink. Plus, I think they felt bad at how grotesquely obvious their denials of all my appeal applications were."

"I don't suppose you got any help from your uncle in Reno, did you?"

"Not yet. They've had a spate of desertions out there. I guess there are quite a few people who aren't as happy about their enlistments now that there is a war on as they were when they were traveling the system on the NTA's tab and hanging out in base bars looking for hookups."

"Oh, well that's definitely more important than this. Heaven forbid some eighteen-year-olds decide they're suddenly afraid to die. We definitely want to get right on that. I appreciate your uncle's ability to prioritize."

"Ensign Pewter, I'm doing everything I can. I'm trying. I swear I am." The dark circles under the woman's eyes verified it. Endless frustrations and conspicuous roadblocks to her attempts to file for appeal had worn her down considerably, and she hadn't gotten any sleep at all.

Orli laughed, more a breath than a sound, a pulse of air through her nose as she shook her head. Twenty, she thought as she watched her attorney fighting with guilt and fatigue. They shouldn't have sent such a bright young mind to do this. They were probably just going to traumatize the poor thing for having failed so miserably in her first assignment. Better they had just let Orli die alone. The charade of a defense wasn't going to mean anything. Except for the official record obviously. It was important for posterity that no one discover how crooked and desperately afraid they all were. They could make up a story about the initial hearings, of course; all of that had happened on the *Aspect*, the records would say. Or on some ship that had been destroyed. Nothing left for evidence. "Such a shame, but these things happen" and all of that.

"It's okay," Orli said, letting Angela off the hook. "We both knew how this was going to work out. I'm just glad you tried. And who knows, maybe your uncle will figure something out at the last minute. If not for me, for the next guy. It's bad enough the Hostiles are trying to kill us, you know? I have to tell you, this is a shitty way to go given the circumstances." She wasn't going to say what she really thought, that she was still hoping Altin would find her somehow. It was as if speaking his name might somehow curse the hope of it.

Angela started to speak, but she looked like she was trying to hold her own emotions in check. She only managed, "I'm sorry."

"So what happens next?" Orli asked while Angela pulled it back together. "I eat, they send me a preacher or something, and then, into my veins with the cocktail that finishes me?"

Angela nodded, composing herself. "Basically. Your record shows no religious affiliation, so they'll send a chaplain if you want. You can refuse it, but it will buy you a few minutes of time if you let him come."

"So what am I supposed to say to him?"

"It doesn't matter. Ask him to read to you from one of the holy books. Hell, just ask him to tell you a story. Tell him one of your own, call it a confession. Just ... I don't know. Get what you can."

"That sounds like shit, to be honest. But it's probably a good idea." She was doing her best to remain glib as her guts twisted nervously inside. She really did have faith in Altin somehow finding her, but if he was going to do it, he needed to get to it pretty quick. The sands in the hourglass were running low, as he might say, and with every grain that passed, she grew more afraid.

Angela looked uncomfortable for a moment, glancing nervously up at the bright light of the diffusion panel, in which she knew a video feed was piping this interview into a monitor somewhere. She seemed to consider saying something for a moment, the pursing of her lips the evidence for a half second before it went away. Instead she blew out a long breath that inflated her smooth young cheeks.

"What?" said Orli seeing it.

"Nothing," her attorney said.

"No, tell me. What were you about to say?"

"It's nothing. I just–. Well, you know, before, you said that Altin Meade might come." She glanced up at the ceiling, choosing her words carefully. "Do you think that is still a possibility?"

Orli's eyes went wide, the mention of his name horrifying. It was as if she hung by a crystal thread above a pit full of spears, and Angela's speaking his name threatened to snip that last lingering line that kept her aloft. It was as if Angela, perhaps fate itself, was trying to ruin her last hope. Her body tingled as if she'd already been hit with the electricity waiting beneath the cell floor, ready to burn her for having spoken his name as well. But she held on to her composure, forced herself to respond calmly despite what went on within her. "I wish he would, but he won't. He has no idea where I am. And even if he did have an idea, how would he find me down here? There is no experience among his people that would make him think to look this far underground. They just don't do that. Maybe in a few mines or something, but they don't build bunkers like this. They have no need. *They* are civilized people." She hated how true all of that was, most of it anyway, even as she was trying to make a lie of it.

Angela nodded, disappointment as obvious in the curve of her mouth as it was in the way she slumped, deflating visibly, if only for the barest of moments, so bare in fact that it suggested she hadn't really thought it possible anyway.

She went to where Orli reclined against the wall and sat down beside her on the bunk. Another long sigh. The two of them stared into the emptiness for a while, neither having anything to say.

Finally, a knock on the door came again, followed by the entrance of the corporal with a tray of food. "I got ham and chicken, and the mashed potatoes are good. I had some earlier. Didn't know if you like gravy, but I got a coffee cup full in case you do. They let me bring three different kinds of pie." His smile was flat and sympathetic, and the mournful droopiness in his eyes suggested it was genuine. He looked back over his shoulders at the two guards at the door, but they weren't watching him all that closely; their eyes were all on her. He reached into his waistband and pulled out a black plastic flask, which he slid onto the tray. "It's really good vodka," he whispered. He glanced to Angela and added, "Just make sure you take this with you when you leave, or I'm screwed."

Angela took it off the tray and nodded that she would. "Thank you," she said in the absence of any gratitude on Orli's part.

The corporal nodded back. He obviously understood. "One hour," he said. "Then the chaplain will come."

Angela nodded once again for Orli's part.

The corporal left, and once more the two women sat in silence for a while.

"You going to eat any of this?" Angela asked eventually. "The gravy won't be any good cold."

Orli shook her head.

"The pie looks good. Look at the color of that strawberry glaze. Come on, have something. I feel terrible."

"I'm sorry to put you out," Orli said. "You don't have to be here. You are free to leave. I release you from your duties or whatever I'm supposed to say. Just go."

"That's not what I meant," Angela said, frustrated. She leaned back and once again silence filled the room.

They were both startled by the next knock. It was the corporal again, this time with the chaplain. He looked down at the untouched tray and sighed, just as Angela had been doing so often since sitting there with Orli. He took it after only a brief exchange of glances with the attorney. He didn't have the heart to look at Orli again.

The chaplain stepped into the room as the corporal went out.

"Ensign Pewter," said the chaplain. "I've come to help you prepare."

Orli looked up at him, and her eyes filled with fire. "Prepare yourself," she said. "It's your conscience that's going to burn for this. Do whatever you need to do to make yourself and the rest of those lying cowards up there feel better about it, but I have no use for you."

"You have no peace to make with your maker? Nothing you would like to say to God?"

"God already knows I think he's an asshole, so there you go. And now that we have that out of the way, why don't you just fuck off?"

"I will pray for your soul then."

"Why don't you pray for someone to figure out that the Prosperions aren't the enemy, that I'm not the enemy, that there's another Hostile world attacking Earth? Pray for someone to pull their head out of their ass before it's too goddamn late. That's what you should pray for."

The chaplain straightened himself, brushed his fingers over his salt-and-pepper mustache and nodded. "Very well, I'll let them know you are ready. And I will pray for you anyway."

"Whatever gets you through the nights," Orli said slumping back against the wall.

When he was gone, Angela looked to her client and shook her head. "I suppose I should admire your courage," she said. "I think I'd be a crying mess if I were in your shoes."

"I've spent enough time as a crying mess," Orli said. "Turns out it doesn't help all that much."

Angela nodded, but unscrewed the cap on the flask. She raised it toward Orli who waved it off. "Do you mind if I do?" the woman asked.

Orli actually smiled. "Knock yourself out." She watched the young lawyer's face contort with each successive swig and wondered if this was the first time she'd ever had a drink. It seemed obvious that it was. Making today a day for new chemicals for everyone.

Chapter 21

Gromf and Kazuk-Hal-Mandik spent the better part of two full days listening and memorizing the summoning spells. They listened to the verses of the song as the woman sang, over and over, slowly committing the sounds to memory. Kazuk-Hal-Mandik had taught himself much of the human language in his time living in the world, but for Gromf it was all new. The sounds were ugly and tasted like rancid meat between his teeth. But he had Discipline, and he learned the sounds anyway. Two days gone, they were out of time for practicing. Now was time to try and see if it really worked.

"Go and tell Warlord we are ready," Kazuk-Hal-Mandik commanded the singer. "Ask that he bring ten warriors. And then you may get some rest." She was careful not to show relief, but the sagging of her features and the hoarse rasp that had become her voice was evidence of how worn down she was. She lowered her gaze and left them, and Gromf was pleased to hear the sound of her bare feet running upon the stone once she had left the room, sprinting to follow the old shaman's orders despite how exhausted she was. She would produce good younglings for the All Clans, strong in spirit and in mind. Gromf approved of her. Perhaps when he reached his hundredth season he would take her for his second mate.

"One time," warned Kazuk-Hal-Mandik when the woman was out of earshot. "Just one demon. From the first verses. And no God Stone."

"I know," snapped Gromf. He too was tired. He hadn't slept in five sunsets. His temper floated near the surface now.

Shortly after, the sound of rattling armor and many heavy footfalls echoed down the corridor beyond the Chamber of Discipline, occasionally punctuated by the strike of wooden spear butts on the stone. Soon Warlord appeared accompanied by ten warriors, just as Kazuk-Hal-Mandik had asked. That was good, the old shaman thought. For all Warlord's mighty roaring, he too believed.

"Slay it when it comes," was all the warning the old warlock gave. "Do not wait to watch and see what it does."

Warlord tightened several straps of his armor and several of the others donned helmets, buckling them on snugly. Gromf was pleased to see nothing but eagerness in their eyes. These were all mighty orcs, fearsome and tested in war. They spread around the room, Warlord with his enormous double-bladed axe standing nearest to the door. He would die before a conjured demon ran loose among his people.

"Bring them forth," commanded Warlord, his teeth wicked sharp and glinting golden in the firelight.

Kazuk-Hal-Mandik took a pouch of sulfur and sprinkled the yellow dust around in a circle, just as the verses of the song had said. He then turned to Gromf and nodded for him to begin.

Gromf reached into the swirling storm of mana as he sang the words that built containment into the yellow ring Kazuk-Hal-Mandik had poured, the words meant to bind the creature inside. He was careful to speak them right.

He let his mind drift away then, falling out of the perfect cube of space that made the Chamber of Discipline, falling out into the mana currents, guided by the rhythms and the words that sought the anger through the center of the world, the anger that reached out with its teeming thirst for blood and the taste of death on its gnashing teeth, the milling sea of ravenousness that leaked its hunger through the very core of Prosperion. He looked for the braided strands promised by the song, the twisting threads that hid in the tempest of the mana, lost in the miasma of so much activity like a bit of leather thong tossed in a roaring fire, consumed by it physically as it was drowned in the light. But Gromf found it because he knew that it was there. He found it by its tiny whirling melody, and he grasped it with the fingers of his mind, tugging on it gently as if pulling himself along, the thread of it the lifeline keeping him from falling out of an abyss.

He pulled and willed the braid to thickening, dragging himself down into the depths of the mana, finding as he did that the twists of the cord, in their windings, seemed to stir the mana itself. He inched along, tugging himself with thoughts like hands over hands toward the circling motion, the pink and purple whorl of everything, crawling slowly down into an increasing chaos that rotated faster and faster as he went.

He pulled along more quickly, the vortex giving him speed. He made good time, and he travelled deeper and deeper, the vortex narrowing. In time he found the bottom, a tiny hole, it might have been the iris of some tiny creature's eye. Light shone through it as if it were an arrow hole in a drying hide.

He leaned down toward the opening, moving in the way of non-action within the mana, and peered through the hole, peeking like a youngling watching grownups mate. He saw them then, the demons, the essence of them anyway, visible in both the realm of light and the mana stream. At first he started, wondering how such a thing could be, but he did not question it. This was a thing of gods, so it could be so if it was so. He watched from his high vantage place, down upon a vast landscape, ragged and profane, edged by ocean on all sides, though somehow he only knew that it was, the sense one has that a thing is true without a way to see. All he could see were the monstrosities, the countless hordes of moving, twisting bodies in a wide valley, the sunlight pouring down into it devoured by huge formations of the yellow stone. The God Stone was everywhere.

He watched and knew that he must be careful. He knew instinctively now what it was that Kazuk-Hal-Mandik had begun, and he knew why it was that the old warlock was letting him experiment with it first. If he could have, he would have spit at such cunning cowardice. But it was foolish to think such things. It lacked Discipline, for the warlock had handed over far more power than he must have understood, and in that moment Gromf understood nearly perfectly.

This tiny iris through which he peeked could be opened at his command. He could open this and let them out of that valley, let them climb up through the tunnel and out upon Kurr, all of them, that valley filled with them like the dung swamps made by the lightning bats in the northern caves, waist-deep rivers of fecal ooze teeming with flesh-eating worms of numbers too huge for considering. The demons were such as those worms, heaped upon one another in a seething mass that lapped like black water up the edges of the valley. He could not help but wonder what kept them from getting out, from cresting their confines and devouring the island they infested so horribly.

Something flashed on the mountainside then, as if calling him, as if reading his thoughts and guiding him to the place, and he focused there long enough to see the misshapen head and elongated, twisted limbs of the rocky-faced creature, the face of God that he'd seen in Kazuk-Hal-Mandik's pond. God grew before him then, laughing, and Gromf could see in that wide, lichen-encrusted face the awareness of his growing fear, Gromf's fear, of which even he was only barely aware.

He quickly cut that vision off, stomped it out like the last embers of an old fire. He looked away from God and sought a lesser demon to bring out. There were so many, crawling over each other like a great bowl of misshapen maggots, it was hard to pick. So he chose just any one. He shaped a spear of mana, straight and with a hard, barbed point, an idea, and flung it down at the first demon that caught his eye. Then he hauled it out as if it were a fish on a line.

With one great yank, he pulled it free of the mana, pulled it free of the island and out through the center of the world. Into the Chamber of Discipline.

The demon stood three times taller than Warlord when it appeared, a thick hulk of ambiguous body and a mass of spindly limbs. It was so black that even the firelight did nothing to illuminate it, though the light did glimmer off its twenty or so insect eyes, red bulbs protruding from what served it for a face, each moving independently as it evaluated its enemies. It blinked at them, regarding them in a wave that moved across all of those glowing orbs, or only some, it was impossible to be sure, and then it leapt into the darkness high above with a roar that sent a rain of dust and pebbles falling down.

Both Gromf and the old warlock conjured bolts of ice as a whisk of arrows from the warriors followed the creature up into the obscurity high above.

"Save that, fools," snarled Warlord. "See it first. Discipline." Then, tilting his huge head backward, he roared up at the demon, calling out the challenge in the private language of the northern clan. "Come and fight, god-spawned coward. Come face death."

Whether by coincidence or by invitation, the enormous black beast dropped down upon Warlord, who only avoided being crushed by the magnitude of his combat prowess and reflexes so bestowed. As it was, he was still struck hard, and he hit the floor as if he'd been flung there from five times his height. The demon fell upon him, mandibles like moose antlers opening wide then slamming shut like things drawn apart by siege craft springs, the clacking of their closing echoing throughout the room like lightning strikes.

Warlord smashed each bite away with the flat of his axe, roaring challenges all the while. Both Gromf and Kazuk-Hal-Mandik sent forth their spears of ice, but the magic rolled off of the creature like raindrops off rocks.

The ten warriors sprinted from their places around the room and leapt upon the creature then, their spears and swords and axes raining down blows that were as furious as their war cries. The demon answered back, and the chamber filled with such sound as no orc had ever heard before, a warped and discordant symphony of a hundred thousand brass horns blown all at once.

The demon spun then and leapt shivering into the air, trying to fling them off, spearing one warrior as it came down, thrusting straight through his body with all nine points of an awful claw, which it then spread wide, ripping the warrior apart as easily as Gromf might open his hand.

One of the warriors, maintaining his purchase on the demon's head, if it could be said to have such a thing, got a spear down in through one of its eyes and drove it deep into its skull, while another orc hacked off the bottom portion of one of its legs with a mighty swing of a bastard sword.

The demon reached back and peeled another orc away, one who was jamming a short sword into a joint in the black armor plating along its spine. It flung him across the chamber with such power that when he hit the wall, he burst like a soft fruit, striking with such force that hardly any meat of him fell wetly to the ground. He became a stain that the chamber would wear for centuries to come.

The demon pinned yet another warrior down beneath one of its several legs. Gromf could hear the warrior's bones crack, but he could not focus on such things. He cast another spear of ice. This spell, like the first, glanced off the demon as if it were little more than a clod of dirt thrown by a youngling at play.

The demon roared as the orc upon its head worked the spear like a plunger through its eye, churning and twisting it around, mangling the soft parts inside. It swiped a long, crooked arm up at the orc, but the orc leapt over the blow and came back neatly where he had been before, gloriously agile and aware in combat, and right back at it with his spear.

Warlord, on his feet again, came charging in as the demon swiped again at the warrior scrambling its brains. He ran in and brought a mighty two-handed swing of his axe upon the demon's chest, the blade of his weapon biting in the full measure of Warlord's extended arm. The demon roared and swiped at Warlord with another of its dexterous limbs, but the mighty orc rolled under the blow, came back and yanked his great axe free. He couldn't duck the return swipe of the demon's limb this time, however, so he dove with it instead, rolling with its momentum and coming right back up on his feet.

The demon took the time to try for the spear-thrusting orc upon its head again, and this time was able to knock him off. It spun round then and with a back-handed—or back-clawed—swat, sent another warrior who was attacking its hind legs into the wall, just as it had done the first. Another stain was born.

Warlord charged back and once again sunk the great axe into the monster's chest, even deeper this time. He swung himself up then, hanging from the haft, and put his feet in the first rent that he had made. His powerful thighs, thick as most orcs' whole bodies, pressed hard against their new purchase as Warlord hauled obliquely at his axe handle like a lever. And lever it was.

A grotesque wet cracking sound erupted like the breaking of a tree, and with a roar of effort, Warlord pried loose a huge chunk of the black carapace that protected the demon's heart, if such a vile pump could be so named. Yellow blood like pus gushed out over Warlord even as the breaking loose of the armored piece sent him flying back and down upon the ground. He rolled to his feet in time to see Kazuk-Hal-Mandik's ice lance fly into the monster's chest cavity, a diseased fissure of yellow and reddish meat. The magician's weapon was followed almost immediately by two arrows and a throwing axe from three of the still standing warriors.

The demon croaked its outrage at that, staggering from side to side and crushing by purest accident another warrior as it thrashed about and even once rebounded off the wall. Everyone still standing sent spears and arrows and ice bolts flying into that oozing yellow and red mess, until at last the demon fell, emitting a low rumble for a time that could be felt through the stone floor. Its limbs twitched for a while after, clacking like falling stones against the chamber floor, its eyes rolling madly in its head, but eventually they went still. A long hiss came from it, and finally the panting orcs knew that it was dead.

They all stared at it for a time, Gromf shaking his head, wondering how he had any chance of controlling such a thing as that, despite what the human writing said. He was certain that Warlord would forbid ever summoning another one.

He was wrong.

"Finally," said Warlord, coming to where Gromf and the old warlock were. "This is magic I respect. Set these creatures loose upon the humans and the golden queen's rule will end." He clapped Kazuk-Hal-Mandik so brutally on the shoulder, Gromf had to catch the aged orc lest Warlord's enthusiasm knock him to the ground. "It will be different this time," Warlord said. "It will be different, and I will finally take a name."

Cries of victory and hope for the great global reign of the orcs rang out then from the surviving warriors, and for a time, Gromf could only watch and marvel at what he had seen. It was power to be sure, amazing power. But was it Discipline?

He also stared at the smudges of yellow dust on the floor where Kazuk-Hal-Mandik had poured out the sulfur meant to bind the thing. The circle was rubbed out in several places, and there ran like a foul river into it a pool of the demon's pus-yellow blood. Gromf shook his head, but he said nothing until Warlord and the other warriors had gone.

Kazuk-Hal-Mandik followed them to the door, laughing with them, and shouting out promises of death to all of humanity, but when he turned back to Gromf, his grin vanished like sweaty fingerprints on a cold blade.

"You could not control it, could you?" the old warlock asked unnecessarily.

"I could not. I would not know how to try."

"Nor I," replied the withered old shaman. "But perhaps we can with the God Stone."

"Perhaps," said Gromf, uncertain if even the yellow stones would help. "And if we can't?"

Kazuk-Hal-Mandik straightened himself and looked resigned. "Then it will be as it was with the dwarves. And we will be with God."

Gromf was sure that was not in keeping with Discipline, but he kept the thought to himself. Before they tried this spell tomorrow, out on the plains beyond the golden queen's gleaming city, he thought he'd better find the woman and listen to the song again.

Chapter 22

Orli didn't fight the Fort Minot security men when they put her onto the table and strapped her down. She'd fought at first when they dragged her out of her cell, kicking and butting with her head, but it had proved pointless. She also thought it pointless that they still followed these dumb old formalities, the meal and the solemnity, the execution itself.

The solemnity was probably the worst. The procession that had brought her into this room, a slow march down the long sterility of the hallways, the mumbling of the chaplain's hopeless prayers, the clicking of Angela's heels in the corridor, louder than they should have been, conspicuous given the absence of other sounds. Just the *tap tap tap* of her shoes and the mumble of the priest.

The execution chamber was made in the shape of a half circle, with windows around the arc looking out into another room where they revealed a laboratory. The lab was full of gleaming machinery and racks neatly filled with equipment and chemicals, and along one wall, several long cylindrical tanks were attached to pipes that ran up and disappeared into the ceiling. The windows, and the view into the laboratory, ended where the arc stopped and the chamber's straight wall began. The upper half of this surface was all one large flat pane of mirrored glass. Orli could not see what was on the other side, but no doubt the witnesses would be watching from there.

Orli saw herself in that mirror as they strapped her to the table, which was tilted nearly upright at the time. They pulled up the elastic material of her plain black uniform sleeves to expose both arms above the elbow.

A stooped man with a ring of hair that had the look of a tonsure to Orli's doomed eyes came in through a door in the back wall, from the laboratory, pushing a cart upon which lay a variety of medical gear. He pushed the cart near the cold stainless steel slab to which she was being bound as the guards secured her knees, waist and head with flat black straps. The guards left, and the stooped figure pressed the lever on the table that tilted it back, moving it slowly toward horizontal.

While she'd been doing a champion's job up to that point of keeping the rush of fear at bay, it came upon her heavily now. She could hear the rise of her breathing even over the whine of the motorized table mechanism, and her heart beat palpably in her chest—though not for long, she knew, a fact of which she was suddenly very aware.

The hunched figure took a bottle from the tray and spritzed brownish-yellow liquid onto a cotton pad. Antiseptic, Orli recognized. What the hell do they need that for? The distant part of her brain was still striving to hold on to sanity, to herself, to that person who had been staring out through her eyes throughout her entire life, so seemingly unchanged over all these years.

She looked back at herself in the mirrored glass, could see herself slowly tipping back. She couldn't even tilt her head forward. She was going to lose sight of herself, denied her own reflection. Maybe that was mercy. She hardly knew.

Thoughts flew through her mind. She thought of Altin. Missed him. Forgave him anything. Apologized for everything. Loved him so thoroughly. She thought of Roberto. He would be heartbroken too. And her father. He would hide in anger. He would only become more fierce. But mostly there was Altin. She wished she could have been better for him. She should have made love to him. She should have forced him to. Pointless morality be damned. She wished she could hold him now, just that, just one last time. She hadn't held him enough. She hadn't held any of them enough.

"Ensign Pewter," came the voice of Commander Adair through a raspy speaker mounted in the ceiling. She could see it clearly now that she was lying almost completely level with the floor. She stared into its tiny black holes as if expecting to see poison gas clouding out. "You have been sentenced to death for crimes against the Northern Trade Alliance, against your country and against the people of Earth. Your sentence is upon you. Is there anything you would like to say before that sentence is carried out?"

At first came a surge of anger, and she felt, for a moment, like spewing forth yet another string of profanity. But, somehow, it seemed too late for that. So instead, she said only, "Tell Altin I am sorry. Tell him I love him. Tell him I tried."

"Is that all, Ensign Pewter?"

She closed her eyes and let the tonsured man do his work. He stretched a tube of rubber underneath her arm and tightened it at the base of her bicep. Her hands shook so violently that, on her other arm, the bones of her wrists and elbows began to drum a dull staccato on the stainless steel. He tapped her arm and then stuck her with a needle attached to a short length of tubing, sliding it slowly into a vein. Blood flowed down the scant inches of the tube but stopped at a small plastic valve.

Commander Adair let his question hang in the air a moment longer, before continuing, taking her silence as her reply. "Then, by the authority given to me by the Northern Trade Alliance and the government of the United States of America, I order that you now be put to death."

A shudder ran down her spine, but she fought hard against fear, if futilely. Not only could she hear her heart beating, she could feel it pulsing in the backs of her knees where they pressed against the cold stainless steel. The terror was so enormous she could no longer think.

The hunched executioner repeated the process with a needle in her other arm. He added a third into a vein on the back of her hand.

There came another series of whirs and clicks, and she could not help but open her eyes. A series of panels had opened in the ceiling and clear plastic pipes, no more than a quarter inch in diameter, were coming down, three of them. Each had a valve at the end and, attached to that, a length of transparent tubing held in place by a metal clip.

The man hooking up Orli took a flexible bit of clear tubing from one of the pipes and attached it to the one coming off the needle in her arm. He did the same for each of the other two needles that he'd pushed into her.

Spots began to swim before Orli's eyes, and her fingertips tingled. She'd started to hyperventilate.

The hunched figure reached under the cart he'd brought and pulled out an oxygen mask, drawing out yet another length of tubing with it. He secured the mask as best he could over her nose and mouth, the task made difficult by how firmly her head had been strapped to the table. He leaned down and opened up a valve on a small tank on the cart's lower rack, releasing a flow up the light blue length of its slender hose. The spots and tingling began to go away.

He double-checked the connections at his three needles and looked out into the mirrored glass with an expectant expression, though, he did not speak.

"Do it," crackled Commander Adair's voice from the speaker on the ceiling.

He nodded, and without looking at his victim, he reached up and turned the valve on the first of the three pipes. It immediately filled with a bright red liquid which dropped from the ceiling, filled the tube completely and snaked down to the smaller valve at the end of the flex-hose coming from Orli's arm, where it stopped. He watched as the long silvery bead of air rose up its length and then bubbled up the pipe and vanished through the ceiling. He turned the small valve and let it flow into Orli's arm.

It felt very cold, whatever it was pouring into her.

He went to the second pipe and once again turned the lever to open it. The fluid in this one was as yellow as lemonade. When the air had cleared the line, he opened the valve at Orli's arm and released its chemicals into Orli's blood as well.

Orli's body started to feel heavy.

The executioner opened the third pipe, which filled with a pale green liquid at the same time a film of red warmth covered her, a thick blast of mist like an enormous sneeze. There was an ozone smell and smoke filled the room. Orli could hear dull shuffling.

Her vision was blurring, a red haze clouded everything. Dimly she felt pain in her hand, and then twice more, once each in the crook of her elbows. Then someone was wiping at her face.

She smelled bacon and garlic, and someone gripped her temples hard. Right after, a heavy weight pressed upon her chest, like someone was lying on top of her, and she blinked to see through a gray haze.

Doctor Leopold's fat face stared blankly at her, his

fleshy cheeks mashed out upon her breast like he was melting there. His eyes had the vacancy of someone listening, his mouth slightly ajar, breathing audibly.

He said something that came to her like sound through water, and he was gone. Light left, or it was blocked, and she realized she was looking at the palm of his hand mashed against her face, his fingers, powerful for all that fat, gripping her head almost brutally again. He shouted at someone. It sounded like "Shut up." Then he began to sing.

She lay there in her heavy body, his hand crushing down on her nose, his song dull in her ears, and then her skin began to sting. She could feel rivulets of sweat running down her face, down her neck, into her bosom, her abdomen growing warm as it soaked into her uniform, her groin and thighs all growing hot and wet. The sting became a burn, a tremendous burn, and it felt as if she were being inflated, squeezed from the inside with terrible force, as if the blood and bile and perspiration, all of it, the very juices of her body, were being forced out through every pore, every orifice, violently. The sting-become-burn became pain, a searing horrible agony in her flesh, pain too overwhelming to endure. She would have screamed, but she passed out.

When she woke up, she was dry again. She lay in a bed near a window. She could hear someone breathing nearby, rhythmic, rich with slumber. Altin lay on couch nearby, his robes brown and crusted with dried blood, his face a mess of the same, and his hair stiffened into short sticks, crackly and all askew. She looked out the window and saw smoke, several white plumes of it gently rising beyond a castle wall. Calico Castle's wall.

She couldn't stop the tears. They burst free in that instant, loosed in the moment of realizing that she was home.

Chapter 23

Colonel Pewter's face was the picture of severity as he moved with his unit across the open plains of Kurr toward Crown City. The thumping footfalls of two hundred and fifty Marines in heavily armored battle suits beat a bass drum to the song of so many whirring servos and the hiss of hydraulic rams as the company approached the capital, still several miles off. Every stomping step splashed up sheets of muddy water in great spreading waves and sent chunks of dirt and grass flying out in a globular spew of green, gray and brown, each footfall an explosion bursting upon the ground so violently it seemed as if grenades were being tossed beneath five hundred steel-clad feet. Nine platoons marched in orderly formation, moving to deliver the ultimatum from planet Earth, the demand that the Queen call off the Hostiles or watch her city burn.

"Canopies unsealed," Colonel Pewter ordered his men as the first of the outlying farms shaped themselves in his view screen. "Their magicians will blend us together like protein shakes if they can. So crack the windows, Marines. At least sixes inches around." He followed his own instructions and tapped the battle suit's console, bringing up the canopy controls. He hit the manual release, then slid the control forward and watched the windscreen break its seal and slide forward half a foot. The distant farm disappeared when it opened, the proper angle for projecting the image on the armored glass compromised, leaving him with only the view of the open prairie upon which they still trod through the canopy itself. He switched on the small console monitor instead. It was barely as big as the palm of his hand, but it would suffice. He knew what he needed to do, and he operated this machine reflexively.

"Contact at two o'clock, Colonel," came Major Kincaid's voice over the com. "Altitude six hundred and sixty feet, bearing north-northeast at fifty-one knots. Looks like they've spotted us, sir."

Colonel Pewter tilted his head back and looked into the gray skies. It took him a moment to find what the major had identified, but he found it, some kind of winged creature flying straight for the city. At first he thought it might be an eagle, but it was too big.

"I can take it out," offered Corporal Chang, whose mech unit marched next to the Colonel's. "I got that bitch."

"No," ordered the colonel. "They need to know we are here. We need them to call off the Hostiles. If we have to kill them, we'll be living here full time. Remember, there won't be anyone back at home if this doesn't work out."

"What the hell is that thing?" asked another Marine marching just behind the corporal.

"If I remember my mythology right, I think that one is called a gryphon," offered Major Kincaid.

"So what is this place, like the original source of fairy tales or something?"

"I've been wondering the same thing, Sanchez," said the Major. "This planet is pretty hard to swallow."

"Keep your heads in the game, people," ordered the

colonel. "Keep the channel clear."

They marched onward, and soon the farmhouse that had appeared on long-range sensors came into visual range. They could see a large group of men on horses charging across a wide plowed field.

Laughter crackled in the speakers of the colonel's battle unit and someone said, "What the fuck? They're literally 'sending in the cavalry'? Someone should tell them that's just a saying. This ain't, like, 1950 or something?"

"They have lances, Sanchez, you moron. It would have to be, like, the 1800s," countered Corporal Chang.

"You're both wrong, now can the chatter," snapped the colonel. "We have no idea what those men can do. A magic trap on a door killed Krakowski easy enough. Don't think their cavalry will be less dangerous than their doors. Spread out."

The nine platoons parted, shaping a long line, gently curving forward at the ends, the beginnings of the flanking maneuvers that would follow. The thunder of their stomping feet splashed heavily upon the muddy ground as they moved. Once in position, they stopped and waited, the press of their great weight squishing ooze out in puddles around them.

Colonel Pewter stepped forward from the line. "Chang, Sanchez, you are with me. Let's go. Major, you know what to do if this goes bad."

"Roger that, Colonel."

The three Marines tromped across the plain toward the forming lines of heavy cavalry, thus far grown to three lines of fifty animals abreast, but more were still racing across the field to increase the ranks.

Three riders came forward, one on the left bearing the crimson and gold standard of the Queen, one on the right in plate armor that appeared to have seen considerable use in its time, and at the center a glorious figure on a prancing charger wearing gleaming plate armor and upon whose helmet bobbed a bright crimson feather, dancing gaily with the motion of his horse as if it were a plume of playful smoke. It was this central figure who removed his feathered helmet as they drew near and tucked it under his arm, revealing a face that was very young.

As a reciprocal courtesy, Colonel Pewter tapped at his control panel and opened his suit's canopy all the way, the whine of the motor sounding until the windshield was thrust straight up into the air where it folded back, conveniently providing cover from the drizzle coming from the dull gray clouds above.

The two officers stared at one another for a time, the Prosperion's horse continuing to dance beneath him, its iron-shod hooves making alternating slaps and sucking sounds in the mud as it pranced and shied, the beast clearly uncomfortable at the proximity of the alien machine and its whirring, whining immensity.

"Why do you bring your war machines into Her Majesty's land?" said the proud figure upon the agitated mount. "You must realize this encroachment cannot be seen as anything other than an act of war."

"I am here to negotiate the terms of Her Majesty's withdrawal of Hostile forces from my planet," intoned the colonel precisely as he'd been told. "Director Nakamura of the Northern Trade Alliance has authorized me to give your people six hours to comply. If you do not, I am under orders to level Crown City and then every other fortified city, town and village on the continent until she does comply. We will not leave this planet until one or the other has occurred."

"We have no hostile forces on your world, and if we did, Her Majesty certainly would not remove them simply because a mob of ruffians riding in iron golems thought to threaten us."

Colonel Pewter's eyes narrowed at that, and he studied the man carefully. He could see the signs of a dangerous collision underway, ego and fear. He decided to change tactics some.

"Listen, son, you haven't got the stripes to make the decision you're about to make, regardless of that feather there. Just send word to your queen and get her out here to talk to us. And you need to get her here right away."

"I will do no such thing. You will remove your ... constructions from this field immediately, or I will remove them for you." The man to the young officer's right made a ticking sound that could be heard despite being mainly muffled in his helmet.

Colonel Pewter looked past the man and saw that the rows of cavalry had grown to seventy-five animals wide, and there were now four lines of them. The back row was comprised of riders wearing no armor, which boded all the worse in the colonel's mind. He figured those would be magicians back there. He looked back at the young officer, locking gazes with him. "That's not going to happen. So, if that's all you've got to say, then we'll be moving on to the city to find her ourselves. I suggest you tell your boys back there to stand aside. We don't want to hurt anyone right now. We only want to speak to the Queen."

"I must insist, sir, that you comply with the instructions I have given you and remove yourself back to Little Earth. If you do not, there will be no help for what comes next."

Colonel Pewter shook his head and tapped the controls to lower his canopy back to where he'd set it earlier. "Look, it's your funeral," he said. "Don't say I didn't warn you." Into his com he said, "Bring them up, Major."

"You are making a terrible mistake," warned the mounted officer. "You have one last chance to call them off before it is too late."

Colonel Pewter only continued to shake his head. Dumb

233

kid, he thought. Probably some rich guy's son. Going to get all his men hosed. They wouldn't even know what hit them.

The sound of the approaching line of mechs rose, the vibrations in the ground more pronounced, until all of them had come even with the colonel and his two companions of the recent parlay. "Tell them to step aside," said the colonel one last time, hoping the young Prosperion would comply. He did not, so the colonel ordered his men to advance. "Steady ahead," he said. "Don't shoot if they don't."

The young officer turned his horse sideways, the length of it directly blocking the colonel's battle unit, about which the animal protested with a wide-eyed whinny, rearing high on its hind legs. But the skillful young rider spun it round in a full circle and sidled it up to where its flanks nearly brushed against the unit's plasma shield. "Halt, I say," demanded the youth.

Colonel Pewter reached down with both of the battle suit's arms, and down it was, for the horse at the withers was only half as tall as the war machine, and as gently as possible, he picked up both horse and rider and placed them carefully aside. Laughter erupted over the com channel as the colonel pressed forward past the officer.

With the young officer behind him now, the colonel did not see the signal the youth gave for his men to charge, but signal he did, and suddenly on they came.

The first line of horsemen lowered their lances and pounded across the wet turf, cries of "For the War Queen" sounding from the darkness inside their helmets.

"Do we fire?" asked Corporal Chang, sounding uncomfortable. "I mean, it's going to be bad."

"Concussion grenades in front of the charge. Give them a fifteen-yard buffer. Try to scare the horses off."

The hollow *thwoop-thwoop-thwoop* sound of two

hundred and fifty concussion grenades being launched from tubes in each Marine's mech filled the air, followed by the dark shapes of the grenades tumbling in the direction of the onrushing horses like lobbed rocks. Almost as one they went off, a tremendous blast of sound and a pressure wave washing out toward the oncoming animals. A few of them reared and pulled up, tumbling riders off their backs. Others stopped short and hard, pitching the riders forward. But only a few. The rest, while angling sideways, reflexively veering away from the unseen force, came on anyway, their eyes wide with fright, but their ears back with anger, trained war beasts with courage in their hearts. Their riders leaned forward even closer to the necks of the charging animals, and it was clear that they would not be scared away. The tips of their lances began to glow.

"Shit," muttered the colonel when he saw it. He knew there would be some kind of magic in that glow, and it was likely not going to be good for his men. Into the com he said, "Take down the animals. One burst. Do it now."

The motors of a hundred mech arms sounded, the armored limbs rising across the line as one, and then came the white flash of Gatling fire erupting from each of them. A spray of fifty-caliber bullets spewed forth, a burst of barely a second and no more, the rush of lead projectiles invisible but for a slight darkening in the air, like the barest shadow had passed across the land. The bullets bit into horseflesh terribly, cutting the powerful heaving chests of the charging creatures into ribbons of slinging hide and bright red meat. Limbs were gone, knees vaporized, and the riders flung into the air.

The burst of gunfire was over as quickly as it began, and the riders lay in various states of disrepair upon the ground. Some lay still, necks broken, while others thrashed about in agony, gripping legs that had been struck by gunfire or bones that had broken and pushed through the skin when they fell. Cries of pain filled the air.

Colonel Pewter shook his head ruefully as he ordered his men to continue onward, toward the city again.

The young officer and his two companions rode fearlessly back through the line of mechanized Marines and rejoined the rest of the cavalry, though from the way the less elaborately armored rider gesticulated, it appeared the next course of action was a matter of debate. Colonel Pewter hoped the young, feathered fool wouldn't do anything as stupid as that again.

"Step over the fallen," Colonel Pewter ordered as they got to the swath of wounded men and decimated animals.

Twenty-eight fireballs, some as big as freight trucks, suddenly streaked across the field as the Marines passed through and clear of the carnage. Someone said, "Oh, shit," over the com. The fireballs had formed in unison, appearing out of thin air in front of the next line of horses, and came on like rockets now. One of them came straight toward the colonel's unit, so fast there was nothing he could do. He couldn't help but squint as the nearly blinding glare struck his plasma shield. The fire wrapped around the shield for a moment, like a ship entering an atmosphere. The flames didn't make it inside, but the heat coming through the gap in the partially open canopy was intense. But that was essentially it. The force of the blow was considerable, causing him to stagger back several steps, just as it did the others whose suits got struck to greater or lesser degrees, but that was the full extent of the damage. And even that could be adjusted for.

"Gravity boost to nine," he ordered. "And lean into those when they come."

"Should we open fire again, Colonel?"

"Not yet, Sanchez. Just keep walking. Maybe they'll figure it out in time."

Lightning played upon the suits next, huge bright arcs of it, sheet after sheet, the energy climbing up out of the ground and streaking down from the sky. The smell of ozone was everywhere.

"Fuck, I'm shorted," called a Marine on the left flank. "I can't believe this shit." Colonel Pewter could hear the sounds of the Marine pounding on his com panel.

"Take it back to base," the colonel said. "Everyone else, keep moving."

More lightning came, and more fireballs, another unit shorted out before they'd covered half the distance to the waiting line of cavalry.

"Colonel?" this time it was the Major's voice.

"Keep moving."

A shaft of ice, thick as the torso of the Prosperions' largest horse and easily five times as long as any of the beasts, formed at one end of the Prosperion line, and it shot out like one of the mineral shafts the Hostiles fought with, a massive battering ram hurtling across the intervening space with incredible velocity. It struck one of the mech units square on and stove it in as if it were an aluminum can.

"Oh, my God," cried a woman's voice. "They got Ashcroft. Did you see that shit?"

Another bolt of ice, again the size of a steel girder, shot out and crushed another Marine. Then two more came. Four after that, and suddenly the attack was on.

Having no choice but to order return fire, Colonel Pewter called for a full-out response. The Marines as one set into high gear.

They ran in long ground-devouring strides, covering the distance at a speed that nearly matched the horses, the cavalrymen having launched into a charge of their own. The two sides closed together rapidly. The fifty-cals spun and sung as the bullets flew. But still the horsemen came.

Electricity sparked from the tips of their lances, flickers of it like captive lightning reaching blue fingers across space at them. None of them went down.

"What the fuck?" Corporal Chang said. "We're not even hitting them."

"I don't like this," said Major Kincaid.

Twenty-eight ice beams streaked over the heads of the riders and crushed in another bunch of battle suits.

"Goddamn," cried Sanchez, watching the Marine to his right get pulverized. "Our shields aren't doing shit."

"They were never meant to fend off freight trains," someone remarked.

Still the cavalry came.

It occurred to Colonel Pewter that something was odd. He kept charging, and yet, as he watched through his canopy, it seemed that they should have closed with the horsemen by now. He squinted into their onrushing line, watching them, the riders bent over the necks of the animals, their mouths moving, their lances level and lit up with magic. But he saw as he stared at them that they moved in a dreamlike way. He could see it if he focused hard enough on them. It was as if they were moving and yet, somehow, the distance was growing as they charged, very subtly, as if the ground were stretching, just enough to make it so they didn't quite cross the field. An effect like in a dream.

"Are you guys seeing this?" the major asked, as if reading his mind. "They're not really coming. Or something."

"What?" That was Sanchez.

"They're not coming. Look."

Twenty-eight more tree-trunk-sized beams of ice bashed in what remained of an entire platoon and a few more to boot.

"Faster, damn it," ordered the colonel. "Get in close.

They aren't missing with those things."

That's when he hit a wall, literally. He slammed into it and came to an immediate halt. They all did. The impact jarred him, stunning him for several seconds. It took as long for the spots in his vision to clear as it did for his control panel to come back up.

"It's a goddamn iceberg," Sanchez said, coming to quicker than the rest.

Colonel Pewter took a second to confirm it and saw that, at least in principle, Sanchez wasn't far off. A huge wall of ice now stood before them, stretching away to the left and right and bending back at a gradual angle, making it impossible to see if there was an end to it nearby. It rose up high into the air as well, perhaps two hundred feet. "Major, see if you can go around. Everyone else, burn it down. Ice melts."

Flamethrowers erupted like the breath of so many steel dragons, licking out from the extended arms of the remaining mechs, melting the ice in waves.

"Readings still showing it twenty-feet thick, Colonel," said Corporal Chang. "It's staying constant. They're refreshing it from the back side."

Colonel Pewter saw the readings on his own console. He called back to Little Earth. "I need air support. Do we have any of those fighters up yet?"

"We're getting close, sir. Ten minutes," came the reply.

"We don't have ten minutes."

"Colonel, they're waiting for us around the end of the barrier," reported Major Kincaid.

Colonel Pewter bit back the profanity that leapt nearly to his lips. His instincts couldn't believe he was being held off by a bunch of men on animals, despite what he knew of magic intellectually. He'd fought alongside Altin once, so he had an idea of what the magicians were capable of, but somehow he hadn't expected this.

He looked up. That wall was very high.

He could shift down his suit's gravity settings and jump, but mechs didn't do well as aircraft, and he didn't want to risk that kind of vulnerability. So he started climbing, jamming the powerful vices that served the unit for hands into the ice and pulling himself up, one yard at a time. Seeing him do it, several other Marines started climbing as well. The colonel wasn't sure what to expect, and he had no ships or satellites in orbit to send him a visual of what was on the other side. At least not yet. He didn't want to order the rest to climb with him. Those that had were enough. "If you're not already climbing, stay down," he said.

When he reached the top, he debated peering over the far edge but quickly put that idea aside. They'd be waiting for that, and he'd take one of those massive ice beams straight to the face.

One by one, the Marines who'd climbed after him joined him. Soon there were twenty-four mechs atop the wall.

"You want the rest of us up there yet, Colonel?" asked an eager young Marine from the ground below. It was clear he felt like he was missing something.

"No. They'll probably just cancel the damn thing and we'll all fall. We're going to see if we can't disrupt this thing. You be ready to come in when it goes down." Without the proper gravity settings, that would be fatal, and the colonel knew what he was doing was going to be dangerous as it was. Better to do it on his own terms.

He turned to the men with him and nodded through the canopy at them. "Let's do this. On my mark, let's jump down and take them out, make them drop this thing. Set your landing for sixty yards out from the wall. Maybe we'll get behind them."

"Roger that." Private Sanchez wore a come-get-it grin as he set his suit's gravity for the leap.

"Flash grenades now, concussion right after. On three, two, one, go."

The grenades shot out in rapid succession, then they all jumped, hydraulic force sending them flying out over the edge of the wall and, as hoped, out over the lines of horsemen and down to the ground beyond them.

Despite the gravity adjustments, the force of the landing sunk the suits several feet deep in mud, and it was the work of a few seconds to get free. In that time, the magicians had turned to see what had happened. They were still too late. Colonel Pewter and his men did not need to move to unleash the Gatling guns. Once again the white flare of fire blew out from the spinning carousel, and in the span of seven seconds a huge section of the Prosperion line lay dead. All of them, mages, knights and animals. Where they had been, what they had been, was now a swamp of mutilated flesh, soggy fabric and rent metal. In patches, leather burned from the heat of the onslaught.

Colonel Pewter leapt from the indents of his landing and made to finish the rest of them, but he saw that they were now in full retreat, the two halves of what remained of their force peeling off on either side and riding for all their worth back toward the capital.

The colonel nodded as he watched them run. "I think their Queen will talk to us now," he said. "But just to be sure, let's wait for the other companies. I suspect our hopes for dialogue alone have passed."

"Which companies, sir?" asked the Major. "How long do you want to wait, since we've got them on the run?"

"All of them, Major. If ten thousand mechs aren't enough to convince her to call off the assault on Earth, we're probably still going to need them to tear that city down. I have a feeling busting into that place isn't going to be as easy as we'd hoped. Not by a long shot."

Chapter 24

Altin led Orli by the hand as they crossed the busy parade ground upon which the Queen's army was forming. They had to dodge the charge of horsemen loping across the field toward the formations of cavalry gathering, and they had to stop and step back to avoid being trampled by sprinting units of infantry making their way to the teleportation platforms, the rattle of their weapons and armor announcing their approach, but only as they were already very near given the general din of the preparations everywhere. Tens of thousands of men and women had already formed into companies, whole regiments, each assembled on the broad tile-work squares around which transmuters and teleporters stood. The transmuters would call up walls of dark solidity, formed from the material of the platform itself, and from it build a box around the warriors, closing them in and making them ready for the teleporters, who would then send those troops by the thousands straight to the orc fortifications that Captain Andru and his team of scouts had found. When it came to moving troops, the War Queen's army had no equivalent.

"Total commitment," is what the Lord Chamberlain had told Altin when he and Orli had arrived at the Palace.

"She's going to send it all in at once and catch them by surprise."

From the looks of the frenzy in the staging grounds, when she said "total" she meant *total*. He thought it was pretty risky to commit like that, but he'd also heard that there were over a hundred thousand orcs. It was probably best if the fight didn't take place here, so he understood the Queen's gamble on that front.

As he approached Her Majesty, who was astride a monstrous warhorse of nearly nineteen hands, he could see in the illusion hanging in the air before her that similar scenes were taking place in the garrisons across Kurr, reserve units gathering from all reaches of the kingdom, and all to be committed to a single swift and decisive fight. As he scanned the images that shifted in sequence across the illusion, he could not help but wonder if, even with all that going on around the continent, she could come up with a force as large as a hundred thousand strong.

"That's enough," she snapped at the illusionist who'd conjured the report for her. "Make sure General Cavendore is ready at Calico Castle, and tell him to send word if Sir Altin ever reappears."

"Sir Altin has reappeared, Your Majesty," said Altin, having come within hearing range.

She turned in her saddle, the leather creaking beneath the weight of her golden plate armor, and regarded him with a level gaze. "I am not accustomed to having my subjects simply exit my presence without so much as a 'by your leave,' Sir Altin," she said, referring to his hasty departure upon learning of the Hostiles in orbit above planet Earth. "I will not tolerate such things, is that clear?"

"Yes, Your Majesty. I was thoughtless, my mind only on extracting Orli from certain death."

"Then it seems that you have done so." She glanced to

Orli and then back to Altin. "I'll be frank: I no longer have any idea where that woman stands in the scheme of things."

"She stands upon my heart, its conqueror, My Queen. But if you worry for where her loyalties lie, I assure you, she is a creature of Prosperion now." He turned to Orli and, by the go-ahead motion of his head, prompted her to speak.

"Your Majesty, you once promised that I would be your subject one day. You promised all the flowers I could pick. I hope that you will still grant me that, if not today, then eventually."

Altin nodded and smiled approvingly. He knew Orli's heart was not filled with that kind of servility, but he also knew where her loyalties were. Orli was doing what needed to be done, saying what needed to be said. Demanding the Queen apologize or demanding that she trust her, neither would be a winning strategy.

"We shall see about that. Right now, I have larger knots in my bowstring." Her face turned stark then. "Sir Altin, what is the condition on planet Earth?"

"I didn't stay long enough to find out, Majesty, but based on what I saw from orbit, they are horribly outnumbered. I don't know how they will defeat the Hostile forces without our aid."

"Yes, she got the jump on them, to be sure. But there's little for it just now."

"They're not Blue Fire's armies, Your Majesty," Orli interjected then. "She spoke to me while I was on planet Earth."

"My dear, while I confess that you are something of an enigma to me, one thing I know for certain is that your judgment on that subject has been compromised beyond measure."

"It's not compromised at all. I spoke to her. She said it's

another being just like her, another living world, a male. Like her mate was. It's not Blue Fire."

"I believe that might be right," Altin said. "I went to Blue Fire and confronted her directly. She insists it is not her behind the attacks on Earth. At first I didn't believe, and if I'm being honest, I still am only partly convinced, but I think Blue Fire may be telling the truth. It really doesn't seem like she's making it up." He couldn't tell Her Majesty that Blue Fire had helped him save Orli, and that this was his evidence for trusting her—that and Orli's impassioned pleas on Blue Fire's behalf, a case made earlier this morning as they were getting her some clothing and preparing to come and see the Queen.

"You are a good man, Sir Altin, but love blinds you. You need only look above the skies of Earth to have all the proof you need."

"That's not quite true," came a voice off to Altin's right. They all turned to see High Priestess Maul approaching along with her assistant, the priestess Altin recognized as Klovis. The two came dressed for war, each in rust-colored robes, the Maul wearing an iron cuirass over hers. She carried a long-handled war hammer with familiar ease, while the young priestess beside her used her spear casually, as if it were a walking stick. "I believe Sir Altin is correct."

"Let me guess," said the Queen. "You've had a drift in the hkalamate pool, and in the grip of that black gas, Blue Fire has promised you, in the same way she has Sir Altin and Miss Pewter, that she's really not as bad as she seems."

"Something like that, Your Majesty, but I have also spent two days in divinations following that conversation, and we have not gotten one drop of dreaming to suggest she is telling us anything but the truth. All divinations point to something red. There is a quality to redness that appears to be the center of it all."

"Ocelot told me to find the red world," Altin said suddenly upon hearing that. "I'd almost completely forgotten. She said Orli would know what that meant."

Orli blinked in surprise at him. This was the first mention that he'd made of any red world, although admittedly, they'd only had two waking hours together since he'd pulled her out of the death chamber back on Earth, and most of those hours had been rather emotional.

Seeing her bewilderment, Altin repeated everything he could recall from what Ocelot had told him, concluding by saying, "She told me that Orli would know how to find the red world, or that she could figure it out. She said we must find it or everyone will die."

"Ocelot is a witch," said the Maul. "She is a primitive and completely removed from civilized events. Her magic has no context in modern politics alone, much less the wherewithal to fathom the nature of alien worlds. She doesn't even know there are such things. She is a spirits worshiper, barely more than an animal."

"She is a Z," said Altin. "And she showed me exactly where Orli was, which you would not, or could not, do. And she appears to know more about the red issue than you as well."

The High Priestess ignored that and turned to Orli instead. "What do you know of a red world?"

"I don't know anything about a red world," Orli answered honestly. "The only red world I know is Mars, which is a small planet near Earth. But there's nothing there but mining colonies and a few oddball cultist enclaves. There are definitely no Hostiles—I mean, no Blue Fire-like creatures there." It occurred to her that the Maul might be offended by the pejorative note that she'd struck when mentioning the cults, and she looked to the High Priestess to see if she had been offended in some way.

"Are you sure there are no other red worlds somewhere

else?" the Maul pressed on, impervious to the Earth woman's blasphemy. "Something you saw on your way from Earth to Prosperion? That is a long journey, during which you must have seen many worlds."

"No," Orli admitted. "Space travel doesn't really work like that. But there are probably millions of them. Billions of them. But I don't know of any in particular. Only Mars."

"Think harder," demanded the Maul.

"It doesn't matter how hard I think. I don't know of any other red worlds. And besides, it might not even be a *world* she's speaking of. Blue Fire is named for a sun, just as her husband was, so it might be a red star you are looking for. There are millions of those too. And that's not even the worst part of it." She paused to look at Altin, who nodded, encouraging her to continue. "Blue Fire and her mate were named for the sun of the other, the sun that gave birth to the one they loved, not their own sun. So even if I did know of a red sun, would we be looking for *it* or for the planet orbiting another sun that loves the planet revolving around it? That's the problem. Are we looking for a red planet, a red star, a planet around a red star, or a planet around another star, which may or may not be red but that loves a planet in orbit around a red star somewhere else? Do you see what I'm saying? It doesn't matter how hard I think. How can I possibly know?"

Queen Karroll wrinkled up her face at all of that, and it was clear she thought it all gobbledygook, but the High Priestess never lost a step.

"You see," said the Maul. "Wild magic to lead us wildly astray."

"Perhaps," said Altin, "or else it is Z-class magic leading us simply and straight to the point that we refuse to see."

"And what point is that, Sir Altin?" The Queen pointed with a golden gauntlet at Orli. "Miss Pewter has just said she knows of only one world, and it is without life. The rest is long-winded nonsense."

"If Orli knows of only one red world, then perhaps that is the only red world we need worry about. We all know perfectly well that divination is all about working with what you already understand. So, perhaps that is what Ocelot is trying to do, get us to work with what we already have between us."

The Maul nodded. At least on that she and Ocelot would agree.

Movement in the sky turned the Queen's attention upward in time to watch a gryphon and its rider come swooping down. The majestic creature landed on a ledge built into the west wall for it, its leonine paws making no sound as they touched down. Its rider, a man in leather armor, threw down his lance as soon as his mount landed, then he leapt off to stand beside the beast, clearly impatient for the gryphon handler to come and take the reins.

At first the gryphon snapped at the handler, its sharp eagle's beak darting toward the woman, who dodged with practiced ease and, with a few utterances, calmed the beast enough to be allowed hold of its bridle. The rider wasted not one moment more and sprinted down the stairs, where he was accosted by an officer, only briefly, and shortly after, the two of them came sprinting toward the Queen.

"Your Majesty," said the rider, his voice rapid, his breathing fast. "The Earthmen have begun landing a force at Little Earth, and they've sent a contingent in advance, moving southwest of the city. Lord Forland's patrol was near and has moved to intercept."

The Queen groaned. "Forland has had that command for less than a week." She rolled her eyes skyward, silently cursing the gods and fate. "How many Earthmen?"

"At least two hundred approaching the city, Your Majesty, in golems of some kind, ogres made of steel. And

I have no good count for how many of them are at Little Earth."

The Queen was silent for a time, chewing on the inside of her lip, then she tilted her head and lanced Orli with her gaze. "Why is it, Miss Pewter, that wherever you go, hosts of invaders follow immediately in your wake?"

Orli could only blink back in bewilderment, wide-eyed and as surprised as everyone else by the news they'd just received.

Chapter 25

Gromf snuck down during the dark heart of the night
to the dark heart of the mountain, far below the great
fortification Warlord had built for the All Clans. He picked
his way down the winding ledges and squeezed through
the narrow places until at last he was at the pool where
God spoke. He did not know how to get the hideous figure
of God to appear in the water as Kazuk-Hal-Mandik had,
but he hoped that God would know that Gromf was there.
God was a god, after all. Did it not make sense that he
would know such things?

Gromf lodged his torch between two rocks near the
edge of the pond and stared at the water for a time. Its
surface looked black as the stone that formed it, and were
it not for the occasional drop of water falling into it, an
echoing plop that sent rings rippling to the edges and
warped the reflections of the ceiling for a time, Gromf
might never have known there was water there at all.

He sat at the edge of the pond, waiting, his eyes growing
tired of staring at the reflection of himself. He looked
about, studying the chamber more closely than he had
before. Empty, smooth and shapeless, an anonymous
formation of time and water passing through. A few

crannies pocked its walls where some element or another had embedded itself and then given way to erosion more readily than the surrounding stone, the evacuation making little shelves and alcoves into which Gromf realized Kazuk-Hal-Mandik and perhaps the warlocks of the northern clan for seasons beyond counting had set lamps and tapers and obscure items of ambiguous use.

In one of these, a very large one at the back of the pond, Gromf saw a skull, a terrible thing, wide and fissured, lumpy and gray with eye sockets that must have held fist-sized eyes and a row of upper teeth that might once have eaten steel. The brow ridges were uneven, large even for an orc, but pronounced more on the right side than the left, jutting out like a bent pinnacle. Whatever soul had housed itself in such a form must have been a fearsome thing.

The water lit up with the bright light of day as Gromf studied the misshapen skull, and once again God sat upon his rock beneath a cloudless sky of blue, the stony rope of his long left arm trailing out of view over a jumble of God Stone-covered boulders, his jointed legs all in a twist before him like a bramble of fleshy cord.

Gromf stared into the pond, keeping his revulsion in check, though the quiver that moved his upper lip might have been obvious to a god.

"You come without your master," said God in the voice of an avalanche. "Already there is divide."

"No," said Gromf, squinting into the glare of so much light. "There is no divide between orc and orc. It is this magic you would have us do. Your demons have no Discipline."

The fissure in his face elongated, grotesque and horrible as it shaped the fault line of his laughter.

"You laugh at Discipline," Gromf accused.

"I laugh at your fear," God said. "I laugh at your

weakness. You crawl down here to beg for power over the power I already give."

"No. I come to seek what the human song does not know. The demons must have Discipline or they can be of little use."

"I will discipline them," said God, his long left arm rising and falling in a whip-strike of elastic stone. It cracked a thunderous sound and several boulders near the impossible figure were turned to glittering clouds of sand.

"And who will discipline you?"

Again came the whip-crack, this time cutting a trench knee-deep into the rocky landscape twice the length of God's long arm, the last half of it spreading along the ground like cracking ice. The ocular depressions of his eyes moved outward in their perimeters as if by rage. The surface of the pond grew choppy then, the water covered with tiny lines like those the night winds draw in desert sand. Storm clouds formed in the skies above the deformity of God.

Gromf watched in silence as fury contorted and pulsed before him in the pond, but eventually it stilled and the storm clouds went away.

"You are strong and clever, Gromf. You will lead the All Clans one day."

"Warlord will lead the All Clans," Gromf said. "I will serve him in my place. It is the way of Discipline."

"And you will serve me, young orc. This too is the way of Discipline."

"Discipline must tie both ends of the rope to cross the gorge."

Tremors crossed the water again, but only briefly.

"How do we control the demons that we bring forth?" Gromf asked directly, feeling confident now. "How do we control them if something happens to you when the fight begins?"

"I am God. What can happen to me?"

"The same that has been done to the old gods."

"That was at my hands. There are no gods left to challenge me. This world is mine. And I will give it to the All Clans, and your beloved Warlord as you choose."

Gromf nodded, seeing what he saw in that. He asked his question again. "How do we control the demons when they come?"

God roared then, no attempt to hide the emotions at all, a great wailing and flailing of all four malformed limbs. "You will do what I tell you, mortal, or I will crush your people and give the world to the elves."

"Then you will not tell us how it is done?"

"They are mine to control. That is all you need to know. The time has come. Open the gate, and open it all the way." The water went dark.

Gromf's face contorted with the tempest of his thoughts, but he quickly brought them in check. The sky might be gone from the pond, but God might still be watching. If he was a god. Gromf was no longer sure.

Gromf stood on the open plains beyond the city of the golden queen, the walls of her vast fortress visible in the distance a few measures off, or at least the image of it as it had been two hours before when the great dome of concealing magic had been cast. Now what he saw was a memory of a time when the plains were empty but for the All Clans shamans arriving, the time of commencement now well underway.

The shaman circles were working together to bring the warriors out of the mountains. In only an hour they had managed ten thousand of them, and more shamans were still arriving from the southern clans. Soon there would be a hundred thousand orcs ready to march on the human capital and crush it forever. Soon Warlord would sit in the high place that the humans' golden queen sat upon, giving orders and eating the cold meat of her dead heart. It was time.

He turned and watched Kazuk-Hal-Mandik directing another circle of shamans, sandy-skinned orcs from the edge of the Sandsea Desert, to their place far from where his own clansmen were. Warlord was smart enough to know that even in this time of pending victory, it was best to keep the individual clans far apart so no accidental fighting occurred. What tragedy it would be to have a clan war break out now, here under the concealment of a great dome of magic, a racial suicide just when they stood at the mouth of humanity's cave ready to take it for themselves. Finally. The humans would find the dead bodies rotting in the sun by the stench, only see them after stepping into the soft mess of their decay. Such was the fate of the undisciplined. It was good to see that the plan made by Warlord and Kazuk-Hal-Mandik was made of Discipline.

When the old warlock was through with his instructions, he came back to where Gromf stood. He wore his God Stone on a leather thong around his neck. Gromf's was in a pouch tied to his waist. Gromf decided to try once more to dissuade Kazuk-Hal-Mandik from opening the gate to God.

"I think we have enough warriors for victory," he said. "The humans do not know we are here on their plain. Much of their force is still encamped at the base of the great peak far to the north of us, guarding the castle with the broken tower. The demons will be trouble for us all. God will not send them back when this is done."

"You continue to blaspheme, Gromf. I accept it from you because you are young. Warlord will not. The spear is thrown. That is the end of it."

"We cannot control them."

"God will control them."

"And who will control God?"

"We've had this discussion before, Gromf."

"This is not Discipline."

"Discipline is how we got here, Gromf. Look around you. We have the power to conceal ourselves from human eyes. We fill their fields with warriors while they sleep and get fat on honeyed sweets. You complain sometimes like a woman. Now is the time to find your heart for war."

Gromf shook his head, but he would not disobey. That was not Discipline either.

By what he guessed was well past midday—it was impossible to tell through the concealment spell for the sky above was stuck fast and still displaying the morning's clouds—all the orcs had arrived, a massive host bristling with swords and spears and axes. All but the southern warriors wore steel armor, another product of Discipline, and more than half of them had at least some form of enchantment on their weaponry. For most, merely the added bite of fire, but for a few, the strongest warriors, more powerful effects were in place, sinuous reaching spells put upon their spears and more than a few with devouring acid dripping from their blades. Even the humans were afraid to use that particular magic.

Warlord came to the front then, riding a horse like a human would. The animal looked small beneath the massive figure, and Gromf wished privately that Warlord stood upon his own two feet.

The other clan commanders came to line up beside him, each of them on a horse of his own. The animals shifted and shied beneath the weight of their riders, and twice one of the gray orc horsemen clouted his beast in the head in an attempt to calm it. The tactic did not work.

"The time has come," shouted Warlord, facing the distant city walls. "I will have the night's feast in that high place there." He pointed with his axe at the highest spire of the palace, which strove above all else in the city, at least a half measure into the sky.

Shouts and calls for victory and glory of various clans followed, which Warlord let play out until they were still. He turned in his saddle and placed a huge hand on the rump of his animal, nearly encompassing it. He looked straight to Gromf and Kazuk-Hal-Mandik standing there.

"Drop the illusion and bring forth the demons," he said. "Let it begin."

Chapter 26

"Take a thousand men and go help Lord Forland hold off the Earthmen," the War Queen ordered the officer alongside the gryphon rider. "Find out what they want."

"Yes, My Queen," said both in unison, and once again they went off at a sprint.

The Queen looked back at Orli who returned her gaze with a frown, irritated by the monarch's implications that somehow Orli might be responsible for the fleet landing a company of mechs on Kurr—not to mention that somehow she might have been responsible for the Hostiles attacking Earth or any other issue of warlike incursions anywhere. She had as much pull with the fleet as she had with the Queen, and Blue Fire certainly wasn't taking any orders from her either. Blaming her was ridiculous.

"So, Miss Pewter, you haven't answered me," pressed the Queen. "Why is it that war seems to follow you everywhere you go? What have you to say for yourself?"

Orli's eyes narrowed as she found her spine. "What I have to say is that Captain Asad believes invading forces follow Altin around in the same sort of way. Which makes the captain just as wrong about him as you are about me.

I would also say that at some point, hopefully, someone in charge of one of these human worlds will stop jumping to conclusions and accept that maybe things are more complicated than is convenient for decision making right now. That is what I would say." She put her hands on her hips and stared up at the resplendent Queen defiantly.

Altin jumped in on her behalf, hoping to avert calamity. "Your Majesty, when I rescued her, her execution was being carried out. The headsman's axe had fallen, almost literally. Doctor Leopold had to extravasate the venom from her body or she would be dead right now."

Her Majesty cocked an eyebrow at that. "Is this true?"

Orli nodded.

"What were you charged with?"

"Being your friend."

Her Majesty rolled the royal lips inward for a time and looked off after the gryphon rider and the other officer. When she looked back, it seemed the subject had changed. "Do you think a thousand riders is enough to hold off two hundred or so of the steel golems your people ride?"

"I don't know," Orli said. "I don't know what your people are capable of. I've only ever seen Altin and Tytamon in a fight. I can say, I don't think fireballs and lightning are going to help very much. They can ground out the lightning, and they have pretty strong shields. Fire probably won't do anything to them at all. Swords and arrows will do even less."

"I've seen those machines at work, Your Majesty," Altin said. "They are very powerful. They have a device that issues shaftless arrows, thousands of them in the span of a few heartbeats."

The Queen nodded grimly. "They must also have the red-light weapons that Miss Pewter wears. The ones we had to enchant against for *Citadel*." She looked down at Orli again and realized the Earth woman wasn't wearing the blaster at her side; in fact, her fleet uniform had been exchanged for Prosperion attire, if perhaps a bit in the style of a brigand, comprised of black trousers tucked into high riding boots and a cobalt blue blouse, all of which appeared to be brand new. Even her dog tags had been exchanged for a light blue sapphire dangling from a golden chain, which the Queen recognized as the amulet Altin had taken from Madame Kenouvier two days past. She wore no weapon at all. "I see you've come unarmed to battle, Miss Pewter."

"I didn't know we were having one," Orli said. "Although I guess I should just assume it now. It seems like that's all anyone does anymore."

"You asked if I would honor my promise to make you my subject one day."

Orli nodded. "I'd like that more than anything."

"Will you fight for the crown as Sir Altin does? As all these men and women do? Even against your own people?"

"I'm not much of a fighter," Orli said with a shrug, "but 'my own people' tried to kill me yesterday. I won't shoot my father or any of my close friends, but I will help you every way I can. This is my home now. I'll fight for it if it comes to that."

The Queen studied her for a time, peering down from the height of her huge warhorse, which itself seemed to be taking the measure of the slim woman standing there. After a time she began to nod. "Very well. You are now a subject of the crown. Swear your fealty."

"I swear it," Orli said, glancing sideways at Altin and suddenly feeling very awkward. Was there something special she was supposed to say, some particular oath? He only nodded at her, his eyes alight with joy.

"Good enough," said the Queen, putting Orli's concern to rest. She turned to the royal assassin and ordered him to send someone for Orli's weapon, the one that the city guard had found during the investigation of Orli's kidnapping and the murder of Tytamon. "Someone might as well put that thing to proper use."

Altin flashed Orli the warmest smile and clutched her hand, his face the very picture of happiness at having Orli officially claimed for Prosperion. It really was her home now, even in the eyes of the law.

"Sir Altin," said the Queen as she motioned for a nearby squire to come and take her horse, "since I have you at hand, take me to the south gate tower, and be quick about it. I must get to the wall and see how it goes with our people and the Earth war machines. We may have to delay our assault on the orc fortress if our patrol can't handle them."

A moment later, the War Queen stood in the high tower at the southern gates of Crown City with Altin and Orli at her side. She looked out over the patchwork of small farms that spread like a quilt across the land toward the prairies beyond. From this distance, all she could see was the endless green of them, spreading away like a verdant ocean leading off seemingly forever to the south and west.

"They must be too far off still," Her Majesty proclaimed. "I need my seer." She started to turn toward the guardhouse and call for one, but Altin reminded her that he was in fact a Seven.

"Your Majesty, I can oblige."

"Ah, yes, I nearly forgot. You are a handy fellow to have about, Sir Altin. And you spare me the noise of a crowd."

Just as Altin was about to begin a spell to search the distant plains for signs of the fleet machines, Orli let out a gasp. "Look," she said, pointing. "Over there."

Following the line of her extended arm, they saw immediately what she had seen: a great dark mass had formed like a blot upon the ribbon of green that marked where the prairies began in the distance beyond the farms, a dark band appearing in an instant as if a great army had been lying prone in the grass and now decided to stand up and be seen. In a manner of speaking, one had.

"Tidalwrath's fits!" Altin exclaimed. "Is that what it appears to be?" He didn't wait for the answer and immediately sent his magical vision careening out across the farmland toward the spreading darkness upon the plain. When he emerged from the spell, he quickly cast the illusion of what he'd just seen into the air above the battlement, just large enough for Her Majesty to see.

"Those are Captain Andru's orcs," declared the Queen. "It seems they have beaten us to the punch." She closed her eyes, and for several moments, she gave orders telepathically to officers back at the compound. Eventually, she returned her attention to the situation on the wall. "This is an inconvenient surprise," she said. "Yet another one."

"But your scout said they were my people in battle suits." Orli sounded genuinely confused. "And he said there were only two hundred of them. How could his count possibly be that far off?"

"Clearly those are not your people, and that's an army, at least ten divisions, out there. So either the orcs have fooled us with an illusion of your battle machines, or the Earthmen are trying to fool us with some sort of trickery of their own. And if not one of those, then we are now being attacked by two enemies together, and clearly collaborating." She looked to Orli and raised her eyebrows. "I don't suppose you know anything about either of those last two?"

"No, Your Majesty, I don't. As far as I know, nobody from the fleet has ever had contact with the orcs. And we don't have the ability to make holograms that big, so it's not fake. Or, if it is, it's not something the fleet did."

"Then either the orcs are casting an illusion of your machines, or I have two enemies who happened to attack at the exact same moment by pure coincidence, which I find difficult to accept."

Orli nodded, staring back out at the enormous stretch of the orc army which spread like a shadow over the land. "The royal assassin has my gun," Orli mused, "is there any chance he has my com badge as well? Maybe I can pick up something over the air. If there is an attack from my people, there will be ships up there." She pointed at the sky to make her case.

"I'm afraid not, Miss Pewter. Your weapon is the only thing we found. The search for Black Sander continues, but I fear he won't be brought to me in time to be of use for this."

Orli shook her head again. "Then there is nothing I can do to help figure it out."

"Wait," said Altin. "What about one of your seeing mirrors? The small frames you carry about. Can you find out in one of those?" He shaped its size with his hands as he spoke.

Orli frowned for a moment before realizing what he meant. "A tablet? Yes, if I had one, I could, as long as I knew the access codes for it."

"I'll be right back. Don't move." Altin vanished, without the least utterance, but he was back in less than a minute, his reappearance announced by a loud rush of air.

"You have a remarkable way of casting these days, Sir Altin," said the Queen. "I'm sure I've never seen a teleporter work like that before."

Altin evaded Her Majesty's point, handing Orli the tablet instead. "Here, see if you can find something."

Both Altin and the Queen leaned in to see what images Orli called up on the small screen. She pressed a portion of its edge, then began touching symbols and small images shining there. "Well, at least I can get in," she said. "Where did you get this? It's one of ours. From the *Aspect*, I mean."

"It belongs to Doctor Singh," he said. "He gave it to me when *Citadel* appeared above planet Earth. I never got time to give it back."

Orli went through several screens and discovered that all her passwords still worked, the one upside of the fleet's having intended to fast-track her straight into the grave. Several long minutes passed as she worked through image after image on the screen.

Altin looked up to see that the first lines of the cavalry had just appeared in the fields a measure beyond the wall, two thousand horsemen suddenly popping into place, indicating that the teleporters back at the parade grounds were already carrying out the new orders from the Queen.

"That's weird," Orli said frowning down into the tablet. "I show several ships in orbit, all with identifiers too low to be starships."

"What does that mean?" asked the Queen.

"Well, for one thing, it means your scout was probably right about there being mechs on the ground. It wasn't a holographic trick."

"Mechs?"

"Marines. Warriors in heavy infantry machines, mechanized battle armor. The ones Altin was talking about. You saw them when you came for me and Thadi— Lord Thoroughgood." She blanched as she said it but pushed the feelings of anger and humiliation aside.

The Queen nodded grimly and motioned for Orli to keep working with the tablet. "Quickly then. Can you find out what they intend?"

"I'm trying," Orli said. "But the *Aspect* isn't here, there's no signal. I can only do so much without its computer to go through. I get open channels and public access, but I'm not coded into any of these smaller ships."

"Do what you can with it," said the Queen. "Sir Altin, I think perhaps it is time you take me back to the staging grounds, given our change of plans. Be quick now."

"Yes, Your Majesty."

"Oh, shit!" Orli exclaimed.

"What is it?"

Orli tapped up the volume control on the tablet and turned it so both of them could hear. "Listen."

"Why are they stopping?" came a voice through the tablet speaker. The screen was blank, Orli had only audio, and that crackling.

"Fuck if I know," someone said in reply.

"Six hundred yards west, Colonel," said a woman's voice.

"I see it, Major. That's a lot of heat signatures."

"They got their reinforcements fast. Bastards led us into a trap."

"What the hell are those things?" someone else asked. "Those ain't horses." He sounded agitated, teetering on the brink of fear.

"Holy shit," said the first voice. "They're some kind of aliens."

"The horse guys are coming back too. What should we do, Colonel?"

There was a long pause before the reply came, calm and analytical. "Those men are in retreat."

"What?"

"The cavalry. They are retreating. Look how they ride."

Silence followed, then a chorus of profanity, many voices, some that made it through the translation spell on Altin's amulet, and some that didn't, indicating many of those being overheard on the tablet did not have enchanted com links like the one Orli and most of the visiting fleet officers to Prosperion had been provided with.

Then came the call from the commanding officer, the

colonel, for the mechs to retreat as well.

The Queen and her Galactic Mage looked up from the tablet to Orli, Altin asking what both thought. "What in the nine hells is going on?"

"That's my father," Orli said, looking grim as she flipped the tablet back toward herself and began stabbing her fingers at it again. "But I can't get video, so I have no clue what's going on."

"I thought that voice seemed familiar," Altin said. "It sounds like they are in trouble."

"They are in trouble," said the Queen. "The thousand men I sent to help young Lord Forland have obviously arrived. Earth people have no idea what a proper cavalry charge looks like, and clearly the illusionists with them are doing a proper job of causing panic amongst your father's men. It seems that now we have them in a rout, making that one less problem I have to deal with for now. Sir Altin, take me to my horse. I have orcs to slay."

"Yes, Your Majesty. Right away."

Chapter 27

Colonel Pewter ran with all the strength he had. Even with the motorized assist to the legs of the battle suit, and with a half g of gravity being channeled off, it still required a great deal of effort to push this hard. These suits were meant for combat, not for speed.

Checking the rearview video feed, he could see that he and his remaining Marines were pulling away from the Prosperion cavalry, if barely, but the black monstrosity that had appeared before the horsemen and brought their flight toward Crown City to a halt was already in their midst. He could see horses and men flying through the air like leaves in a whirlwind and the huge ... alien, whatever it was, tossed them about like toys. From the havoc it wreaked among them, he knew that his initial assumption had been correct. While the horsemen may have been running toward that giant army that had suddenly appeared in the distance, they had not been running toward whatever that giant black thing was.

He radioed little Earth, asking about the air support. "Two fighters in four minutes, Colonel," was the reply, just as the colonel was suddenly airborne himself. "Four more in sixteen."

The grass spun down and out of view as the video feed went suddenly haywire, and for a moment he saw, upside down from his vantage, the figures of several hundred Prosperions leaning over the necks of their horses, still hell bent on their getaway. He also saw that a second creature, like the first only with many more legs and a strange bulbous head, had arrived to torment the Prosperions further in their flight.

Then, for a moment, all he saw was sky, the gray mistiness of a cloud-filled expanse monopolizing his vision entirely.

Then he saw something black, a flash of grass again, and then the horses rotated through his view once more as well. He realized he was spinning in the air, flung somehow as the rotation repeated itself twice more like that. And after a half rotation more, he landed on his back, once again staring skyward and hitting the ground so hard it set the mech's controls to static for a time.

He clambered back to his feet in time to see the incoming blow of one long, pitch-black limb, thick as an oil drum, swinging toward him, the strike sent his way with an accompanying roar from a creature so hideous he had no words for it. Once again he was flung into the air, his battle suit whirling like the blades coming off a windmill. He could hear the shouts of his men nearby as he landed hard, many enduring similar treatment he supposed.

"Four companies in formation here at base, sir, you want me to send them out?" crackled the voice in the speaker near his ear. "The rest are still inbound."

"How long till we have a starship in orbit?"

"At least nine more hours, sir."

"Get the suits out of the fortress. Those walls aren't going to matter against ... whatever this is, and we can't fight in a box. Spread out by company. Get the rest of those goddamn fighters in the air." It was with some difficulty that he kept the calm in his voice despite the rapidity of his beating heart.

He got back to his feet again and spun to check the status of his men. A few of them were still pounding off toward Little Earth, but most had come back and were fighting over the downed machines of their comrades. The Prosperion cavalry was streaking past as he watched.

The beast that had hit him stood like a mutant spider over the mech unit of Corporal Chang. Its massive limbs fell in rapid succession upon the battle armor like giant fingers drumming the cadence of Chang's demise.

Colonel Pewter could see the blue flicker of Chang's plasma shield, which was both good and bad. He only had the two tumbling flights he'd just taken to gauge by, but he was sure the power unit wouldn't hold up for long if Chang had suffered multiple hits like that.

He sent two anti-aircraft missiles at the monster and then opened up his fifty-caliber cannon as he ran in to assist. The missiles blew off four of the creature's legs and the spray of bullets opened up a huge rent in the black angles of its body, spilling out rivers of pale yellow goo.

He was on the monster in twenty quick strides, the Gatling gun still unloading bullets into the beast at point-blank range. He switched on the jackhammer blade of the mech's left arm and punched through the hard shell of the monster just as it spun on him.

It tried to throw him off, but he spread the claw hand of that left arm wide, like a grapple stuffed into the beast's abdomen, and the creature could not shake him loose. He triggered the jackhammer and pulverized the creature's guts. It was dead in moments, and soon Corporal Chang was back on his feet.

"I thought I was fucked, sir," admitted the wide-eyed Marine.

"Not this time," the Colonel said.

They both spun and realized the monster they'd just fought was the third of its kind, for the two that the colonel had seen as he spun through the air the first time were still in action, making a ruin of two mech units in Major Kincaid's platoon. The colonel didn't have to say a thing, and both he and the corporal charged in. Four more missiles threaded their exhaust trails over the plain, and one of the monsters erupted like a grenade pie. The second felt the fury of both fifty-caliber cannons and spun toward the two incoming Marines.

The colonel and the corporal had cut it nearly in half by the time the downed Marine was back on her feet and adding her own weapon to the mix. Soon there lay a smoking pile of black plating floating on a swamp of red-and-yellow ooze.

"They may be big," shouted Corporal Chang, "but they go down like little bitches." He just started to sound off a long and profane battle taunt when the colonel cut him off.

"There are more," Colonel Pewter said, turning back in the direction from which they'd just come. "Lots more."

And there were. Six more. None of them quite like another. Some much smaller, one much bigger, but all black as a moonless night and all hideous and indescribable.

"Get these other units up and keep on to Little Earth." He switched to the command com. "Get the transports in the air. I don't want those ships caught on the ground if this goes bad. Fighters up, bombers up and mechs down, then I want those pilots at twenty thousand feet until I say otherwise."

"Roger that, sir," came the com officer at Little Earth.

Little Earth was in sight by the time the six misshapen monsters caught up to them. Colonel Pewter almost made it back to his reassembling platoon when one of the smallest of the monsters caught up to him, leaping into the air and landing heavily on his back.

The computer-controlled gyros and gravity compensators did their best to keep him on his feet, but he still stumbled forward and had to brace himself with one arm to avoid having his mech sent sprawling face first into the mud. He twisted his head around to see the beast pounding on the canopy and trying to push one of its twisted claws in through the gap he'd made by opening it as he had.

He had faith in the shield, but he didn't want to trust his luck too far, so he tapped the control and sealed himself back in. If one of the Prosperion mages decided to teleport him into the center of the planet, well, then today just wasn't his lucky day.

Reaching back with the suit's left arm, he clutched the creature by a portion of what might have been a tail. With a mighty yank, he whipped the creature off his suit back and pinned it to the ground, stuffing the end of his Gatling gun right into its twenty-eyed face and letting go a ten-second blast. Its pus-colored blood hissed and steamed off the plasma shield, and its legs were still twitching as the colonel finally rejoined his men.

He could see the formations of the other companies spreading all around. More ships were landing even as others took off. Very soon he'd have his ten thousand Marines. It might only barely be in time.

Looking back out over the plains, he saw at least twenty more of the black monsters on their way. Long-range sensors showed others appearing in the distance, popping into existence as if ... by magic, which he knew was, most likely, exactly what it was.

He'd trained for a lot of things over the course of his forty-two years in the corps, but never for battle against wizardry. He told himself he needed to stop underestimating them. Every time he did, they ratcheted the surprises up another notch.

The twenty beasts crawled across the prairie like animate tumbleweeds, their speed unnervingly fast, but they stopped inexplicably, holding up just over five hundred yards away, the lot of them twisting and reaching limbs and claws into the air, mandibles and jaws and vacant orifices filled with teeth shaping the sound that could only come from such manifest monstrosity. The colonel hoped they might be considering a retreat based on the number of Marines forming up, but the movement from the others behind them, the new creatures appearing in the distance, proved him wrong. These were waiting for the rest to come. From the looks of it, the army itself, those behind the creatures, had no intention of breaking ranks. They appeared, at least for now, committed to letting the misshapen black behemoths deal with the colonel and his men. He couldn't decide if that was good news or bad, but either way, more of the giant creatures were on their way. Lots of them.

More and more of them appeared, and at a rate of escalation that went from exhilarating, given his recent victories, to something out of a nightmare. In the course of eleven minutes, the number of the black beasts had tripled and would soon approach the same number as his Marines.

"Colonel, this is *Raptor One*, reporting. Do you want us to engage?"

He looked up and saw two fighters hovering above him at a thousand feet.

"Roger, *Raptor One*. Let's see what they think of Tiny Tim."

"Roger that. A quarter kiloton of *fuck you* on its way, sir."

"Visors dark, people," ordered the colonel. "Gravity set to *dig in*."

No sooner had he said it than the contrail of a long slender missile streaking from one of the planes above drew its chalk line across the sky. Even with the canopy nearly black, the blast seemed blinding, and the colonel had to squint and turn his head away.

He turned off the dimmer right after and watched the mushroom cloud rising even as the pressure wave came at them. It blew by and then, a moment later, sucked back, pulling with it a few bits of cloth that made the colonel turn around.

The Prosperion cavalry had reformed its lines some forty yards behind where he stood, or at least, they seemed to have been attempting to do so when the concussive wave set all their horses to bucking and more than a few, along with their riders, tumbling through the grass. He counted them damn lucky they'd been as far off as they were.

He looked into his monitor. There was no movement in the area where the monsters had been gathering. That was good. However, in the time it took for the dust and smoke to settle so they could view the crater where the monsters had been, long-range indications showed there were over twelve thousand of them now near the main host of the army.

"That's not even possible, is it?" came Private Sanchez's voice. "You guys are seeing all this, right?"

"*Raptor One* reporting no survivors at impact site, Colonel. Total kill."

"Well, they're not hard to destroy," said Major Kincaid from her position, fifty yards off with her platoon. "But there's a crap-ton of them now."

The young Prosperion officer with the red plume in his helmet rode up to Colonel Pewter's battle unit then. He moved boldly out in front of it and tapped on the canopy with the end of his lance. Which made the colonel laugh good-naturedly, for it was a curious thing for the officer to do.

The colonel switched on the megaphone and turned the volume down low enough that he hoped it wouldn't startle the officer's horse. "What is it, son?"

"On my world, sir, we say that 'my enemy's enemy is my ally.' I feel that, given what I have just observed, that you and I may be in a circumstance so described."

"I can see how you'd want to see it that way just now," observed the colonel. "So what happened? Your magicians lose control of their monster brigade?"

The puzzled look that came upon his features struck the colonel as genuine even before the clean-shaven rider spoke. "These demons are no work of my men."

"So, what are you trying to tell me?" asked the colonel. "Whose ... demons are they then?" He watched the man very carefully as he spoke, his years of command, years of working with young men who often had a tendency to manipulate the truth, serving to filter every movement, every twitch of the face, every word of the young Prosperion.

"I assure you, sir, I have not the least idea. But you have my word, on the honor of the House of Forland, that those things are not the work of any of my men."

"So, assuming I assume you're not setting me up, what are those things?"

"Demons, sir."

"You said that before. Do you mean demons like, well, like fire-and-brimstone demons? Wrath of God and all that stuff?"

"Yes, sir. Precisely, sir."

The colonel wanted to laugh, but the absolute solemnity upon the Prosperion officer's face, and the newfound humility, was such that the reflex died before it had wind enough to fly. "You're serious, aren't you?"

"As death itself, sir."

"So why don't you undo it. Send them back to hell. Isn't that the point of all that magic you people do?"

"It can't be done. There is no spell for it. Or at least none that Her Majesty would allow. We are witnessing the very thing that marked the end of the dwarves of Duador."

"Yes, I remember hearing about that a time or two from my daughter and her boyfriend. Unending hordes still running around somewhere. Total genocide."

"That is correct."

"How do I know this isn't the work of your Queen?"

"The legions of orcs that have gathered at the outskirts of the city are evidence enough to my eyes," he said. "But I can't say how you would know that this was true. But even if it were some incomprehensible plan of Her Majesty's, which I do not believe for a moment, then I am as troubled by it as you."

"Orcs?"

"If you could not see it, there is an orcish army gathered out there beyond all those demons."

"Orcs. The people that hit Tytamon's castle a few months back?"

"They are not people, but yes, the same. They are less of a problem than the demons. Those must be stopped immediately. If such a thing is possible."

"Well, I think we can kill them easy enough," said the colonel, pointing to the crater a half mile away. "That was a little one. But if their numbers keep growing like they are, I don't think your Queen is going to be too happy about what we have to do to the countryside to finish them. She may have to find a new place to live for the next few centuries."

The officer looked as if he at least partly understood, but he returned to his original point. "May we then, for the time being at least, call off hostilities between our forces, until such time as this new threat has been abated?"

The colonel laughed and nodded. "Yeah, we'll call a truce for now. But if I see any of those ice blocks busting into even one of my people, I'll turn my guns on you personally."

"Very well. Thank you, sir. I will let my men know we have an arrangement for now."

"You do that."

The young officer started to turn away, but the colonel stopped him, having thought of one other thing. He released the canopy on his suit and let it open all the way. "What's your name, son?"

"I am Manduval Forland, son of Gustemore Forland, Baron of Dae and Westmore, and I am second lieutenant in Her Majesty's Seventh Cavalry, sir."

"All right, Lieutenant," said the colonel as he unpinned his com link from his uniform. "I'm Colonel Pewter, First Marines, Northern Trade Alliance. Glad to know you."

"Glad to know you too, sir."

He tossed the com link to the young man, pointing at it with the purse of his lips as the cavalry officer caught it. "If I understand these enchantments of yours right, I won't be able to understand a word you say once you get out of range, but at least you'll get the gist of what we're up to. Don't make me regret giving you that."

"On my honor, sir."

With his canopy closed once more and the lieutenant on his way to rejoin his men, the colonel radioed the new situation with the Prosperions to his own troops, some of whom protested via muttered profanity, but all accepting it as fact.

The sensors read five thousand of the "demons" now.

"Colonel, there are going to be over two hundred thousand of those things within the hour if my calculations are correct." There was an edge to Major Kincaid's voice as she gave the report. "If we're going to do something, we better get it done."

"How many suits we got now?"

"Nineteen hundred," answered Little Earth control. "Six birds in the air. Fourteen more in prep. More troop ships still inbound."

Colonel Pewter supposed that was good news, but he couldn't help wondering if ten thousand Marines suddenly didn't seem like remotely enough.

"Incoming," said the Major then. "And look, they're spreading out. Looks like they learn quick."

Sure enough, the mass of the black beasts was scattering as they ran toward them, separating out from the orc army like sand thrown into the wind. He almost had to laugh. The only thing worse than the real-life discovery of a demon horde was the discovery that such a horde might be even marginally intelligent.

"Keep them pruned back, Raptor squadron, and laser support down here where possible. Marines, hold this ground. And protect the Prosperions if you can."

And so it began.

Chapter 28

Gromf and the crooked figure of Kazuk-Hal-Mandik made their way to the eastern edge of the formation while the shaman working the concealment spells brought down the dome that hid the army upon the plain. They came to a halt a hundred paces away from the main body of the orc host.

"Let us summon only one at first," said Gromf. "Test the resolve of God."

"Still you doubt," said the old warlock. "Even here, at the brink of victory."

"I wish not to fall from it."

"Summon your one if that is all you have the stomach for. I will bring God forth."

Gromf shook his head, but he knew that Kazuk-Hal-Mandik would not be convinced of the risks he took.

Leaving his God Stone in its pouch, Gromf began casting the demon summoning spell he had learned from the human song. He didn't bother with the circle of sulfur this time. He once more found and followed the hidden threads of mana that wove their way through the deepness, through the great hole in the world and down through the furious rotations of the massive vortex that emptied into the valley of God's demons. Gromf again went down and peeked through the tiny opening at the tip of the vortex, down into the writhing mass of black deformities, the heap of twisting limbs and gnashing teeth, the claws reaching up to him as if calling for him to choose them over all the rest. They knew that he watched; their hateful eyes turning up at him proved it even as he looked down.

Again Gromf felt the presence of God, saw the flash of his eagerness like a signal fire on the edge of the valley. He tried not to look, but he could not help it. God smiled his earthquake smile. Gromf tore himself free of that hollow gaze and speared a demon at random with a shaft of mana that he made. He hauled it out, up through the funnel, and like a sling this time, he flung the demon out to the northeast of the army, far from himself and his people.

It appeared in the air above him and landed three hundred paces away, a five-legged form of darkness like the shadow of a long dead tree. It landed heavily and stood upon the plain, its red eyes turning this way and that, taking in the scene.

Gromf looked to Kazuk-Hal-Mandik, but the old shaman was still casting his own spell. He looked back to the demon and waited for it to charge. It turned and glared at him, all of those eyes narrowed in obvious hatred, but then it spun and roared.

It roared to the east. Which Gromf thought odd.

But then Gromf saw the cavalry charging in, over a thousand humans on heavily armored horses, thundering at the orc flanks at breakneck speed. Already!

How could they have known? Gromf wondered. The counter-magic had always been in place. Here, while summoning, but also in the mountains, all these months, all the plans carefully concealed. The hiding magic the great promise of Discipline. And yet there they were, humans riding into the army's flanks the moment the concealment spell was gone, as if they'd been waiting there all along.

The ground shook then, terribly, and even beneath the cloudy sky, a shadow fell over Gromf as something large loomed nearby. He turned to see what it was just as he heard Kazuk-Hal-Mandik cry out, "Behold, God has come."

The army behind them all fell to their knees, though Gromf didn't see it, for he was too busy staring at the arrival of this figure that had seemed small in the bright light of the subterranean pool or, at least, not much larger than Gromf himself. But here, on the surface of Prosperion, standing beside him, God was huge. As tall as ten orcs at least, and that one long arm ran off for fifty paces like a rope of stone, the girth of a pine trunk. God stood upon his crooked legs, seeming to surmount the plain, and he roared so loudly birds fell dead from the sky, their bodies falling like feathered hail to land with dull thumps upon the grass.

Gromf looked again to Kazuk-Hal-Mandik, who had eyes only for the face of God. The old warlock raised his God Stone to the giant before them and muttered prayer words in the old language, the language before Discipline. Gromf shook his head.

God looked down at Gromf and that crevice in his head cracked across his face again. "Now do you believe, tiny mortal?" God asked him in a voice that nearly knocked Gromf down.

"I have never doubted that you would come," said Gromf, holding his ground.

"Open the gate, and I will show your people to glory."

"Why do we need them all? You can slay the humans alone, for you are God." He pointed across the plain to where the human cavalrymen were nearly upon the demon Gromf had brought. "There is your first taste of human flesh."

The five-legged beast Gromf had summoned was almost among the humans then. He could see as it approached them that several of their magicians cast giant fireballs and long lances of ice. Those washed over the demon uselessly, the lances broke into pieces, burst into mist like snow. Gromf laughed. He had learned that lesson too: magic was of little use against them.

The cavalry charge pulled up short as they came upon the demon then, or perhaps they were thwarted by the size of the army they saw formed upon the field. They may have thought a thousand cavalry a nice flanking move, but it was not enough with a demon now in their midst.

Gromf looked around for signs of the main body of the human army, for surely there was more, this thousand just a feint, but it was not there.

So much for human intelligence, Gromf thought. How foolish did they think orcs were? Or how feeble. This small group of horsemen spoke of a human insult.

The demon he had brought forth grabbed horses and flung them wildly about, plucking them out of the grass like tubers and tossing them high into the air. The cries of the terrified humans, the shrieks of the tumbling mounts made Gromf happy, and it occurred to him that he might have been wrong about God.

"Open the gate," God commanded again.

"I will do it," Kazuk-Hal-Mandik said, rising from where he had fallen to his knees.

Behind him, Gromf could hear the clink and clatter of armor and weapons as the army rose to its feet again as well.

Gromf waited for God to go and help the other demon with the humans, but God did not move. He seemed to teeter there as Gromf watched, and the young shaman wondered if perhaps God could not walk at all. He spent a moment in study of God's misshapen limbs, the absurd angularity of so many joints. God's legs looked as if they might crumble with little more than a kick.

Gromf would not be opening the gate for him. Not now. Let the old warlock try.

He turned back to see how Warlord viewed the unfolding events, and it was with pride that Gromf saw the leader of the All Clans content to let the demon do the work on the human cavalry. Warlord watched, and made only the motion for Gromf to hurry up when he saw that the young shaman had looked to him.

Gromf nodded but could not help feeling reluctant to summon more. The one alone had just set the humans into retreat.

Or had it?

Suddenly thundering into view came a new army, an army of metal-clad humans like none Gromf had ever seen. They were tall and thick like mountain ogres, yet ran with the speed of mounted men. Their whole bodies were covered in steel, and yet they were angular and thick. Even upon the muddy turf, their feet pounded loudly, shook the ground, like the thunder of the migrating mammoth herds.

"What new magic is this?" he asked God, but God seemed to be glowering into the distance at what he beheld as well.

Gromf thought it might be best if he did summon at least another demon or two to help the first one deal with the golden queen's new surprise.

Once again he went into the mana stream, followed the braided cord into the valley of demons. He speared two more, not sure he could pull them both forth without the God Stone.

He could.

He threw them out to where the first one was chasing after the horsemen who were now in full retreat. He saw immediately that the steel-clad human giants had now also turned to run away. That was a good sign. Perhaps this new magic was not a threat after all.

He chastised himself for his moment of fear. There was no amount of steel plating that could harden the weak human heart. Even wrapped in their brand new magic, they didn't stand to fight against one demon, and in the time it took to bring forth two more, they ran away like younglings from a bear cub. He laughed and watched as his new-flung demons landed amongst the fleeing enemy.

The largest one he'd summoned, a great black bubble of a thing with a flat head and several thick legs, landed near one of the steel giants, the impact of its landing rocking the ground so mightily that the armored human was thrown twirling into the air. Gromf laughed as he watched the magic armor land hard on its back. He wondered if it would get up again or if the human inside had turned to mush on impact.

Apparently not mush yet, the steel giant rocked and twisted itself back to its feet, turning just in time for Gromf's hulking demon to bash it with a massive forelimb. Again the human in the bulky armor spun through the air. Gromf's contentment continued, and he could not help but question what had made the golden queen think such armor could be of any use. Her warriors were an embarrassment to her people, and it made him wonder how orcs had ever been defeated by such feeble things as men.

Gromf's demon crawled with amazing speed to another armored human nearby, whipping its steel-encased legs out from beneath it and then straddling it when it fell. The demon began to pound upon the armor with its mighty limbs, hammering the bulky steel suit deeper and deeper into the muddy ground with each blow. Gromf leaned forward, willing his keen eyes to see better across the distance so that he might watch the blood spill when that armor cracked open like a nut.

That's when the first human, the one who'd been knocked about just moments before, somehow, remarkably, got up despite how hard it had been hit and how far it had been flung. Gromf realized that perhaps that magic armor was stronger than he'd allowed. He watched as the first human ran to where the demon beat upon the downed one in the mud. Two streaks of something white burst from the ribs of the running human's armor, the smoky lines shooting across the intervening space and then exploding in bright yellow flashes of light and a mighty sound. The explosion destroyed four of the demon's legs, causing it to tilt sideways and sag. Meanwhile, the upright human continued to close the distance, its right arm upraised and directed at the demon, the end of it emitting a bright plume of fire and a high-pitched metallic whine. Gromf could see that the fire was not long enough by any stretch to cover the distance, but the human was too stupid to stop trying as he ran. A few moments after the too-short fire erupted, Gromf heard the demon roar in pain, though he could not explain why.

Then the human was upon the demon and somehow managed to jam its left arm up inside the massive creature with greater ease than Warlord had with his mighty axe. The human simply thrust his arm up through the armor plate and began, what Gromf could only assume, to grip and tangle the demons guts with a steel-clad fist. Soon the demon lay dead upon the field.

Gromf realized now that the humans had tricked him into thinking they were weak. He looked back to see if Kazuk-Hal-Mandik had opened the gate yet. He closed his eyes and forced himself to listen to where the old shaman was in the casting of the spell. From the verses he heard, it would still be some time before the gate was open to let the demons out; opening the gate was much different than cracking it some and pulling a demon or two through.

Gromf did not want those armored human giants coming this way. There weren't very many of them, and he did not want Warlord to have to send the army to brush off this small flanking threat. He and Kazuk-Hal-Mandik should be up to such a task. He would conjure more demons.

He reached reluctantly into his pouch and pulled out the God Stone. He could get many demons with it. He would get enough to deal with the humans' new armor magic. By then, Kazuk-Hal-Mandik would have opened the gate. Then, they would have to trust in God to stem the tide and control them.

God laughed then, and Gromf wondered if he had read the thought in his mind. He looked up to see that God was looking down at him, smiling with that great creviced face.

"Now you believe," said God. "Now that you face the children of another God."

Gromf shook his head, not to disagree, but because he did not know what God's words meant.

That's when Kazuk-Hal-Mandik gasped. The sound was followed by a wet thump upon the muddy grass.

Gromf looked to the sound, which came from nearly at his feet. Kazuk-Hal-Mandik lay there, still as a windless night.

Gromf knelt and shook the old man, but he did not move. He rolled him onto his back and listened at his chest. The drum of his heart was still. Gromf looked up to God then.

"Take his stone," said God. "He is weak. It has always

been for you. Take his stone and yours together, one in each hand. You will need them both to open the gate. The golden queen's armies will soon appear, and your Warlord is waiting for the hordes you promised him to tear down her enchanted walls. And now the children of a new God have come to help, so you must hurry or it will be too late."

The fighting demons were out of sight now, chasing the humans off, but he could hear the sounds of the new magic armor in the distance, the explosions and strange metallic-sounding fire. He knew that God was right. He was a fool to have questioned him. He bowed his head then, steeling himself for what he must do. He snatched the God Stone from around dead Kazuk-Hal-Mandik's neck, breaking the cord with the violence of it. "I will open it," he said. "Let them come."

Chapter 29

"**D**ad?" Orli said for the twentieth time at least. She held the tablet close despite its sensitive microphone. "Colonel Pewter? Is that you? Come in Colonel Pewter." She repeated it several more times, still not knowing if the message was getting through. The infernal effects of magic, especially here in Crown City, made electronics almost pointless, and her tablet hadn't been picking anything up since Altin had taken the Queen away. She'd been trying for well over ten frantic minutes, and when she saw the bright flash and the mushroom cloud, she'd nearly been in a panic the whole time as she tried to raise him again.

It took several long minutes before he answered after the flash, and when he did, he was more than distracted by the sound of it. "Orli? What are you doing on this frequency?" The signal was broken in a few places, and she still couldn't get video feed, but enough of his message got through that she could make it out. "Are you guys operational already?" he asked. "That's incredible, and your timing couldn't be better. We need orbital support, and we need it now. Call up my location, and then get the *Aspect*'s lasers to drill these things some new assholes

ASAP. Tell the rest of them if they're back up and running too. It's bad down here, and the shit storm is only starting to blow."

"No, I'm not on the *Aspect*. And you need to call off the fight. It wasn't the Prosperions. I don't know how you guys got back here, but stop. Stop attacking them. This is all a big mistake. And there is a huge army outside the capital. Are you close enough to see it? It's really bad."

"No shit it's bad. And yes, I'm right on top of these things. Some kind of aliens. One of the Prosperions called them demons. And there are at least ten divisions of regulars on the other side of this demon mob. One of the Prosperions says they're orcs."

Altin reappeared beside here then, looking impatient at having been kept at the parade grounds so long by the Queen. He started to complain but gauged immediately by the look on her face that there were more serious things afoot.

"Demons?" she asked, as she worked through what her father had said. "We knew about the orcs."

Altin frowned when she said it, the very word jarring to any learned magician of Prosperion. He could not understand what the colonel had said, however, for the translation spell seemed no longer to be in effect for him. Altin repeated the word back to her, echoing her question almost exactly as she had spoken it. "Demons?" But even as the word passed his lips, he felt the chill of dire epiphany hit him like an ogre's fist. Of course demons! How could he have been so stupid as to have not anticipated it long before? He closed his eyes and started a seeing spell immediately, dreading what he might be about to verify.

"Yeah, big ugly things. Hard black casing, legs everywhere," the colonel replied to Orli's repetition of the word. But he had to give orders for a time after that, and for a long string of minutes Orli could only listen to the grunts and breathing of a fight that she could not watch. The voices of other Marines filled the air as well, cries of agony, shouts of triumph all intermixed. Then her father's breathing sounded as if he were running, which rushed his words as well. "Orli, we just tore up a bunch of them. They're big, but they're not too smart and they die easy enough. Problem is, there's going to be too goddamn many of them. And what do you mean you're not on the *Aspect*? Did Altin come get you out of that mess in Earth orbit? Tell him I owe him one for that."

"Yes. Well, sort of. He did come get me. They tried to kill me."

"Who, the Prosperions? Or the Hostiles? I saw what was happening before we came back here."

"The fleet. Captain Asad and the rest of them. I'm pretty sure the director was in on it too."

"What? For what?"

"Treason and lots of other bullshit. The court martial was a sham. But I'll tell you about it later. I'm fine now. Altin did come, and I'm safe in Crown City. Well, not really safe, because there are tens of thousands of orcs outside the city, and the numbers are growing. They're using magic to bring more and more, just like the Prosperions do."

"They're all Prosperions from where I'm standing," said the colonel. "Although we've made a truce for the moment with a bunch of them, the same ones who attacked us earlier. Turns out they didn't know these demons were coming either. At least this group here didn't. No clue what's going on with that queen of theirs, though."

"She didn't know about them either. I was just with her. You have to call off the attack against her people. This is all a bad mistake, and it's going to get worse if you join with the orcs against her."

"We're not fighting her, at least not for now. We've got bigger problems with these goddamn monsters crawling out of the ground."

"Monsters coming out of the ground?" she gasped aloud.

"Yes, monsters out of the ground," said Altin then, now finished with his cast and knowing exactly what she was talking about as he came out of the spell. "The orcs have opened a portal of some kind. They got the spells for it when they stole Melane Montclaire's spellbooks from Calico Castle. This is really bad. This is what happened to Duador."

"Orli, what's he saying? I can hear Altin's voice, but I had to give my com badge away."

"He said it's a spell. He said the demons are what happened to Duador. Remember what I told you about that small continent in the northern part of Prosperion, the genocide?"

"Yes. That's what I heard from their officer here. He said we're all fucked. Major Kincaid figures there will be two hundred thousand of them in less than an hour."

She turned to Altin, "So what do we do?"

Altin shrugged. "I have no idea. As far as I know, there's no way to stop it. I would have to find Melane's books, but even if I did, I wouldn't have time to read them and figure it out. This is really bad."

"What did he say?" asked the colonel.

"He said it's bad. He said he doesn't think there's a way to stop them. Definitely not soon."

"Hey, Colonel," came another voice then. "I got this dude with the feather tapping on my window with his stick. Should I let him in?"

"Yeah, Chang, let him in. See what he wants. He probably wants to talk to you. I gave him my com link."

"Roger that," said Corporal Chang.

A few moments passed, and then a new voice came on, sounding distant but clear enough. "Sir Altin, this is Lieutenant Forland, Seventh Cavalry. Tell Her Majesty that the demons are resistant to magic, or at least they are to elemental spells. Our transmuters are having some luck turning them to stone, but getting close enough to touch them is dangerous, and even those spells they seem to resist half the time. So far it's the best we've been able to do. Swords and spears are the only certainty."

"Can they be teleported?" Altin asked.

"They're all rage, Sir Altin. We tried. It just won't work. If Her Majesty can get some stone transmutations enchanted for the archers, that is the city's best chance. It takes several men quite a while to hack even one demon apart. And the numbers are stacking against us very fast. Were it not for the Earth people's magic—the weaponry of their machines—my men and I would all be dead."

"Well, Her Majesty left the wall a few minutes ago. She's convinced the Earth people came back to make war on us."

"They did come back to make war on us," said the lieutenant. "But things have changed. At least for now."

"What are they saying?" asked the colonel then, unable to understand what either Prosperion had said.

Orli summed it up for him. The colonel hummed but didn't answer right away. "Orli, can you and Altin get the Queen to call off the Hostiles now? Maybe us helping her man Forland out here will be enough to make her play nice now." She relayed that to Altin.

"That's not the Queen's doing," Altin said even before Orli could. "Colonel Pewter, I swear to you on the love I have for your daughter, Her Majesty did not order that attack."

Orli translated that for him, adding for her part, "And what's more, it's not Blue Fire doing it either. There's

46:09

something else going on. Something about a red world. There is another planet like Blue Fire somewhere, and that's the one responsible for the attack on Earth. It's not Blue Fire. I'm sure of it."

"I think the timing of the attack suggests otherwise. There are no coincidences that big."

"Yes, there are. Blue Fire tried to explain it to me. Something about ripples in space. And how she found Altin's world. I didn't have time to figure it all out, though, not before those NTA assholes tried to kill me."

"Holy shit," came the cry from another Marine. It was echoed by more than a few others as well.

"Baby, I'm going to have to go for now. Things just got ugly over here. Tell the Queen to call off the Hostiles. The director has ordered Prosperion be destroyed if she does not comply. He's serious. Earth is done for if it doesn't stop, and they're fine with evening the score. It's bad at home, Orli. I don't know when Altin got you out of there, but it's bad. We can't stop them. This is our parting shot. There's more ships inbound and a whole heap of bombers and low-altitude fighter craft coming with them. If she wipes out our planet, we'll be planting the NTA flag here in the radiated rubble of her kingdom right before we all move to Andalia. That's a promise you know we can keep."

"Here they come, people, formations tight. Open up on them," said a woman's voice, her tone even but clearly tense as she gave the command. "Colonel, we need you up here."

"I have to go, baby girl. I love you. Stay close to Altin. He's a good man. Let him keep you safe."

"I will," she promised, tears forming in her eyes. He rarely spoke to her so tenderly. She didn't like how that sounded like goodbye.

And then her father's attention went elsewhere, and the sound of heavy breathing came across the connection, his every word one of command. The battle was on in earnest where he was.

Altin sent a seeing spell out across the plains, intent on seeing what was going on. Orli had to content herself to just listening to the sound of the colonel and his men fighting for a time, but the cries of the dying Marines were too awful for Orli to handle for long. She felt helpless and, after a few moments, weak and worthless too.

"We have to do something," she said, looking up at Altin with frightened eyes. "We have to do something now." He did not see the fear, but he heard it in her voice, even as transfixed as he was by the battle he was witnessing. He let the seeing spell go. She repeated herself when she saw that he was with her again.

"But what?" he asked in reply. "We can't get Her Majesty to 'call off the Hostile attack' because it isn't hers. Blue Fire says it's not hers either. And now, it probably doesn't matter because there is no way to cork the bottle spewing forth those demons." He pointed out to where the black spot was still growing on the field. "Your father and his men are making hay with the demons from what I just saw, but even that won't be enough. Look how the numbers grow."

He had seen that the fleet's mechanized units were increasing in numbers too. There were many standing with the colonel, and many more coming in and disembarking from ships landing at Little Earth. There would be thousands of them soon, and not a small number of flying craft.

In addition, from their place on the wall, he could see that her Majesty's troop numbers were increasing on the field as well and, for a time, even more rapidly as the teleporters hit their stride. But even with those forces combined with the mechs from Earth, it wouldn't be enough for long. The parade grounds inside the city would eventually empty. The staging areas filled with assembled warriors in cities across Kurr would empty. So too would the bellies of the Earth ships empty all their warriors in their various fighting machines. Soon they would all be here. But that fissure in the plain out there beside the orc host would not run dry. The demons would come until there were millions of them, and only when the numbers were so great that they could consume each other as fast as new ones came forth would their numbers level out. And there it would stay in perpetuity, an ongoing spew of death that eats death, forever and all time, just as the stories of Duador told.

"So where are they coming from?" Orli asked, watching as he did the spread of the black stain on the prairie where the demons arrived. It had begun to flow toward the Queen's army now, and the orcs had also begun to advance.

"From hell, I guess," said Altin. "I don't really know."

"There's no such thing as hell," she said. "They have to be coming from somewhere. Is there like a cave or something? Are they some kind of subterranean animal? Like field mice or ants or something?"

"I really don't know. The study of demon conjuring has been forbidden for five hundred years. Nobody knows what it is. It was deemed too powerful, as the forever-absent dwarves will attest. Since then, the worship of the evil gods hasn't even been practiced in secret. Her Majesty's diviners find anyone who even thinks about it, and she has them hauled off to the headsman's block."

"I hope they get better hearings than I did back at home," Orli said.

Altin nodded, but his mind was not on the ways of justice just then. "We have to get word to the Queen about what Lord Forland advised. We haven't time to waste. The battle will be upon us soon."

"What will we do then?" Orli asked.

Altin shook his head, making a sound like a grunt deep in his chest. "We'll fight."

Orli's mind raced for an alternative, but there was simply nothing that came to mind. Turning away from the wall she leaned into him. He enfolded her in his arms and let go a long warm breath into her hair. He was right, of course. They'd have no choice but to fight. And, worse, even if they won, it would still be over for Prosperion. The War Queen couldn't call off the attacking orbs on Earth, and so they were going to die anyway. All of them. Everyone would be dead. What a great time to be alive.

She allowed herself to draw strength and comfort from Altin, who seemed to do the same from her. She loved how his clothes smelled of Prosperion, how they smelled of the wind that blew across Great Forest and permeated the fabric with the authentic scent of this world, or what it had been before today. She'd come close many times to having this world to live upon in peace, as a home, a place to be happy, but no matter what she did, no matter how hard she tried, it seemed the universe, or perhaps some laughing god out there somewhere, really just didn't want that for her. Violence lived everywhere. The Queen was right, it followed her.

But if that's how it was, then that's how it was, she thought to herself as she listened to Altin's heart. It beat so steady and strong. She would be strong too, like he was. She wouldn't go out simpering like some frightened child. With one last inhalation of beech and elm and the scent of the man she loved in his clothes, the scent of the man she was probably going to die with very soon, she leaned back far enough to look into his emerald green eyes. She smiled up at him. "Let's get it done," she said.

He kissed her, long and with passion heated by the burning down of two whole worlds, crushing her to him for a time. He pulled away then, holding her face in his hands, smiling back at her. "I love you," he said.

"I know. I love you too."

And then they were with the Queen, who had just learned of the demons herself.

Chapter 30

Captain Asad sat upon the bridge of his dark ship swearing under his breath. His crew had done this restart ritual over twenty times between practice and traveling to Goldilocks, or Blue Fire as it was thought of by some. And yet at the nine-hour mark, his people had insisted it would still be at least two more hours. "Other crews will have gotten it done in ten," he'd insisted. "We have no idea what's going on down there. Get it done."

The two hours was up and he was still sitting in the dark.

"Nguyen, what's the problem down there?" he barked into his com badge.

"It's almost ready, sir. I'm on my way back now. They said five minutes."

"They said two hours, a hundred and thirty-one minutes ago."

"Yes, sir," came the ensign's tactful reply.

Captain Asad rose from his command chair and paced the bridge. The older man sitting at the weapon controls glanced up at him as he passed by. He too had been around long enough to recognize when silence was the best option.

Several steps past the weapon station and nearly to his chair, the lights came back on. All of them. High-pitched sounds were emitted from speakers, and monitors flashed, and then normalcy returned to the *Aspect*'s bridge. A moment after that, Ensign Nguyen appeared from the lift and took his place at the controls. He quickly tapped in several commands, and after a few minutes ticking and clucking to himself, he had his station fully operational. "Ready to go," he said. A similar report came from the weapons officer seated next to him.

"Take us to Prosperion. Get it on the monitor as soon as we're close enough. Report on the status of the other ships."

"Yes, sir," said the ensign as his hands flew across the controls.

The time it took to make the jump and cover the distance from exit to orbit passed so slowly for Captain Asad that he might have burned holes through the hull were his eyes actually capable of generating the heat that seemed to radiate from them. But at last they arrived at the planet and quickly set themselves to finding out how the landed troops had done.

As soon as video was available, they called up the fight taking place on the plains of Prosperion. Even the bellicose Captain Asad was taken aback by what he saw.

Crown City was awash in black monsters, demons according to the brief they'd been given from the controller at Little Earth as they approached the planet. Wave upon wave of the monsters swarmed around the city walls like an ocean of black tar, and they could see where in places, a few of the larger ones had been able to jump over the walls and were wreaking havoc in the streets. The space fortress, *Citadel*, hovered over the battlefield along with what looked to be several hundred smaller cubes of stone, which the captain recognized as the small towers dubbed *redoubts* by the Prosperions. They hung over the fight raining long blue shafts of ice and huge balls of fire into the black mass, but not to any significant effect the captain could appreciate. Occasionally, a particularly agile monster would leap high enough into the air, or perhaps was thrown that high by its fellows, and would grapple with one of the smaller blocks, but each time, the redoubt would simply vanish and reappear somewhere else over the battlefield.

Meanwhile, the base at Little Earth was under similar siege. All ten thousand mech units had landed, but the status report showed that over a quarter of them had already been destroyed. The fighters and bombers were laying strafing runs across the ranks of the black monstrosities, and the bombs they'd been dropping had dug a trench that was over a hundred feet deep, two miles long and nearly a mile wide. The trench separated the beleaguered base from the huge army that was embattled with the forces of the Queen, but the monstrous things seemed to flow from the flanks of that host like a river of black oil, pouring down into the trench, and then climbing up the other side. The edge of the crevice served as the front line for the fleet forces, and the mechs and fighters were blowing the beasts to pieces by the thousands as they tried to clamber out of the trench. And yet, despite uncountable losses, the demons continued to come.

"That is not what I expected," admitted Captain Asad as he looked on.

"You seeing this, Asad?" came the voice of Captain Metumbe over the all-com.

"I'm seeing it," he replied.

"What do you make of that?"

"I'd say the arrogance of the so-called War Queen has finally come back to bite her. It looks like she tried to let loose some kind of Prosperion attack dog, and they turned on her somehow. If anything, it's going to make our job easier."

"I agree. Maybe we should get our people out of there though. I'm not sure they're going to be able to hold out for much longer against all that, despite how well dug in they are. And maybe there's no point now anyway."

"Nguyen, get me Colonel Pewter. And if he asks about his daughter, don't say a thing."

"I won't, sir. Right away, sir."

"Get the director online as well. He should be seeing this."

"Yes, sir."

The colonel did not reply right away, but less than a minute passed before Director Nakamura's face lit up the ensign's com. Captain Asad got up and went to it, leaning against the panel with one arm. "Take this feed, Director," he said. He nodded to Ensign Nguyen to send the video feed they'd been watching since coming into orbit above Prosperion.

The captain observed the sequence of expressions that moved across the director's face, at first confusion, then recognition, then shock and last stoic determination. "What happened?" he finally asked.

"We don't know. We're trying to get Pewter up."

"Is his mech still up?"

"Yes, he's still showing operational."

"*Transport Nine* is inbound," reported Ensign Nguyen then. "Commander Levi has requested ammunition. He says he needs every crate on the ship. And I have Little Earth control relaying Colonel Pewter's request for orbital support from any and all ships available."

Captain Asad looked to the small monitor where the director was still visible, looking tired as he stared at the video feed of the battle on Prosperion. "Do we pull them out, or do we resupply them and help them cut a path to the city walls?"

"Did they give the ultimatum to the Prosperion leader?" asked the director. "We've seen no lessening of Hostile attacks here, and forty-one cities in the NTA alone are gone, or at least no longer communicating with us. We've got to put the pressure on the Prosperion ruler or you folks won't have any place to call home."

"I don't know, sir. We're trying to raise Colonel Pewter now." Captain Asad touched the ensign on the shoulder. "Find out if Little Earth control knows if Pewter or Kincaid got to the Queen."

"Yes, sir."

"Do you think, given the situation, it would be safe to send a ship straight to the capital now?" the director asked as he continued looking on. "She's got to be sitting in a pretty deep puddle of piss right about now, even if Pewter didn't get through all that."

"The magic screws with flight controls. I expect whatever that effect is will be much worse right now. I would bet everyone who can use that power is using it to defend the city."

"Captain, I have Colonel Pewter," reported Ensign Nguyen.

"Get him on screen."

A moment later the colonel's face appeared, looking haggard and sweat-soaked. "Asad, we need starships to cut us clear and get us time to get out. This is pointless without a lot more suits and air support."

"We're working on a solution for that, Colonel. I have the director on the feed. We need to know, did you get to the Queen? Did you give her the ultimatum?"

"No, I couldn't get there in time. Not before all this went down. But she knows. Orli is in the city with her. I told her to get the message to the Queen."

"Pewter?" the captain said, eyes wide as his gaze shot

to the image of Director Nakamura.

The director's expression flattened, grim, and he was nodding, as if a suspicion had just been confirmed.

"Yes, my daughter is alive," said the colonel watching Captain Asad. "And she told me what you did. You and I are going to deal with that if I get off this planet alive."

"In the meantime, Colonel," said the director, redirecting that subject for now. "What was the Queen's response?"

"No response. I've been busy, and Orli said it's not the Queen attacking Earth. Altin Meade confirms it."

"They're lying, and both are servants of the crown. So that's the end of it," said Captain Asad. "Earth is finished." He shook his head and looked as if he wanted to send a nuke down into the capital city right then.

"Maybe not," said the director. "If that woman really has miscalculated as bad as it appears she has, maybe she needs to soak in the juices of her mistake for a while longer is all. When it gets ugly enough down there, she may be forced to stop playing this stupid game."

"I don't think it's a game, Director," said the colonel then. "We've been working with a company of royal cavalry down here, and their C.O. swears this isn't the doings of the Queen. He says this is an invading army from the mountain, a population they call *orcs*. They're the ones that brought the demons out."

"He's lying, just as she is," said Captain Asad. "They're a race of liars. We had a run-in with the orcs a few months ago. They're savages with bows and pointy sticks. This is just another attempt to buy their War Queen time. For all we know, those orcs aren't even real."

"The demons are real," said the colonel. "And faking the rest doesn't make any sense. I think she's got a real problem, and it popped up at a really bad time. We'd have been screwed if those orcs came at us, but they never have. They've been engaged with Her Majesty's regulars the whole time. And since these black devils have started showing up, the total number of invaders has more than quadrupled. The only reason we haven't been overrun is that trench. Well, that and the fact that half these bastards are too busy either eating the dead or eating each other to come at us properly. If you guys start helping out from up there, and we don't run out of ammo down here, I think we can hold out for a while. But I don't think it's going to go as well for the Queen."

Both the director and Captain Asad nodded at that. The captain spoke what the director clearly thought. "If that's the case, then she will want our help at some point. Let's just hope it is in time to save the Earth."

"We need to get in touch with your daughter, Colonel," said the director. "We need to tell her to let the Queen know we can help her clean up her mess. Tell her to call off the Hostiles."

"Pretty goddamn ironic, isn't it?" said the colonel. "You two jam her straight through the system, behind my back, and you send me here to do this at the same time. Me fighting your battles while you're murdering my daughter. You're like a couple of snakes, and you even fucked that up. And yet here you are, needing me and my girl to pull your ass out of the deep shit you got us in. I'm not impressed, gentlemen."

"We didn't get us in it, Colonel. We never asked to be at war with the Hostiles, or that queen. You can have your day in court when this is all over, but that day will only come if there is a court for you to come back to. So, secure the sour grapes for now, do your job and get your daughter into the feed."

Hate warped the colonel's features like heat coming off the hot barrels of a Gatling gun, but he seemed to relent some. "I'll see what I can do." His feed went dark.

Chapter 31

The line of Orli's laser cut a clean gash along the ridge of spines running down the demon's back, toppling several of the sharp protrusions, like severed stalactites, and sending them tumbling over the sides of its body toward the cobblestone streets. Two of the city guardsmen beneath it, pestering its lower hemisphere with the sharp points of their halberds, had to jump out of the way as the huge spines crashed to the ground.

Taot's flight path took them low, and Orli spun her head around in time to see three other guards diving out from between the demon's legs, just in time to avoid its vicious bite. But another was not so lucky. She watched in horror as the monster plucked a fourth guardsman up from the crumbling cobblestones in one of its claws, held him dangling by one ankle, thrashing and screaming for a moment, before passing him into the nasty shears of its awful visage where it mashed and masticated the man in its bloody mandibles. Orli turned and pressed her forehead against Altin's back, trying to clear her mind of what she'd witnessed. She had to stay focused.

Taot swung back around, and once again Altin threw down an ice lance that was as thick as Taot's tail and nearly half again as long. The huge frozen shaft crashed into the cut that Orli had made and split it wider, though, as before, the ice broke up more easily than it should. Altin had concluded early on that the creatures were resistant to magic in some way. Fire was useless and lightning almost as bad, but this strategy, working together, was garnering some results. The creatures were less resistant inside than out. Their hard outer shells made magic largely ineffectual, but his magic seemed to hold together almost half the time if he could get a shot through a break in that carapace.

They flew back hoping for a killing blow. Taot swooped down on silent wings as the air whistled through Orli's ears. They came up level as they sped toward their quarry, then Taot stretched his neck out before them and blew his dragon's breath into the hole that Altin and Orli had made, a long, roaring spew of infernal heat, so bright it made Orli shield her eyes. The fire blasted back, some of its heat bouncing off the demon's shell, and Orli couldn't help the reflex that had her pressing hard against Altin's back as well. She could hear the fire crackle as they flew the length of the monster's body, the sizzling noise of its fluids being brought to heat. Unlike Altin's magic, dragon's fire was real enough, and the demon had naught to do for it but boil and burn. The heat and gas from Taot's expulsion filled the cavity the ice lance had opened, burning into the soft innards of the demon mercilessly, and as the momentum of Taot's pass carried them by the demon, the dragon kept up the flames. He curled his long serpentine neck back and downward as they flew past, still blowing fire as they began to rise. When the yellow tongues of flame were no longer concentrated enough to inflate the beast effectively, the dragon cut off the spew, but it was enough, for in the moments after Taot's terrible breath stopped, the demon burst apart. The explosion of superheated flesh and expanding gas blew fragments of its hard black armor everywhere, the shrapnel of its demise breaking windows and snapping balconies into twisted smiles of splintered wooden teeth on both sides of the street. It was messy, but it worked.

When it was dead, the remaining guardsmen stood up from where they'd been crouching behind their shields, shouting up at the dragon and his riders, their grateful expressions obvious even though their voices could not be heard over the triumph of Taot's roar. The cry of the dragon had been reverberating across the city for hours, at first frightening the populace, but later the cause for cheers—cheers from all but the gryphon riders anyway, who now had to work twice as hard to stay in their saddles whenever Taot flew near.

Altin did his best to give the Queen's men their space, but the fact of the matter was that Orli's laser and the dragon's fire were the best weapon the city had for fighting in the streets, picking up the demons here and there as somehow a few them continued to find ways into the city despite the tremendous effort at defense. Orli cut them open, and Taot steamed them to death from the inside. Altin's ice lances were merely the lever to simplify things a bit.

"There's another one coming over the wall. Look, over there." Orli had to shout to be heard over the wind of Taot's flight as she pointed to guide Altin's eye. "See it? To the east, like a giant lobster."

"A lobster that's half melted and has a second head growing out of its back, maybe," he said even as he directed Taot with the pressure of his knees toward the giant, misshapen oddity.

He sent a message to Taot not to get too low, pointing out through an image and sense of dread that the demon's second head came with a second pair of claws that could grope up and snatch them out of the air. The dragon's thoughts returned impatience, a mental growl, annoyed that Altin felt inclined to tell him, a natural born aerial killer, how to fight.

They swept across the cityscape then, just above the chimney tops, and came in range of the demon that had managed to get over the walls. Orli could see white robed medical mages busily casting healing spells on the men who had fallen where the lobster-demon had jumped up and landed atop the battlements. If the airborne trio could kill the thing, the soldiers and mages down there might be able to hold the expanse of wall again.

If there were anything good about fighting demons from Orli's point of view, it was that they were almost impossible to miss with laser fire. She aimed down for the monster's uppermost head, intent on trying to cut a line at the back of its neck, maybe even deeply enough that Altin's ice lance could break it off. She missed badly, however, when Taot swerved around a four-story inn, and instead she cut a line down the creature's side, just above the line of its several projecting legs.

Altin conjured an ice lance ten spans long and two spans thick as Taot swept past the monster and soared out over the wall, over the battlefield, in a long, banking arc that would ultimately bring them back round to confront the lobster-demon again. Orli still couldn't believe how many of the monsters there were down there, so many throwing themselves against the wall now that it seemed impossible they could ever hold them off. There had to be hundreds of thousands of them. It was a miracle of the magical prowess of Crown City that the walls hadn't yet been overrun. Only a few of them were occasionally able to breach the great height and powerful enchantments on the walls. At least for now. The city was still, all things considered, relatively safe, at least as long as the dragon and his two riders could keep up with the demons that did get through.

The tragic sight of Her Majesty's armies in the field was less encouraging. The orcs and humans, strangely isolated on the field beyond, continued to fight, the combatants now climbing over the dead, orc and human alike, knee deep in gore as they battled on. She knew that someday, if she lived through this, she would never forget the carnage that she had witnessed on this awful day.

Altin loosed his ice lance and two more slightly smaller ones, sending them streaking down and smashing into the seething mass of darkness pressing against the walls. The first burst against the humped back of one monster, shattering uselessly and flying in all directions like so many thousand bits of hail. The second had even less effect on another demon, but the third managed to find a purchase between two sliding plates of boney hide near what might have been the neck of a smallish demon that had been trying to climb the wall. The shaft of ice didn't kill it, but it did knock it off the wall. It fell at first onto the heads and backs of those beneath it, and for a moment it lay atop them, bobbing and surging with the movement of the invaders, its legs upward and thrashing like a great upturned beetle floating on a stormy sea, but then it slipped sideways, sunk down into a momentary space between its fellows, where it ended up trapped beneath their tromping feet and unable to rise. Orli hoped that would be the end of it, but she had no way to tell. It seemed unlikely, given what she'd witnessed thus far that day. And it was worse for Altin. All his great power, and yet that was the best he could muster, one shot out of three, and that barely enough to flick one small demon off the wall.

They passed back over the fray and into the city's air space. Altin's next ice lance formed quickly as Taot dove down toward the lobster-like creature again. He guided the dragon's angle with the press of his heel, causing Taot to tip his right wing. The massive ice spear flew true again—Orli had noticed that they seldom missed—and once again a large rent opened in the demon where her laser had cut through its armored outer shell.

As before, Taot's long, sinewy neck curved down and stretched for the opening, but the creature saw them coming and shot out one of its thick pinchers, which snapped at the dragon's head. Taot jerked his head out of the way, a powerful reflex, which sent a surge of energy up his spine like a wave running up a rope, and the force of it nearly flung Orli off. It would have, too, had Altin's arm not wound around behind him, whipped back in anticipation and reflex of his own as he caught her and kept her pressed firmly to himself. She clutched him tightly about the waist with her left arm, her fingernails nearly digging through his robes as terror chilled her thoroughly.

Meanwhile, the S-curve that had formed itself in Taot's long neck with his defensive retraction now worked like a wound-up spring for his counterattack, and in the instant following the demon's defensive move—almost the same moment Orli heard the loud snap of the demon's closing claw—Taot's open maw darted forward again and nipped that claw off right where it formed at the end of the demon's leg, removing it as easily as if he'd clipped a rose bud off its stem. The warm spray of the demon's reeking fluids spewed out from the severed opening, splashing across Orli's leg and down the dragon's flanks as they flew past and then up and out of range.

The dragon, with two powerful flaps of his wings, drove them even higher than at first it seemed he needed to, much higher, almost straight up and yet angling sideways some. Orli continued to clutch Altin about the waist and craned her neck to see around him, looking for a reason for the sudden and precipitous quest for altitude. Then she saw it, a rising spire, the dragon's efforts meant to avoid collision with a needle-sharp minaret. Still they struck it, though they missed most of the stonework from which it emerged. They ran up against it at an angle, and the dragon's huge talons reached out to absorb the shock, though in doing so, he squeezed Altin and Orli together in the curve of his back. The impact was jarring, and both Altin and Orli gasped as the breath was knocked almost entirely from their lungs. The minaret snapped off, breaking clean and sending down a jumble of large stones. They gasped, the three of them sounding off together, but the break in the minaret and the dragon's noble efforts took enough off of the collision to avoid calamity for them all.

Taot pushed off against the stump of the spire with his powerful back legs, sending more bits of broken stone down into the courtyard below, and in four more mighty strokes of his wings the climb was done. He let the upward momentum die off—at the peak of it they were all weightless for that one half heartbeat—and then he folded his wings and let gravity call them back toward the ground. His broad head, with its long curving teeth shaping the very grin of death, was at one moment high above his riders, seeming to lead them up, but then, in that moment of weightlessness, he curled it down from the apex of the ascent and let it fall past his riders, its downward arc shaping the turn that would lead them back down and back into the fight.

Orli gasped at the suddenness of the ordeal, the pass by the demon, the minaret and the sudden altitude, all in the span of a few breaths. In doing so, the cold air of the lofty moment filled her lungs with chill as she clung to Altin like a sweater all through the stomach-churning turn. Plummeting down, she could see the city spreading beneath them like some huge holographic map. She might have marveled at its myriad styles and mottled disparity of architecture had she not been so afraid that they were now going too fast to pull up.

They weren't, but barely, or at least so it seemed to her. The g-forces she endured as the dragon pulled out of the dive felt like they would grind her into the dragon's spine, splitting her in half. It was all she could do to lift her chin off her chest and turn and watch as the streak of Taot's flames filled the split in the demon's side as they shot by again. They were already soaring out over the battlefield when the monster blew up, its guts painting the inside of the city wall in disgusting pus-colored hues.

Orli saw spots for a moment as Taot banked, caused more by the last turn than this one, and again they were headed back toward the city's heart, Altin sending spears of ice down into the demons as they flew past the wall, and, like before, it seemed they had very little effect.

There came a sound through the wind then, a high-pitched tone, accompanied by a sensation upon her back. At first she attributed the sound to internal ringing in her ears, a pressure effect as she continued to recover from Taot's rapid shifts in altitude and hard-grinding turns. She attributed the touch upon her back to the movement of her new Prosperion clothing in the wind; she was hardly used to her new attire yet. But the tone came again, three short, equidistant beeps, and the vibration this time was definitely pressed against her back. Where the tablet was tucked into her waistband.

Quickly, she holstered her blaster and pulled the tablet out. A pair of taps and her father's face appeared.

"Orli, girl," he said. "Thank God you are still alive."

"I am. We both are." She had to shout to be heard over the rushing air.

Altin looked back, startled and fearing she'd been injured, but she turned the tablet briefly so that he could see. He nodded and sent instructions to Taot to maintain altitude.

"Are you okay?" she asked when she'd turned the tablet back around. "It's a disaster here. More and more demons are getting over the wall."

"We're not good. But we're holding them off. The *Aspect* and a few other ships are in orbit now. More are coming."

"Tell them to use the ships' lasers to clear off the city walls," Orli shouted over the wind. "Tell them they need to hurry or Crown City is going to fall."

Director Nakamura's face appeared in the lower left quarter of her screen, Captain Asad's in the lower right. "That's actually what we wanted to talk to you about."

Orli had to turn the volume all the way up, and even then she had to bend right down near the tablet to hear, hiding in the relative calm to be found at the base of Altin's back. "Save the city, Asad, you prick," she said as she leaned in. "Do one decent thing in your whole goddamn life."

The director nodded as he spoke. "That is exactly what he will be doing, Ensign, the moment you get your friend the Queen to call off the Hostiles attacking us here on Earth."

"It's not her attacking! For the love of God, how blind can you possibly be? Look at the fucking city." She held the tablet up, tilted down so they could see the battle taking place beyond the city walls. "Do you really think she'd be using any of her power anywhere other than here right now if she had a choice?"

"We know all about the situation there," said the director, perfectly calm, as Orli hunched once again into the shelter of Altin's warm body. "We are prepared to burn the area around the city clear the moment the War Queen does what we ask. Have her call her ally, Blue Fire as you say, and demand that she withdraw her orbs. The moment they leave our system, Crown City will be ready for picnics in the park again."

"They're in the city," Orli pleaded, anger giving way to desperation. "Right now. Look." She held the tablet out again as Taot's flight carried them over a large courtyard near the center of town. The twisted shape of a demon, a crooked mass like a bent bit of lumber, was pulverizing a warhorse as they flew by, its rider already dead, lying in three pieces on the ground not far away. Several townspeople were fleeing down a nearby street, brooms and wood axes in their hands, no longer willing to fight with the loss of the knight. Orli turned the tablet back and looked down into it. "*They* don't have time for this, Director. Don't do this. Don't play this game. People are dying. Innocents."

"Tell it to the *War* Queen," he said, once again putting emphasis on the bellicose title. He sounded exactly like Captain Asad.

Orli's frustration and helplessness came out in one long scream. Altin turned back, as did the dragon whose head rose up and peered down at her over Altin for a moment.

"What do I have to do to convince you Blue Fire has nothing to do with the attack on Earth either? She didn't send the orbs. She's not working with the Queen. Are you really going to let a million people die here just to make a point?"

"Billions of people are going to die, Pewter," spat Captain Asad. "And it's your fault, you and your friends on Prosperion and your pal Goldilocks. You are going to get those people killed if you insist on clinging to naive fantasies while ignoring the obvious truth. We all agree this isn't a game, but it's your powerful friends who are playing one anyway. We never asked for any of this."

"There's no goddamn game," Orli screamed. This time all the volume was in the service of her rage. "What possible benefit is there to killing absolutely everyone? Nobody is that stupid. Not even you, Asad. Clear off the fucking walls. Help those people out there in the fields. They are dying. This is real."

The director's face seemed to pinch in for a moment. Clearly he was thinking. For the barest moment, Orli had hope, but Captain Asad's face was stern as stone. The director saw it, seemed to waver for an instant more, then shook his head negligibly. "When the orbs leave, it will be done," he said, though with perhaps the barest note of regret. "Not before. Talk to the Queen. This channel will remain open for her reply. Hopefully it will come before both planets are destroyed." The director's quarter of the screen went blank.

Captain Asad started to say something, but Orli cut the power to the tablet, uninterested in what he had to say.

"We have to get to Her Majesty," Orli shouted to Altin then. "We have to figure out what to do."

"Her Majesty is out there," he replied, pointing over his shoulder toward the battle raging out in the fields beyond the city gates. "Assuming she's still alive."

A long growl rumbled in her chest, her whole body quaking with the ferocity of it, until it finally released itself in a howl of impotent fury. "Fuck!" she screamed after, as a point of emphasis. "Fuck, fuck, fuck."

Altin, growing used to the alien word, nodded. He'd only snatched bits and pieces of what had been said out of the rushing wind, but from what he had heard, there was little he could do but agree with the sentiment she so violently expressed.

"We have to stop them," she said.

"Stop who?"

"The other Hostiles. The other Hostile world."

"I agree. But how? How many will die if we abandon the streets now, given that the fleet isn't going to help?"

"They're going to die anyway."

Altin grimaced at that bit of cold logic. But part of him knew it was likely true. There was so little time. "We should go find Ocelot. Though I fear how long that might take."

"Why don't we just do what she already told us, do like you said before, go with what we know, what I know: Mars."

"You said there's nothing there. We can't go off hunting around on hope. How many red worlds, how many red suns, did you say there were again? Millions? Billions?"

"Yes. But you said Ocelot is a Z. So, that matters. We're not doing any good here. We're only buying these people time. But for what? Look out there, Altin. This isn't going to end in anyone's favor. Everyone is as good as dead. Everyone! What difference does another hour, another three make, if the end is the same?" That's when she realized she'd cut off her father when she shut down the tablet. "Shit, my father," she said, and set to calling him back.

Altin nodded, chewing on his cheek as he considered what she'd said. "Let me at least see if Ocelot is poking about her home." He set himself immediately to casting the seeing spell.

Orli got her father back quickly enough, and she apologized, though he perfectly understood. "I'm going to do more than cut Asad off when I see him again," the colonel vowed.

"So are you going to be okay?" she asked him. "You saw what they said. I can have Altin come teleport you out."

"The ships will be cutting our guys some room here in a minute or two. And we have more ammunition on the way. Roberto and the other pilots ought to be back soon. We'll be all right."

"You're not really going to help them destroy Prosperion, are you? Asad and the director?"

"Right now I'm just trying to keep my people alive."

"What about these people?" She shoved the tablet out for a moment but was too frustrated to aim it well. He couldn't see but a portion of her arm reaching out into the air, but he got the sense of her meaning as she snatched it back and pressed on. "You're not going to stand there and let them all die? You can't."

"No. I can't, and I won't. If I can help, I will. But there's not much I can do right now. We're pinned down."

"Can't you get the mechs into the city? And the Queen's men you've been working with? Get Roberto to bring you all here. Surely he'll fly you in."

"I don't think flying into the giant tornado of magic those people are casting is a good idea."

"There's not going to *be* a giant tornado of magic in another few hours," she said. "Altin says the Prosperions are going to run out of mana."

"What does that mean?"

"It's the stuff they make magic with, and they're going to use it all up somehow. Altin says it can actually run out. There's a bunch of priests in the middle of the city doing something with a piece of Liquefying Stone right now—the one we lost when we crashed Altin's tower that day. A high priestess in Leekant had it, and she turned it over to the big-shot priests here in Crown this morning. They've started some kind of ritual to funnel mana into the city, which is working according to Altin, but he also says they're still going to run dry. If they run out, the city will fall and the streets will be overrun. At that point, the starships won't be any help at all. Nuking the city or cutting it to ribbons with laser fire isn't really much different than letting the demons tear it up."

"Why didn't you tell the director that? Maybe that would make a difference."

"He would have told me that was another reason why the Queen needs to stop the attack on Earth. You were listening."

The colonel nodded at that. "You're probably right," he said. "A sad truth about politics and power. But this brings brinksmanship to a new low."

"Except that's not what Her Majesty is doing. She's out there stabbing demons with a fucking sword right now. Don't you see? She isn't playing this game with them. There is no game. So will you come? Altin said he saw your guys hammering the demons when he cast his seeing spell. He says you guys are doing better than we are with a tiny fraction of the numbers that we have."

"Yeah, at first we were doing fine, but I've only got a few thousand suits left. It's been grim. We'd need ten times that, probably more, to defend a city street-by-street. A hundred thousand would probably barely be enough given the numbers they have now."

"Earth has a hundred thousand mechs."

"Yeah, well, Earth is a long way away."

"Not for a Prosperion."

"Orli, there's nothing I can do. You need to just stay with Altin, and when it gets too bad, get out of there. The two of you can go to Andalia. Find a place to hide from Asad, because if both worlds go down, you know that's where the fleet is going to go. If he finds you there ... it's never going to end for you. Just be safe, you two at least. Promise me."

She started to protest, but he waved her off. They had another wave of demons climbing up out of the giant trench. "Stay safe," he told her. "I have to go, baby girl. I love you. I'm sorry I ever dragged you into all of this."

"I have a feeling I would have been in it by now either way," she said. "And I love you too." She hated how final that sounded. Again. "Stay safe, and come help us when you can." That seemed better.

He nodded, then cut off the feed. She stared into the empty screen for a moment, fighting off the wave of regret that washed over her, all those years their relationship had been surface only, a fondness conveyed in packets of transmitted video bits. She'd been so selfish all those years, so ungrateful, so careless of what he'd been through. Happy to simply use him as a way to get out of trouble, or to get under Captain Asad's skin. And now it was going to be too late to make it up to him. Unless they figured out where that goddamn other Hostile planet was.

She forced her emotions back and leaned in, speaking over Altin's shoulder. "So what now? We can't just let this all fall apart. What about Mars? Is that just stupid and desperate, or is there a chance we'll find something there?"

Altin shook his head. "No," he said. "It's not stupid, though it may be desperate. It's definitely me being a fool for letting myself get sucked into this fight. I chose the course of action, but not the course of intelligence. The panic of the moment got us both. I hate leaving them like this, but I think you are right. It's the only chance we have, however slim it is."

"You were ordered into this fight," she said defensively. "Things got crazy fast, remember?"

"I do. Let's not waste any more time. I looked for Ocelot, but she's not there. Or she doesn't want to be found. So let's do as you suggested. Let's go to your red planet, Mars, and see what it has to say."

They were at Calico Castle in the time it took her to say, "Okay."

Chapter 32

They stood together looking out through the narrow window of Tytamon's great tower, Altin shaking his head as they beheld the incredible cloud of Hostiles swarming above the Earth, and Orli covering her mouth in absolute disbelief.

"They are fools to think this is any doing of the Queen," he said. "But I don't blame them for blaming Blue Fire."

Not mine, came the distant voice in his head.

"Yes, I know." He spoke it as well as sending the thought, for Orli's benefit, even though she could not hear what Blue Fire had to say.

"What do you know?" Orli asked, tearing her gaze away from the crumbling wreck of fire that of one of the few remaining Juggernaut-class war ships within their view had become. She'd been transfixed by the tiny flecks of debris spewing out of its broken bays and cracked open corridors, like crystallized blood from exposed capillaries, sparkling in the light of the distant sun like flashing gems. Tens of thousands of men and women had died just then, were dying as they watched. A shudder ran through her as she looked up into Altin's face.

"Blue Fire didn't send them. She must have read my

thoughts." He half expected Blue Fire to confirm it, but she did not. "Where is your red world from here?"

"Let me look." She still held her tablet, but it was the work of several minutes to find a satellite she could access. "They've destroyed most of the net feeds," she said. "There are hardly any satellites left. This one isn't even in English."

"I don't know what that is."

"My language. I know enough Spanish from Roberto to get by. Give me a second." She poked at the tablet for a time while Altin looked back out the window. A starship that looked just like the *Aspect*, the place he'd first met Orli, blew up at the eastern edge of Earth's blue disk. His thoughts, like Orli's, could not help but tally up the loss of life.

"Got it," she said. "We're on the wrong side of the sun."

Altin didn't need to ask questions about that, and he immediately cast a seeing spell and sent it plunging toward the sun, Sol, light of the beleaguered Earth. He took an angle just over its northern pole and tempered how much brilliance he would allow as he passed over it. With no seeing stones to use for this, he found himself grateful for the time he'd spent trying to catch up with the fleet ships several months ago, so long ago now it seemed, back when they'd been fleeing from Blue Fire and her orbs, before they'd known there was a Blue Fire at all. That was when Blue Fire was simply a Hostile. Like the new enemy they faced. Just Hostile. He couldn't help wonder as he pushed his vision along at meteoric speeds if this other Hostile might not be like her, if it might not be making a terrible mistake. However it had found Earth, perhaps it could be reasoned with as well. Assuming they could find it.

It was still a long bit of work for Altin to get past the sun, nearly forty minutes, and he was half tempted to stop and just go make a few seeing stones, but every time he thought about stopping, every time he imagined himself and Orli running around looking for river rocks, he shook the idea off, unwilling to waste the time. At least two hours if not more. He hoped this decision wouldn't be disastrous, but such was the nature of decision making during crisis.

Finally he was well over the sun, far enough that he thought the star posed no threat to the integrity of the protective shielding he'd cast over the tower, the tower that should still be Tytamon's ... so much lost life recently. He pulled out of the spell, and before even mentioning it to Orli, he teleported the tower to where his magic sight had been.

"Here," he said, even as Orli's indrawn breath revealed that she already knew they had moved. "We're on the other side. I've oriented this window facing straight away. Your sun is somewhat near and directly through that wall." He pointed across the circular chamber to where it was. "So where is Mars?"

Orli turned back and leaned through the window, feeling as she did as if she were about to stuff her face into empty space. Survival instincts willed her body to stop, but she reached out to the sides and grabbed hold, pushing past the natural fear. In doing so, she nearly knocked a decanter off the edge of the windowsill, a beautiful thing crafted to look like a pair of palm trees whose glass-flute trunks had wound around one another as they grew. It teetered there on the narrow stone ledge, began to fall, but she scrambled to catch it, grasping it by the stopper just before it fell. It was heavier than it looked, and the palm fronds of its stopper, like jagged blades of flat green glass, jabbed into her hand, causing her to nearly drop it anyway. But she got her other hand under it and managed neither to drop it nor smash it against the wall.

She straightened herself, holding it steadily, and studied for a moment, fearful that she might have come close to breaking some dangerous or powerful artifact. She handed it to Altin apologetically, expecting some word of warning from him, which did not come. He only shrugged, gesturing with a movement of his head to the stack of artifacts lying in a heap near the table. "I've done worse," he said.

The palm fronds of the stopper spun easily as he took it from her, by design he thought, like a child's toy for a windy day, but he could tell it was not a thing for children. It was far too stout, despite its apparent delicacy. By workmanship alone, it was obviously a thing of the elves. But whatever had been in it was gone now, and there was no sign of what might have been, nor was there any way to gauge how old it was. But it was pretty, and it had belonged to Tytamon. In times like these, times of such destruction and misery, he couldn't bring himself to treat it roughly or toss it aside like he had those others not so long ago.

As he set it on the table, it made him think of Tytamon. He wished Tytamon were there. They needed him. And he missed him terribly. He realized as his eyes lingered on the decanter that he'd never really faced his grief. He gazed down at the object, both recognizing it as a thing he'd gazed upon absently a thousand times before and yet really only seeing it for the first time now. How many times had he noticed it over the years and not asked about it? How many times had he noticed any of it, any of the many things in this room? How little time he'd spent learning about Tytamon, the person, the friend. How little effort he'd put in. He wished he could have just one hour with him now. One hour back to ask about the decanter, or any little thing. But now it was too late. He hadn't taken the time. Not for Tytamon, not for anyone. And now everyone might be gone. Oh, how he wished Tytamon were there. If not for his own regrets, for the sake of all those in peril now. Tytamon would have known what to do. He might have prevented it all from getting so far out of hand.

Altin shook his head ruefully at the decanter sitting there, sending a silent apology to his lost mentor for all that had gone wrong on his brief watch. He gently spun the fronds again, watching them turn for the barest moment, and then, with a sigh, went back to Orli, who had stretched herself through the window again.

She was practically hanging out of it, leaning so far out he was afraid she would fall. It was many floors to the scant stretch of stone below. Just as he was reaching for her, she shouted, "There!" Her proclamation was triumphant, evidence of success. She pointed into the night. "Right there. That one. In that clump of four bright ones. See it? The one that looks like a really big red star."

Altin bent at the knees and stared down her arm, sighting the length of her finger as if it were a quarrel and her arm a crossbow. He still had to look around a little, but he spotted it quickly enough. "Got it."

Once more he was in a seeing spell.

Shortly after, they arrived in a low orbit, and Altin immediately remarked how much Mars reminded him of Luria back at home.

They stared out the window for several minutes, shoulders touching, hands touching where they lay side-by-side upon the stone of the windowsill. They watched intently but soon realized there was nothing going on.

"So what are we looking for?" Altin asked. "I don't see a thing. There are no clouds of coconuts flying around destroying anything. There are none of your ships flying around in a way that suggests some sense of urgency.

Which means we probably need to go down to the surface, eh?"

"Let's check the other side. Victoria is the biggest base here anyway. Then we can check on the water stations at the poles. And just in case you do decide to go down there without asking me first, there's no air down there, so it is like Luria in that."

Altin nodded, but his expression was grim. He hated wasting more time pushing his sight around, but he didn't waste time getting to it. In less than a minute, he had found the other side of Mars.

"Gods be damned," he swore as he came out of the spell. "I think I know why we are here."

"Why?"

"Look," he said, then cast a teleport spell that took them halfway around the red planet. "There."

She didn't need him to point out the colossal Hostile orb orbiting there. She couldn't have missed it if she'd tried. "My God, look at it. It's huge. And over there, look; there are little ones coming off of it." She let go a bewildered breath as she stared out at it. "How big do you think that thing is?"

"I don't know how big this planet is," Altin answered honestly. He'd learned from his discovery of Naotatica that gauging the size of a planet was not an easy thing to do, a difficulty that explained much of the meticulous measuring habits the Earth people had when it came to traveling in space. "Nor do I know how far away we are. Scale is difficult out here, but it has to be approaching six hundred measures across."

She nodded. "Probably not a bad guess. I don't suppose you can just teleport it into the sun, can you?"

His face withered, and he made a squishy dismissive sound with his lips. "No chance. Far too much mass for me in something like that."

She watched as tiny specks, like motes of dust, moved off of its surface and shot away, at first toward Mars, or so it appeared from the angle she had been looking at it, but she soon realized they were going right by and heading toward the sun. "You seeing that?" she asked. "There's a little ant trail of those things leaking out that way."

Sure enough, a faint line of the small Hostile orbs—which only moments before would have counted as normal-sized in their sense of the things—was steadily making its ragged way out over the northern pole of Mars and straight off toward the center of the solar system.

"What do you think the odds are that this is where the orbs attacking Earth are coming from?"

"I have no idea what the odds are," he said, "but I do know how we can find out. I'll follow one."

"They're moving pretty fast. Do you think you can catch one?"

"Oh, I have a trick for that," Altin said, thinking of a spell he'd recently learned called Wake Sight, a powerful pursuit spell developed by a lowly-seeming C-ranked caster by the name of Speekes Beeglethorpe. "I knew that spell was genius when I saw it the first time."

Once again the cast was instant, and soon his sight was streaking toward the unspeakably huge Hostile they'd found lurking behind Mars, sending its smaller orb minions off in the direction of Earth—unless it was doing something nefarious to the sun. There was only one way to find out.

When his magical vision arrived upon the surface of the colossus, he couldn't stop the gasp that emitted itself from his distant body.

The orb was as they'd thought or, more precisely, as they'd feared: nearly six hundred measures across, large beyond any Hostile they'd seen before. Its surface was exactly as the others were, if perhaps a bit rougher and redder. The only real difference was its size. He did not want to think about how large the projectile shaft this orb could throw would be, but he was certain it would eradicate everything on Earth if it decided to pulverize the planet. His lessons from Orli on meteor impacts and even the missile attacks her people were capable of had taught him enough on that. Which meant, since it was here, that it didn't want to pulverize *everything* on Earth. A frighteningly familiar story shaped itself from that.

He had to slow his pace considerably as he cruised along the surface of it, which once again reminded him of his first days in space, his first exploration of Luria, pushing his vision along its red surface. Things had certainly gone wrong since that propitious-seeming time. He had been such an innocent. So naive. About literally everything.

As he cruised over the giant orb's surface, he noticed a pockmark forming itself, not unlike the craters he'd seen on Luria. Except this one was forming as he approached.

Suddenly the surface of the giant Hostile buckled, then fell away, as if a sinkhole had opened up. A perfectly circular orifice shaped itself, and then from it, like coral letting loose an egg into the sea, a Hostile popped out. A "regular" one, he thought to himself as it streaked off, maybe seventy spans in diameter.

He tried to catch it, but it was already too late, it gained speed rapidly, and by the time his wonderment at its formation gave way to lucidity and the point for his being here, it was already out of reach.

He did, however, have the advantage of now knowing how the Hostiles formed, so he simply moved around long enough to find another fissure in the process of opening. When he saw it, the tell-tale pockmark shaping suddenly, he shot himself over to it, observed the flesh-soil of the Hostile falling in and then doming at the bottom of the new crater, the new Hostile emerging like the crown of a child just being born. And as easily as that, he attached the Wake Sight spell to it.

In moments, he was streaking toward the sun, this time heading the way that he had come and at the speed of the Hostile to which his sight was bound. The Hostile he trailed soon joined with others coming up off of other parts of the enormous "mother" orb, and by the time Mars was fading in size behind him, he was part of the ant trail Orli had spoken of.

He oriented his vision forward as they approached the sun, and he half expected to plunge into the brilliance of the burning sphere as he got close. But he did not. Instead, and much as he had done earlier, the Hostile took an angle over the sun, on a curving but direct line straight to the other side. They were definitely heading past it.

Soon the sun was behind him. He couldn't be sure where Earth was yet, but there were three bright stars ahead, any of which might be the world that had given him Orli. One of them grew brighter and brighter with greater rapidity than the rest, and he nodded, or his body far behind him did, as he determined that must be Earth.

But not long after, that bright light began to move to his right, drifting slowly farther out of the direct line of the Hostiles' course until it was finally whipping by in the distance, closer than before, definitely round and planetary, but not with the least trace of blue. It wasn't Earth. He figured it must be an inner planet, just as his own solar system had planets that resided inside the ring of Prosperion's orbit. Which meant he still had to wait.

He turned his attention from the planet and again looked directly ahead. One of the stars before him did seem to have a bit of blue to it. In the time he had to watch it, it made him think of Blue Fire and of the blue star that had given life to her lover, the lover that she had lost. It seemed there was a lot of red and blue in the universe.

Thinking of Blue Fire and her lover filled him with sorrow, and the more he thought on them, the worse it got. Soon the sorrow became alarmingly profound, oppressive and crushing. Which is when he realized it wasn't his. Blue Fire had sensed his thoughts and was filling him with her unfathomable lament.

No, he thought at her. *Get out of my head. I'll lose the spell.*

Blue Fire faded once more away, the presence of her vast sadness draining from him as if from a great basin of private agony.

Free to think his own thoughts properly again, he realized that the Hostiles he was following were coming together with another glittering line of them, another ant trail, the two merging like streams and becoming a river in the black emptiness of space. He could trace the new line back in the direction of the planet he'd just passed, and he wondered if there wasn't another giant orb there, an orb like the one hiding behind Mars, sending its own spherical warriors against the people of Earth.

Soon enough the second bright light of the three "stars" appeared big enough and far enough to his left that he knew it was yet another inner world. Like the last, it was not blue as he knew Earth would be, but was still bright and circular just the same, if only in the smallest measure his eye could make. It must have been much farther off than the last one had been.

He flew on in the endless silence for a few minutes more and was not surprised to encounter another line of Hostiles joining from off to his left. Three tributaries converging into one steady river of death.

Soon enough, the blue "star" of earth finally shaped itself round as well, and at length there could be no doubt what it was and what was happening to it. The giant

Hostiles were sending orbs at Earth, adding to the already absurd number of its attackers from three giant sources hiding behind nearby planets. It was clear enough to Altin that Earth had no chance of staving all that off. They weren't even fighting the one at Mars, despite Orli's having mentioned the existence of bases there. He released the seeing spell and returned his vision to his own eyes. He quickly related everything he'd just seen to Orli, who looked mortified as she heard.

"That's it then," he said when he was done. "If this is what Ocelot wanted me to find, then, well, we found it. Now we know Earth is doomed to Andalia's fate, and Kurr to that of Duador." He had to laugh at that, though it was a dismal sound. "I wonder what the elves will do now that they are all alone on String. I guess they win. The last man standing."

"Not if we can stop it," Orli said. "There must be something we can do. You said Ocelot told you to bring me here. She said bring me here 'or else' everyone will die. Right?"

Altin nodded. "If this is the right red world."

"Then there is something we can do."

"I'm afraid you have more faith in her than I do at this point."

"No. I'm just tired of everyone screwing up my life, and I'm not going to roll over and die. So think. Use that big size Seven brain of yours and help me figure this out."

Altin laughed again, this one touched by at least some vestige of mirth. If he had to die, if all the worlds were ending and there was nothing to be done, at least he would finish his life beside her. Given the circumstances, he couldn't think of a better way to go. "All right, General Pewter, what's your plan?"

"Don't 'general' me. I'm in no one's fleet now, remember? I'll settle for one of those 'Lady' titles from your world when we work this out. Now quit screwing around and think. People are dying."

She was right, and her words sobered him.

"Blue Fire," he said. "Gods, I'm dumb as rocks." He sent the thought, but Blue Fire had already heard. He spoke his thoughts aloud. "You saw what I saw. Who is it? What world is that? Is it someone you know?"

Not know.

"Well, you must know something. More than us anyway? Think!" He echoed the inflection of Orli's last words.

He saw then, in his mind's eye, an image of himself standing naked on the ledge deep inside the world where Blue Fire lived, the world that she was. She projected that almost violently into his thoughts, just him, standing on that ledge.

"I see it," he said as she pressed the image insistently. "Yes, me, there. What about it? A ledge. Me on the ledge." He scoured the memory that was his own. He'd been far inside the planet, deep below, guided there by a glowing emissary of some kind. He sent the image of that thing, the stretching, amorphous wheel that had led him down into the darkness. "That thing?" he asked.

No. The negativity shook inside his mind. She remade the image of him standing there on the ledge.

He frowned. "Yes, me. On the ledge. The huge space of your outer chamber. Lots of Liquefying Stone. Is it Liquefying Stone?"

He saw a blue star then. It came upon a mixed wave of love and grief.

"Blue Fire. Your Blue Fire. It's your husband, I get it," he said, his impatience obvious. "It's another Hostile. Is that what you're saying? We already know that." He felt bad for using the pejorative term, but what else was there?

No, she thundered in his mind. Once again he saw the

image of himself on the ledge. Then he saw Orli standing there. Naked too. He'd never seen that before. He was struck by how beautiful she was. But no sooner had he seen it and realized what he was seeing, Blue Fire snatched the image away. There was negativity to the removal then, harshness. Once again he saw himself standing naked at the edge of the precipice, alone, though this time the blue star of Blue Fire's lover hovered in the darkness at his back.

Still nothing made sense. She repeated the sequence, adding Orli, then taking her away. Always nude.

Finally it hit him. "By the gods I am dim as a cave. It's a male. The Hostile attacking Earth is male."

Blue Fire's emotions told him he was right.

He turned to Orli. "She says this one is male."

Orli nodded that she'd heard. Altin's eyes lingered on her then, his gaze tracing the line of her throat, over the exposed flesh above the line of her blouse, which clung to her shoulders low in the southern style of Kurr. He looked down to the rest of her, his expression shaped by a fleeting hunger spawned by the things he'd just seen. In that moment he forgot himself, and his thoughts ran freely, in his mind and upon his face, if only for the span of that one glance.

"Oh, you have to be kidding me," Orli said upon seeing it. "Now? Of all the times we've had, of all the beaches and all the hours and hours we've had alone on your world, now is when you look at me like that?"

Altin shook himself. He grinned a sideways thing. "Yes," he said. "I guess we're no longer on Prosperion." He could not pursue it further, however, for the press of so much peril came creeping back like cold fog to smother the warmth of the exchange. "So now we know that much. Can you think of why that might help?"

Orli shook her head at first, but turned and walked

about the room, stepping around and over fallen works of Tytamon's magical contrivances without seeing them at all. She bypassed artifacts of most ancient Prosperion history, pushing aside this wicker weave, the work of people ten thousand years dead and gone, bumping aside that book, some dusty tome filled with pressed flowers from a place where long-extinct creatures had once roamed spectacularly, not even knowing what treasures she ignored as she passed them by. "Maybe it isn't me that needs to know. Maybe it's your friend, Ocelot. Or even just that priest with the big hammer, the one from Leekant that you said found your stone. She's a diviner, right? And of course there's Doctor Leopold. Maybe this is what they need to know."

Altin nodded. "You're probably right. But divining takes forever. I don't think we have that kind of time. In fact, I'm sure of it. And it's still nothing to go on, really. What does gender change? And even if it was significant in some way for the findings of a divination spell, it would still have to be a powerful one, which means hours and hours at best. Doctor Leopold spent several hours the last time I asked him for help, and some spells take days."

Orli made a face at him, pushing out her lips in an elongated pout. "You're so negative, sometimes," she said. "We can at least go back and ask."

"We can," he agreed, "but that will also eat up time. Neither planet can afford to wait."

"Then let's buy them time," she said. "If these big Hostiles are supplying the reinforcements, let's get rid of them. Are you totally sure you can't send that thing into the sun? Or even just send it farther away so it takes them longer to get to Earth? Even just to try? Maybe if we can do at least that much, we can convince Director Nakamura that the Queen is genuinely trying to help, maybe even prove her innocence. Then the starships at Prosperion can hose down the walls of Crown with lasers and drop a few tactical nukes into that demon orgasm that's happening out on the plains. We might even buy enough time to send your guys to Earth to teleport more Marines to Prosperion to defend the city, even to save it." Her voice rose in pace and pitch the entire time she spoke. "Altin, it really could work."

Hope lit her beautiful face with such radiance. She was so exquisite to look upon, her blue eyes sparkling as she stared up at him, the lights of the nearby candles glinting golden in the satin hair that framed her loveliness. He hated to dash her hopes. But he had to. "It can't be done. It's too big; the mass would be well beyond me."

"What about the mages on *Citadel*? Get Aderbury. Get all those guys, and the weird guy in the red suit."

"Even they couldn't do it. There aren't enough of them."

"You can help them. You're a Z. You're the most powerful wizard on your planet, damn it. Surely there's something you can do. Use the goddamn ring Blue Fire gave you. Or something else I don't know about. Please, you at least have to try."

The *no* that had begun to form on Altin's lips stopped, and for a moment he froze as if turned to stone. He looked down at his ring and slowly began to nod.

"Blue Fire," he said slowly, to Orli but also to the being by that name, speaking with his thoughts to her. "Can you help us? Can you help me like you helped me with the fleet? Your power should be enough to send this thing away. Help us fight."

Not fight. She followed that with the essence of dread, of feebleness. He saw himself once more standing naked upon the ledge, the blue sun of Blue Fire's mate at his shoulder again.

"What do you mean, 'not fight'? You fought with me before. We sent the fleet all the way back to Earth."

The thought came as simply a negative, again with the image of him and the blue sun.

Altin growled, frustrated. He didn't have time for another set of Blue Fire's riddles. "Fine, then give us Liquefying Stone. Will you supply us with enough for *Citadel*? At least that?" He sent an image of the concert hall on *Citadel* filled with mages, each of them holding a piece of the yellow stone.

His mind, his heart, what felt like it must be his very soul, filled with hatred, envy and greed. It flooded with avarice, lust and need. The wave of it all buckled his knees, and he fell to the floor, clutching his head, shouting, "No!" But despite his plea for her to stop, on it came, a great blast of such horrible emotion, such awfulness, all he could do was collapse and curl into a ball.

The onslaught went on for what seemed like forever, all the while Orli kneeling beside him, shouting his name at first and then weeping, crying out into the void for Blue Fire to stop whatever she was doing to him. But on and on it went, Altin writhing in his fetal knot, shaking, sweating, tears running from the open faucets of his tightly shut eyes.

But at last it abated. The torrent of human depravity went away. It was replaced by the images of the humans Blue Fire had come to know, Altin, Orli, and the priests of Anvilwrath. All twenty-five of them and High Priestess Maul. There was even a flicker of Thadius Thoroughgood's face, though she'd only known him through the images in Orli's mind, the taste of his elixir left in the mana cloud that had poisoned Orli's mind.

Altin came out of it trembling and looked up through horrified eyes at Orli bending over him. She pulled him to her, clutching his head to her breast and holding him tightly. He sobbed for a while, his body shaking and wracked by flashes of memory. His robes were damp with sweat.

Finally he calmed himself, his wits returning to him, and at length, he could think again.

"Are you okay?" Orli asked, hating how empty that question seemed. "I thought she was trying to kill you."

"I think she nearly did," he said, his voice weak, his body still twitching in her arms.

Eventually she helped him to his feet and together they got him into a chair. She stroked his damp hair as he fought to breathe normally. Many more minutes passed before he spoke again.

"She knows what my people will do with them," he said at last. "She knows the forces of greed and lust that humanity will set loose with the Liquefying Stones if they are given out."

"They won't," Orli protested. "This is serious. And we're not all like that."

"We are. Look what we did to the dwarves, and we didn't even have the Liquefying Stone at all. And think of it; look what the orcs have done with only two stones. Imagine a thousand stones in the hands of a people capable of doing what the orcs are doing now. What we did at Duador. Them or us. There's no difference in the end. Only the stories we tell ourselves when it's done."

Her cheeks flushed red. She could see the emotions Blue Fire sent were smothering his ability to reason. "So what you're saying, what you're both saying, is that, for fear of your people killing themselves, we should just let them die." Her eyes widened, bewildered, and she gasped at the very idea. "That doesn't make any sense, Altin. You're not thinking it through right now." She turned and stormed to the window, blowing out an exasperated breath. "Tell Blue Fire that Altin Love thinks she's making a mistake. Tell her Altin Love thinks Blue Fire is going to do on purpose what she did by accident to the Andalians.

341

Tell her I said she's about to add two more worlds and billions and billions of lives to the list of deaths she's caused. Tell her I said I think that's bullshit. Tell her I think she's just as bad as any humans have ever been."

Frustrated tears ran down Orli's cheeks but she wiped them away angrily. She would not let Altin see them. She had to be strong, she had to stay strong, but this felt like one blow too many for her to take, one too many punches in this whole big fighting joke of a universe. The stupid joke of absent gods laughing at the futile plight of the feeble creatures who never even knew if they were real. She was so sick of feeling helpless all the time.

She stared for a long time out the window, her thoughts running through memories and time. She wondered if Roberto was still alive. If her father was. She hoped Asad was dead but had to take it back. He would take others with him if he died. At least by an attack on the ship. She wondered what kind of person it made her for thinking that, for wishing such hateful thoughts. Maybe Blue Fire *was* right. Maybe it was better if humanity was gone.

She caught herself and shook the feelings off. She liked to think she was one of the good ones amongst her race, and look where she had gone almost in the same breath in which she'd tried to argue that not all humanity was so bad. She had to keep it together.

That's when Altin's voice broke into her silent reverie.

"She said she'll do it," Altin said. "She says you are right. But first, let's go talk to Maul."

342

Chapter 33

Altin stood beneath the vast crimson dome of *Citadel*'s concert hall, the tentacles on the dome's ceiling high above writhing slowly like golden snakes warming in the morning sun. He was explaining the nature of the Liquefying Stone to the *Citadel* mages, trying as he did to convey the nature of the danger they all now faced. Conduit Huzzledorf, seated as always on the plush upholstery of the ottoman that occupied the very center of the room, turning slowly round as it did and making him seem as if he were some crimson-clad doll on display, seemed bored and impatient to carry on. When Altin began what would have been his fourth repetition of the facts, starting once more to explain how fast the mana would come to them, the conduit could finally take it no more.

"Sir Altin," he said, running his hands through the frizzy fringe of white hair that, if one counted his eyebrows in the mix, ringed his head nearly perfectly, "you've made it quite clear already. And it won't be them casting, it will be me, so all will be well. Have Miss Pewter hand them out and let's be on with it."

"Not until we are there," Altin said. He looked to Orli,

who stood next to him with a small wooden chest at her feet, the container provided by High Priestess Maul at the conclusion of their visit with her in Crown City. The box held the Liquefying Stones that Blue Fire had given them. The chest was filled with eight hundred bits of the frightfully potent yellow stone, one for each mage in the concert hall.

He looked back up into the chamber, so many faces staring down at him that it made his time teaching at the university seem like an intimate gathering. But he didn't have time to be uncomfortable. "Does anyone have questions? There are no stupid questions, and if you have one you don't ask, you are stupid, because, as I have said several times, we will all die for your ignorance. Contrary to the conduit's confidence, the fact that *you* are channeling the mana matters almost entirely. You pull too much, it's over."

"As a motivational speaker, Sir Altin, I have to say you are terrible." This of course came from the conduit, whose rotation upon the ottoman had him facing the other way, and since he did not deign to turn his head, it seemed as if he were speaking to himself in his own reflection in the chamber's giant bronze doors. He waited until the rotation brought him around far enough that he could look up at the Galactic Mage and raise his eyebrows at him with an irritated air. "Would you like me to get them in a more suitable mood for this undertaking, now that you have sucked all the enthusiasm from the room?"

"No. I would not." He reached a hand out toward the conduit, his fingers opening and closing twice in a row, rapidly, demanding. "Give me a seeing stone."

"I am perfectly capable of casting the seeing stones for *Citadel*, young man," said the conduit.

"Give me the gods-be-damned stone," Altin nearly yelled. "There is no time."

The violence of Altin's command startled the normally implacable conduit, and he reached into a leather satchel that he wore and pulled out a diamond the size of an avocado seed. "No need to get snappish, young man. I won't tolerate much of that, you know."

Altin ignored him, and in the span of an instant the diamond was gone, leaving the conduit to stare, blinking, into Altin's empty hand. Altin glared down at him and gave the barest of nods, all but imperceptible. "Now, Conduit, you may take us to where that stone has gone."

The conduit was still gaping wide-eyed into the space where the seeing stone had vanished without Altin's having uttered a single word, but he pulled himself together straight away. "Cebelle, let Aderbury know we're moving," he began, speaking to the concert's primary telepath. "Teleporters get ready. Seers get me that stone. Let's go, people, let's go."

Orli watched in awe as the concert hall mages came to order, and then, looking rather like slices of a colorful pie in the sections where they sat together in matching guild robes, they all moved in unison by school. The gray-robed teleporters sat swaying slightly in their seats, their hands on their laps, their lips sequenced so perfectly they might well have been reflections of a single mouth. The seers in their ochre robes also sat swaying and singing a single song, though their hands were uniformly out before them with fingers splayed, reaching together as if searching for something. The other sections of the hall sat completely motionless, coming at the call of the conduit to stone-like rigidity, no one even so much as twitching or tapping a toe. All eyes were closed, all waiting for the call for mana channeling if required.

"Aderbury is with us now, Conduit," reported Cebelle. Her eyes were still closed as she spoke from her place at the front row of the seers' section, veins like purple roads on a parchment map visible through the thin skin of her ancient eyelids. "We can go."

Conduit Huzzledorf looked straight up then, right into the center of the tentacles twisting slowly above him. His eyes, unlike the concert mages', were wide open, staring upward as if he saw something in the core of those groping ropes that mortified him.

Orli watched him and could not stop the reflex that made her grip Altin's arm tightly in her hands. There was something terrifying in the conduit's look. Something psychotic, she thought. Suddenly she was frightened of the idea that the red-clad man with the crazy fringes of hair and the slightly insane look in his eyes would be the one casting the spell that would carry her across the universe. He struck her as unstable, broken even, his wild-eyed expression seeming near madness or, perhaps worse, mad with a love for power.

And then it was done. His eyes snapped shut, then reopened purposefully, blinking a few more times. He looked to Altin and announced, "All right, we're here. Now hand them out, my boy."

Altin ignored the pejorative, but this time Orli did not. It ignited her anger inexplicably. She nearly leapt upon the man. "Knock it off with that crap already," she snarled through clenched teeth, her face pressed almost into his. "Sir Altin is here to save your sorry ass and the asses of everyone else on your damn planet. Show him some respect. You forget whose ship this is and what your place is on it."

Altin put a hand on her shoulder and smiled at her, shaking his head in a way that said it was okay. He didn't want to have to explain the nature of conduits to her, and there was no amount of reason that would make one of the enigmatic mana handlers behave socially anyway, at least not in any consistent or predictable way, much less get them to properly abide by the structures of military discipline. Even the Queen put up with a great deal of insolence from them. They were a sort of magical celebrity, oddities that were well aware of their usefulness and, like mad artists in their way, prone to misbehave.

Fortunately, they were also the sort of creatures who did not care if they were yelled at or insulted very often, at least not when it was convenient to be so cavalier, and so Conduit Huzzledorf only laughed a merry laugh and clapped Altin on the arm, saying, "There's a keeper for you, lad. She'll fight your fights for you, and you can lie about the house eating confectioner's delights and reading low literature as you please."

Altin ignored that as well and nodded down to the box sitting at Orli's feet. "Let's hand them out." He stooped and opened the chest, then loaded his pockets with as many as he could carry comfortably. With his pockets full, and his robes hanging heavily for it, he then took a large handful to carry as well. "I'll start up there," he said, pointing with his chin to the pie-slice section of seats to the left of the concert hall's large brass doors. "You start back there, Orli, and Conduit, if you would be so kind as to split the difference and get the healers' and illusionists' sections."

The conduit made a big fuss about being told what to do by "children," but he complied, filling a pouch on the front of his satchel with handfuls of the Liquefying Stone until there were only two layers of the crystals left, stacked neatly in rows in the bottom of the chest. Orli picked the chest up, which was still quite heavy, and went to the section of the room she'd been assigned to, climbing the stairs and directing the nearest mage on each side of the aisle to take one and pass it down until the whole row had been given a stone.

"Not one breath of magic," Altin must have said at least twenty times before the whole room had been equipped.

"Don't let them touch your skin until you need them. And not one single syllable of magic until you are all linked to Conduit here. If anyone so much as tries to light a pipe with a summoned flame, we will all be incinerated on the spot."

Everyone nodded that they understood, and any marginally close observer of humanity could see fear on more than a few faces in the room.

"Let's get the illusion up, Cebelle," Altin said, "so everyone can see what we are up against. Don't touch the Liquefying Stone while you do it."

The old woman nodded at him, as if grateful for that reminder, redundant as it was, but the conduit protested in his way. "Sir Altin, if you don't need me anymore, perhaps I shall go have a nice hot bath."

"Oh, for God's sake, Conduit," said Orli. "There are two worlds at stake. Give it a rest."

"No, he's right," said Altin, trying to be diplomatic. "I'm sorry, Conduit. You know your job. Please carry on."

Counting that a victory, the conduit looked as if he might press the issue, but Orli took a step forward looking as if she might throttle him on the spot, so he refrained. He returned to his seat upon the slowly turning ottoman, and tilted his gaze up into the air above him expectantly.

The low notes of Cebelle's chanting soon became the only sound in the room, the lights dimmed, not that Orli could have identified where those lights came from to begin, and soon the large glowing globe of red Mars filled a space in the air ten paces in diameter above the conduit's head. Orli heard several mages mutter, "Luria," under their breath.

Mars rotated slowly in the illusion, which struck Orli as being much like a hologram, and orbiting the planet were its two small moons, Phobos and Deimos, both visible just now. Orli wondered if, given the absence of the giant Hostile in the scene, perhaps it had left. But then that too entered the image hanging in the air, dwarfing the two rocky lumps of Mars' circuitous companions like a starship might dwarf crew carriers docked next to it in port. And even in this illusionary image, seeing how big the Hostile beside Mars was triggered more than a tingling sense of dread. She nervously wondered if perhaps all of *Citadel*'s mages, even with Liquefying Stones in hand, could possibly be enough. Had she been too hopeful in assuming it? While they had been in the cavern on Blue Fire's world getting the yellow stones, Altin had made it more than clear that in all likelihood, the mages were going to kill themselves.

"Let us begin," Conduit Huzzledorf said, holding aloft one of the big diamonds from his satchel. "Seers get this seeing stone now, before it goes. Sir Altin tells me it may disappear fairly quickly once it arrives at the sun. Apparently that thing is rather hot." A few mages laughed at his joke, but most were either too nervous or too terrified to be amused.

So began the process of getting *place* for the teleporters, using a seeing stone to find a place of familiarity into which they were going to try to teleport that vast Hostile orb. Before they could send the orb into the sun, they had to know where they were going to send it, and they all had to know it if they were going to send something that big that far. That was step one.

The first seeing stone was cast, but as soon as it was gone, all the seers let out a collective moan, the sound of a hundred disappointed casters all as one.

"Try it again, people. I told you to look fast. Pay attention."

As Altin waited, leaning against the stool in the central ring of seats where the lead casters from each school sat, a circle that ran around the conduit's ottoman, he got a telepathic nudge from Aderbury, who was far above the concert hall, manning his post in the tower that looked down upon the assembled redoubts and out into the space beyond *Citadel*'s protective shell.

"My people want to take the redoubts out and go help the fleet ships fighting above Earth," Aderbury said. "They're getting antsy up here. Do you need us for this?"

"Tell them they need to wait. We need to contact Director Nakamura first. Our redoubts will still be fired upon if they go out right now. Wait till this works. Orli will contact them on her mirror and make sure they are going to cooperate."

"If they don't?"

"Well, let us hope they do. I'll let you know."

Aderbury let go of the tendril that connected their thoughts, and Altin turned to see how the conduit's seeing went. Another of the enchanted diamonds had just left Conduit Huzzledorf's hand. Not long after, three voices shouted, "I've got it." One other said, "I think I saw it too."

Conduit Huzzledorf looked annoyed and, in a little fit of impatience, mussed the already-spastic frazzle of his hair with his hands. "For the love of Mercy, we're going to spend all day on the easy part," he growled. "Let's do this properly, people, so we can get to the Liquefying Stones."

Altin wanted to jump in with a warning, to point out that eagerness was a terrible idea, but he knew that would be a bad idea too. There was no point in pointing it out again, nor was there any point in arguing with the man. Besides, who knew what kind of difference having a conduit could make while using the Liquefying Stone. Perhaps Altin was worrying about nothing now—though he sorely doubted it.

He was half tempted to take Orli back to Tytamon's tower, just in case something went horribly wrong, but he'd vowed never to leave her like that again. They would face the danger together from now on—together, so that he could keep her safe.

Several more attempts to cast seeing stones into the sun were made, each in hopes that the seers could find them before they evaporated, and eventually all but four of the concert hall seers had found the place before the diamond was gone.

"Good enough," the conduit announced. "You four can sit it out since you obviously can't handle it."

Orli's mouth dropped open in her horror at how rude that was, but Altin was nodding that he agreed. They didn't have time for weakness or incompetence because they didn't have time at all. Now was not the time to mollycoddle people just so they could feel good about themselves.

"Healers get your sections now, and watch for injuries," ordered the conduit. "Diviners, stay ahead of them so they don't have to guess. Seers link the new place. Teleporters shape it; Sir Altin has the lead. Everyone, in order, you know how channeling works. Let's go, let's go." He watched as the sections shuffled and shifted in their seats, nerves calming, and finally the room was ready for the attempt. "Get your stones, people. Let's hitch the teams and quarter this titan."

Altin waited until he saw the rest of the room had closed its eyes. He glanced back at Orli one time and smiled, a wan thing with love in his eyes, then turned to face the conduit who was watching him, waiting with an eyebrow raised. Altin nodded and closed his eyes.

Orli watched the two exchange the look, and she saw, or thought she saw at least for a moment, a look of humility flash upon the conduit's face, as if, in that one moment, he was willing to let Altin know that he too was afraid. She couldn't decide if that made her feel better or not, but at least it made the crimson-clad man seem human again.

Twelve mages fell over in their chairs immediately. Orli saw them fold as if they'd been gut-punched, first one, then two more, then the rest, with no particular pattern as to where it happened around the room. Just slump, slump, slump, twelve of them nearly all at once. None of them moved again. Nor did anyone get up to help. She thought about running to them herself but decided that might make things worse, getting in the middle of the concert like that.

Then began the wait. The time spent waiting for the seers to find the sun had seemed long enough, but now the time simply went on and on. After a while the beating of her heart subsided some, the fear spawned by the slumping mages exchanged for curiosity. She marveled at the haunting beauty of the song the concert hall magicians made. It was like a chorus of accident. No words together, no direction at all, and yet, there was a harmony in it that seemed to suggest orchestration anyway.

She listened to it for a time, but soon the sameness of it lost its hold on her. It became background sound like frogs and crickets chirping in a springtime field or the soft crash of surf over the course of a day at one of Prosperion's many beaches. Thinking of that set her to watching Altin as he cast. She wondered what he was doing right then, wondered what was going on in his mind, what he was seeing. He sat motionless, where most everyone else in the room swayed. She wanted to walk around to the front of him, to look into his face, but she was afraid she might disturb him somehow. She was way too terrified of interrupting something to move, so instead she closed the lid on the empty wooden chest and sat down on it, using it for a low stool. She leaned against the half wall that separated her from the front row of the concert hall mages, staring mainly at Altin's back. She watched him for a time, but then came a shout from across the room, a man in purple robes, an illusionist, seemed to bark then slumped forward in his chair.

Movements in the white-robed section adjacent to the illusionists seemed to become more frantic then, the healers, as Orli recalled. The pitch of their songs rose, and the weaving of their hands grew faster and faster, making it seem as if they stitched something together in unison through the air.

Someone else cried out behind her, somewhere above. She stood and looked, saw that a transmuter had also slumped forward in his seat.

Two more went down in the enchanters section, and a teleporter near where she stood, seated nearest the aisle, fell out onto the stairs. The woman's body slid down the steps until she bumped against the wall, her robes pulled up so far as to expose her to her underclothes. Orli stared at the woman's stomach and chest, willing the movement of breath. She watched the taut flesh below the mage's ribs, waiting for it to rise. It did not. The woman was dead.

She looked frantically back to Altin, but he remained motionless upon his stool. The conduit too remained exactly as he was, seated on his ottoman, rotating in the dim light cast by the illusion of Mars still above him, its moons and the Hostile floating there. Nothing was changing. The only thing happening was people were falling out of their chairs. Dying.

Orli wanted to scream. She wanted to run to Altin and shake him out of the spell. Did he even know people were dying out here? Was he so lost in the magic he didn't know? She knew better, though. If she touched him, they might all die.

Three more shouts. Another teleporter and two more purple-robed illusionists. An orange-robed conjurer after that.

Time continued to pass. A ridiculous amount of it. Four

more mages slumped like melted things as what had to be another hour passed. Orli was frantic now. The Hostile was still floating above Mars, looking exactly the same. What could possibly be taking them so long?

She'd known that it would take time. She understood that mass and distance mattered somehow in doing this thing. But *this* long? She had no idea how long she'd been sitting there since it began. Many hours at least. If this was the time it took, it was going to be too late anyway. Crown City was probably already overrun.

And then the Hostile was gone. She knew it because the light in the room changed, the red light of Mars suddenly brightened in the absence of the darker Hostile. The wall beyond where the Hostile had hung in the air suddenly lit up with the glow coming off the illusionary red world, its glowing light no longer blocked by the intruding orb in orbit above.

As one, the entire room gasped as they came out of the spell. It was as if the lot of them had just come up from beneath the surface of some horrible lake, all rising out of the water in need of a single collective breath. A teleporter right behind Orli stood, looked as if she were going to say something to Orli, then fainted, her eyes rolling up into her head and her body pitching forward over the long brass rail. The railing worked like a fulcrum, and her feet flipped up, and over it she went, tumbling toward the floor where Orli was.

Orli caught her as best she could and lowered her to the ground. She glanced back over her shoulder toward the healers section and saw a white-robed mage jump the rail and come running toward her. Others were making their way to the rest of the wounded magicians lying around the room, and even the conduit went to see what he could do to help. Orli had expected him to gloat.

Orli gave the healer room to work with the fallen

teleporter and turned back to see if Altin had come out of the spell. He had, though he sat rubbing his temples and shaking his head. She looked back to the healer, who nodded that the woman would be all right, and then she went to Altin's side.

"So it worked," she said. It was only half a statement, the other half made inquiry by the rising lilt in her voice.

"Yes. It did. I think we lost a lot of magicians though." He squinted as his eyes played through the room. Several of the wizards in the rows above were weeping now, standing in small knots around fallen comrades. He nodded. They'd lost more than "some." The count would be twenty-one dead when it was done. Twenty-one dead, eleven magically blinded and unable to ever cast spells again—for some a fate worse than death—and four more unconscious but otherwise relatively unharmed.

"So, did it go all the way into the sun? Is it dead?"

"Yes," he said. "I could actually sense the heat when the spell released. That's never happened before."

"But it's dead. So we did it. I can call the director and tell him to start helping Crown?"

"Yes," said Altin sounding weary. "Call him and tell him it is done. One of them anyway. To be honest, I'm not too sure we can do that again."

She nodded and pulled the tablet out from her waistband. She could only hope the public feeds at Mars base Victoria or on one of the orbital stations were still operational.

Chapter 34

Director Nakamura's face was all condescending smiles and faux friendliness, his eyes flashing like storefront glass as Orli appeared on his monitor. "Ensign Pewter, I wondered when I was going to hear from you again. It's been six hours. Captain Asad reports Crown City's southern wall fell twenty minutes ago. I'm surprised Her Royal Majesty took this long to recognize—"

Orli cut him off, forcing herself to keep anger and revulsion in check. "Her Majesty isn't here. I am. Altin and the *Citadel* mages have discovered the source of the Hostile attack. They're sending the small orbs to Earth from giant feeder Hostiles hiding behind Mars, Venus and Mercury. Altin saw them himself. The magicians have killed the one at Mars. You can check with Victoria to verify."

"We know what they're doing. And we haven't heard from Victoria in sixteen hours, so I can't have them show me anything."

"There must still be a video feed. I'm using their relay. How about Armstrong station? Are they still up?"

"Armstrong was the first thing to go. But I can pull up the telescope at the water plant. Give me a second." The screen went blank, leaving her to stare impatiently at the NTA crest for an interminable seeming length of time. Finally the director came back. "It appears you are correct. It is gone. Or at least, we cannot see it anymore."

"Then tell Asad to help them. Please, hurry. And my father says he needs at least a hundred thousand Marines, suited up and cleared for street-to-street fighting in the capital. If the wall has fallen, he probably needs more than that, since it's been this long."

"Easy there, Ensign. I think you are getting ahead of yourself. I said we can't see it anymore. I don't have any way of verifying it's really gone. If we've learned anything about your medieval friends, it's that they know how to make things invisible, that sort of thing. For all I know, they've just ... I don't know, maybe tossed a cloak of invisibility over it or some other trick out of the storybooks."

"Oh, for God's sake, Director, please. People are dying. They're still dying, six hours later." She spun the tablet around, panning across the room, showing one by one the groups of wizards working to help those who had fallen. She showed him the mage who'd fallen down near the base of the wall, showed the white-robed magician still chanting over her. Then she went right up to the rail and showed him the lifeless teleporter, lying so indisposed in the heap of her ignominious demise, limbs askew, her Prosperion modesty as dead as she. "Look at her, Director," Orli hissed at him, letting him stare at the dead woman for a time. "Look at what you are doing. These people are real. This isn't a joke. They came here, they died here, for us, for our stupid, arrogant, ungrateful world." She spun the tablet back around and leaned right down into it. "So stop fucking around and help them already."

Her gamble appeared to have worked, at least in part, for the director did look somewhat mollified. "All right,

Pewter, I'll give the order to Asad and the other starships to strafe the walls. But our Marines are defending our cities. Here. The Hostiles are everywhere, and I'm not pulling even one mech out to go save Crown City. Not until the skies above Earth are clean. The *Aspect* and the rest, that I'll do, but that's it. I don't believe that Queen you so worship is as innocent as you want me to. Not for one second. I want the orbs gone. And don't make me regret this gesture I've just made."

"Well, we just killed the big one here at Mars, so you'll see the last of the regular Hostiles from this direction pretty soon. And as far as gestures go, Altin said he will send some of the redoubts to help with the fight above Earth once he knows you guys aren't going to shoot them down. So, if he sends them, will you give the order not to fire?"

"And if they decide to start ... turning our ships into pixie dust, what then? Should I just apologize to everyone and tell them we've made the mistake of trusting that Prosperion woman's word again? Trusting *your* word again? That's a lot to ask, all because you showed me one dead wizard."

"Tell them whatever you want. It doesn't matter whose *word* it is. If the redoubt mages turn on you, you'll just be dead that much sooner. What difference could that possibly make to me or the Queen? Dead is dead. Wake up, Director. Go look out the goddamn window at what is happening. Does it really matter who kills you at this point?"

He laughed, or at least half of his mouth laughed. "You grew into your father's daughter, that's for sure," he said. "Fine, I'll give the order not to shoot ... first. But we aren't going to tolerate any funny business up there. One false move and you'll see what we developed while you were gone. I don't think Her Majesty's little crystal ball is ready for what my new Juggernauts can do."

"Yes, Director. Yours is the biggest one. We're all in awe. Now tell the ship captains around Earth that the redoubts are on the way. I'll talk to Altin about what can be done with the other big Hostiles at Venus and Mercury. And let those Marines know they need to be ready to teleport. Crown City isn't going to hold out forever."

The NTA insignia came back, and Orli looked up into the concert hall. Several of the downed magicians were being carried off, others were being teleported directly to the hospital floors below.

Altin saw that she had finished speaking to the director and came over to see how it had gone.

"Not good," she said, "but better than I expected. He said he's going to order the fleet ships in orbit over Prosperion to help defend the walls, but he also said the south wall fell, which means ... well, you know what it means."

Altin nodded grimly. "It means we need to hurry up."

"He cleared you to send the redoubts, but he wants us to get rid of the other orbs before he'll send any ground troops to Crown City. The big Hostile here disappearing doesn't make him believe. He said we could just as easily be hiding it somehow. He says he wants the skies above Earth cleared first. But I know he's watching the numbers of the incoming orbs, so if we can cut them off as proof that we are for real, I think we can get him to send the battle suits sooner than that."

Altin nodded again. "If I were him, I'd probably be doing the same thing. They don't trust us, and as infuriating as it is, that is the reality of it. We have to get to the next planet and see if we can repeat this little trick of ours." The way he shook his head as he spoke didn't bode well for his expectations in that regard.

"But you've lost so many people. You said you probably

can't pull it off. Do you think maybe you can?" She had to hear it anyway.

"I'll pull some teleporters from the redoubts. I doubt a handful fewer of them will make much difference in the fight around Earth just yet anyway."

"Will those magicians be strong enough?"

"They will be. We've got a lot of pretty high-ranked wizards up there. We tried to keep the rank-balance even between upstairs and down. We'll just have to undo that for now."

It was her turn to look grim, and her bosom heaved with the magnitude of the breath she drew. He watched it and smiled. She saw and smiled back. "If we get out of this ...," she said, but she didn't finish.

"Yes," he said. "If."

Twenty minutes later, all the seats in the concert hall were filled again, and the redoubts whose crews were not conscripted into service in the crimson room were sent off to aid in the defense of planet Earth. Altin spent the duration of that time locating Mercury and then Venus with a seeing spell, and by the time the conduit was ready to move *Citadel* again, Altin had seeing stones in place above both planets.

"All right, Conduit, let's get there and see if this will go better than before. I had a peek, and it seems we might be in a bit of luck. Both of these Hostiles are smaller than the one we just killed, so perhaps we're on higher ground than we thought."

"I thought we did famously last time," replied the conduit, the gangly mess of his hair radiating out from his head like frozen filaments of static electricity. He turned and looked up into the chamber at the magicians sitting there watching him confer with the Queen's Galactic Mage. "What do you say, people? Did we not just hand the gorgon her head? I say that was a fine bit of magical work, don't you?"

A tentative, discordant variety of cheers broke out, half-hearted from some, absent in others, but a few, "Hell by hells, huzzah!"

"We just killed a creature well over six hundred measures across," the conduit went on, exaggerating its size some, but Orli wasn't going to point it out. "Us. The people in this room, the people on *Citadel*. You are galactic mages, the first of Prosperion's great space warriors. And you have struck the first great victory for Kurr. Raise your voices, people, and recognize your own cosmic authority. I say, Hell by hells, *huzzah!*"

Much louder this time came a chorus in echo of his own.

"Where are the children mousing about in this room," he shouted at them. "I said gods-be-damned *huzzah!*"

This time the *huzzah* that sounded rattled the concert hall seats. Orli could feel it in the bronze railing upon which her hand rested. She could feel it in the floor.

"That's what I thought you said," shouted the conduit. His face was nearly as red as his tunic and matching pants for all the shouting, but he looked happy then. "And it seems that Sir Altin has found us another giant Hostile to kill. Granted this one is much smaller than the last, but I hope you won't feel bad about killing it just as brutally as before."

Orli could see relief flicker on more than a few faces at that last part, tactically delivered as it was, and all voices once more raised the mighty *huzzah*.

"Then to the lists, my friends. Cebelle, find Sir Altin's seeing stone and let us be on our way."

A brief wave of muttering and whispers passed through the room as people who had leapt up in their fervor retook their seats. The newly arrived redoubt mages asked last questions about using the Liquefying Stones. A few others said prayers to favored gods.

And then they were at Mercury.

As they had for Mars, the seers and the illusionists worked together to get an illusion cast of the hot innermost planet, setting it once more in place in the air above the conduit's head. Its light, set off by the brilliance of the bloated sun nearby, filled the room with a much brighter, almost ochre hue. It was less discomforting than the red light of Mars had been. This light felt like the fires of war, and most everyone in the room had a much better sense of what they had to do. While anxious hands wrung and nervous bowels churned and rattled like old wagon wheels, all were convinced this time would be a better go.

Soon Orli found herself sitting quietly on the empty chest again, watching as the wizards worked in concert together, the diviners seeking to know who might fall first, the healers ready to get ahead of it, as many as needed, plunging their minds into the body of whomever it might be, healing in advance, willing health and growth in anticipation of the bursting tissues and burned-out minds. For the most part, it worked perfectly. Three of the newcomers, the redoubt mages, went down immediately, but the others managed very well. Nobody else went down, at least not right away. One of the diviners leapt up, screaming and clawing at his face, thirty minutes in. He threw himself down the stairs, and Orli thought he was going to break his neck. But he did not. He got up and ran, screaming, out of the concert hall. The chamber filled briefly with a bright wedge of artificial daylight as he went out, the light an illusion in the next room, a warm summer sky on Prosperion beaming through the open doors like a slice of happiness, perhaps a promise of it, though it was devoured quickly as the doors swung shut again. They closed by their own enchantments, cutting off the man's raving lunacy like something corked along with the illusionary sunlight. All that screaming and then, silence once again.

She looked about, thinking that his noise would have broken the concentration of the other mages, but it had not. Everyone else remained rigid in their purpose even as their bodies swayed.

After that, all was calm, and the time passed slowly like before. Not in the count of hours, for she had no clue how long she waited while the spell was underway, but in the helplessness of those hours. Time in that room was agony. She wanted to check her clock, thought about doing it many times, but each time decided it was too dangerous. Who knew what even her tablet's small electronic pulses might do to a spell like the one that was being cast? So she sat. And sat. Until finally the giant orb above Mercury disappeared.

Once again the sound of eight hundred people coming up to breathe, a single symphonic gasp, filled the hall.

The conduit let out a loud and rapturous laugh. "Behold, oh gods of the universe," he shouted up into the red, writhing ceiling of the room. "Your children have risen and come to show you how powerful they have grown."

Scowls and grumbles followed that, mutters of warning from the sections where the mages wore robes of white or black, the healers and the diviners, who were the most disturbed by the conduit's words, near blasphemy if not right over the line. Even Altin shook his head at what he'd heard.

And, as if she had heard it herself, High Priestess Maul wrote a note in smoke above Altin's head. "Come." That is all it said, but Altin knew what it meant and where it came from. No one else Altin knew used that kind of spell.

Altin looked back at Orli to see if she'd seen it there, which she had. He turned to the conduit then. "Conduit, I assume you saw it too."

The conduit nodded. "I did. Go do your thing, boy. We don't need you or your Z." He stood up from his ottoman and strode to the railing, rallying his people again. "Do we, mages of *Citadel*? Sir Altin has had enough glory on his own. It is our time now. We can kill one Hostile without him, can't we? It's practically a baby next to the two we've just sent to the great cook fire of that sun anyway. I for one will be thankful to have him gone."

A few of them cheered half-heartedly, though most did not cheer at all, and Orli could tell the room was not happy to be losing the power of a Z. But he had to go. If the smoke script message meant what she thought it did, High Priestess Maul had learned something about the mysterious male Hostile.

Chapter 35

Gromf sent a wave of fire sweeping across the muddy furrows of the farm, now battlefield, catching a cluster of humans in it and setting their crimson capes on fire. He'd killed the magician that protected them with a spear of ice moments before, and now they had no one to put this fire out. They screamed and rolled in the wet soil, trying to extinguish the blaze, but Gromf sent another wave over them, pausing it, letting it rest in their midst like a wall of agony. The noise of their pain was barely audible over the roaring of the demons at the city wall nearby, countless thousands upon thousands of them comprising a writhing plague in the service of God.

Gromf wondered at such an endless throng, a churning mass of legs, claws, teeth and horns like a black river flowing around the city, a great mote of spidery limbs reaching and clawing against the towering obstruction, the enchantments of the humans making it impossible to climb. For now. Still, a few of them, leaping like giant ticks, would fly out of the mob and sail over the magic, or through it, into the city beyond. He had realized hours ago that the demons were too stupid to open the city gates, or perhaps simply too large to get inside the towers where the mechanisms held. Or else they didn't care. Perhaps the anticipation pleased them. Who could know what served for pleasure in the hearts of these great and brutal things?

It wouldn't be long now, however. Warlord would open the gates as he pleased, for the golden queen and her men had fallen back to defend a great rent in the city walls. They all had, the remainder of her forces driven all the way back to the broken expanse where they fought desperately to slow the trickle of demons making their way into the city streets. And they were failing at it. Their numbers, once nearly as large as the orc host, were now nearly all gone. Perhaps twenty thousand humans remained on the field, and that number thinned near the walls as more and more of them chased after demon invaders that got past them and ran into the human neighborhoods beyond. The golden queen's army was nearly all destroyed, and the carnage had been sublime. The rabble defending the walls would die easily after that, pinched between orcs that Warlord would let into the city and the demons outside.

Behind him for nearly two measures in every direction lay the feast of death, the demons gorging on the dead, on all of them, their own as much as the orcs and humans lying there. Their huge shadowy forms hunched and stooped over bodies, giving the battlefield the appearance of lumpiness as far as he could see, mound upon mound of darkness, as if it were covered by ten thousand heaps of pitch. They were everywhere, and the sounds of their gluttony slunk into Gromf's ears like wraiths, the slurps and smackings, the crunching of bone and crinkling rip of metal, all weaving audibly under and amongst the shrieks and wails of the attackers at the wall, and, occasionally, marked by the cries of some fool who had not had the sense to die before a demon came to make a meal of him. Gromf allowed himself a smile.

The remaining humans fought now to protect the slow movement that drained them back into their city, the soldiers leaking into that fearfully defended break in the wall like a stream through a rotting beaver dam. But there was still hope for personal glory in this, for the golden queen herself still fought at the front of their lines. She, in her shining armor, was there, still hacking and mangling Gromf's allies with that brutal sword. And the wicked elf was there too. Keeping her safe. But not for long. Warlord had nearly hacked his way to them now, and soon, Gromf would be at his side. Together they could beat that awful pair, where so many others had failed.

With the soldiers who had rushed him dying in the fire now, Gromf was free to make his way to Warlord. Warlord was struggling to get close to the human queen, for her people threw themselves at the mighty leader of the All Clans as if he were a mountain and they an angry wind. They died in great leaking heaps, but still they came. And Warlord cut them down again and again as if he were gathering thistles to make tea, the mammoth force of each swing chopping through two and three of them at a time, their bodies falling in pieces and their weakling guts spilling out into the mud.

Gromf saw a woman with a crossbow taking aim at Warlord then. He cast an ice lance that took her through the face. He had no joy in it, however, no delight in the brains that leaked out through the back of her skull, for they had only ever been filled with woman's thoughts and no glory could he take from that.

The golden queen was the one exception, and as if she were trying to mirror the greatness of Warlord, she cut down three orcs on her own, the massive broadsword she swung nearly as long as she was tall. The bite of that weapon was furious and, though she was female like Gromf's last victim, hers was a different heart. She fought like a great animal, and for her Gromf had grudging respect. Not to recognize the danger living upon the edge of her blade would mean certain death, just as it had for those three fools lying at her feet as he watched.

Warlord crushed in the head of another stupid human that had thrown himself in the path of the great warrior's quest for the human queen, the butt of Warlord's axe pulping the man and dropping him like a stillborn falling from the womb. Warlord roared his challenge at the queen, at the same moment that Gromf's quickly conjured ice lance, so easily made with the two God Stones now, flew through the intervening space like a spear aimed perfectly at her head.

The ice lance struck her directly on the side of her helmet, and for the briefest moment Gromf thought he had stolen victory in that, but then that blue shaft he'd cast was hurtling back toward him, deflected by some cowardly human enchantment of the golden queen, and it hit him in the shoulder, driving through him and jutting out the back, right beneath the bone, a length of ice protruding nearly as long as half his arm.

Blood leaked from the wound in front and back, and Gromf knew the wound would be fatal when the ice lance melted down enough. Blood would pour too rapidly from such a hole to heal. Even with the God Stones, his medicine magic would not be fast enough for that. He would have to keep it cold. He touched it and kept the spell alive as he ran to Warlord's side.

The vile creature that he recognized as the golden queen's servant, the hateful elf, suddenly appeared at Warlord's back. The slender figure held bloody knives in each hand, straight and narrow things nearly as long as short swords, and Warlord did not know the elf was there. The powerful orc was just then staving off the furious chopping onslaught of the golden queen, and his back was briefly exposed.

The reflex came before he could stop himself, and Gromf yanked the ice lance from his body and hurled it at the elf, drawing the slick, cold shaft from his flesh and sending it whistling through the air.

The elf saw the bloodied ice lance coming in its peripheral vision and leapt backwards with reflexes quicker than a dung fly's, cart wheeling out of danger so fast it could barely be seen.

Blood puked out of the massive hole in Gromf's shoulder. He bit back the pain and summoned another ice bolt, which he jammed through the hole again. The agony of doing it set a swarm of dots swimming in a graying haze that came into his eyes, and for a moment, Gromf thought he'd killed himself. But gradually his vision came back, mainly by the pure force of his will.

He watched through the fog as it cleared, expecting the elf to come at him in his weakness. Which it did. The agile creature, armored in leather that rendered it as black as any of the demons were, ran at him with its two wicked daggers dripping the blood and gore of all the orcs and demons it had killed today.

Gromf conjured another ice lance and sent it on its way. The elf vanished, flickering out of view, only to reappear again when the ice lance had passed through the space where it had been, and worse, it was now two steps closer than before. Its teeth shone white behind the curl of its lips, growing brighter as Gromf's vision returned, and Gromf wondered if there would be joy for it when it saw that Gromf was dead.

Then God struck it. God's long, stony arm whipped across the field and smacked away the onrushing elf like the pesky insect that it was. Gromf saw the elf flying away, tumbling head over feet out across the field like a wet deerskin that's been flung away. He was glad, grateful to God for intervening on his behalf, though he also saw in the next moment that the elf righted the helpless-seeming spin of its flight and vanished well before the arc of its path could bring it crashing into the midst of several demons feasting upon the heaps of gore. It reappeared directly below where it had vanished, on its feet, still clutching its knives. Running back again. It ran more quickly than any orc could. Even a mounted one.

Gromf supposed such a creature could not be killed so easily as that, not even by God.

He looked up to where God now stood, the towering figure turning its attention from the elf to smile down at him. "You must live a while longer, Gromf," God said. He reached down and, with his shorter arm, took the ice out of Gromf's wound. Again came the pain, and the dimness once more returned to his eyes. And then he was whole again.

He realized that it was so, even as God took the stone rods of his fingers away from Gromf's injury. Gromf looked at himself, where the hole had been, but it was gone.

He wanted to praise God for healing him so well and so quickly, but God was staring into the sky. Gromf wondered what God might be doing now, wondered if God might be calling down some great power from above.

There came then a bright light, a red thing straight as a spear, so long it seemed as the distance between the mountains and the moon. It cut a hole through the clouds above and landed with a hiss not twenty paces from where Gromf stood, stable on his feet again. The mud in that place erupted and splashed Gromf with wetness that burned as if it had been boiling. Steam came in a blasting cloud right after it, and Gromf had to stagger back or be scalded and killed where he stood.

He ran back out of it, and then gaped as he watched the

spear of light move away, marveling at God's new and awesome display. The shaft of light cut a deep trench in the farmland for nearly forty paces and then moved into the ranks of demons on the far side of the city gates. It brutalized the monstrous bodies of the demons, paring them instantly, their black armor bursting and their guts inside spraying out like the steaming geysers of the western Daggerspines.

Gromf watched it as it cut through a swath of demons along the wall like a sharp knife through the belly of a trout. They fell in heaps and the beam of light never paused at all. He wondered why God was doing it.

Soon other beams like the first came from above. They came from different places, at different angles, burning holes in the very sky it seemed, long shafts of nearly blinding light, lancing down from above and moving around like sticks stirring a cooking pot, leaving in their wake heaps of hissing death, opened-up demons in piles oozing lakes of gore and issuing clouds of fetid smoke and steam.

He looked back at God who still looked up into the sky. "Why?" he asked the towering figure then. "Why would you bring this down upon us now, when victory is near? What have we done?"

God looked down at him and shook his vast, misshapen head. "This is made by the children of another god. A new one."

"You said that before. What other god?"

"The god of humans from far away."

"You slew the other gods. You can slay this one too."

"Perhaps," said God. "But we must hurry now."

Gromf nodded, and he turned back to help Warlord with the golden queen. Without her elf nearby to guard her so efficiently, she was falling back now, as more and more orcs surrounded her and her remaining men. Even sorely pressed as they were, they backed toward the hole in the wall slowly, still bent on defending it to the last. Gromf gave them credit for that. But the demons fought their way toward the gap just as eagerly, and there was an endless supply of them. One of them ripped three humans apart near the edge of the broken stone wall and went skittering through the open space into the city before any more humans could close the gap.The golden queen turned and tried to cut it down as it slipped inside, but another demon confronted her. And Warlord leapt at her as well.

She went down under Warlord's weight and the weight of the demon's pounding limbs. They grappled together, Warlord and the golden queen, but their efforts at each other were confounded by the blind rage and blood thirst of the demon, who continued to hammer upon them both for a time, mashing and stomping with all its heavy feet. Gromf feared both might die in that.

Then came a roaring from above and a hot blast of wind. Gromf thought the dragon he had seen earlier had returned and begun to breathe on him. He looked up and saw, briefly, something large, bulky and angular, spinning over his head. It pitched and turned as it came overhead, with strange fire shooting out of round openings on its underside, and then, like a bird that's been shot down, it whirled awkwardly and smashed into the city wall with a loud crash and a blast from one of the large fiery openings. The heat and shock from the blast sent everyone nearby, orc, human and demon alike, tumbling away like leaves in a wind, and even Gromf, farther from the impact than others had been, rolled backward twice from the force of it. He was a moment in getting his bearings again.

The strange metallic object lay against the city wall, bent and looking broken, though he could not be sure, for he knew not what it was. It was made from a substance he'd never seen before, not quite white and not quite gray, seemingly of metal, but not in any form he knew. It had symbols painted on its side. Symbols he did not recognize. It was human writing, he thought, the two largest symbols in red: a vertical line with a shorter horizontal line at its top set beside a second vertical line with a squat circle attached near its top and jutting out to the left. Gromf stared at the symbols, searching his memory. But they did not match any of those symbols he'd seen in the human book, though he knew he hadn't studied it very carefully. For a moment he wished Kazuk-Hal-Mandik were there to interpret the message, to read what it might tell them about the new god. But only for a moment. For as he looked on, he saw that there were beams of metal thrusting out from the twisted structure that had crashed there, bent and twisted, pushed through its metallic outer skin at strange angles like broken ribs thrusting through the dead flesh of a defeated warrior.

For a moment he feared that this was some unanticipated trick, a weapon of the new god, but the smoke and fire that came from the protruding ribs of metal convinced him that whatever it was, it was a broken thing. And as evidence of that, at the very moment he realized it, a piece of it fell away, a square section at the narrowest end of the broken thing, revealing as it fell that the object was hollow inside.

Out from this opening came first a handful of humans on horses. Gromf had never seen cavalry emerge from such a vehicle before, a thing that seemed to have fallen out of the sky. But right behind them came several of the steel-clad humans Gromf had seen at the beginning of the fight. They came out, and already their whining metallic arms were shooting the fire that was too short. From this much-closer proximity, Gromf could see that whenever the humans pointed the too-short fire at a demon or an orc, that demon or orc burst apart in chunks. Not so powerfully as when struck by the red lights from the sky, but still, the metallic whine coming from the fire must have emitted something else, for despite the flames never reaching the bodies of God's forces, they fell open just the same.

Gromf watched in horror as more and more of these armored humans came out. He counted thirty-five.

He looked back to where Warlord and the golden queen had been grappling beneath the demon's feet. Both leaders were just then struggling to their feet. The human queen shook herself and clearly had been dazed, her sword hanging limply for a moment in her hands. Gromf thought about hitting her with an ice lance but remembered what had happened with the last one. She was like the demons in that, worse even, not simply resistant but actually reflecting magic back. He would have to leave it to Warlord to strike her down.

And the great orc was in a position now to do it, too, for he saw the golden queen's sword drooping as it was. He raised himself up out of the mud, steam rising from him, made by the heat of the blast, and quickly retrieved his axe. He roared as he started for the queen.

The humans in the strange steel armor were moving that way. Gromf worried what they might do to Warlord if they saw what he was about to do to the golden queen.

Gromf knew what he had to do. He summoned his mightiest ice bolt, made it twice as thick around as Warlord himself, and five times as long, letting the full power of the God Stones fill the object with colossal mass. He sent it hurtling at the last one in the line of the armored humans with their whining spits of fire. The ice struck the human like a landslide and carried it, armor and all, into the wall where it was crushed like a bug. Gromf laughed. The magic of the new god was not so great. And better, none of the others had seen him do it. He moved closer and repeated what he'd done, once again picking off the one at the rear of their formation. That ice beam had the same effect, and another human died.

Exultant, Gromf did it four more times, running closer with each cast and chanting the spell more violently.

Then someone shouted at him from the open place at the back of the broken thing that had crashed into the wall, a human voice, an obvious challenge for a fight.

He spun to face the fool, expecting another human in the steel armor like the rest. But it was not. It was a male human, shorter than most, bulky in the chest and with darker skin than the flesh of the golden queen's kind. This man wore no armor, though his clothing was still unlike any human garment Gromf had ever seen, black and gray, with a strange glittering button near his neck. He carried in his hand a strange weapon, similar in ways to the shape of the small crossbows humans used, but this one had no bow at the end, nor did it seem loaded with a bolt. It glowed in places along its shiny black length with a type of fire Gromf had never seen before either, in all, its use beyond reckoning. But Gromf knew it was a weapon by the way the human leveled it at him. The human said something, wiping as he did at a trickle of blood on his forehead. The human's finger moved on the weapon and, for a moment at least, Gromf saw a thin red beam of light.

Chapter 36

Altin and Orli arrived at the Temple of Anvilwrath in Crown City only moments after the smoke-lettered summons from High Priestess Maul had appeared. Altin's teleport placed them behind a huge column at the top of the front steps, a vantage of such altitude that it granted them a view of the city stretching away to the east, west and south. From that lofty locale, they could see that fires burned in many locations along the southern wall, and in places, the smoke rose from neighborhoods much closer to the temple than the wall, as much as a half measure into the city, the black plumes blowing eastward in jagged smears, marking the path of the demon disease as it began to encroach. Around the city they could see the red streaks of laser fire coming through the cloud layer above, the starships in orbit doing their part to burn back the attackers around the city. That was heartening, as were the small mushroom clouds in the distance, bright flashes that had Altin gawking for a time.

"It is as if the nine levels of hell truly have opened," he said. "These are the things of myth, the things of gods."

"No, these are the things of human history," Orli replied. "This is what's wrong with us."

That was true, and Altin nodded. It was all he could do to suppress the urge to get back to the wall and help them. Orli saw it in the look that came across his face, the way his lips rolled in and the inclination of his posture toward the stairs. She touched his arm, turning him to look at her. She shook her head.

The tension bending him toward the fight released as he saw the truth of the situation in her eyes. It wouldn't be enough. He faced back toward the temple interior again. "All right, let's go."

If the Temple of Anvilwrath in Leekant could be said to be immense, grandiose and spectacular, then the temple in Crown City was nothing less than the absolute manifestation of architectural strength and power. Nothing in the city besides the Palace competed with it in terms of scope, scale or awe. Where the Palace was audacious, ambitious and elegant with its spires climbing a half measure into the sky, the house of Anvilwrath was vast, stalwart and brutal. Though he had been there before, Altin couldn't help wonder as the two of them ran inside, moving deeper and deeper into the maze of its thick colonnades, if either demon or "tactical nuke" could do such a place any harm. It seemed to possess a solidity that must be invincible. The sheer scale was hard to comprehend, not in height but in endlessness. They ran and ran and ran, and yet the rows and rows of massive columns seemed never to stop. No end appeared, no change in the sameness of all those trunks of stone, every one thirty spans high and at least half that in diameter. The carvings changed, the runes changed, but never the scale or density. It was as if they had come into the realm of squat colonnades, some strange place where there existed only cylindrical stone and the space between them.

So run they did, on and on, winding through what

seemed at least a full measure before coming into the "outer courtyard," which was a term, given the distance they'd come, that might have made them both laugh at some other time, some less dire place in history.

The young priestess Klovis was there to greet them as they emerged into the open air of this expanse. Her rust-hued robes were torn, a long rent straight down the front of them, gaping and revealing a red line of dried blood running down between her breasts clear to her navel.

She saw both Altin's and Orli's eyes go to the wound and gave a grim smile as she too looked down at it. "That one was close," she said, nodding as she did. "Yet Anvilwrath seems to have further use for me."

The two of them nodded at the priestess, glad to see her spirits were still high. "I got the Maul's summons. Where is she?" Altin asked.

"She is with the Grand Maul below. We've just come back from the field. Anvilwrath has shown us where you must go. Come." She turned then and took off at a run, leading them across the courtyard and deeper into the heart of the temple. They ran for a long while, longer than before. Orli was in exquisite shape, but Altin began to tire. His was not a runner's heart, which forced the two women to slow their pace.

"Don't you people recruit any teleporters?" he asked after a time, panting with the effort of going on.

"We are here," said Klovis nearly as the words had left his lips. She stopped at the end of a corridor down which they'd been running for what seemed to Altin at least a hundred years. It ended abruptly in a cul-de-sac, around the edge of which were twenty-five candles burning in fluted glass of cobalt blue. In the center of this ring, inlaid into the mottled brown stone of the floor, was the image of a pair of crossed war hammers in polished steel.

Klovis hoisted her robe up as she stepped between two

candles and motioned for them to stand with her inside the ring. They did, and a moment after they were far below.

Huge braziers lined the walls at intervals around the chamber into which they appeared, each alight and filled with burning orange flames that licked up the walls like dragon's breath. The space into which they had come was enormous, and looking up, Altin could see stalactites sparkling in the lofty darkness. The natural vault, the glimmering work of nature, gave way to the work of men as Altin's gaze traced its surface around from high above, its angles and seeming imperfection flattening closer to the floor, the coarse stone transformed to polished smoothness which, farther down, was hung with tapestries. The whole of it, the transformation from the wild to the worked, gave the room an unfinished feeling, as if the priests had only been allowed to work up the first twenty spans and then left the rest alone, a compromise between man and gods taking place up there. He supposed there was probably some mystical reasoning for such things but had no time to seek the story behind it all.

Gathered at the center of the vast chamber, some hundred paces at least beyond where the three of them had just appeared, was a small crowd, most in the rusty robes of Anvilwrath, but a few figures that were not. Altin recognized High Priestess Maul right off, as well as two other figures, a young woman in the gray robes of a teleporter and a skinny young man in brown trousers and a tunic of homespun: two of his former students, Tribbey Redquill and Caulfin Sunderhusk. That gave him pause. He looked the question of their presence to Klovis, but she was already moving off the crossed hammers upon which they now stood, stepping through the ring of cobalt-housed candles and heading toward the assembly deeper in the room.

The group, almost as one, turned to face them at the moment of their arrival, and High Priestess Maul stepped forward out of the group right away. "Good, you came quickly," she said to Altin. "There may still be time."

From the center of the crowd emerged a tiny figure, a man so old and frail he seemed on the very edge of turning straight to dust. He sat upon a wicker chair which had been set upon a plank with wheels attached. A young acolyte pushed him toward Altin and Orli, and High Priestess Maul, in deference, gave way.

The little man slowly thrust his head forward like some gristly tortoise emerging from its shell, and he stared first at Altin, then the Earth woman standing nearby, his eyes glittering in the firelight as he considered them in turn. The arm he raised to point at them was little more than a pair of sticks wrapped in the splotchy velum of his skin, and the mangle of his old fingers shook as he marked the two new arrivals with what served as a pointing motion in the air. "They have come," he said in a dusty croaking voice. A proclamation for the room. "The Seven and the Alien. Come to beg the mercy of Anvilwrath."

Orli glanced to Altin, who glanced back and shrugged. He'd never met the Grand Maul before, but he knew who the man was, and he had no intention of showing disrespect, no matter how farfetched or even ridiculous whatever might be coming turned out to be.

"Five worlds," rasped the man who had held the highest office in the Church for nearly six hundred years. "One for each hand of Anvilwrath. Three human worlds, plagued by arrogance. Hope weeps for Feydore in another. And the fifth grips the hammer of his judgment. Justice comes and even Hope's sorrow is not enough. Our time nears its end."

He motioned for the acolyte tasked with pushing his chair to move him still closer to Altin and Orli, right up until the plank's edge bumped against Orli's shins. His tortoise head stretched to its fullest length, the wattles of his neck hanging loose like pale, soggy prune skins draped from the tendons visible beneath.

Altin glanced back to Orli again, but she was staring into the old man's eyes as if hypnotized. Perhaps she was. Altin couldn't know. He looked back and saw the Grand Maul's gaze narrowing at him. "The Seven doubts," the old priest said. "And the Alien does not believe."

"We believe," Altin said. "Sort of. We need to know where it is. The big one. The male."

"You would disarm Anvilwrath," hissed the old man, his face shaking with the violence of the expulsion, the waddles swinging wildly. "You would kill him if possible." His body was old, beyond crumbling, held together by willpower alone, but those eyes were steady and strong. They compelled Altin to speak.

"Yes," he said. "We would."

"No!" Orli exclaimed almost violently in response. "We would ask him to stop. We would plead our case to him, as I have, as we both have, to Blue Fire. If she can be reasoned with, so can the new male. But you have to tell us where he is. If you know, please, we don't have time to wait. The demons are in the city now, and all of Earth is being devoured. Tell us. Let us try."

The Grand Maul smiled then, his cracked lips a rip in the brittle pages of an ancient book. "It will not be enough."

"If not, then we die and your prophecy comes true," Orli said. "No surprises for you people at least, right? So let us try. Where is he?"

The Grand Maul laughed then, a deep and honest laugh that rattled out from the cage of his storied bones. He raised the gnarled palsy of his left hand and, without a word, the acolyte behind him pulled his chair away and turned him around. The youth wheeled the Grand Maul back through the crowd of priests, which parted before him like city pigeons beneath the tread of tourist feet. He came to rest at the top stair of a wide, circular pit, five concentric rings leading down to the bottom of what Altin knew was a hkalamate pit. He'd been in the bottom of one of them before.

The Grand Maul waved again and the acolyte turned him back around to face the rest of the room. "These children will show you the way," he said, pointing at Tribbey Redquill and Caulfin Sunderhusk with his eyes. "And the Alien will show us what their maps mean in her device. Then *we* will speak to Anvilwrath. Not you." He slid icy scorn across Orli and Altin in turns. "Unbelief is what brought us here."

Altin shrugged. He didn't care who talked to the new Hostile world. Just so long as someone did, and did it quick. Part of him was willing to admit that these priests were probably better suited to it than he was anyway.

The Grand Maul made a hissing sound and jerked with his head in a way that sent Tribbey Redquill and the slender Caulfin Sunderhusk scurrying to where Altin and Orli were. Caulfin unrolled a parchment and held it stretched before them while Tribbey started to explain.

"This is a basic star map we made," she said. "It's not to scale because, well, we'd have had to do it on enchanted mammoth skin, which we didn't have time for. But, it's a start. This is where we are, here." She pointed to a symbol like a tiny sun drawn near the bottom of the chart, three finger-widths left of center. "Over here is Blue Fire." Again she pointed near the lower edge, a little higher up and two finger-widths right of center this time. When they'd seen it, she moved her finger again. "And this one here is Earth." The mark was a third of the way up the map, a half hand from the left edge. "Now this is where the scale issues came up, but this makes the point." She flicked

Caulfin's fingers where they covered a portion of the top edge of the map. He moved them without complaint. "This is what we believe is the location of ... Anvilwrath." She glanced to the cluster of priests nearby and smiled, then gave Altin and Orli a private look, which each understood entirely.

The map in between and all around these three sun-symbol shapes was dotted by various other symbols, the shapes of constellations Altin had known all his life and that Orli had learned only recently. They both stared at the map for a time, Altin looking up first. He looked askance at Orli, then back at the map. Eventually she looked up too. She saw that everyone was watching her expectantly, waiting for her to explain what the map "meant" in her "alien" device.

"I don't think I can do anything with that," she said bluntly. She glanced to Altin and then back across the gathering. "There's just not enough there."

"There's more," Tribbey said. She took the map from Caulfin and motioned for him to go on with his part. "Do your map."

"So," stuttered the youngster, growing nervous now, "I'm not sure how good this is, but we came up with this one too. It's a spell I wrote based on the models the fleet's computers make." He started casting immediately, and a moment later, an illusion appeared in the air just behind the green-eyed mage and the Earth girl. They turned together to look, following the direction of so many other pairs of eyes, and saw it there, a huge three-dimensional star map twice Altin's height and twice that again both deep and wide.

Upon seeing it, Orli took the scroll from Tribbey and walked into the illusion, unfurling the parchment as she went. She looked back and forth, trying to find Prosperion's sun. Caulfin, guessing her purpose, helped her by having one star amongst them all pulse and give off a note like the striking of a tiny bell. The star was near her foot, near the nearest edge of the illusionary map.

"That's Prosperion's sun," he said. "And here is Blue Fire." Again a star pulsed brightly and once more came a single sound, though a different note this time. The star was higher, up at the level of Orli's calf, but it too occupied space close to where she'd stepped into the area of the spell. If she spread her feet apart, she could touch them both with her legs. "Here is Earth," he said, and again came a tone. Two steps into the illusion another star pulsed, this one about chest high.

Orli walked right to it and stared at the golden speck of it for a moment, almost expecting to see tiny planets revolving around the depiction of Earth's sun, Sol. She turned back and looked through the illusion at Altin and the rest of them standing there. She could not help but think they were a remarkable people, and though she dreaded what was to come, she was glad she knew that they were here, living on this world that was so different, yet so terribly the same as the place she'd come from.

"This one way back here, near the top, is the one I'm calling Red Fire," Caulfin said.

That drew Orli up and spun her around. She went straight to where the ringing sound had been, tipping her head back and seeing a bright red spot pulsing near the uppermost edge. "It's a red sun," she said.

"Yes," Tribbey jumped in. "That is what you suggested we might be looking for in the male Hostile, and with the help of the priests here, we've divined this star map. I couldn't verify it, of course, with the fleet being gone and us having lost access to all their machinery, but we were hoping you could do that for us now."

Orli was already pulling the tablet out of her waistband, and soon she was tapping up the star maps in its memory.

JOHN DAULTON

If Caulfin's illusionary galaxy was even remotely accurate, the star in question was a long way from Earth. If the spell depicted the distances even remotely close to reality, she estimated the red star must be hundreds of light years from Earth at least.

Once she had the charts called up, she moved back to the golden speck that was Sol and, from that vantage, pointed the tablet's input lens up toward the red sun at the far upper edge of the illusionary map. She saved the image to memory and then checked the star patterns against what she had on file, wondering as she did so if an illusion would even register on video. What if that kind of magic was all in the mind? She'd never thought to ask.

It did not register.

"It's not working," she said. "It doesn't pick up on video."

Tribbey pointed at the map, which Orli had rolled up and tucked under her arm. "That's why we made that one."

Fortunately, the parchment star pattern did register when Orli scanned it with her tablet, and with a bit of resizing, Orli was able to query the records for a pattern match. She found one almost immediately, a red supergiant star listed as Cep 128a1. It was an extremely young star by star standards, barely forty million years old, and it was huge, over ninety times the mass of the suns that nurtured Earth and Prosperion. It was also very far away, over a thousand light years from Earth. And rounding out the bad news, the entry said nothing about planets around it at all.

She scanned through the article, but there was little else she could use. There was little there at all, just a name, coordinates and the brief estimates about its size and age. But at least she knew where it was in relation to Earth. She could have pointed it out to Altin from Earth if they were there, or at least from near Earth once they were beyond the glare of all its lights.

She became aware of everyone staring at her again, and the weight of their expectation was nearly physical.

"Well," said Altin, "do you know where it is?"

She nodded. "I do. But I don't know if there are any planets there, much less life. This thing doesn't have much detail on it at all. Worse, I don't know how we can possibly get there in time. It took you days to get to Blue Fire, and she is so much closer than that one is. You have no idea how far. We'll never get there before it is too late."

"That doesn't matter," said High Priestess Maul. "We don't need you to 'get there.' We will speak to him from here. What we do need from you is all the information you can give us to guide the divination spell. You must tell us everything you have just learned and what it means. Every scrap of information will get us closer to finding him."

"And," Altin added, "try to tell it as if you were explaining to me. You know, someone who is not understanding more than half of what you say."

"Of course," she said. She called up a few relevant files on her tablet and then started right in. Over the course of twenty minutes, she told them everything she learned from the short computer entry about the star Caulfin had designated Red Fire, and she gave as much technical background as she could in such a short period of time. She explained as precisely as possible in the absence of meaningful Prosperion terminology the distance involved, and this was augmented by periodic input from both Altin and Tribbey, who stood as something of a bridge between the technologies of the two cultures, much as Orli was, and had gotten through their own efforts more understanding of intergalactic things than anyone else on Kurr. The explanation was further assisted by frequent references to the illusion Caulfin continued to maintain, where Orli would step into it and point out this detail or that, and reference images to go with it on her tablet. She explained the nature of red supergiant stars, and even tried to explain star collapse, dwarf stars and black holes as best as possible. But they were running out of time and everyone knew it.

Finally the Grand Maul said, "Enough." He touched her soft hand gently with the wreck of his own, and bade her shut off her device. "And let us hope it is." For the first time Orli thought he might not be rooting for the end of humanity after all, or at least part of him anyway.

"Places," said High Priestess Maul, after which she went directly to the edge of the circular pit. Without the least thought for modesty, she slipped out of her robes and handed them to Klovis who folded them neatly and took them away. The Maul was strong and lean, and she looked confident and proud as she made her way gracefully down into the pit. While Orli had no idea what the reasons for it were, her composure gave Orli confidence. Maybe they really had a fighting chance.

The assembled priests took places around the middle stair, just as the priests in Leekant had done when Altin went into the hkalamate pool in the temple there. The acolyte powering the Grand Maul's chair pushed him around to the far side of the pit where the square block of an altar sat. The youth cast a levitation spell, and a moment later, the ancient figure was atop the altar, chair and all, ready to conduct the spell.

"What are they doing?" Orli asked as she watched the ritual being prepared.

Altin explained as best he could, but the hissing *shush* he got from the Grand Maul prevented thoroughness. It was enough, however, and Orli settled in close to Altin and waited patiently.

Klovis came up beside them and motioned that they remain silent. Orli had to resist the urge to say, "Duh."

Shortly after, it began. The fires of the braziers lowered around the walls, and the crushing darkness from above descended, as if it meant to join with the equally-crushing silence that filled the vastness of the chamber now. Then, slowly, and with rising volume, the Grand Maul's old voice became audible. It creaked like old ship timbers as he sung the spell that would start the hkalamate dream, and Altin stared all the while into the bottom of the pit where High Priestess Maul lay, her arms and legs spread out nearly to a cross, exposing herself, making herself, mind and body, a target, open and vulnerable. Just as he had once done.

Soon the black vapors of the hkalamate came pouring out from the edges of the lowest step, swirling around the Maul like a graveyard fog devouring the light. She remained motionless, calm, the pace of her breathing apparent for a time by the rise and fall of her chest, until eventually that too was gone. Then there was only the darkness, a pool of coal-black mist.

The priests around the ring began their part, echoing the words of the Grand Maul seated above them in his chair. He guided them in their quest for Red Fire. His mind, his power and experience, shaped the chant of the rest, each of them on their own willing High Priestess Maul into the place of the one they knew as Anvilwrath, yet guided also by the things Orli had explained.

The chanting went on for well beyond an hour. Altin was used to such things, but Orli became restless and her feet itched to move. She wanted to pull out her tablet and see if her father was okay, and Roberto, though she knew she'd never get a signal down here. She had no idea how far beneath the surface they were, but somehow she knew instinctively it was very far.

Something warm hit her then. Something wet on her lips. It came upon an explosive squishing sound, and as it struck her, she saw that Altin was recoiling from something sudden striking him as well. She wiped at her mouth and pulled away a bit of something soft and gray. She looked to Altin who had dark spots on his face and a long bit of the gray stuff sticking to his robes, which he picked off and studied for a moment with an arched eyebrow. His attention was pulled back to the hkalamate pool, however, as many of the priests had begun falling forward, tipping into the dark cloud like felled trees.

Both Altin and Orli glanced to the Grand Maul, seeing that he stared wide-eyed into the pool just as they did, his expression horrified.

They looked back into the pool and saw that the dark cloud was melting away, the mist receding as if down a drain opened by the cessation of the Grand Maul's chant. Altin's eyes strained for the sight of High Priestess Maul as the pit emptied. She had not sat up yet, nor made a sound, but soon he saw her bared breasts appear, a pair of pale islands that soon grew to include ribs, stomach and, slowly uncovered, the rest of her. Most of her was just as she had been, strong limbs, the taut body of a warrior priestess. But her head was gone. Or, at least, most of it was gone. There remained only a ruptured shell of skull, like the bottom half of a broken egg laying where her head had been, and the splattered evidence of where the rest of it had gone in the radial lines of wet darkness slung outward, tracing the explosive path of her demise.

Altin looked at the bit of gray substance in his hand and, suddenly mortified, flung it away. Orli looked sickened too, and wiped at where the bit of the Maul's brain tissue had been upon her lips. She could still feel the sticky wetness there. She shuddered and turned to Altin, who was staring once again at the Grand Maul.

The Grand Maul stared back across the space at him and shook his head. "Anvilwrath does not wish to speak to us."

There followed a long silence. More than a few looks of fear among the younger priests. Tribbey shushed Caulfin from something he started to say.

"Then it is too late," muttered Klovis from her place beside Orli after those first few moments had passed. "We must prepare for the end. Judgment has come."

"Fuck that," Orli said. She turned to Altin, clutching his arm tightly with both hands. "Get me back up top. We know where it is. Maybe the director will listen now."

Altin nodded. Whatever she had in mind, they had to try.

Chapter 37

Altin's teleport spell brought him and Orli out of the hkalamate chamber far below the temple and placed them back at the spot at the top of the temple steps, near the first of the giant columns and with a view out over the southern half of the city. They'd been down in the ritual cavern for well over an hour, and in that hour, the number of fires burning along the southern wall had grown considerably. There were too many plumes of smoke to count, and a large section of Crown City's southern district was slowly turning black as fire consumed it, the ruin spreading like a disease whose malignancy the two observers could follow visually as it progressed. Still, horrid as it was, Altin supposed it could have been worse given how long they were down below. The defenders were doing what they could. Unfortunately, he also noticed that there were two new plumes of smoke to the west. That was not good news. If the west wall was breached, the stain of that disease so visible in the south would infect everything there as well, and likely straight away. Even with the help of the starships and bombers, they were still losing ground.

Orli was tapping the icons on her tablet as Altin

surveyed the city. She uttered a few profanities, most of which ended with the director's name.

"What is it?" Altin asked.

"I can't get the director," she said. "It's either the magic or fucking Asad is blocking the relay."

"Why would he block it?"

"I don't know. It's probably magic."

"Can you get Asad directly?"

She was punching buttons and sliding images across the screen as he asked. A moment later she shook her head. "No. I'll try my father."

"Maybe he can get Asad?"

"If he answers, he can patch me into his ship, the *Livermore*. I hope he's okay."

Altin could see her hands shaking as she said it, and he put his arm around her. "I'm sure he's all right. I fought with the man. He's an incredible warrior, and clever. He'll be fine."

The colonel's voice sounded from the tablet, and with a touch of her finger, Orli made his face appear, though it flickered and the sound crackled horribly. "Good," she breathed. "You're still alive."

"So are you," he replied, the relief apparent on his face. "Where are you?"

"We're inside the city, at the Temple of Anvilwrath. Altin's with me. We're both fine. Where are you?"

"I'm with nineteen Marines and eleven of the Queen's Seventh Cavalry, near the south wall. The demons opened up a section of it, and it's all the Royal Army can do to hold the gap. We're chasing demons through the streets when they get through, but it's like drinking from a fire hose over here."

"There's more than one breach," she said. "But Director Nakamura says he's willing to send a hundred thousand mechs, just like you said you'd need, if we can figure out the Hostile problem."

"Well then you better do it quick. I've lost almost half my team, and these guys on the horses are insane. They're the only ones left of their whole regiment. You've got to give them credit for balls, but balls aren't going to be enough forever." His hand moved up and touched his ear for a moment, and his eyes darted to another section of his control panel. "Your pal Levi says 'hello.'"

"Roberto? Is he there? Why is he there?" She sounded almost hysterical.

"Yeah, he's here. He flew us into the city when the director ordered our people off the ground."

"Off the ground? Why did he order you off the ground? He's supposed to be reinforcing you guys, not pulling you out."

"I don't know. We got the order right before the starships started scraping the walls. It was a good call though, we were being overrun."

"So why is Roberto with you? Does he even have a mech?"

"No. No suit. He's running around on foot. For a guy who sits on his ass all day flying spaceships, he's pretty handy in a firefight."

Orli's expression conveyed that she was absolutely appalled by the idea.

"Don't worry; I'm keeping an eye on him."

Orli shook her head, knowing that could easily not be enough. But what else could she say, especially since Roberto was obviously hearing at least half of the conversation right now.

"Listen, you have to hold on a little longer," she said, forcing herself back on point. "We figured out where the Hostiles are coming from. It really isn't Blue Fire. It's another being like her; we're calling it Red Fire for now. It's a red supergiant in Cepheus, Cep 128a1."

"So can we get some nukes to it and take it out?"

"We don't even know if there's a planet there."

"I thought you said you found it?"

"Well, we think we found it."

"How far out?"

"About a thousand light years."

The colonel didn't have to say anything. The turn of his mouth made his feelings clear—he knew as well as Orli did what that meant in terms of time. He put on his best believer's face, though. "Well you better tell your boy Meade to get his ass moving."

"Blue Fire!" Altin blurted, listening in but only getting half of what was being said. The way he said it suggested he'd had a revelation of some kind.

Orli and the colonel from his place on the tablet in Orli's hands both looked at him. "What?" Orli asked.

Altin's eyes were already closed, his thoughts at work making their appeal to Blue Fire. *Are you there?* Speaking to her was much like the way one walks in total darkness, hands out, steps coming tentatively, reaching through oblivion for what should, or might, be there.

Always here, came the reply.

Can you see this? He sent the images he had in his mind, the red stars from the images in Orli's tablet, the supergiants, and he conveyed the image of the little red spot in Caulfin's illusion. He included a reminder about what she herself had said, about the red star, or whatever it was, being male. *Do you know this ... do you know him?*

No.

The abruptness of her reply, the totality of it, struck him with finality. There was nothing like curiosity or anything. Just, no. He frowned. He could hear Orli talking to her father on the tablet, her voice rising. He tried to push it away. *Can you look for him? Can you find him like you found Altin Love?* He thought it carefully, focusing on the question of it, conveying the sense of Orli dreaming, of her as she had been the first time Blue Fire found her while she toyed with the Liquefying Stone. He shaped the idea, but he sent with it the sense of seeking, of curiosity, he imagined himself poking around in tall grass, kneeling and looking under a bed. *Look.*

No find, she sent back. There came after that the image of Altin naked on the ledge in the center of Blue Fire's world, the blue star of Blue Fire's dead mate above him. A definite essence of maleness came with it, a concept she was learning from her human friends. She sent back the image of Altin looking in the grass and under the bed, this time with Blue Fire's mate above him. He saw Orli's face under the bed. *Must find Blue Fire.*

"Harpy spit," Altin swore aloud. He tried to work through the riddle. He and Blue Fire's mate, looking under the bed and finding Orli there. He just about swore again, but realized it might actually be perfectly clear. *Are you saying that males must find females? That he has to find you?*

Truth. She showed him an image of Prosperion surrounded by an endless expanse of pink light, a plain of it, or perhaps a vast unmoving sea. She put a sound in his mind, a note like a plucked cello string, a sound taken from his memories. The image pulsed and ripples moved across the pink expanse toward a planet that appeared in the path of the outbound rings. Orli had described seeing this, though they hadn't had time to work out what it meant. They'd been in such a rush, he couldn't be sure.

Blue Fire changed the image, borrowing again from Altin's memory, this time the illusion that Caulfin had cast. She sounded another note, this time emulating Caulfin's bell. Pink rings moved out from the image of Prosperion in the illusion to where Blue Fire was. *Blue Fire see Orli Love world.*

A gradual sense of dawning came upon him then, augmented by what Orli had surmised, that somehow Blue Fire had found Prosperion because its people, or its creatures, had been using magic. "It's mana," he said, once again speaking aloud by habit now. "You found us in the mana. Or you found our world in it somehow."

Truth.

So, can't you find Red Fire in the mana? He must be using it too. His orbs are using mana all the time?

Not mine. No find. Again came nude Altin on the ledge with the blue star above him. Then he saw a pond, and across the surface of the pond blew a small cloud of dandelion seeds. A small version of Blue Fire floated in the water at the edge of the pond. The dandelion seeds blew into it. *Find Blue Fire.* She sent back the image of one of the red-hued Hostiles attacking Earth as she'd gathered from his mind. *Find.* That was followed by an image of the dark orbs he'd first encountered, the ones he deemed coconuts.

He scrunched up his face, fighting hard to understand. He became aware that Orli was no longer talking into her tablet. He opened his eyes. She'd put the tablet away, tucked back into the waistband of her trousers.

"Well?" Orli asked, clearly impatient and having been watching him for a while.

"I asked her to try to find Red Fire. She seems to be saying that she can't. I think he has to find her. Something about his orbs and hers. Ripples in the mana and dandelion seeds. It's giving me a headache. Maybe you need to talk to her in a dream. I don't even know if I'm conveying the red sun idea properly."

"Like there is any chance I can get to sleep," she said. "My father patched me through to the director via the *Livermore*, and the director says he's given the ready order for the mechs to redeploy to Prosperion. But nothing else has changed. The inbound orb count remains steady, so he's holding off on giving the go-ahead. He's not going to pull anyone off Earth defense until the Hostiles pull out. And frankly, I still think he thinks Her Majesty is bluffing somehow."

"What about *Citadel*? Did they get rid of the other big one? It's been long enough; they could have done it by now."

"Yes, it's gone."

"Then what is the director waiting for? Why are your warriors on standby? What could be the bluff?"

"He's waiting for the orb count to go down. He says when his people aren't dying by the thousands, he'll give the go-ahead."

Altin nodded. He thought that was a stingy interpretation on the director's part of the deal he'd made with Orli, but there was nothing to be done about it for now. He sent Aderbury a quick telepathic nudge. His longtime friend and the acting captain of *Citadel* answered right away.

"You're alive," said Aderbury. "Thank the gods. So tell me, are we sending teleporters somewhere down on Earth to get their warriors to Crown? We need to know where to go. My seers tell me the sand is running out."

"Not yet. The director is stalling, insisting on significant reductions in the Hostile count. But be ready for those directions when they come." If it comes, he thought, though he kept that part to himself.

"We're ready. We're making hay with these Hostiles too. Conduit's team had an easy time of the last of the big ones, so they're pretty confident downstairs. Give us a few more hours and that director will have his 'significant reductions in the Hostile count.'"

Altin looked out over the smoke filling the city. There were three more fires in the west. A few hours would be disastrous. The city would be overrun.

Altin cut off the contact with Aderbury and turned back to Orli. "So what do we do? What do you think about all that stuff Blue Fire said, the seeds and orbs and all of it?"

"The dandelion seeds are the orbs," she said. "I'm thinking that either one of Red Fire's orbs needs to find one of Blue Fire's, or one of Red Fire's orbs needs to find Blue Fire herself."

"These ... beings are millions of years old. You said it yourself. How could they not have found each other by now?"

"Space is big. And who knows, maybe there's some kind of territorial thing with these creatures, whatever they are. It's hardly unprecedented. Maybe the red one never came over here because Blue Fire already had a mate. Maybe out of respect, maybe out of fear. I mean, all we can do is guess."

Altin listened and tried to convey what Orli said as best he could to Blue Fire. He tried to construct images and send emotions that got at the heart of Orli's ideas, throwing it all at her like a plate full of food, hoping that somehow she might catch at least one morsel in her mouth.

She did. *Truth*, she sent.

Which part? The territory part, the orbs—seeds—finding-each-other part, or the part where his seeds find you?

All truth.

All of it? He showered Orli with a look of pleasant surprise. *So what then? If you get one of your orbs to Earth, the red ones can find it? Then you can talk to him, to Red Fire?*

Truth.

That's it?

Altin looked as if he might get mad, his gaze playing

out over the city, over the carnage and death, the destruction. He fought back the tide of it, and glared down at Orli instead, venting some, "All Blue Fire had to do was send an orb to Earth to start the conversation with the red one. It's that easy."

Fear came to him then, first a little, then more and more, heated to a boil. The emotions weren't his.

Orli saw it on his face. "What's the matter?"

"I don't know. Now she's afraid." He was clearly irritated, despite the emotions Blue Fire pushed into him.

"Maybe that's why she didn't go talk to him. Maybe she's shy."

"Shy?" He looked incredulous.

"I'm only guessing," Orli said. "But maybe that's how her species operates."

"Well how many people have to die for that?" He was shouting, though he didn't realize it until it had already come out.

"Don't yell at me," she said. "Your people have some pretty strange customs when it comes to male and female relationships, *Sir* Altin." She put a heavy emphasis on the title to make her point. "You waste lots of time on 'honor' and 'propriety' while life ticks by. Look around, the universe doesn't always give us time."

He started to respond, but thought better of it. He knew he wasn't angry at her anyway, just at the circumstance. Besides, she had a point. "You're right," he said. "I'm sorry. We have to keep it together. Both of us."

Orli nodded.

Altin let go what remained of his tension and spoke in a calmer voice, filtering Blue Fire's feelings as best he could. "Fine. But if Blue Fire is shy, now is the time for her to get beyond such things. She needs to go talk to him." *You need to go talk to him*, he thought, directed toward Blue Fire.

No nest.

"What?"

The hole in the desert known as the Great Sandfalls appeared before his mind's eye. *No nest.* He saw a series of images after, creatures building nests and burrows, animals in caves, some of the animals unrecognizable, others recognizably Prosperion.

You don't need a nest. If thoughts could be spat, that would have been, exasperation propelling it. *Just talk to him. We're not asking you to marry him, just tell him to stop attacking Earth. Explain what you did at Andalia. Why it was wrong.*

Fear came again, much greater than before, so great it drained the color from his face. He could only filter so much.

"Stop!" He thought it and shouted it aloud. "Stop." The fear abated some. "Why are you so afraid?"

There was a long pause, so long he thought Blue Fire had cut off the communication, pulled herself out of his mind. He actually checked beneath his ring to see if the green light still pulsed there.

No love, she sent at last. Then fear came back. Intimidation and helplessness that somehow filled a space he knew as forever.

He thought he knew what that meant right away, but he clarified anyway. *So if your orb and his orb*, he paused and shaped the thought that went with it into dandelion seeds, *... if the seeds meet, are you saying you are stuck with him, even if you don't love him? Is it like a mating ritual or something?*

Truth.

"Oh, for the love of Mercy," Altin moaned, completely at wit's end now. He turned a full circle atop the stairs where they stood, his arms out helplessly and his eyes to the sky. "We are doomed."

"What?" Orli asked. "What did she say?"

"If she sends an orb to Earth, somehow that's like a marriage proposal. Or the actual wedding. Something like that. All I know is she's afraid and doesn't want to send one of her orbs over there. Apparently they can't just 'talk.' And she doesn't love the new fellow, so she doesn't want to go."

"Well, what about the other option?" Orli said. "About Red Fire's orb finding Blue Fire's world. What did she say about that? Is that any better? Maybe the orbs are like gametes, and if they meet, well, you know how it works. We know she thinks of them as her eggs."

"I have no idea what a *gamete* is, but I think I know what you are saying anyway. I'm not sure, however, why bringing one of the red orbs to Blue Fire would be any better than simply having two orbs meet."

"Maybe she doesn't have to offer one of her own that way. Maybe he has to do something to impress her first. Some sort of intergalactic first date. If he isn't a gentleman, then she doesn't have to release an egg to him." Orli wrinkled up her face in a way that acknowledged the speculative nature of what she'd said, but it was in keeping with much of what'd she'd read of other species in the world, at least her own.

Altin let go a long impatient gasp, but he sent the gist of that along to Blue Fire. "So, is that it?" he asked, speaking the thoughts aloud now as well so that Orli might follow along. He sent that and tried to picture Orli in a room alone, but with Blue Fire's world hovering near her in the air. He imagined Thadius walking in, and conveyed a sense of hate. Thadius went away. "If he comes to you, then you can decide if you like him or not?"

Truth.

Trying to preempt unexpected complications down the road, Altin added, "And what happens if you don't like

405

him? Or he doesn't like you?"

Blue Fire sent emptiness, not loneliness, just absence or vacancy.

He frowned, but translated for Orli as best he could. "I don't think she knows what happens. I don't think that's ever happened before. Maybe that's the territory thing."

"Ask her if she wants another mate." Orli said.

"By the gods, she doesn't need to mate with it. She just needs to get it to stop killing everyone."

Orli put her hands on her hips and glared at him. "Just ask her."

He did. Blue Fire clearly did not want another mate. She sent waves of love back at Altin, carried on images of the blue sun that had once warmed her long-dead beloved.

Altin would have laughed if it all wasn't so cosmically ridiculous. "She says 'no.' She's still in love with the dead planet."

"Altin!" Orli snapped, her mouth and her eyes flung wide. "What's wrong with you?"

He recoiled from the shocked expression on her face, and his hands went out helplessly to his sides. "What? This is absurd. And it's taking a lot of time. And we're not getting anywhere."

"What's absurd is that somehow you ended up being the one who can speak to her easily while I cannot. My God. How insensitive can you possibly be?"

"If you want to try, go ahead," he said. He tugged off the huge silver ring and handed it to her.

Orli grimaced as she watched the light pulsing inside the curve of the ring, glaring at it as if it might burn her on contact. She well remembered what had happened to her when she'd touched the yellow Liquefying Stone that day long ago, the day she'd met Blue Fire and the day both she and Altin had nearly died. That stone had been far less potent than the green one in Altin's ring. Altin had made it more than clear that this thing, this secreted part of Blue Fire's very innermost self, was something more dangerous than the yellow stone alone. But she reached out and took it anyway. "Do you think it will work?"

"I doubt it, but I'm sure in the nine hells not getting anywhere on my own. She did find you when you were holding the Liquefying Stone, so who knows. You were a lot closer to her then, and sleeping, but it's worth a try."

Orli slid the ring over her thumb reluctantly. She cringed, waiting for the mental onslaught of Blue Fire's inner voice. It did not come. They spent several more minutes waiting, but to no avail. Orli handed the ring back to him and shook her head. "Guess not."

"Of course not." Both of them were frustrated. Frustrated and tired.

Blue Fire's fear came washing into him when he put the ring back on. It was fear and love and remorse. *Orli Love not leave Blue Fire. Hate alone.* His mind swelled with the immense loneliness that resided eternally in her, loneliness the size of a galaxy. But there was more to it, something penitent. He realized it was an apology.

What? He sent back, confused by the rush of such anxiety. *What do you mean?*

Orli Love not leave. She had no word for "please" but it was clear that she was pleading with him.

It took him a moment to sort through the torrent of anxiousness and fear, the sense of abandonment, but finally he made it out. She thought he'd left her, cut her loose forever when he took off the ring.

No, he thought back to her then. *I'm here.* He did not speak it, thinking it just to her. He showed her in his memory what he tried to do, how he'd tried to help Orli talk to her with the ring. He tried to explain. He could sense she mostly understood, but she was still shaken by the experience. And so quickly too.

Blue Fire talk Red Fire, she sent then. It came on a wave of complicity, servile, though definitely afraid and filled with echoes of loneliness. He saw then an image of himself walking across the pond where the dandelions blew. In his arms was a red-hued orb. He carried it across the pond and placed it in the water where it floated next to the round globe of Blue Fire's world. It was obvious what Altin had to do. *Blue Fire speak Red Fire. Orli Love not leave.*

"Orli Love not leave anyway," he said to that last fearful thought, trying to comfort her. But, though he didn't say what came next, the thought rose unbidden in his mind. *Altin Love will be dead soon, but he won't leave you until then.*

And with that, she conceded to meet Red Fire and speak on their behalf. Altin would have been relieved by that, but he couldn't shut off the fear that came from her after giving in. He tried to calm her, thought soothing thoughts at her, promised to keep her safe any way he could, but all to no avail. Blue Fire was simply terrified, a great colossal fear that seeped into him across all that space and despite his best efforts to filter it.

"Well?" Orli asked, once again lost given the absence of many spoken words during the last exchange.

Altin's hands still trembled from the ferocity of Blue Fire's anxiety, and his voice shook as he replied. "She says she'll do it. But I have to bring a red Hostile to her."

"You what?"

"You were right, or at least I think you were right, about it being better if the red orb finds her planet before it finds one of her orbs ... her eggs. So she basically asked me to go get one of Red Fire's 'seeds' and bring it to her. After that, I guess we'll just have to find out."

"Do you think it will work? Do you think she can get Red Fire to stop the attack on Earth?"

"I hope so. If she can't, then we just wasted ten minutes

that we should have spent trying to get to him ourselves."

"She'll convince him," Orli said, finding confidence. "She understands the gravity of what she did on Andalia. They aren't evil creatures, you know. Look how sensitive she is. It's going to work."

"We're about to find out." He looked grim as he said it, but the expression was more a product of his continuing efforts to at least mute some of the throbbing terror Blue Fire was pumping into his head. He forced a grin. "Let's go catch a Hostile."

Orli nodded, her expression as bleak as his. She really didn't want Blue Fire to get hurt.

Chapter 38

Calico Castle's tall central tower appeared above planet Earth, another chunk of lifeless debris to the sensors of the Earth ships, which was fortunate for Altin and Orli. Despite the director's suggestion that there wasn't a significant reduction in the number of Hostiles around Earth, to the eyes of the tower's occupants, the swarm seemed noticeably diminished. It was still a swarm, and in large patches above the continents there still hung hazy gray clouds that could only be Red Fire's orbs.

"He's such a liar," Orli snarled. "There are obviously less of them."

"He's a politician," Altin said. "That is what they do. Now help me find a little one so we can get this underway."

"Can you get us closer?" she asked, knowing that he could. "I can't see well enough from here."

A moment after, and they were closer. "How's that?"

Startled by the suddenness of it, the instantaneous expansion of the planet beyond the window, she nodded. "Better."

They leaned through the window together, shoulders touching, each of them scouring the frenzy of Hostile orbs, tens of thousands of them still shooting and darting through space. Some had ships chasing them, missiles streaking in between the weaving movements of their flight and lasers striping the space with crisp bright lines. Others dive-bombed fleet squadrons, sending their pulverizing shafts of stone hurtling down at the ships in hopes of bashing them open as easily as if they were simply ceramic things.

Despite the overwhelming numbers, however, several of the massive Juggernauts remained, and the smaller starships coupled with the little groups of low-orbit fighters managed to continue to fight effectively among them, the network of all those computers synchronizing gravity pulses and popping open Hostiles like so many lanced boils. It couldn't be said that the battle was under control, but a case could be made for the fleet holding its own. For the most part. Explosions now and again marked where practice and light-speed computations still weren't good enough.

"There," said Altin pointing. "That one, chasing that gray ship."

She saw the orb he was referring to and nodded. "Yes, that's small for a Hostile. Get it quick before it catches them."

Here it comes, he conveyed to Blue Fire in his thoughts.

With that, he plunged his mind into the mana, the serenity of its new consistency, a purplish vapor that filled everything thanks to his ring, like a fog with no wetness, no temperature. It was simply everywhere, waiting for him. He shaped the link across the space between himself and the Hostile chasing the ship, a thought only, no words, no gestures, and as easily as that, he had it. He thought then of the space around Blue Fire, the place where once the fleet ships had been, where they'd rained down their mighty missiles at her, where they'd unlocked the power in the tiniest of things, unspeakable power stored in the smallest bits of less than a molecule. It was there that he sent the little Hostile, in an instant, fast as the flick of a hummingbird's wing.

"Do you see it?" he asked Blue Fire, sending his thoughts after the Hostile across that space and once again speaking them for Orli's benefit as well. "Is it there?"

He saw in his mind that it had arrived, like watching it through a seeing spell, but the image put there by Blue Fire. Her entire being seemed to tremble around it, her thoughts quaking like the ground beneath an army's marching feet.

"Does she see it?" Orli asked.

He nodded. "Let's go in case she needs our help." Almost as soon as he'd said it, the tower appeared above Blue Fire's enormous world. The blue disc of Earth vanished and the brown mass of Blue Fire's filled the view, a nearly waterless planet capped at the poles by huge oceans upon which seemed to float the tiny continents where life went on, where plants and animals were blissfully unaware of the cosmic events unfolding just about everywhere else but there—happily ignorant like Altin had been but a scant two years ago.

"Should I say something to her?" Altin asked. "Or leave her alone to talk to him?"

"How should I know?" Orli asked as she leaned out the window and looked around.

"I'm no matchmaker. You're the one with the perfect grasp of what is going on."

"I wouldn't call it perfect," Orli said, leaning even farther out the window and looking left and right. "And where is the orb? I don't see it."

Altin looked too, though he couldn't lean out to do it now, given that Orli had climbed up into the windowsill to get a better view. "I don't know. Should I ask her? It's the same question really. I don't want to interrupt."

"I don't know either. Maybe give her a few minutes first. Does she still feel afraid?"

"Terribly."

"Well, she's probably nervous. I was nervous when I first met you."

Another time he might have smiled, but the thrumming of Blue Fire's terror prevented such a thing. Still, the memory was a fond one. "I was beside myself," he said, recalling the first time he'd seen Orli in person, standing before his hospital bed in the *Aspect*'s sick bay. "Never had I beheld such beauty."

He couldn't see it, but she smiled, hers unhindered by waves of someone else's fear. "Yeah, you were pretty obvious." She sighed, very briefly, even without receiving broadcast terror, she was unable to sustain pleasant thoughts for long. "Maybe that's what's happening to her. Maybe she is smitten by the big red hunk." She climbed back into the room. "I sure hope so."

"As do I," he said. "But I'm worried. I'm not getting anything like that from her at all. It's still just her afraid, like she was before we sent the red one here."

They waited nervously for a while, but still nothing changed.

"I'm going to try to talk to her," he said at length. "It's been ten minutes at least."

"It's been longer than that," she said. "Go ahead."

Nothing.

"She's not answering me."

"Maybe they're making love."

He harrumphed, the sound deep inside, unconvinced. "If they are, she's still horrified."

"They do live for millions of years. Maybe courtship takes a really long time." She turned and leaned back out the window again, peering down at Blue Fire as if somehow the raw desire to know would be enough to let her see.

"I should have asked, shouldn't I? Should have found out more."

"Yes. But we didn't think of that. That's usually how it goes."

"What if we're locked out now? What if that's it? What if I can't speak to her anymore, for ... for years. Maybe tens or hundreds, even thousands of years."

Orli bit her lip. A low sound rumbled in her chest now too. She turned back from the window and went to sit at the table that had so long served Tytamon as a desk. She ran her fingers through her hair, over her forehead, exhausted and frustrated. She stared silently into the wood grain, as if seeking the answers there, but there was nothing. She looked up at him, and shook her head. "Then that will mean we have made a very big mistake."

She put her forehead in her hands as Altin turned back to the window, staring out at the silent world below, the world whose terror buzzed inside him like blood returning to a limb that's gone to sleep. He spent several minutes trying to find the Hostile with seeing spells, but it was no use. It had moved. Rapidly no doubt, and who knew where it might be. Somewhere in orbit around the vast planet. Somewhere on the surface. Somewhere far below.

All he could do was wait. But for how long? How much time should they invest in this strategy? He should be moving off, trying to find Red Fire on his own. That was the only hope left if this plan failed. But if he left, what would happen if it didn't work? Or only sort of worked. What if Blue Fire suddenly needed him? What if he exhausted himself trying to find Red Fire and couldn't cast himself back again? Blind casting, even with the ring, could still do that to him, he knew. He hadn't had much rest these last few days.

He watched the emptiness around Blue Fire for a while longer, but still no sign of the orb. He turned back to where Orli sat and saw that she had drifted off to sleep. She had to be exhausted. She'd only gotten a few hours' rest after he'd snatched her out of the executioner's grasp. She was in worse shape than he was when it came to that.

But he had to keep going, to keep moving. And there was some work he could do while they waited for this idea to play out.

With a thought, he was standing at the creek in the meadow beyond Calico Castle, the area strangely silent now in the absence of the army that had been encamped near the castle walls. Their tents were all still there, the outbuildings, he knew it by the thin lines of smoke rising into the air, the gray plumes snaking lazily up toward the clouds from fires that still hadn't quite burned out. Total commitment, the Queen had said. And this was it.

He spent a nerve-wracking quarter hour searching out suitable rocks to use as seeing stones. He enchanted as many as he had patience for, stopping between each enchantment to cast a seeing spell back to the tower for a peek at Orli, who still lay slumped over the table getting a few moments' desperately needed rest. He'd take an extra second after checking on her to peek out the window, hoping for some signs of blossoming planetary romance, whatever that might be, but there was nothing. Then he went back to work on the seeing stones. Find a stone, enchant, check on Orli. As quickly as he possibly could. And even with that casting regimen, with that furtive speed, he was only willing to make eleven of them. He had to get back and begin the work of finding Red Fire's world. Eleven would have to be enough.

He quickly sent himself into the castle proper, to a storeroom below the kitchens where he found a basin, which he brought out into the courtyard with another teleport and began filling with water at the well. It was tedious work, but he wound the crank furiously and the physical exertion of several buckets full helped calm his nerves a little bit. Perhaps because it was a familiar task, a thing he'd done, here, in this place, so many times before, it was strangely soothing to do. After a time, midway through his task and, as he found himself staring down into the dark hole of the well watching the bucket slowly creep up out of that sloshing abyss, he began to fill with nostalgia again. How many times had he done this? How many hundred times? All better times, for sure, though he'd appreciated them little enough.

He brought the bucket out and looked at it, an old wooden thing, gray with age, its outsides soft with having been so wet so often over the years. Just then it seemed a familiar friend. An old companion of his youth. He turned and looked across the courtyard at the wooden scaffolding where the work had begun to rebuild his tower—the east tower, which he would always think of as his. No one was working on that now.

Definitely better times.

He heard a sound behind him, back the way he had come. He turned to see Kettle, who had just spotted him.

"I thought I heard someone a crankin' at that old thing," she said. She tried to look calm, but tears burst upon her face, and she came running to him. "Oh, Altin, 'tis all gone wrong, hasn't it?" She clutched him in arms made strong by the daily lifting of sacks of flour and grain, the toting of water pails and the mashing and chopping of vegetables and meat.

He held her long enough to let the wave of her emotions pass, and he wiped his own tears away with a quick shrug of his shoulder on the right and an absent-seeming motion of his left hand, while she pulled away and dabbed at her face with her apron strings.

When she was composed, he smiled down at her, all confidence again. "It's not pretty in Crown City," he said.

"But the Earth people are helping, and ... well, if Blue Fire can get through to the Hostile world that is attacking Earth, they'll have more men to spare. If that happens, I think everything will be all right again. At terrible cost, but all right."

Movement in the doorway caught his eye, and he saw a small blonde head peering out of the shadows within.

He looked back to Kettle. "Pernie's home?"

"They sent her back. Her Majesty called up all the instructors at the school ta fight."

"That was good thinking," he said. He sent Pernie a smile as best he could given the ongoing thrum of Blue Fire's fearful agony.

Taking that as encouragement, she ran out to where they were. Altin expected her to bounce into him and hug his leg, but she stopped short. She stood very straight and looked him directly in the eye. "I can help, you know."

This time his smile moved all the way to his eyes. "You are a brave little sprite, I'll give you that," he said. "But I think we've almost got it won. Besides, Kettle needs you here to guard Calico."

She thrust out her lips then, and crossed her arms over her narrow little chest. "Everyone knows all the orcs are at Crown City trying to kill the Queen," she said. "Nothing is coming here."

"You're probably right," he said. "But it's best to be safe."

"I'm not a baby anymore."

Altin smiled again. "I know you aren't."

She was looking at the basin he'd filled. "What's that for? Are you going to scry out the enemy? I know what that is, you know. Even if I can't do it, says Master Grimswoller." Her little frame straightened to its fullest height, clearly pleased with her ability to recognize magic purposes by name.

"Yes," he said. "That's exactly right." He took the bucket from where he'd set it on the edge of the well and poured it into his basin. He flipped the catch and tossed the bucket down again.

"So you might still need me to fight."

"I don't think so," he said as he wound the bucket back up again. "Besides, where I'm going is no place for a little girl."

"I'm not little."

"Well, it's no place for a big girl either."

"Is Miss Orli going?"

He stopped winding for a moment and studied her. She had a strange look on her face. "Yes," he said, once more working the well handle. "Blue Fire speaks to her, so I have to take her along." It wasn't exactly a lie, and he didn't want to deal with whatever that look was on Pernie's face.

Pernie stuck out her lips again. Altin looked at Kettle, who merely shrugged. In the old days, Kettle would have sent Pernie away, sent her off on some time-consuming errand that would give Altin his space. A lot of things had changed.

"I have to get back," he said. "I can't leave her out there all alone."

Kettle nodded. Pernie stalked away.

Two more plunges of the bucket and Altin had enough. Kettle watched him in silence the entire time. When he'd dumped the last of the water into the basin, he let go a long sigh. "It's going to be all right," he said, just as he had said before.

The edges of her mouth crept upwards a bit, a wan crescent below the uninhibited love misting her eyes. She hugged him and then watched him go, hoping he was right.

Chapter 39

Colonel Pewter tapped the glass on the inside of his battle suit canopy, hoping the reading was wrong. It read under forty thousand rounds left for the Gatling arm, and the unit's power core was down to a quarter charge. He figured he had about two hours of fight left in the suit, but he wouldn't have half that for ammunition. If he used the laser, he'd have less than twenty minutes. After that, the suit would be nothing more than a toy for the demons to toss around.

"Down to twenty-eight thousand," came Corporal Chang's call even as the Colonel was tapping on the glass. "This is going to be a bitch when it's down to jackhammers and grips."

"Roger that, Chang. Make your shots count, people," the colonel said for perhaps the tenth time that day. He'd been saying it since the transport ship hit the wall and they all came scrambling out. He wondered how much more careful they could be.

Private Sanchez's unit came charging back around the corner as the colonel gave the order to conserve. Cobblestones flew like dark sparks from the smashing impact of each of the battle suit's footsteps, and Sanchez cut the corner tight enough to splinter a wagon that had been upturned earlier by a demon. Bits of wood flew from it as the Marine burst through its frame, the whipcords of leather straps flapping as the long traces flew skyward, turning slowly in the air before landing behind him. "We got company," the panting Marine yelled as he ran to where the colonel stood. "Four of the big ones, and about sixteen orcs." Another Marine rounded the corner right behind him, his suit smoking from a segment at the back, a short length of red hose waving spastically and spraying red fluid in the air.

"Fire Team Two, can you get to my location?" the colonel asked.

"In a minute, Colonel," came Corporal Chang's reply. "We have to finish this fucker first." The sound of gunfire and the profanity of the other Marines in Corporal Chang's fire team served as background noise as he spoke. "Can you bring them to us?"

"We've got a man on foot here," he said. "Just get here ASAP."

"Roger that."

The colonel ordered his men to cover, marking the one building on the block not burning yet as the one not to hide behind. "Commander Levi is in that one," he admonished as he fell back and positioned himself behind the glare of the burning inn. It would give him a chance to get off a first shot. Sanchez moved down the street a bit further and hid as best he could behind a marginally shattered tree.

The first of the three demons that had been chasing Private Sanchez didn't bother rounding the corner as sharply as the Marine had, and it erupted through the side of the two-story structure as easily as the mech had run through the wagon. The roof collapsed in its wake, sending embers climbing into the sky, and the demon crawled straight for where the private stood behind the splintered remnants of the great oak tree. It paused only for a moment, looking farther down the street where the Marine in the smoking mech was still running, seeking cover of his own, but mainly hoping he might draw the pursuit after him a bit farther, pulling the demons deeper down the gauntlet his companions made and giving them as much advantage as possible, if only for a time.

The demon watched him running off, but turned back to Sanchez, who must have seemed as if he were cowering there. It rushed at this near victim, just as two more demons essentially finished off the house on the corner and came pounding into Colonel Pewter's view.

The colonel waited as the first demon ran past, holding his fire and watching through the flames as twelve stilt legs ate up so much ground so rapidly. Right behind it came another, this one twice as large, a top-heavy monstrosity similar in ways to the very first one the colonel had fought, a massive black body like a wide-bottomed beaker tipped upside down. Where the spout would have been was its neck which thrust out before it as it ran upon the five great clubs of its legs and feet. This one did not see him either, and it chased after its fleeing prey farther down the street, leaving Sanchez for the first.

"Steady, people. Wait for the third one to clear me. Levi, watch your fire, there will be orcs after. Take two good shots, then stay down so they don't figure out where you are."

"Don't think I won't," said Roberto from his place inside a room looking down on the street, three buildings down from the corner and nearly in line with where the colonel was. "I'm done trying to be a hero after that last one."

The third demon came past as he said it, a long sinewy thing, low to the ground like a reptile but with a body that was little more than a consecutive set of lumpy mounds.

If it hadn't been moving in the direction it was, Colonel Pewter could not have identified which end was its head. Even then he couldn't truly know, for the creature had no eyes, no horns, no mouth, no identifying features at all. Just several sequences of bulk, like bulbous sections in a knotted rope.

When its last segment had nearly passed him, the colonel opened up with his Gatling gun, charging into the trailing section of it as he did. The jackhammer blade was already moving as he drew near, intent on plunging it into the hole his bullets cut into the demon's hard outer shell. But when he got to it and punched into the jagged place where the fifty-cal had been doing its work, he found that he could not penetrate this one. He backed off a step and opened up again, a waterfall of brass casings pouring onto the street. The ammo counter on his canopy ticked down rapidly.

Rather than spin around to face him, the demon simply stopped running and raised up its back half as if it had changed its mind as to which end was its head. It curled back on itself like a serpent about to strike and, quick as a whip, slammed its bulbous mass down at him.

He dove to the side just in time to avoid being smashed, and the rounded bulb of the demon bashed through the cobblestones that remained and punched a six-foot hole into the gravel and dirt below. It wrestled with itself for a moment to extract its hammer head, and once again raised it up into the air. The colonel expected to hear it roar like the others had, to feel the vibrations of its awesome size through his suit, but it made no sound other than the hard plastic sound of its clattering feet. For a moment most of it was lost in the dust and flying debris of its first strike.

The colonel rolled his battle suit back to its feet and ran at it again, guns blazing into its exposed underside, though with what appeared to be the same results as before, which was nothing, or so little it might as well have been. That's when the streak of Roberto's laser cut across the street and bust out a chunk of the black armor, so the colonel moved the line of his fire to that spot as well. The place where the beam hit had already begun to glow some, becoming molten, and a second line of laser fire sent a melt of black fluid running down the demon's side and onto the street. Two steps was all the colonel needed before he could jam the jackhammer into the hole, but already the massive stone-smashing bulb was on its way down again, intent on driving him into the avenue like an old-world railroad spike. Again he had to dive out of the way, and this time the momentum of it carried him into the fire raging in the building behind which he'd been concealed.

The monster clattered after him, still silent but for its many feet striking the broken ground, and a second swipe, this time of its tail section, or perhaps of its original head, came swinging back at him. It caught him full on in the back, smashing him through the flaming wreckage of the house, flying through the wall and tumbling back into the street. He immediately checked to see if his console was still operational, even as his machine was still sliding to a stop against the unmolested steps of the building where Roberto was. He saw the *Aspect*'s top gunner peering down at him from the window with a grim look upon his face.

He quickly got to his feet, just as the demon was nearly upon him again. The beam from Roberto's laser lanced out across the street and burned into the demon again. Three bursts in rapid succession, at first a slow melt of black fluid began, but that quickly became a smoking stream like hot oil pouring down.

The colonel managed to turn back to face the demon head-on as it rammed him, and this time he plunged his jackhammer arm deep into the huge bulbous end where Roberto had softened it up. Fortunate timing too, for the penetration came barely in time to prevent his bulky war machine from being flung through the frame of Roberto's only sanctuary by the demon's wild thrashing.

He triggered the jackhammer's blade and chewed up everything he could reach inside the creature's head, or tail, whichever it might be. He had to resist the urge to open up point-blank with the suit's other arm and finish it off more rapidly, but he did not. He knew how precious every round would be, and they'd be wasted on armor as thick as this. He knew he had to hold on and wait for it to die from the wounds the jackhammer could make.

As if reading his mind, Roberto started in trying to open another soft spot on the other side of the demon's massive bulb. A long sustained shot, followed by two more.

The colonel saw the beams and barked for Roberto to stop through clenched teeth, straining as he spoke with the effort of keeping the tenuous hold he had on the demon's hammer head. He'd managed to stuff the mech's right vise claw into the hole he'd started when he'd first rushed it, and opening the claw wide, got a purchase, though not reliable he knew.

A group of orcs came around the corner then, several of the seven-foot brutes and a handful of the shamans that the colonel had come to dread. They, like the Queen's cavalry earlier in this long, long day, had figured out the effectiveness of the massive ice rams. It was like fighting the goddamn Hostiles all over again, huge shafts of primitive solidity crushing Earth machines as if they were made from cardboard. They'd been designed to withstand high speed, armor-piercing rounds, and energy weapons of all kinds, even some heavy impact resistance was built in, but only to the point where it would not impact mobility. But nobody had ever expected them to endure being hit by veritable freight trains with any regularity. And these green barbarians had begun casting just that. Only one of them at first, but soon others got word, and he'd been losing men ever since.

He saw the orcs forming up in the flashes of vision afforded by the demon's thrashing, its bulb head waving him in the air in the spasms of its rage and agony, all the while his battle suit whining and hissing as it was put to the limits of its design in his efforts to avoid being flung free, perhaps even flung several blocks away. He had a feeling this might be his last fight if that happened, no telling into what kind of mess he might be thrown, and so he made a point of pushing the jackhammer even deeper in.

The huge shaft of ice came at him at the same time the demon died, and with the barest flick of his legs, he was able to yank the demon's body in front of the incoming missile right as it struck. The force of the impact reverberated through the largely hollowed-out bulb of the slain demon, but its armor held, and both the suit and carcass were sent sliding down the street with the momentum of the giant ice lance. It finally came to rest against the broken tree where Private Sanchez had been.

The demon lay across the colonel's mech heavily, and he labored to get the body off quickly. The hydraulics jolted powerfully against the limp mass as he shoved at it, but he could not throw it off. He could hear the footfalls of the orcs coming down the street, their alien war cries, bass and resonant as they ran. The rattle of their armor got louder and louder the nearer they came, as loud as the motors of the suit while he worked frantically to lift the carcass even just a little bit. He realized that Roberto would try to save him if he could not break free.

He looked back out through the top of the canopy,

hoping to see the other members of his team. Neither was in sight, nor was Corporal Chang and his fire team.

"Don't do anything stupid, Levi," he called out. "Wait for Chang to get here before you show yourself."

"Negative, Colonel. Orli will kick my ass if she finds out I sat here and watched you die."

"Stay where you are, Commander, that's an order."

The colonel heard the confusion amongst the orcs before he heard Roberto say, "Not going to happen, sir." There was shouting and growling, and the noise of at least two orcs in pain.

"Oh, shit," said Roberto, not sounding entirely pleased. "That got their attention."

"Idiot," snarled the colonel. "Get out of there."

He heard ballistic rounds go off, four of them in rapid fire.

"Head shots, bitches," proclaimed Roberto. "You want some more of that?" Three more loud bursts followed.

"Levi, get out, goddamn it," the colonel ordered again. Then, to Fire Team Two, "Chang, where the hell are you?"

"They keep coming, sir," the corporal replied. "We can't get clear."

He could see in his console that his two team members were still moving, the flashes on the grid map indicating the frequency of their fire. He pushed against the demon pinning him, but again met with futility. "Goddamn it," he spat.

One of the orc shamans came into view as Colonel Pewter looked past the curving bulk of the demon into the gray skies above. The orc bent down from his perch atop the demon's body and peered into the mech's canopy as if the colonel were some strange specimen in a jar. The colonel tried to pull his Gatling out from under the demon, but it was stuck. He made a futile swipe at the shaman with the left arm, the jackhammer spitting its staccato at the orc, loud, but useless. He flipped on the flamethrower, but didn't even get one fiery gasp. It had been out of gas for an hour now.

A second shaman climbed up next to the first, and they spent a few moments seeming to discuss what they were going to do. All the colonel could do was watch.

"Shit," shouted Roberto again. "They're in here now."

"Get out," shouted the colonel, feeling useless and weak.

That's when he heard the sound of hooves pounding on the ground. He could feel them in his back where he lay pressed against the dirt. He tilted his head back and saw Lieutenant Forland and his crazy cavalrymen charging in. Six of them had lances lowered and ran at the front of the group, with a seventh on the right side of their line with only a sword. Behind them followed four more horsemen, each of them standing in their stirrups and chanting what the colonel knew would be some kind of spell.

The two shamans looked up, startled, and one of them began a chant of his own, while the second one slipped back out of view on the other side of the lifeless demon. A moment after, a fireball struck the chanting shaman in the chest, blasting it off the demon corpse, burning and howling in agony. Seconds later, the horses charged past him and the air filled with the sounds of steel on steel and the grunts of combat being fought hand to hand.

A movement beside him caused him to look left where he saw a man in chainmail, wearing a brown tabard splattered with blood, placing his hands against the body of the slain demon. He closed his eyes and began to sing, and after a few moments, the demon vanished, changed in that instant to a great splash of water that fell heavily upon the colonel and then washed out into the cobblestones, turning quickly to dirty little brooks that ran away through the wreckage of the street.

The colonel, marginally used to magic by now, had not expected that, and it took him a few moments to realize he was free. When he did, he regained his feet and spared no time for thanks, wading instead right into the combat taking place in the middle of the block.

He was in its midst in nearly an instant, and in no time he'd punched his jackhammer fist through the chest of one orc and the head of another. It only took a three-round burst from the fifty-cal to bust open a shaman a few paces off, one in the middle of casting a spell, and a sweeping backhand right after sent another shaman flying over the house where Roberto was. The colonel could not be sure if it was dead or not, but it turned icy blue in the air, which suggested something might have backfired with the spell it had been working on.

That's when Roberto came leaping out of the second-story window. He flew out over the colonel, arms and feet churning, and he landed heavily on the street, rolling as he hit. The roll absorbed most of the momentum, but he hit hard enough that his assault rifle went skittering away. In the moment it took him to recover and start for his weapon, an orc had also burst through the window and leapt down after him, its giant mace poised to pulp the Spaniard in a single swipe.

The colonel yanked his mech's arm back, its length still extended to maximum from the last swing, and just managed to get it under the mace before it made jelly of Orli's best friend. The mace clanked heavily against the extended limb and a mist of hydraulic fluid began spraying out where a hose was torn free from its mount.

A second orc was jumping out through the window after the first, and the colonel hit it with a short burst from the Gatling gun, shaking his head ruefully as he did. Ammo wouldn't matter now, he knew. He could tell by the spray of oil that he was going to lose control of that arm anyway.

"Thanks, Colonel," Roberto said as he reclaimed his weapon. "I wasn't sure how that was going to turn out."

The colonel didn't waste time to answer, and instead charged back to help the Prosperions with the remaining orcs. They'd made pretty good work of it before he got there, proving how it was that the eleven of them still remained alive when so many others had died. These were men any officer would give anything to have with him, any commander, in any service, at any time in history. Such combinations of heart, mind and skill transcended time and type of weaponry.

By the time the group of orcs were dispatched, Private Sanchez had returned. His companion had not had the same luck that he and the colonel had, and the private conveyed it wordlessly with only one long look. The colonel nodded. That made one less of those rare combinations to help them here today.

There was no time to mourn losses, though, and he instantly checked back on Corporal Chang. "Chang, can you get clear?"

"Sir, they're coming from everywhere. We need to bug out. I think the south wall is completely gone. I can see the Queen coming up the street with a ton of other Prosperions. It looks like a rout. And, sir, there's a really big one back there. I mean, like really big. With a long-ass arm that it's flinging around like a busted coolant hose mashing everything."

"We'll come to you then. Protect the Queen as best you can. We'll be right there."

He popped open his canopy to look the red-feathered cavalryman in the eye. "It's all going to shit now," he said. "Your Queen is in trouble two blocks away." The Prosperion said something back to him, but he'd moved off too rapidly at the news for the colonel to make it out. Within seconds, the eleven horsemen were gone, galloping off to protect their monarch.

He called up to his ship, asking about the reinforcements from Earth, but all he got was the same "they're forming up, and will be there as soon as it becomes possible to spare them" that he got the last three times he asked. He knew exactly what that meant.

He looked down at Roberto, who, standing in the street as he was, looked so small and fragile compared to the battle suit the colonel wore. The young commander stood ready, however, with only his rifle, his side arm and a bulletproof vest. Not much for fighting ten-ton, or even just two-ton demons, that was sure.

"You're probably going to regret having offered to fly us in here," said the colonel with a crooked grin. "They won't evac us now, you know, because of what we did. Technically, we're AWOL."

"I know. Shit happens, right?"

"Yes, it does. But for whatever it's worth, I know why my daughter thinks so much of you."

"That's funny," Roberto said. "Because your daughter usually tells me I'm a pervert and only have a one-track mind." He flashed a wide smile, however, and was clearly proud of his alleged misdeeds.

They both laughed, though it only lasted as long as it took to transform itself into a pair of coinciding sighs, a few seconds of levity before reentering the storm. "Well," said the colonel, "let's make sure you have a chance to continue building that reputation, Commander. Stay low, stay close and, for God's sake, stay out of sight."

"Roger that. I'm definitely done playing the hero this time."

They both knew that wouldn't be true if it came to the precipice once more, but then, that's why they were both still alive.

Major Kincaid's voice crackled over the com as the colonel's canopy was snapping shut again. "Colonel?" She didn't sound pleased.

"Yeah, Kincaid, go ahead."

"Sir, a quarter-mile stretch of the west wall just fell."

Chapter 40

Altin returned to the tower, bringing his small supply of seeing stones and the basin he'd filled into the bare little room that had served as Tytamon's private teleportation chamber for all those centuries. Wanting to set straight to work, he took only a moment to glance out and check on Orli, assuming she would still be sleeping at the table where he'd left her. She was not. She stood at the narrow window looking out on Blue Fire's world again, her back to him. Slight upward movements of her shoulders coincided with soft sniffling sounds as she gazed out upon the planet, and Altin knew immediately that she was crying or, at least, that she had been recently.

He rushed to her side, peering around her to confirm in the glow of Blue Fire's planetary light that there were in fact tears running down Orli's face, lines of shimmering reflection drawn down her soft cheeks and into her bosom where they disappeared. She did not look back at him, only down at Blue Fire. She sniffled again, but that was all, the eye of the storm's sorrow having already passed.

"Orli, what's happened?" he asked. "What's going on?" She had been sleeping soundly only a few minutes ago. He hadn't spent that much time with Kettle in the courtyard.

When she did look at him, it was with distance in her eyes, as if she were far off somewhere in her mind. She shook her head, barely enough movement to discern. "He's going to rape her."

"What?"

She pointed down, out through the window at something far below. He followed with his eyes and saw it then, the huge round mass of a giant Hostile orb, a titanic thing, twice as large as the one they'd seen at Mars, hovering down near the lowest edge of the visible disc of Blue Fire's world. A threadlike line of smaller orbs made their way out of it and into Blue Fire's atmosphere. They glowed like a string of bubbles moving through a bottle of space-black champagne, a steady penetration of the thin veil of Blue Fire's atmosphere.

Altin tried at once to get Blue Fire to speak to him, but she could not. He tried again, sought it in the way of a telepath, a press of mana rather than a simple thought. Still nothing. He could still feel her terror though, the lingering essence all through him, around him like an atmosphere of his own.

"I can't get through to her now," he said. "She's blocking me."

"*He* is blocking you."

"He? He who? Red Fire?"

"Yes."

"How? Why?"

"They block other males. It's why he never found her before. Her mate blocked him from finding her all those years ago, scared him off with his great power and secured this territory."

Altin whispered some Prosperion profanity under his breath, but it was inaudible. "It even blocks human males?"

"So it seems."

"And now we brought him here."

Orli nodded as Altin began to catch up.

"Why can't she fight him off?"

"He is too strong. Many times stronger than she is. She said there is nothing she can do."

"Are you talking to her now? Is she in your mind?"

"No. I fell asleep. She cried out to me in my dream." For the first time she turned to face him. "She cried out to me, Altin. She begged me to help her. He's tunneling toward her right now, forcing his way through the surface of the planet, in search of her, in search of her womb."

"Her womb? I thought they did something with the orbs. The whole gamete thing you were talking about."

"They do. When they are being civil. When they are in love."

It was Altin's turn to stare out the window nearly paralyzed. He watched the thread of orbs streaming into her, a constant press of hostile intent sent to bore into the very core of Blue Fire's body.

"So where is the womb? Maybe I can help her."

"It's where you took me when we got the yellow stones for *Citadel*, the cavern with the ledge."

"Mercy's sweet breath. Then I should go."

"You'll die." She said it so bluntly, so matter of fact. There was no emotion, no emphasis, simply a statement of totality. "He is waiting for you."

"Waiting for me? How the hell does he even know I exist?"

"He's known about you since the first taint of you arrived near Earth, on the Liquefying Stone."

He didn't have to ask it, for she saw the question on his face.

"The one Maul carried to Earth when she first arrived, with the conduit. Huzzledorf brought her with him, and she had your Liquefying Stone. Your essence was in it, or on it, somehow, left over from using it or something. Your DNA maybe. But that's how he knows. That's how he found Earth. That's how he found out about Blue Fire too. She's the first he's ever scented. His lust is ravenous."

"She told you all of this?"

"It is her will."

His face showed complete and total perplexity, his mouth open, dumb. "Her will? Will to do what? Orli, you're speaking in riddles almost as bad as she does. There isn't time for this."

"Not her will to do anything. It's her final will. A last will and testament. She's going to die, going to let go. She doesn't want to live through this."

"But why?"

"Because, Altin. Because she can't take another tragedy, another layer of it in her long life. You don't know what utter hopelessness is. To be helpless and powerless. I do. I've seen it. She doesn't have the strength to fight back. And she doesn't have anyone to come and save her before it happens like I did. So she's going to wait for it and then let it smother her, let the horror of his violation crush her until there is no more. She can finally be free."

"We'll save her. We'll prevent it somehow."

"It's already begun."

Altin frowned, furious, helpless in his own way. Frustrated. He paced away from the window and back. "I thought she couldn't kill herself. That's why she's suffered so long as it is."

"She can't. But she can let him snuff her out."

Altin leaned out through the window, watching the events unfold. His heart raced. His mind raced. His whole body trembled with rage layered atop the horror he felt from Blue Fire.

He screamed inside his head at her. Screamed for her to speak to him. To tell him what to do. But still there was nothing. He was beyond impotent to help.

"We have to do something," he said. "Orli, we have to stop it."

"He will kill you. His power is ten times greater than hers. A hundred times greater. She has no words for it, but it's massive. He will kill you as easily as he did High Priestess Maul. If you let him find your mind as the Maul did, you will be killed. It will be quick."

"If that's the case, why can't he find me now? I have this." He held up the ring. "If my taint was on the Liquefying Stone that Maul had, and if he somehow ... what, smelled it? Then why can't he smell me on this?"

"I don't know, Altin. I have no idea. I only know what she told me. He's striving for her inner core. He means to take her seeds by force, since she would not give them up willingly. And when he does, when he finds her and breaks in, she is going to let her life flow out through the wound."

"That's not going to happen."

She looked at him, something in the intensity of his tone sparking the tiniest bit of hope. He spun and stormed back into the teleportation chamber. He slammed the door. She heard the lock slide into place. Then she didn't hear anything.

She turned back to look down upon Blue Fire, but she was gone. The window frame lit up with bright red light in that instant, the glare of it intense and coming so suddenly it startled her. She stepped back, and for a moment thought somehow Altin had transported them to the vile red world somehow. But then she saw the familiar shapes of rocky Phobos and Deimos. This was Mars. Of course he hadn't brought them to Red Fire. How could he have?

Looking to the right, she saw that there was another of the giant Hostile orbs in orbit again. Not quite so large as the first one had been, but there it was nonetheless. Apparently Red Fire had sent another already to take the place of the one they'd sent into the sun. The new one, like the other, sent a trail of small orbs running off over the sun, toward Earth again. She sighed when she saw it. Director Nakamura would take the arrival of the new orbs as evidence of Her Majesty's deceit. He'd call off the air support. No ground troops would be sent to Prosperion from Earth. Her father and Roberto would die. Everyone would die.

It really was all going to end. Even Blue Fire. And only the red world would survive. The ultimate victor, Red Fire.

Their last hope lay in whatever Altin was doing now. Whatever madness struck him. She knew him well enough to know he was up to something.

Then Mars was gone. She blinked, and it wasn't there anymore. She blinked again, a few times, a quick fluttering, waiting for something else to appear in its place, the next great cosmic sphere. She knew it was foolish, but hoped that it might be Red Fire next. She hoped Altin was in that room, that teleporter's room, doing what he did best, consuming vast distances with his potent genius. She hoped somehow he could cross a thousand light years in only a few moments' time. That's what she hoped, and she blinked and blinked, wishing Red Fire to appear.

Nothing appeared. They were nowhere. All was emptiness. Stars upon a black void. Billions of burning cores serving to heat something, or nothing, and destined to die one day. To die like everything else, like Blue Fire, like Tytamon, like her mother so long ago. There were only the good people to make it matter at all. Sweet, beautiful Altin, in there probably about to blow out his brainstem trying to save the universe. Her father, distant, aloof and brave, but he loved her too—for all the misery his decisions had made of Orli's life. She'd never really thought much about what he'd gone through way back then, what had led to the decision to bring a little girl aboard a spaceship like he had—a shitty bit of parenting that was. But she understood. She could allow herself to now. His heart must have broken when her mother died. She'd never thought about it like that before, from his point of view, not very hard anyway. What wreckage a lost love like that must cause. The misery of Blue Fire stood as the galactic font of that kind of misery, the colossus of pain pouring fountain-like into the black veil of eternity, every star yet another tear. In a way, Orli thought Blue Fire might be better off dead. At least that torment, that eternal wound, would be over for her. Blue Fire seemed to lack the one thing humans had, hope. Blue Fire seemed to have nothing she hoped for, not survival, not the chance that tomorrow might be okay.

She thought of Roberto and a long list of other friends, old fleet friends and new ones on Prosperion, Aderbury out there in *Citadel* right now, thousands of magicians trying to defend a planet that wasn't even theirs. It was all so beautiful in its love and human association, and so horrible in its irony. The beauty of humanity at war with the evil that it made.

For the barest moment, she wondered if maybe the universe might not be better off rid of humanity. At best it was equal parts good and evil. At worst something less favorable.

She knew even as she thought it that it wasn't so. It wasn't so because of those same people she'd been thinking of. As long as they lived, there was hope. They were the hope of humanity. She was.

The stars shifted noticeably outside the window, like a movement seen at the edge of vision, a phantom motion that, when caught, freezes to stillness again. She had to stare hard to decide if their position had changed. In the absence of planetary light, there were so many stars out there. She spotted a greenish nebula far off to the right and high above. She wasn't sure if that had been there before. But she decided to use it for a landmark. She knew what Altin was doing in there. There could be nothing else.

She stared up at that nebula for a long, long time. It felt like an hour, though perhaps it was less. And then the nebula was gone.

Still there was nothing out there. She ran to a window on the opposite side of the tower and looked out through it. More stars. A binary system was very close, so close she instinctively feared for the radiation coming off of it, though she trusted in Altin's shields. They'd preserved them much closer to suns than this. It was frightening though, for despite how much she loved him, she also knew that he was ignorant of so many things. He was the truest manifestation of the early explorer, daring to do what no one else had done, doing it out of courage, true, but also out of having no fear of things that, had he known them, might have given him cause to turn back. Although, probably not. Not Altin. He would have figured something out. That was who he was.

The binary system vanished sometime later, and Orli knew then that her assumptions had to be correct. Altin was chewing up the expanse of the galaxy, hell-bent on getting to Red Fire. But then what? What did he plan to do? Was he going to blink down to the surface and challenge the being to a duel? Blue Fire had told her that Red Fire was far more powerful than she was. Given how much more powerful Blue Fire was than Altin, Red Fire would be godlike by comparison.

She had to help Altin. If she knew the Galactic Mage as well as she thought she did, he was in all-action mode.

Which meant he probably didn't have a plan for what would happen when they got there. So she would make one for them. She would try to anticipate their needs.

Moving away from the window, she took her seat at Tytamon's desk and thought through everything she knew. Everything Altin had told her about Blue Fire, everything she had seen and experienced in all her dream exchanges with the giant living world. She sat amongst the clutter collected by a once-great mind and willed herself to the same kind of exercise, the pooling of imagination, learning and discipline. She pulled out her tablet and went to work making her best guesses at what they would find if—when they found the distant star. If Altin could somehow get them there, they would not arrive without at least some kind of strategy.

Chapter 41

Gromf woke slowly, the sound of tearing flesh all around him now. He lay in a pool of mud, made runny with his own blood. Something heavy lay upon him. He lifted his head to see and saw that a horse had fallen across his legs. Its rider, a human female, lay dead nearby, her mud-splattered face looking at him, eyes wide, perhaps in shock that she had been slain. Her mouth was open in a scream that Gromf had not heard. He'd heard nothing since the strange human had shot him with the beam of red light. He touched his forehead where the light had struck, just above the bridge of his nose. His finger slipped into the hole that was there, two knuckles deep into the bone.

Someone had healed him again. He knew it had been God. Few shamans had the gall to conjure healing. It was a coward's craft. Death was welcomed in the clans.

Looking about him, he saw scores of demons everywhere, the smallish ones, the ravenous ones who ate the bodies of the dead, slurped and gobbled all around. There were two near him, sucking the last marrow from a human skeleton.

One of them looked up from its meal and saw him. It

flashed long and pointed teeth, a row of spikes like blackberry thorns grown half the length of Gromf's arm. Gromf wondered if it would eat him next, though it should not be so. He was the opener of the gate. They should leave him alone. Respect him. But he knew that they did not.

There were worse deaths than to be eaten by the servant of a god.

The demon leapt across the field and landed upon the carcass of the horse. It tore into its new meal hungrily. Gromf tried to push the horse off of his legs, but he could not. He would have to wait.

In time, the second demon came, and Gromf thought that the two of them would have him free very soon, but the second one started on the human female instead. It snatched her up like a freshly caught fish and bit into her head. Gromf watched, testing the weight of the horse, and the course of the demon's progress, in doing so. He could not move the horse off of himself yet. The demons scooped out the soft parts of their meals, sucking entrails into their mouths like strands of boiled salt grass.

Eventually, as the demon ate, Gromf was able to work himself out from beneath the animal. He slowly rose to his feet and stood upon wobbly legs. Perched upon the horse, the demon raised its head and pushed its hideous face near his. The reek of the offal, the copper scent of blood, and something indefinable, assaulted Gromf's sense of smell.

Gromf pushed the demon aside, or made to, but the effort staggered him to the side instead. It was as if he'd pushed against a boulder twice his size. So he stumbled toward the sounds of fighting in the distance now.

He saw that the south wall of the city was in ruins. A measure in either direction smashed down by the might of God's minions and the great army Warlord had made. Though Gromf himself had fallen, or at least had lost a great deal of time, the All Clans were nearing the height of victory.

He turned back and fished through the mud, looking for his two pieces of God Stone, fearing someone might have taken them while he was unconscious. But no one had. No one knew of them. All those who knew had died in the great arena. All but Gromf and Kazuk-Hal-Mandik, and the old shaman had died in the first moments of summoning. So there was only Gromf now. He found the stones right where he expected they would be. He picked them out, wiped them off, then gripped them triumphantly in his fists. There was still time to help.

He made his way to the wall, passing through the blocks of its falling as if through the aftermath of an avalanche. Inside the city, smoking ruins were everywhere, the jagged lines of burnt timbers thrusting like blackened limbs reaching to the skies, pleading uselessly for aid that would not come. Fires crackled and popped as he walked onward, regaining his equilibrium a little more with each new step. From time to time, he would follow the line of those reaching timbers as they pointed skyward, directing his gaze up into the clouds. He scanned all around in the air above the city for signs of the huge red lights, the beams sent by the children of the new god. But they flashed no more.

He smiled, knowing that his god, the true God, had defeated the new one. That was good, and Gromf was happy in his heart. Gaining strength from this, he increased his speed, trotting up the ruins of the street in hopes of rejoining the fight. The fires burned darker, blacker and thicker the farther into the city he went. He knew that Warlord would be pressing for the golden queen's palace, for that was where victory would be. That was the seat of power upon which Warlord would sit.

Faster and faster he went, and even at near full speed,

he had to run for some time, tracing the progress of the fight by the smoke and the trail of bodies everywhere. He had never realized how huge the human city was, and for a moment, even in this moment of humanity's obvious downfall, he found himself wondering if such a people could be killed. But it quickly passed, and on he ran.

He dodged around smoking hulks of dead demons, waded through swamps of gore, great lakes of innards flowing from wide areas of death where human, orc and demon corpses lay jumbled together like some vile stew. He sloshed through it without hesitation or rise of bile, sometimes deeper than his knees. Bones snapped under his feet. Skulls rolled like loose rocks unseen in the riverbed. Occasionally some broken human moaned. Humans whined like younglings when they died.

He passed through several such sites, low places of mire. Other areas had perhaps less gore but far greater devastation. He crossed broad intersections in which he beheld the complete obliteration of what must once have been places of great pride for the golden queen, and increasingly so the farther on he went. The buildings that burned as he pressed through the city grew larger in their ruin, more spectacular in their collapse. Grand columns toppled and smashed here and there, demolished statues of humans carved in careful likenesses, their weak faces and fragile limbs hewn ironically of stone. Gromf laughed at these, spat on the careful polish of the white marble pieces lying all about, lying there dull and dust covered, a cracked and empty glory slowly being buried in the soot of all that smoke. As it should be.

The sound of fighting was louder now. He heard thunder cracks and knew that lightning was coming down. Lots of lightning. The shouts of humans fighting sounded like swarming bees to him in the distance, the noise of thousands of beating wings. He heard the roars of demons echoing from buildings beyond as well, buildings that had yet to be pulled down and burned. It was the song of the battle, and it cheered him. It raised his spirits and helped reduce his shame for having fallen as easily as he had. There was still time for glory. He would fight again.

Running at top speed now, he raced down the human city's streets. The fighting seemed to have cut a great wedge into the city, and it was easy to find where the brunt of the fighting was, as the wreckage drove him right to it now.

He came upon a vast city square, a broad flat space which was lined all around with buildings that climbed high into the air, each rising in tiers of stone stacked one upon the next like flat rocks, but unbelievably large, wide flat squares piling up toward the clouds, making it easy for humans to climb the steep slopes to the fanciful human structures at the top of each. Most of these were made of the shiny white stone he'd seen in other statuary as he'd come into the city, though one was made of darker stone. It was the largest of the buildings. A blocky colossus that dominated the square at the farthest end. The mountain of its construction had at the top such an immense assemblage of columns Gromf could not fathom the reason for such a thing. They'd made a forest of fluted stone, for what purpose? To prove to someone that they could? Stupid and vain humans.

However, it was a structure that must represent the seat of some power, for atop its steps were hordes of humans in robes the color of rust. Lightning forked out from these humans like the fury of a god, and it licked around the man-made mountain and burst orcs like stomped-on fruit.

Demons threatened them on all sides, however, and only one lightning bolt in ten gave trouble to the crawling black death that came at them. The humans fought these with weapons of steel, and Gromf was surprised at the efficiency. But he knew it would only be a matter of time before that great structure was overrun and destroyed. All those columns would come down, toppled in the demise of human arrogance.

He looked past it to the palace in the distance, its taunting spires reaching so unfathomably high. That too would fall, although perhaps not physically. Gromf thought it would be good to keep. Warlord could look out upon his lands from that great height and see all that he had conquered today.

Gromf had to find Warlord. He had to return to his side, show him that Gromf survived. That Gromf still made war for the All Clans. That he still fought for God.

He ran past the scene in search of him. The demons would take the square, even if all the orcs aiding them were turned to stew, the same as they had been in so many other parts of the city. They died in the glorious cause, and their deaths were welcome.

He ran past the wide square and followed the sounds of fighting deeper in the city.

He heard the metallic whine of the warriors of the new god, for what else could those giant things be? Weapons of other humans come to aid the golden queen. He ran to that sound then, enraged by it. He wanted to find the human who had shot him in the head with that red light.

He found two of the humans in the ogre-sized armor suits. They fought together against a demon and a pair of orcs. A burst of the short fire emitted from one of the armored arms and the nearest of the orcs turned to mush. The demon bashed the other armored human and sent it flying into an artificial pond, a large thing, perfectly round, and layers of water pouring from stone troughs climbing into the air. Water spat from its top like a geyser and ran down its layers like little waterfalls, but the flying human in all its armor crashed down through it, shattering its tiers one by one with its weight until it landed with a splash. Water and bits of marble flew all around. The white-stone water tribute was destroyed, and the human did not move, its armor lying motionless just beneath the surface of the pond. Gromf saw the human's hands press against the clear surface of its armor then, the flat white pads of its hands pounding on the transparent substance near the top of the great metal thing. It was clearly desperate. The human's face lifted up—a male human, Gromf thought—and by its wide and frightened eyes, Gromf knew it was in trouble. He watched the human for a moment and realized its armor was filling up with water then. He watched the human drown and was satisfied.

The other human crushed the remaining orc with a backhanded swipe of an armored arm, and made sure the job was done by stomping the limp body under foot even as the demon lunged with a huge crab claw that caught the armor firmly in its grasp.

It lifted the human up and slammed it down once against the ground, while the human punched at it with its left arm. The powerful arm had a protrusion, a long iron spike that looked to Gromf like a short spear, though the human never threw it. The spike moved in and out rapidly and made an awful sound, but never flew away. The human did thrust it into the demon's claw, though, and it drove the point into the shell with rapid vibrations and a tremendous hammering noise.

At first Gromf thought the demon's shell would be sufficient to prevent such an attack, but it was not, and soon the human had thrust its armored limb elbow deep into the claw, breaking it apart. A moment later the human was free and the demon reeling back and roaring in outrage.

The human ran forward and punched its other arm, the

fire-emitting arm, into the demon's open mouth. Gromf heard the muted sound of its metallic fire weapon going off inside. The demon's back opened up in a spray of yellow guts. It pitched forward, dead, its weight driving the human back.

Gromf ran forward, calling up his giant ram of ice as the human yanked its armored arm free of the dead thing. The human saw him coming and raised the fire-emitting arm. Gromf had to let the ice lance go early and smaller than he would have liked as he dove to the side, rolling behind a piece of the broken water structure lying nearby. A few of whatever it was that the short-fire weapon spewed ticked off the street nearby, sending up bursts of broken stone and dust in a line that chased Gromf as he rolled away. The unseen projectiles careened off into the distance behind him with warped and whining sounds, but that stopped right away as the human was spun around by the impact of Gromf's ice lance.

He laughed and regained his feet, starting another lance. The human inside the armor was shouting something that Gromf couldn't hear, but he could see it was a human female again. The humans must have sent all their women into war. Which was just as well, for there would be no men to mate with them. They might as well all die. Their time was done.

He reminded himself to stay disciplined. They had also ruled for well over a thousand years. And he could not let a woman kill him.

He sent the new ice lance at the woman in the giant suit of steel. Her mouth was still moving when it struck her and sent her flying down the street. She landed a hundred paces from where she had been, and Gromf could see the flailing of her armor as she struggled to get up.

He ran toward her, grinning. He would kill her and teach her that women were too weak to fight.

The transparent portion of the armor opened then, it popped up and swung away. The woman climbed out of it, struggling to free herself of some tangle of thin flat ropes, some of which appeared to be jammed into her skin. She wore clothing just like that of the human that had shot Gromf with the red light, the light that was like the light that came from the sky, though not nearly as thick as that.

She pulled something from a long rigid pouch strapped to her thigh, drawing it out and raising it like a weapon at him. It was too late though, for Gromf's ice lance was already away. A small one now, at least compared to the last. Warriors threw spears as big in practice every day. But it would suffice.

It struck her through the heart and drove her back against the upraised expanse of transparent material that had come open on the armor suit. She hit that hard, and nearly crumpled, but somehow stayed upright, leaning against it, her blood running down the clear surface behind her, visible between her legs as it poured into the hollow from which she'd emerged. She looked down at the shaft of ice in her heart, her eyes wide, clutching it, then looked up at him again. She spat a spew of blood at him and then pitched forward, dead, falling back into the armor in a heap.

Victory felt good, and Gromf's confidence continued to renew. He did not have to face God or Warlord in shame.

He ran on, looking for them both. He came across two more skirmishes and stopped both times to help his side. He shaped a wave of fire using his God Stones, and in one great splash set a hundred of the golden queen's warriors on fire. It was joyous.

It was much the same elsewhere along the way. Finally, he heard the sound that he was looking for. The deep roar of God and the lashing thunder of his vast reach, that arm that wrought death like a granite whip. He heard the crisp retorts of the humans of the new gods too, their armor undoubtedly spitting fire at God. That Gromf could not tolerate. God had spared his life twice today. He knew he would never understand it, never know why God would preserve his weakness and failure, but he must not ever doubt again. God had a plan for him, and he would not fail it, whatever it might be.

A few minutes at full speed brought Gromf to the heart of the battle. They were perhaps a measure away from the golden queen's palace on a broad expanse of carefully laid stones, every one of them cut into perfect rectangles and set together edge to edge. These stones ran the full distance to the palace, and from side to side nearly a quarter as wide, a tremendous level expanse made for what? Yet another monument to human arrogance.

Such were their ways, their ostentatious displays. But today would be the end. The demons with their crushing feet were chewing up huge chunks of the carefully placed and carefully cut stone. Even the children of the new god trampled that work under with the stomping of their metal feet. More delightful irony.

But the most glorious thing he saw was God. God towered above them all and wiped swaths of humans aside like insects crawling in the dirt. That awesome length of his great arm swung back and forth to the roar of his immensity, splashing humans into the air as if he were stomping in mud puddles. The humans flew away from him in waves, flung out over the battle, over the buildings, and looking like flocks of wingless birds clawing at the sky as they tumbled and spun away.

Gromf looked for one of them to gleam with gold, hoping to see the human queen land at his feet. He would pull out her tongue and push in her eyes with his thumbs. Then he would drag her to Warlord to eat.

She did not land near him, however, for such was not

his destiny. He saw it when he spotted her, still in combat with Warlord. He found them by the sound of Warlord cursing her in the secret language of their clan. Gromf knew what he had spoken, though the golden queen did not.

How long had that battle raged? How long had Gromf been unconscious? Long enough for the army to cut this deep into the sprawling city. Long enough for God to stop the lights from falling from the sky. And still the two leaders fought.

He wondered why God did not strike her down, and yet he knew. It must be Warlord. Such was the prophecy.

But Warlord hadn't done it yet. Why?

And then Gromf saw why.

It was the wicked elf.

Warlord ran at the golden queen and swung at her with his axe. The queen parried it aside and then dove back, away from the upward thrust of the axe haft as Warlord swung it toward her groin.

Then the elf was on Warlord's back. It raised its daggers and went to plunge them in, but Warlord reached back and snatched him off and threw him into the crowded melee all around.

The golden queen leapt on Warlord in that moment and somehow drove him to the ground, where the two of them grappled for a time. Finally, with a mighty thrust of his legs, Warlord threw the queen in her gleaming armor off of him. She flew back several paces and rolled right back to her feet. Warlord was back on his. They circled each other warily again, and Gromf knew then that this had been going on for hours.

It was Gromf's fault. He was meant to kill the elf.

He looked to the crowd where the elf had vanished. He could not find it, but he could tell by the way the crowd seemed to fall in on itself where it was. The thrusting spears and swords of the orcs trying to kill it dove and slashed, yet they found nothing to bite into, no flesh to cut, no bones to break. Such was the elusive nature of that awful thing.

The elf cut his way clear and once again moved to get behind Warlord. Then it disappeared.

Gromf shook his head and ran toward the fight. The elf would not cut Warlord down from behind. He sent a wave of fire at an angle, the farthest end of it just missing Warlord's back.

The elf appeared when the fire passed over him. He spun and faced Gromf coming on even as he patted at places where the black leather of his armor smoked. The snarl that formed on his wicked face was an invitation to death.

Gromf sent two ice lances, each as long as the elf was tall, thick as his fist, both sharp to a needle's point.

The elf vanished, avoiding Gromf's missiles, and reappeared running straight for Gromf. Gromf had done this before.

This would be for the glory of God, Gromf thought as he gripped his God Stones tight. He had been given a second chance, and this time he would not fail. He would see how much fire the elf could endure.

The elf's daggers were already on their way.

Chapter 42

Altin was down to his last seeing stone when he found the red sun. Ten stones to get there, a massive and desperate undertaking, but there it was, a giant red sun. It was still far away, barely bigger than a button in the distance, and perhaps a bit more orange than he'd expected, but it was where it was supposed to be, and there could be little doubt. Altin knew this was the one.

He also knew from what Orli had taught him about Blue Fire's mate, and even about Blue Fire herself, who the fleet people had named Goldilocks for a reason, that there would only be planets capable of supporting life in a certain area around that enormous red sun. Too close, and it would be too hot for life. Too far away, and it would be too cold. And while that made perfect sense to him, he'd still have to guess at where that band was, and even if he got it right, he'd then have to hope there were planets in orbit there. And if there were, he'd have to find them and then determine if there was actually life living there. It was a lot of *if*s.

Now certain that he had found the star they sought, he took up his last seeing stone and drew a deep breath. "Get me close," he said as he gazed down upon it. Its surface was smooth, polished by time and the flow of water down that sweet little creek, a gurgling brook on a planet that was now so far away, a distance so great that measurements meant nothing, and the best Altin could do to comprehend the scale of it was through the way thinking of it made him feel. It was that far away. He almost felt bad for the little rock. It would never see that place again. It would be stranded out there forever. Thinking it reminded him of his first seeing stone, cast successfully onto the surface of Luria. He'd felt the same way then. His will sentencing something to eternal banishment. How easily it could be done, anthropomorphosis or not. He shuddered at the thought.

Then he sent the stone on its way, sent it to the place that needed to be right, that seemed right, which was all he had. It was a guess, a placement based on what felt like the right distance relative to the scale of what he already knew. He knew where Prosperion was in relation to its sun. He knew where Earth was in relation to Sol. He even knew where Blue Fire was in the same sort of way. He measured those distances and used that to guide his last seeing stone. It was surely not science, and he knew that some suns burned hotter than others. He'd listened to all that he'd been told. But he sent the stone, and it would have to be enough. He would have to begin the search for life from there.

He checked the scrying basin a moment after to see if there was anything to see. He immediately saw that the red sun was as he had hoped, or mainly so, a bloodied orange sphere glowing brightly and similar in size to the suns he knew, if perhaps a bit bigger than they were. He gauged he'd gotten a little closer than he ought to have, but he hoped he hadn't missed by much. The rest would have to be done by casting seeing spells anyway.

He wasted no time and began looking for a planet

nearby, plunging his vision out into the silent blackness and pushing it around.

As always, the distances, even within a solar system, were infuriatingly large, and quite despite Altin's considerable experience moving his sight as quickly as he was. And this solar system seemed even worse than the three other solar systems he had explored so far. Orli had said the sun would be much bigger, nearly a hundred times more, but such things were intellectual concepts, abstracts for the mind that somehow never struck one properly until experienced for real.

Eventually, after a great deal of searching and wondering which angles he pursued might intersect the plane of planetary rotation, and wondering even if he did find it whether there were any planets anyway, he finally saw a "star" in the distance that was growing rapidly as he moved. It started out as a tiny dot of light like all the rest, but it began to expand in his vision, drawing attention to itself as Altin sped along. *Finally*, he thought as he rushed toward it.

It grew and grew as he approached. It was very red, and the closer he got to it, the more he began to despair that he would find water there. Closer and closer he went, and still no blue oceans shaped themselves as he approached. No white clouds or snow appeared, not the least brushstroke of color beyond ever-present red, though he did begin to notice a few dark spots, like freckles growing slowly as he drew near.

When he was close enough, he realized the freckles were moons. The planet had several, and he made a quick circuit of each of them. Blue Fire's mate was, by Orli's theory anyway, a moon around a colossal world, and that gave him hope. He'd almost forgotten about that. The planet didn't need water if the moons had some.

They did not. They were all barren things, dark and

rocky. Clearly without atmosphere, and certainly no large bodies of water anywhere. Frustrated at the lost time, he pushed his way down to the planet itself. He raced around it in a high orbit as he had the moons, looking for signs of small seas, large lakes, rivers, glaciers, anything that might give him a place to start looking for life. All he saw was red and the occasional whorls of what looked to be mustard-colored clouds. At least there was some kind of atmosphere.

He pushed his vision downward, and came upon the surface, discovering as he did a red place that was as much like Mars as it was Luria. It was barren, just like its moons, though heaped in places with mountains that seemed to Altin's magical eye as if they must thrust hundreds of measures into the sky. They dominated huge portions of the landscape like bloody teeth rooted in an enormous jaw. The roar of the wind in places sounded the shouts of that violence too. At times it roared with such power that Altin had to tweak the spell to mute the sound. The frenzy of this place, of the wind that blew beneath the mustard smears of that sky, was everywhere.

A few times he paused, awed by it, in particular, mesmerized by the great snaking tubes of enormous tornadoes that would suddenly pounce upon the land. They were thick and furious flutes of wind that, from nothing, would instantly appear, scores and scores of them like a mighty herd, tightly wound things that stretched upward as far as he could see, twisting and writhing ropes of turmoil that bound the violence of the land to the violence of the sky. They wove and danced around each other like the ghosts of awful giants celebrating hate and rage. It was both fantastic and horrifying at once.

Surely no life could live in such a place.

He spent a long time pushing around that seething red

world, racing back into orbit and diving back down somewhere else, probing into the shadowed places between and around mountain ranges that seemed as large as Prosperion itself.

He even pushed through the surface, ran around in the darkness for a long time, hoping to chance upon some series of tunnels, some underground rivers or lakes, some winding passages filled with the dim glowing substance that lined the walls of the caves around Blue Fire's core, the porous planetary tissues of a planet-sized organism.

But he found none of that.

After wasting what he knew was far too long on it, he pulled his vision back into the darkness of space again. He gazed out upon the sun. What had he missed? Why was there no life here? There had to be life. If not, well, then there wouldn't be life anywhere.

Or maybe he'd just gone too far. Maybe this world was too close to the sun.

Or too far away.

How much time should he waste guessing again? But what other choice was there? He couldn't go back and try divining now. Or perhaps he could. Perhaps Ocelot would know. She'd known before. Maybe she'd be home this time. Maybe she'd be waiting for him. Maybe.

If not, he'd lose even more time.

The debate with himself wasted time too. He let the seeing spell go.

When he came out of the teleportation chamber, he found Orli seated at Tytamon's desk and busy at work on her tablet. He realized for the first time that she must be wondering what he had done, perhaps thought he'd lost his mind.

She did not. She looked up when he came out and smiled a tired smile at him, her teeth and the whites of her eyes bright and reflecting the bluish light of her tablet where it lay on the table before her. "Did you find him?" She asked it in a way that said she already knew he had, that she knew he'd never have come out otherwise.

"I don't know," he said. "I found the red sun. And a big red planet. But I can't find water. No oceans, no lakes, not even a puddle anywhere. And no ... no womb, or whatever chamber a male would have in its place. I found nothing. I don't know what to do."

"Where did you look? Where in the system, I mean. How far away was the planet? How many are there, do you know?"

"I remembered what you told me about distances from the sun. About habitable zones. I guessed at it. I made the red sun the same size as yours and mine in my mind, and on what felt like the right relative scale, started looking there. And as I said, I did find a planet too. But nothing on it. I don't know if there are other worlds."

Her mouth shaped the hum that followed, and she set herself to tapping on the surface of her tablet again. She tapped for a long time. Altin started pacing, his mind racing, his heart beating with the urgency of a task he was afraid he wouldn't accomplish. Finally he said, "We need to go see Ocelot."

Orli looked up at him. "Do you think she can help? Do you think you can find her?"

"I don't know, but I can't waste more time guessing. Guessing got us this far, but now we need something else. If this is the red world she spoke of, then perhaps she will know more."

"All right," Orli agreed. "I think it's just as well. There are some things I need too. Things from Earth."

His eyebrows shot up, curious, but only for the briefest span of time. They both knew the stakes, and if she thought there was something they needed, then that is how it would be.

They went to seek Ocelot, and in the barest flash of time after returning the tower to its place at Calico Castle, the pair of them were standing at her door. She hadn't been home when Altin looked upon returning to Prosperion, but Altin was determined to try in person anyway. An ocelot could hide itself easily, he supposed, if it had reason to, but maybe he could scare her out.

A full moon shone above the flat-topped stone in the clearing, and a gentle breeze blew the scent of pine and a hint of ash at them through the trees. The serenity of it was startling.

Altin knocked on the door of the dilapidated wooden hovel as Orli gazed out over the edge of the upthrust rock upon which Ocelot's hovel sat like a hat. She wondered at the long streak of burnt forest not so far away, a wide black cut dark enough to be visible in the pink light of Luria, the gentle hues of it seemingly a reminder that even here, in this peaceful place, she could not forget that there was violence everywhere.

The door opened and a child stood before them both, a girl, no more than fourteen. Her hair hung lank and bedraggled around her dirty face, and her clothes were barely adequate to cover her. She smiled an even smile at them, something marginally feline and turned back inside, leaving the door open behind her. She disappeared into the shadowy darkness immediately, as she had no fire tonight.

They stepped inside and Orli tried to make out the contents of the shack's singular room, but the bars of moonlight striping the interior did little to illuminate anything. A dull thump came from across the darkness, almost inaudible. Spots of black and gray crossed a moonbeam.

"You've found the red world, haven't you?" came the child's voice from somewhere across the room.

"I have," said Altin, disappointed that she'd had to ask. "Sort of. I found where it should be. But I cannot find where it hides. We were hoping you could help us the rest of the way, since it was your guidance that brought us to it to begin."

Orli shrieked then, a brief outcry, and her hand darted to her leg. She clutched her calf, gripping it in the same place Black Sander's accomplice, Belor, had cut her that night in the rain, the inkpot incision into which her clothing had been dipped, colored with her own blood to throw off any pursuit. She briefly saw the ghostly glow of cat eyes in the wan light of another moonbeam, but they vanished into the shadows with a blink.

"Alien blood will guide us," said Ocelot, her voice changed and older now, shaped by the tiny organ pipes of her wildcat form. She leapt up onto the stack of firewood near the nearly crumbling stones of her fireplace. She licked at her claws, lapping Orli's blood from each in turn. She did a careful job of it, the pink tongue emerging over and over again, seemingly at the task far longer than cleaning would require. "Make some tea," she said in a sleepy voice when she was done. And then, as if sated by a full meal, she curled up against the wall and went to sleep.

At first neither of them could believe it. They watched and waited, neither daring to move. Ocelot obviously knew what was happening, so how could she possibly just curl up and go to sleep?

They exchanged a pair of glances, Orli's far more incredulous than his, but both in similar states of impatient disbelief.

They looked back at the sleeping cat again, watched in the dim light as her sides moved up and down slowly, regularly, as she breathed. Every so often, her long whiskers would twitch, just touching a narrow band of moonlight coming through a crack, the tip sparkling like a tiny firefly before vanishing again.

They turned to one another once more, both too afraid to say anything. What if the slumber was part of some wild Z-class divining spell? Not even Altin knew.

"Well?" Orli mouthed, taking care to move her face into a bar of light shining down from a hole in the ceiling so that he could see. "Now what?"

He mouthed back, "I don't know."

They watched some more, but still the cat slept.

Altin's eyes ran around the room, more in frustration than seeking anything. He saw the teapot sitting near the fireplace next to the little box of leaves. Glancing at Orli, he saw that she saw them too. She gave him a helpless look. They both seemed to realize they had no other choice. They'd committed to this course, and now they had to see it through. And Altin knew that Ocelot had seen things with the tea before. It wasn't such a long shot, perhaps.

He went straight to the fireplace and found the pot already filled with water. He directed Orli to the woodpile with a gesture as he measured out enough tea and made the pot ready for a fire. Orli filled her arms with wood and brought it to him. He took the load from her, and tossed it all into the fireplace, then conjured a flame that set the stack ablaze. The tea began to brew, and shortly after steam began to drift up from its spout.

They continued to watch and wait. They watched and waited, and the tea brewed and steamed. It steamed and brewed so long Altin was afraid that it would be too strong to work and then he was afraid that the water would all boil away.

Finally Ocelot woke up.

She cast a long shadow up the wall behind her as she arched her back and stretched, a wide yawn setting the curve of her tongue briefly upon the gray planks as well. Without the least hint of urgency, she jumped down onto the floor, another dull thumping sound, and padded to the fire. The young girl sat cross-legged before it then, her hands out and savoring the warmth. She took a handful of broad, flat leaves from a basket and used them to grab the teapot. She poured a cup which she handed to Orli. She filled another for Altin, and a third for herself.

Orli took hers reluctantly, but a nod from Altin reminded her that they were in a place in time where they had no other options but trust.

"Drink up," he said. "It doesn't seem to have any noticeable effect. At least, it didn't last time, but I didn't make it then either." He looked to Ocelot as if she might support his claim, but the child stared absently through the steam of her cup into the fire.

Orli blew across the top of her tea before taking the first sip. It burned her mouth anyway.

"It's too hot," Ocelot said.

Altin, having just done exactly as Orli had, agreed. "It is," he said. "I will cool them as I did last time." He cast three small ice lances, finger length, handing one to Orli and reaching another to Ocelot.

She made no move to take it.

He held it out a moment longer before pulling it back. "Ocelot, please," he said. "We really haven't got any more time. And we still have other things to do. Just take it."

"Not the tea, teleporter."

Altin glanced over his shoulder at Orli, who shrugged. She was doing her part by drinking the tea. Altin's ice stick helped a lot.

"What then?" He saw the Z-class child staring into the fire. It was burning very high. He shouldn't have thrown in all the wood.

Impatient that she chose this time to be so particular

about that kind of thing, he teleported half the logs outside into the burnt place where he'd fought the troll, confident there was nothing there that would catch fire. "There, are you happy? Please, I'm begging you. We must hurry."

"Too close to the fire." She dipped her finger into the tea.

"Oh, for the love of Mercy," he groaned. He teleported the rest of the fire out where the first half of it had gone. "How about now?"

"Altin!" Orli said, fearing he would aggravate the girl with his temper now.

Ocelot turned and looked past him to where Orli stood, a touch of a smile curving on that smudged and dirty face. "The alien would see what the teleporter cannot."

"What's that supposed to mean?" Altin asked. "People are dying in great piles all across the galaxy. An entire world is about to be raped, and you make wordplay."

Ocelot continued to look at Orli now. "He is too close to the fire. Get him away. Then he will find it when the time comes."

Orli nodded. She knew exactly what it meant.

"Men fight while women do the suffering," Ocelot went on. "So you must let them. You will hide in the noise of their combat, a song sung beneath the echoes of mashing rams' horns. You must find your way into his heart. That is a woman's way. Find it, and cut it out."

"But how will I find it?" Orli asked. "The planet will be big. How can I possibly find the heart chamber?"

"The blue one knows. The blue one has seen it. She will show you the way."

"But I can't speak to her. Only in dreams. We can't wait for me to sleep. Or for me to wake up from sleeping drugs. There just isn't any more time."

"Hide in the thunder of the rams' horns."

"I don't understand that part."

"You will."

Altin stood watching this exchange, the side-to-side motion of his head growing more intense.

"I knew this was a mistake," he said. "I knew I got lucky the first time. Worse than cryptic answers were inevitable at some point from you."

Ocelot continued to ignore him, eyes locked on Orli's just as Orli's were locked onto hers. "When the time comes, you must act quickly. He will not fight long."

"Why not?" The way Ocelot said it frightened her. "Why won't he? Who is *he*, Altin or Red Fire?"

"The teleporter."

"So what do I do?" Her desperation was obvious.

Altin wanted to get out of there. He wanted to get to Earth. To get the nukes or whatever other things Orli had in mind. He knew that had to be her intent. His people had nothing for destroying entire worlds. Hers did.

"You will see," said Ocelot. And for the first time in a while she looked to Altin directly. "When she does, you must let her. You will have to do your part."

"So what is my part? I'm fighting. I already got that. Are you going to at least tell me what kind of fight it is?"

"Yes." She smiled and dropped another droplet of the tea onto her tongue. "For you, it is the fight of faith."

"Faith?" He sounded incredulous.

"Yes."

"Faith in what, the gods? Even you resort to that?"

"You will see."

He turned to Orli. "Faith?" He practically spat the word. "I could have gotten this nonsense from the priests." He reached his hand out for Orli's. "We are done here."

Orli didn't take his hand. Her gaze went to Ocelot, who had gone back to staring into the fireplace as if the blaze were still there. "Is that all?"

"Yes," Ocelot said. "*If* you can make him go."

"She can," Altin answered for her. He leaned down and took her hand himself. "We're going."

"Wait," said the girl, finally rising. She walked across the room into the darkness, bending over and rummaging through something. There came scraping sounds of something small, woody and dry.

"What is it now?" He could barely contain his impatience.

She came back and handed him a small cluster of something dark and brown, a stem from which grew a kind of seed, large and wooden, split open along one edge. They were irregular shaped, looking as if someone had folded each of them together rather hastily.

"What is this?" he asked impatiently.

"It's a peppercorn," Orli said, the trained botanist recognizing it instantly. "It's exactly like the species we have on Earth."

He looked to Ocelot and, with the last of his reserves, asked, "Are you going to tell me what it's for, or is this another one of those 'you will see' things?"

"I don't know," was Ocelot's reply. "It is what I saw."

The rumble in Altin's chest was the only warning Orli got, and with that, they were back at Calico Castle again.

Chapter 43

Altin took a moment to cast a seeing spell back to Crown City, placing his vision at the top of the lofty steps that climbed to the Temple of Anvilwrath. He saw that the temple was embroiled in a bitter battle, right up to the last stair. The priests of Anvilwrath fought hand to hand with orcs by the score, and huge demons were bashing against the columns, trying to knock them down, a few at least that they might squeeze their huge bodies in between to get farther inside, cracking the shell, as it were, to get where the soft meat was. He could tell immediately that the columns had been enchanted with great strength, for the size of many of these creatures was simply astonishing. Altin wondered as he observed if this moment was the explanation for why that insane-seeming forest of columns had been built, remembering how long it had taken him and Orli to run through it to the courtyard only a few short hours ago. He suspected it was. They must have divined it, the builders, hundreds and hundreds of years ago, saw the need for it this day and made it so. Or else it was simply a clever tactical design. Either way, the demons would not get inside any time soon. At least he hoped.

He couldn't afford to wonder about it long, however, and he made a quick survey of the rest of the city. A huge section of Crown was burning, a great wedge cutting in wide from the decimated southern wall and funneling straight through the city, bashing down and burning through buildings on a straight path to the Palace. He knew instinctively that was the goal even before he pushed his vision around the temple to verify.

Sure enough, beyond the temple, the broad sweep of once majestic Unification Avenue seethed with activity. It was the point of the spear thrusting toward the city's royal heart, all its glorious towering oaks had been ripped out like weeds, the statues of the great kings and queens all gone. Now it was broken and swamped with a tumultuous crowd of war. At its farthest end, the Royal Army was being compressed against the Palace walls like twenty thousand grapes in a wine press made of demons, the libation of their bodies, their red blood, running through the filtering heaps of the hacked apart and dying, an intoxicant for the invading horde.

Altin wanted to look for Orli's father, but knew he couldn't take the time to sort through all that activity. He also realized as he thought about the Earthman that there was no laser fire coming from above. He looked skyward and recognized that the fleet had stopped helping them, even from the safety of orbit. He also noticed that *Citadel* was back. The great sphere of it hovered, barely visible against the clouds. He saw no redoubts in the air and figured that the wizards must have gone to the Palace walls.

He came out of the spell right after and went to where Orli sat at Tytamon's table, once again tapping away at her tablet.

"Asad and the others are no longer helping them," he said. "The laser fire has stopped, and *Citadel* is back at

Crown."

"I figured as much." The quizzical look that ensued upon his face prompted her to fill him in. "When you brought us to Mars, on the way out to Red Fire, you stopped in orbit, and I saw another one of the big Hostiles had returned. Not as big as the one you guys sent into the sun, but big enough. I had a feeling Nakamura would take that wrong."

"They could have just taken *Citadel* back and gotten rid of that one too."

"True. If they'd known it was there. But how would *Citadel* have found out about it? It's not like anyone on Earth could call them up and tell them another one had come."

Altin wanted to shout, to vent the pressure of his frustration, but he held it back, plunging his fingers into the muss of his dark hair instead, blowing out exasperation in a long, low hiss. "Surely the director must realize by now ...," Altin began, but let it die. Of course he didn't. "I need to let Aderbury know."

Orli nodded that she thought that was a good idea, and so Altin sent *Citadel*'s leading wizard a telepathic nudge. Unlike last time, he did not get an immediate response. In fact, he knew he was making contact, but Aderbury wasn't answering. That did not bode well, and wouldn't if they'd needed *Citadel*. He needed Aderbury alert up there, ready to go.

Altin sent another nudge, letting go the first and trying anew, this time more urgently. He still had to wait for a reply, but finally one came. "Tidalwrath's fits, Altin. It's about time. Her Majesty has ordered us back. The fleet stopped helping, and Crown is about to fall. I've been trying to contact you for over an hour. We cut down tons of the Hostiles above Earth. Another hour or two and we would have had them all. Half a day at most."

473

"What are you doing out there? Why didn't you answer? What if I needed you?"

"I'm transmuting these harpy-spawn demons," he snapped back. "They aren't as resistant to stone as they are the elements ... so long as you don't mind getting close enough to touch one anyway."

Altin could feel the pulse of Aderbury's battle rage in the message as it came.

"I'm sorry," Altin said afterward, imagining his friend running around, unarmored, dancing between the crushing footfalls of those giant demons, muttering transmutation spells that would turn them to stone, but only if he lay a hand on one. Brave. And insane.

"So who is in command of *Citadel*?"

"Peppercorn," sent back Aderbury. "There's not much an enchanter can do down here, and all the available conduits are already working with the Enchanters Guild to keep up the supply of arrows with transmutation spells. Not that it's really helping much."

"All right. So do you still have teleporters ready to go? Can I contact her if the time comes?"

"Yes, they're all still up there waiting. They're working with the seers and dropping broken columns and pieces of the wall on the demons. Most of our healers have gone, though. They went down into the Temple of Anvilwrath with the Liquefying Stones. They've got some kind of spell down there to help with mana flow into the city, so we decided to give a hand. It was running pretty low."

"That's good. But please, make sure the teleporters are ready."

"They are. We didn't send the redoubts out."

"I saw."

"Where are you?"

"I'm at Calico Castle. Orli and I found Red Fire."

"Who is Red Fire?"

"The other Hostile world."

There was a long pause and Altin knew Aderbury was working through it and forcing himself not to ask. He was as much aware of the time constraint as Altin was, perhaps more so given his circumstance. Altin hoped he wasn't putting his friend's life at risk distracting him, even as he realized he clearly was. So he cut it short then. "Be safe, Aderbury."

"I will if you hurry up and do whatever you are going to do."

"I will."

"Mercy be with you."

"You too." And then Aderbury was gone.

When Altin turned back to Orli, she could see how pale his face had gone. She asked immediately what he had learned.

"Aderbury and the rest of the transmuters are fighting on foot at the Palace walls. Peppercorn has *Citadel*. The teleporters are waiting for us, but I'm not sure to what end. I don't even know where to go. Ocelot was useless, and the Palace is going to fall."

A wave of emotion overcame him, and he stalked away, trying to force himself to think, but with no direction to think in.

Orli watched him, could sense the feelings of impotence and rage.

"Altin," she said, giving him only a minute to deal with himself. "I need you to get me back to Earth."

He stopped his pacing, straightening stiff as a stick, his back still to her. She saw by the movement of his shoulders that he drew in a breath. He turned back, his cheeks puffing as he let the breath back out. "Where?"

"Back where you found me, back at Fort Minot."

He let the admonitions, the warnings, the comments about the risk of her being retaken, die on his tongue. He nodded. "Where? The room I found you in?"

"No, that's too far down. We need to get to a supply depot."

"How?" He was going to need a diviner to make sense of where she wanted him to go. That place had made no sense to him at all. Everything about it looked the same.

"Just get me there."

"And then what? We run around?"

"No. I can find one from the air. I'll know what I'm looking for when I see it."

"I can't fly. It will take too long to learn the spell."

"Taot can."

"I don't have time to cast all the enchantments we need to hide us from the heat eyes your people have. The invisibility enchantment that we would need. I'll have to find more perfume to coat the dragon, or they'll see us."

"Then they see us."

"We'll be fired upon."

"We'll fire back. You said yourself our war machines are 'in the box.' That's the big vulnerability. So, teleport them. Isn't that what you do? Let's go!"

"Orli, do you realize what you are asking me to do? To your own people?"

"They're not my people, remember? And you already know the rest." The look she sent him was so severe, so frightfully determined, that he knew she was right. He would do what had to be done.

He nodded and sent a message to Taot that was not really a request. The urgency of it was enough to get the mighty beast's attention, and he agreed, though he hadn't cared much for Earth the last time they were there.

In the span of five minutes, the three of them were soaring between the upthrust buildings of Fort Minot's uniformity, winding through the low-slung cityscape of black mirrors and blinking lights. They didn't even have the advantage of darkness to cover their approach, the sun high as they swooped in. Not that it mattered much, for the air defenses of the base were busily engaged with the Hostiles swarming all around. There was some luck in that.

Red orbs, smaller than the planetary variety, draped themselves over buildings everywhere, flattening out and then oozing like melting wax down the sides. They clung to the mirrored surfaces and ran in long rivulets, dripping elongations of their substance, the once rocky and hard transformed into something different, something malleable, fluid and clearly corrosive in high degrees. Other orbs came speeding down from above and simply crashed through things, blasting into buildings or punching through hangar doors like meteors. In places, the dragon riders could see through the holes and observe the orbs flattening themselves out upon floors or over ships and equipment, forming undulations and lumps that marked where fighters and freighters and vessels of every type and size were being unmade by the oozing Hostile goo, the acrid smoke coming from them testimony to the materials being dissolved beneath.

Orli immediately set to looking for signs that would lead them to a central supply depot. "Take us lower," she shouted into the wind of Taot's flight. "So I can read."

"What are we looking for?"

"Hangars," she said. "Really big ones, big enough for ships like the *Aspect*. Or garage doors, lots of them, set up for large-scale delivery trucks."

"I don't know what that is."

"Just take us lower."

Altin guided Taot downward, and soon they were only a few spans above the lowest of the rooftops. Orli's head pivoted quickly from side to side, her eyes scouring the fronts and backs of buildings down long streets, piercing the shadows of alleyways, seeking.

Meanwhile, Altin, in his nervousness, watched the skies for signs of pursuit, be they from Earth or another world. For the first several minutes, there was none, but soon enough, in came a long, angular flying craft with a bank of red and blue lights that flashed in sequence on its canopy. It fell in right behind them.

Altin sent the image of it to Taot, but the dragon did not need to be told to avoid it as best he could. He'd heard it coming long before Altin knew it was there.

"I knew they'd find us," Altin called back to Orli, who glanced behind them nervously.

"Attention Prosperions. Land the ... vehicle immediately or you will be fired on," came the command from the pilot of the hovercraft.

"Are you fucking kidding me?" Orli said. "Is he even looking around?"

Altin only shrugged, hoping Orli could do something. Apparently she could not because she went back to looking down into the buildings below.

"Are you going to do something?" he asked anyway.

"Do what? You need to take him out. They probably won't give you another warning."

Reluctant to do such a thing, he pressed Taot to fly faster, knowing even as he did that the creature could never match the Earth machine for speed. The dragon dipped and wove through buildings, tilting sideways through the narrowest of openings, skimming surfaces by the barest margins, his agility incredible. But the pursuing craft simply moved above the buildings and followed from higher up. They could dimly hear it repeat the previous command.

"We can't lose it," Altin called back to Orli.

"No shit. Take him out before he gets a heat lock on us."

"He wouldn't shoot us down without provocation,

would he?"

A stripe of blue light streaked through the air, just missing them. It struck the road beneath them, which exploded, a huge hole forming and a spew of black asphalt flying up and all around.

"How much more proof do you need?" she said as she drew her blaster and fired several shots at their pursuer.

"Dragon's fire!" he swore. "But he's not the enemy."

She fired several more shots. "He is now."

Taot swerved, banking so hard he nearly threw his riders off. A missile hissed past them and blew out the corner of the building Taot had barely missed himself. He roared in fury as shards of glass nicked them all, blown out from the blast.

Altin knew then that she was right. He still didn't want to kill the pilot, though.

He turned back and, with a few moments to formulate a plan—and several more shots from Orli, one of which blew off one of the ship's flashing lights—Altin teleported the hovercraft and its occupant into the execution chamber where Orli had once been. He was careful to make sure the cockpit ended up in the center of the room, but he had no time to really consider the relative space beyond that level of detail. With a thought the pursuit came to an end.

"About time," Orli said. "That was cutting it pretty close."

"I didn't kill him."

"Good." She went back to looking for the main supply depot.

They flew down several more streets, trying to use the buildings as some sort of cover, hoping not to be discovered by any more Earth ships. But those were not their only enemy.

As they crossed over a series of small hangars, headed

into another section of taller structures, Taot suddenly went into a roll, a long corkscrew maneuver, as he dodged an incoming Hostile. It was an orb nearly as wide as the avenue over which they flew, plummeting at them from above, coming in at a long, shallow angle.

Taot's roll wrapped them around its passing, his wingtips brushing the glass of a building on one side of the roll and his talons breaking through on the other as he pushed off. The orb just missed Altin's head, and had he thought to, he might have reached up and touched the thing as it passed through the tube formed by Taot's evasive flight. They felt the wind of it as it rushed by, and they watched as it crashed into the base of a building to their left. Taot righted himself as he flew through the shrapnel of its impact, and once again they were showered with bits of glass.

As they flew free of the row of buildings, Altin looked back to see that the lower part of the building struck by the orb was brutally smashed in, so much so that the building began to tilt, sagging on that side and considerably off from vertical. He was sure it was about to fall.

"There," Orli cried above the wind as Altin watched the reflection of the three of them diminishing in the mirrored glass of the falling building far behind. He turned to see her pointing toward a long flat expanse of black glass that he guessed must be a thousand paces long and perhaps a third that wide. It was perfectly rectangular and recessed from the surrounding area by several spans, like a strange dark pool had been built there waiting to be filled. Lights coming from ragged holes in its surface, however, showed where Hostiles had punched through and gotten inside. Altin didn't know if it had once held water, but if it had, it would now all be drained away. "Take us through one of those openings," Orli said.

"There are Hostiles in there."

"This is what we need." She motioned into the air all around them, at the fighters and the missiles and Hostiles plunging down from everywhere. "Do you really want to keep looking for another one?"

"No. I suppose not." He sent the message to Taot.

The dragon banked hard and swooped in low, rolling over backward as he dove into a large hole that had been bashed through the massive hangar door by the Hostiles. It was a hard and sudden roll, and the arc and twist of the maneuver had them both free falling for the briefest moment before the maneuver completed itself in time to catch both riders again. Altin was used to such things, but Orli suddenly gripped Altin about the waist like a docking clamp.

Taot swooped down toward the floor of the hangar some five hundred spans below, he and Altin conferring on where it would be best to land.

Altin saw Hostiles spreading themselves out over a half-built spaceship of some kind, three of them, and another was oozing itself out flat like spilled liquid upon the floor. Several people in uniform were busy shooting at the latter one with various forms of weaponry. Streaks of laser light and the concussive blasts of ballistic rounds echoed from the thick concrete walls. Busy in their fight, and far across the hangar, they appeared not to have noticed the dragon flying down.

Taot's head snaked back and forth as they came in, and he blew several blasts of fire into the air, seemingly at nothing.

Altin found a place clear of the fighting and far enough away from all the Hostiles, to which he directed Taot with a thought. The dragon landed so rapidly and so heavily that the impact knocked gasps from both riders as if they shared the same set of lungs.

They slid off immediately, and the moment they were

clear of him, the dragon stalked off and began blasting fire into the air all around again, just as he had done during the descent. He sniffed and rumbled and blew, his head moving up and down at the end of his long neck, swinging high and low, side to side. He growled and the floor shook beneath his feet. Altin sent him thoughts to warn him from getting too close to the Earth men with their weapons, but on and on went the searing of the air. First here, and then there, all around them in the air. Altin sent a quick query to his friend then, asking if he'd been hurt, hoping that he hadn't come unhinged from the pressure of flying through a battle-torn alien atmosphere.

Altin got back an image of rotting flesh, of an animal, a moose he thought, in the throes of some wasting disease. Taot sent that to him and then went back to blasting the air again and again and again, pacing about like a mad thing in its lair.

"I think I should send him back," Altin said. "He's going to blow one this way by mistake and then we're all in trouble."

Orli had been looking for something and turned back to Altin only long enough to say, "That's fine. We can get what we need here anyway. Send him back."

Altin prepared to send the dragon home, sending him a warning that the teleport was about to come. He saw as he looked back to Taot that the Earth people had spotted the dragon by the brilliance of his fiery display. He spent the instant it took to make sure Taot's cave was unoccupied, and then sent the dragon back to Prosperion. The last licks of his most recent fireblast, curling upward in the moment before he was gone, were sucked down by his sudden absence, the remnant flames forming a twisting yellow sheet as the air rushed in to fill the space where the massive reptile had been.

"We're going to have some more of your friends over

here," Altin said as he looked through the last vapors of Taot's breath.

"Come on," Orli replied, grabbing his hand and dragging him at a run. "Over here."

They ran across the hangar as the sounds of shouts and the splash of laser beams upon the wall in front of them announced that the others were now in range. Altin felt the heat of one beam on the back of his neck, and knew from the smell that hair had been more than singed.

Orli came to a door and tried the handle, but it would not open. "Hold them off," she shouted as she drew her blaster and started firing into the door.

Altin spun back and sent a huge fireball, big as a house, flying across the room at the fleet people running at them. He directed it just over their heads, but close enough to fill their noses with the smell of their own burning hair. See how you like that, he thought. They stopped, and even fell back a step, but another lance of red light shot by, just missing Orli.

A more powerful weapon than hers, the soldier's shot actually finished the work of opening the door, and Orli practically dragged Altin through it by the back of his robes as bullets ricocheted off the metal doorframe. Another three rounds cracked the heavy glass window that looked out into the hangar from where they were inside, smashing white impact marks like spindly stars into it.

"They're going to get through that pretty quick," Orli said. "Do something."

Altin thought about another fireball but decided against it. He thought about an ice lance, but that was just as bad. What he needed was an ice wall, but he didn't know the spell. A bullet hit the window again, this time pushing the glass inward in a nearly perfect dome, cracks like spider webs covering its surface like a drapery of lace.

The next one would get through. Improvising, he quickly conjured an ice lance that was ten paces long and five in diameter. Rather than throwing it, he flipped it sideways and let it drop across the front of the room. It landed with a heavy thud as several bullets struck it even as it fell into place. A laser did likewise, and he could hear the hiss of steam as it hit. He wasn't sure how long the ice lance would hold, lacking the solidity and powerful cold of a true ice wall, so he cast a second one beyond the first, then cast a third stacked atop those two as if they were all little more than stacked ice logs. A grenade struck his barrier then, which shook the whole room. In the span of moments, he'd added three more, making the stack roughly fifteen paces thick. The laser fire and heat from the bullets and blasts would melt them together even as they blew apart. At least he hoped.

"That's only going to hold them for a while," he said as he turned back into the room.

He saw Orli running between long rows of shelves, spindly metal units filled with boxes of various kinds, all with writing on them that Altin could not read. The place was very organized, and Altin could tell every box and crate was in its proper spot, part of a systematic storage plan.

"What is this place?" he asked running down a long row of shelves after her.

"Supply locker. Parts and supplies," she said. "There will be others nearby. We need suits. And a Higgs prism."

"Suits? Like the ones your warriors wear?"

"No. Spacesuits. For breathing where there is no air. You don't think we're going to be so lucky as to find a nice comfy climate on Red Fire, do you?"

"I hadn't thought about it quite that far," he confessed.

"Well, I did," she said. "While you were jumping us across the galaxy, I came up with a list of what we might need. It's going to be a big world if it's like Blue Fire at all, so gravity might be really bad, maybe more than we can handle."

"But it wasn't a problem on Blue Fire."

"I think she was doing you some favors."

He nodded and followed her like a dog, tailing along and feeling somewhat useless. He paused long enough to cast a seeing spell out into the hangar. Two of the fleet people were trying to melt through the ice with lasers, but the others had gone back to shooting the Hostile spreading out across the floor.

"Here," Orli called out triumphantly. "Just right for us. Except there's only one." She held a box that was roughly the size of both his fists pressed together.

"What is it?"

"Higgs prism. Small. Low power consumption, too, way better than the ones the *Aspect* uses—twelve years is a long time." She looked up, a grim smile of satisfaction on her face, but she saw that he still didn't know what it was. "It redirects gravity. We can stay at Earth normal no matter how bad Red Fire is. We'll just have to stay together."

"We will." He had no intention of leaving her side. Ever. Not until this was all done or they were all dead.

"Good. Now come on. If there are any suits, they won't be in here. We need an equipment locker. There will be one somewhere close." She took his hand again and ran toward the back part of the room, through several unlocked doors, and out into a large, dimly lit central corridor. They looked both directions, but the length of it, as far as they could see, was empty. "Just as I thought. Everyone is up there fighting. Let's go." She took off running again, dragging him along.

"How do you know where we are going?" he asked as he struggled to keep up with the athletic Earth woman tugging at his arm.

"It's the upside of boring fleet uniformity. I spent my childhood on a base like this. They're all the same."

They ran for some time, Orli reading the placards on the doors that had them, until finally they came to a place where she started trying some of them. The first two were locked, so she kicked in the third when it wouldn't open either.

Altin practically ran into her back right after, assuming she'd charge straight in as she had been, and he intent on following. But she didn't go in. She glanced into the room, made a quick survey of the sorts of equipment she saw inside, then turned away. "Not this one," she said.

Apparently boring fleet uniformity was only so uniform, Altin thought.

She kicked in four more doors and finally found what she was looking for, a room filled with rows and rows of strange, stiff-looking suits. They went in, and Altin, out of curiosity, reached out to touch one, but she called back to him as she ran down a long row and turned right and out of sight. "Not those. They're too thin. We need heavy ones, with big-time power packs."

He didn't ask why and simply ran in the direction she had gone. He found her by the sound of her shuffling through some very dense-looking suits, stuffy and thick like they were made from several layers of heavy hide, or whatever served for hide on this strange world, a substance seeming almost metallic, though soft and just off white. Each suit had a panel with colorful buttons on its front, another on the left sleeve, and a bulky, box-like apparatus on the back that was a convolution of alien objects too complex for Altin to bother trying to take in. On a shelf above them, each suit had a bulbous helmet to go with it, big cumbersome things with rounded face plates of dark mirrored glass.

"These," she said as she made her way down the row of them, her hands touching the sleeves of several, turning them to reveal tags attached and dangling from each. "Come here."

He stepped toward her, and she held one of the suits up to him, pressing it against his chest.

"Close enough." She pushed it at him, obviously intending that he take it, which he did. It was heavier than he expected it would be, much heavier. They wouldn't be able to move very fast in them, he thought.

She went down the row a bit farther and grabbed another that seemed to satisfy for herself. "Now all we need is the *kaboom*," she said.

"What?" Altin felt lost. They'd been moving so quickly through such completely alien space it unsettled him, adding to his anxiety. He had no idea what the end of this running about looked like; nor did he know when it would end. They needed to get to Red Fire and do something soon. He had faith in Orli's ideas, but this was taking a great deal of time.

"We need mining charges."

"All right." But he couldn't help asking, "What is that?"

"Explosives. To kill Red Fire when we find his heart."

"I thought we would use one of your missiles. The big ones like they were going to use to destroy Blue Fire's planet."

"Good luck finding one," she said. "You left them all floating in orbit when you sent the fleet back to Mana's Edge. And even if we had one, I have no idea how to set one off. You can't just light a fuse on those things, you know? But that doesn't matter. The charges will be fine. Remember, we dug a mile-deep mine on Tinpoa in a matter of months. If we can do that, I can dig out a tiny heart chamber that's, what, barely as big as you are tall?"

He nodded. Blue Fire's heart chamber, the only one he

had any experience with, hadn't been very big, all things being relative. "So do they keep that sort of thing here too? In a place filled with spaceship supplies? Or will we be running around some more?" He glanced down at the heavy suit in his arms and didn't think that was going to be a good idea. At least not for him.

"They might, but I'm not willing to run around guessing. I already know where there are plenty of them."

"Where?"

"Tinpoa."

"But your people abandoned it. I heard that they took it all. The machines that power everything, and the ones that make the air. There will be nothing there to breathe."

She slapped the suit folded over her arm. "Can you cast in one of these?"

"I don't see why I couldn't."

"Then we'll be fine. Let's go."

"Where?"

"Back to your tower. Unless you want to change in here. But I think we might be pressing our luck in terms of not running into anyone. Battle or not up there, someone is liable to find us. You don't want another qualm of conscience, do you?"

"You're right, of course," he said. "Back to Tytamon's tower then."

She put her hand on his arm. "It's your tower, Altin."

The left side of his mouth twitched up as he nodded. "That is what Kettle said."

"Let's go."

And then they were back on Prosperion.

Chapter 44

The trip to the Tinpoa mines went quickly. Orli, having spent so much time there, knew exactly where the explosives were kept: in a heavy vault in the supply locker. Altin was able to teleport them inside after a brief exercise with seeing spells and two blind trial teleports into the darkness with a pair of glow sticks that Orli gave to him. Once inside, Orli filled a leather satchel with all the charges that would fit, then took him to the tool room where she got a rock drill that was so heavy she grunted when she lifted it. With that slung over her shoulder, she turned to face him and announced that she was ready to go.

"Go where?" Altin said, still not used to the tinny sound of his own voice in the dome of the spacesuit helmet. At least Orli had shown him how to clear the dark tint so he could see. That had been a few moments of perplexity a few minutes earlier. "We still haven't found Red Fire yet, not the world anyway. I have to admit, I've been sort of hoping some epiphany would strike while we were at this, but it's been nearly an hour since we left Ocelot's hut, and I still don't have any ideas leaping to mind."

"I do," she said. "Ocelot told us where it was. Or at least mostly. She said you were too close to the fire. So, obviously, you were too close to the sun. You need to back out."

He frowned at that for a moment, but then saw how obvious it was now, in hindsight. "Yes, but even if I do, that only widens the band of space around the sun we have to search. There has to be a better way."

"These suits have great optics. We can find it. Come on, let's go. Clock's ticking."

Altin stared down into her helmet, into her impatient, eager eyes. He saw such strength there. Such confidence. She'd rolled up her sleeves and set herself to work, as it were, and it was inspiring, even when it felt like all hope might easily be lost.

Moments later they were back out at the farthest distance Altin had ever been from Prosperion, so far that the distance between Prosperion and Earth became inconsequential by comparison. There comes a point where a handful of light years starts to wither to nothingness, a new sense arises as new scales reveal themselves, and they'd found just such a distance as they approached the huge red sun.

"So now what?" he asked, but she was already moving to the window nearest the table. As she tipped herself out through the window, her bulky suit, with its huge helmet and the clumsy-seeming cluster of strange Earth machinery, filled the opening almost entirely. Altin watched her, watched the suit back with all its blinking lights and its levers and dials, the function of it all completely alien, and marveled at her. He was so grateful to have her there, even if he had no idea what she had in mind.

She turned back to him almost straight away. "I can't see anything. You have to take us closer to the system.

The helmet optics aren't *that* good."

"He may detect us," he said. "He may detect me. So, be ready." Even as he said it, he knew that it was pointless. What should she be ready for?

Orli didn't call him on it. "If he does, you must fight him off. You have the ring."

"Maul had the Liquefying Stone."

"Did she? Was she using it in that black fog? You said she gave it over to some other priests, that there was a ritual preserving mana for the city somewhere. Would she have taken it back from that?"

"I don't know," he admitted. "It seemed so important to reach Red Fire, I just assumed it would be in play. A tough decision that must have been, how best to use one stone to save so many people, but you're right, she probably did not."

"Then you will be fine. And even if she did have it, you said yourself the ring is better."

Altin nodded. It might be true. He also recognized that Orli was playing the optimist now, far more than she was when she'd relayed the assessment of his chances from Blue Fire, which was essentially a promise that Altin had no chance to beat the powerful male Hostile at all.

"Come on," said Orli. "Go already." She even managed a half-hearted smile.

Altin closed his eyes and returned to the place where the last seeing stone was, in the empty space between the planets swinging around the red sun. He rotated his view in all directions to make sure that it was clear, and then he released the spell. A moment after, the tower was there as well.

Orli set herself straight away to scanning with the spacesuit's long-range optics. She spent a long time leaning out all three of the room's windows and finally turned back to Altin, looking irritated. "Can you turn this thing a little bit? Like a quarter rotation? I can't see all the way around it."

Altin obliged and once again Orli set to staring out each window in turn.

"I still can't see anything. It must be on the other side of the sun."

Altin shook his head and grumbled. "Just the same as it was with Mars. I swear it's an ogre's fortune we've got out here."

Right as he said it, something came crashing into his mind, crushing the sad telepathic blocks he'd put in place, not just blocks to keep out distracting thoughts from fellow magicians while he was out here, but strong blocks meant to stave off just such an attack. He thought he'd come prepared, thought he'd taken the warning Blue Fire had given him to heart, but in that instant his vision filled with a blazing red heat and the seismic force of anger that wasn't his, a force like a thousand tons of rock being dropped on him all at once.

Reflexively he reached out for more mana, and had he not been wearing the ring, his mind would have been torn asunder, even physically blown apart just as Maul's had been. But the ring was there, and the mana was there, all of it, no channeling required, in the instant that he needed it.

He staggered back under the press of the assault, his mind gulping down mana in quantities for which there was no measure, fighting to push back against the crushing magnitude of all that fury, but still the onslaught came and mashed down at him. He saw hatred in the red heat, could feel it in the core of his being, hatred and the most unspeakable rage and, shockingly, inexplicable jealousy. There could be no doubt that this was Red Fire.

Altin tried to shout back at the attacking entity in his mind, tried to speak to it with the brute force of his own will, blasting back against the currents of Red Fire's hostility with a sense of peace, an offering of friendship. *We don't have to be enemies.*

There came in response a veritable blast of contempt. It felt as if the whole universe shuddered with revulsion, disgusted by that pathetic, simpering suggestion that there might be anything other than absolute mortal combat. Revulsion added itself to the press of anger and jealousy, and with it came even greater confidence. Red Fire knew now that Altin was weak.

And then Blue Fire was there.

Altin felt her terror open up in his mind, the familiar sense of her presence that he'd had before, though now awash in fear and agony. She came into his mind with a feeling of furtiveness, like she was hiding, like she'd had to sneak out to be here. But mostly fear and trembling concern, worry even, all of it woven together with the great strains of resignation and pain, and exhaustion, a great bruising sense of utter fatigue and battery. Together it all played in his mind like a symphony of awfulness. But, through it all, despite it all, she was there. She came because she was afraid for him.

Get away, she sent. Her voice filled his mind like a child's cries carried upon a distant wind. *Leave. Orli Love not die.* There came a sense of pleading. Begging.

He'd never experienced a sensation like that before. Not from her. Not in such a way. How could he possibly be so important to her as that? Humbling wasn't remotely enough to describe it. It was almost horrifying. To imagine someone so desperately in need of him as that.

Red Fire knew that Altin was speaking to her. He could hear everything they had to say. His mind engulfed them both. The crush of his wrath dropped Altin to his knees. Though he could not feel it, blood had begun to run from his nose and ears. He was too caught up in greater miseries to notice such things.

Orli noticed, she'd seen it all, and she'd run to him, stood before him in that moment watching the blood run free, screaming for him to let go, to take them out of range. She pleaded for his safety like Blue Fire had.

We are going to help you, Altin sent to Blue Fire, an effort requiring all his strength. *If we can find his heart.* Everything was in the open now.

And then he knew where it was. And why she'd taken such a risk. He saw it all. The red planet, the heart chamber, all of it. He knew, because she knew.

She'd seen it in Red Fire, took it from him as he invaded her, the assault requiring by its very nature that he expose himself, that he open up and make himself vulnerable. Red Fire had no reason to fear, however, no reason for caution, for she had not the strength to repel him. They both knew it. Red Fire could see into her mind as easily as she could see into his, as easily as she saw the way into his heart. He saw that she'd seen, and he even saw as she gave the memories to Altin. If Red Fire had known what laughter was, he might have mocked them both. She could do nothing to him. She was too weak. And Altin would be dead in moments. And nothing would stop him from getting what he wanted.

Altin was vaguely aware of Orli screaming at him as well, the dim noise of more chaos beating on the exterior walls of all that agony and rage. He could open his eyes and almost make her out, right there in front of him. Her mouth was moving and making sounds. What was she saying? It looked like, "Get out."

"Get us out," Orli shouted at him. Over and over. "Altin take us away, please."

Get out, echoed Blue Fire, forcing her own thoughts into the round shapes of Orli's cries. *Get out. Get away.*

Altin tried to do something with it. But none of it made

sense. He recognized the words, but he couldn't hold on to them. He had to keep pulling in mana, more and more and more. He knew, at least some silent part of him knew, that if he didn't, they would die.

He watched through a dark and hazy gauze as Orli dug into the neck of his spacesuit, clawing at his throat like a dog digging frantically to get at something. He wondered what, a slow question, thinking like grasping mist in a dream. He thought it might be his amulet. That was probably it. He dimly wondered what would happen if she broke his contact with Red Fire in that way. If she could.

That's when it hit him. He'd never added extra mana to the amulets. There wasn't enough. Not out here. He was going to do it to her again, going to get her killed this time by his incompetence. If she struck it, they would die. Which meant he had to get her out.

Die, came the volcanic hatred of Red Fire's rage and jealousy.

A teleport. That was what he needed. But even thinking of it was an effort. A spell to take them home. It was all he could do to conceive the idea, his mind so busy sucking down mana still. He could feel the shell of himself beginning to collapse, pressing in and cracking in places like the window in the hangar bay on Earth as it was being shot, the strength of his defense covered with cracked lines like spider webs, just as the glass had been.

Orli's hand thrust through the tight elastic material at his throat, her knuckles nearly choking him as she pushed inside. She jammed her arm down into his robes and fished around violently against his chest. He felt her nails cut into his flesh. She was cursing. If she struck the amulet, that would be the end.

He gulped and gulped the mana. Tried to shape the thought. The spell. Fought for it. The place in Calico Castle where the tower belonged. That place he knew.

Orli was screaming in his face, the amulet tangled up in his robes and the tight elastic seal of the suit around his neck.

Shape it. Shape the space. Close it. Put us there.

Die.

He slumped to the floor. He could barely breathe, struggling to do it, gasping. His vision swam before him like a cloud of flies. He could smell bread. Phantom smells, he knew. He thought maybe he had died. Or he was dying.

But then Orli rolled him onto his back. She was leaning down over him, her face ravaged by fear. "Altin! Altin, say something. Are you all right? Say something, please!" He heard it as if she were talking to him through a wall.

He blinked a few times. Reached up and wiped at the trickle of blood coming from his nose. He could still smell baking bread.

Orli's expression softened some. "Can you hear me?" she asked.

He nodded and tried to sit up. She helped him, and together they got him into a chair. A few more deep breaths came and went before he could speak. "What happened?"

Orli's eyebrows fell as her mouth opened in disbelief. "You're asking *me*?"

He blinked off a bit more of the dizziness and nodded.

"You tell me what happened," she said. "One minute you were fine and the next you were bleeding everywhere and calling out to Blue Fire. You stumbled, then you fell to your knees for a few seconds and then we were back here."

"Back here?"

"Yes, at Calico Castle. You brought us back. I was about to use this." She held an amulet in her hand. He closed his eyes and let out a long, agonized breath. How close it had come. And how stupid of him not to make sure he'd put enough mana in them. *A hasty mage is a tasty mage upon the tongue of death.* How many times had he heard that tired old cliché, and yet there he was. Again.

But there wasn't time for recrimination now. He reached out and took the amulet from her. "Give me yours," he said.

She looked down at her bosom for a moment, touching the stone absently. "Mine?"

"Give it, please. Quickly. We must get back."

She handed it to him. He spent the next several moments working on them, resetting the destination from *Citadel* to a safe place in Calico Castle instead, for fear of Orli's ending up in the middle of a fight if things went wrong. He loaded them with mana, taking advantage of the misty everywhere that the mana was to speed the process along. He need not trickle mana in like he had before, not now. He could pack it in like snow, gathering up great clouds of it and pushing them all in, and endless stuffing like mashing cotton into a box. When he was satisfied there was more than enough, he handed hers back to her. He gave her a grim look, glancing quickly to the sapphire and then back up at her. "It would have been bad. Worse than last time."

She looked horrified and suddenly realized what that meant. She stared down at her amulet as if it were a scorpion on her palm. When she looked back up at him, he was nodding.

"Yes," he said. "*That.*" He shook himself and stood up. "Now we have to go back. I know where it is."

"Where what is? Red Fire?"

"Yes, and not just where, but I know where the heart chamber is. Blue Fire showed me."

"But how can we go? You can't do that again. Look at you." Her gaze painted a path down his face and into his spacesuit, which bore the dark stripes of running blood, smears of it everywhere.

"Then we'll have to do it fast. I think this must be the fight Ocelot was talking about. I have to fight him off while you use those things you got from the mine. It has to be."

"Altin, you were on the ground in less than a minute. I'm going to need a hell of a lot more time than that."

"We have to try." He looked as if he were about to cast the spell that would send them back again, but Orli caught his face in both of her hands, stopping him.

"No," she said. "Not like that."

"We have to. You should have felt what I felt coming from Blue Fire." Speaking her name reminded him of her terrible misery. He reached out to the beleaguered being, intending to reassure her and let her know that help was on its way, but in that moment realized that Blue Fire was gone again, blocked and muted by the strength of Red Fire. Only the constant murmur of her suffering remained, returned to the quiet whimper in his mind that it had been before, like the sound of a brook in the distance, only this one filled with liquid misery.

"You're not going to help her if you are dead."

He slumped into a nearby chair, absolutely exhausted to the center of his being. "What is left then?"

Orli stood and turned, pacing to the window and back. She stopped briefly as she made a return trip to the window, stooping to pick up her helmet from where she'd thrown it in her urgency to get to Altin. She came back and set it on the table near Altin's, nearly knocking over the palm tree decanter that they'd moved from the window not all that long ago. It might just as easily have been a thousand years. Time was moving at such a vicious pace. She caught it reflexively once more and set it right, then continued to pace. They were missing something.

"So, let's say you are right, and that is the fight you are

up against," she said. "How can we possibly get into the heart chamber and destroy it if you've only got a minute at best?"

"Ocelot did say I wouldn't be able to fight for long. Perhaps that is enough."

"It's not. If I'm supposed to sneak in under the radar while you two go at it and set the charges, how can I do it that fast? I mean, when you say you know where it is, do you *know* know, as in you can teleport us right to it? Or just, you know where to look? A minute isn't a lot of time for me to be running around trying to figure things out, much less drill holes and set charges."

"I know where to look."

"Then that doesn't help us yet. So what are we missing?"

"Divination is the problem. You can't count on it for everything. You have to figure some of it out yourself."

"We have. That's why we have the suits and the charges and the drill."

Altin looked to where she'd set her helmet next to his. The heavy bulk of the drill lay on the floor beneath them, with the satchel of explosive charges leaning on it, as if casually, as if it were reclining there with no concern for the immediacy of literally everything.

More out of a desire to buy time to think than to find out what he already knew was going to be terrible news, he cast a seeing spell back to Crown City. The situation there was just as he had feared it would be. The army was falling back into the Palace proper now, what was left of the city's defenders draining slowly inside its walls, orderly and steadily, but clearly retreating inside, into the last bastion of the beleaguered War Queen. As he watched, men moved through the Palace gates in clumps, others guarding flanks that were sorely pressed as the enemy tried to choke off that tiny gap and keep them from safety. The demons themselves tried to gain access to the soft insides of the War Queen's empire as well, pressing not just to stop the retreat, but to get inside and suck out the last marrow of the kingdom. But the Queen's warriors held. They somehow maintained discipline even still, worked together as a people and held the enemy at bay, defending one another as the army slowly trickled through the gate, the lake of the Queen's crimson in the grand avenue beyond the Palace being pressed tighter and tighter together, the body of them surrounded by the black mass of orcs and demons, seeming to be squeezed inside, passing through the gates in a slow osmosis of inevitable defeat, oozing from outside in, into what would be the last stand for them all. But the orderly retreat was painful to watch, too many of them trying to push through that singular opening. There couldn't be many more than a thousand warriors left out there, two thousand at most, trying to hold off the scourge of that massive enemy long enough for everyone to get in. It was improbable that such a plan would work.

He didn't want to watch it any closer than from where he was, at an altitude above the Temple of Anvilwrath. He didn't want to watch people die. Maybe watching Aderbury die, or someone else he knew and loved. No way. Not now. That would finish him. Looking was a bad idea.

He glanced up and saw *Citadel* hovering above, shining like a jewel in the late afternoon sun. Beautiful, powerful, and worthless in the end, reduced to providing a hail of broken stones as the teleporters picked up and dropped giant chunks of debris, broken bones of the city, time and time again. It was effective, but not enough and, in the end, disheartening to watch. The greatest magical achievement of all time, utterly useless. They might as well have no magic at all, really. Their last hopes had lain at the feet of the magicless Earth fleet all along. The irony was painful.

Which is when he realized how obvious it was. The solution had been there all along.

He dropped the spell and leapt from his chair. "I know what we're forgetting," he said. He strode quickly to the table and pushing Orli's helmet aside, he picked up the little sprig of peppercorns. "It's peppercorn! She meant Peppercorn, on *Citadel*."

Orli was staring back at him wide eyed, hopeful, surely, but not understanding what he had in mind. "What about her? You already spoke to her, before we left."

"Peppercorn gave us anti-magic," Altin proclaimed. "Anti-magic was what the fleet was doing to avoid Blue Fire. How could I have been so stupid?"

Orli caught on immediately, looking excited even. "Yes. Oh my God, I'm an idiot too. That's how we can get into the heart chamber undetected. You can ..." she looked around for a moment, "... you can put it on these suits."

"I can," he said, "with one problem. I don't know the spell."

"Well, you better learn it fast. Can't you just, you know, drink something or something? Surely your people have ways of doing this."

He smiled at her, this time a real smile, one with actual joy in it. She was as brilliant as she was beautiful. "You know my world better than I do. There is a diviner's trick. Ocelot actually did it to me the other day."

She smiled back, but waved her hand in the air, a gesture to say that they should be moving on, not talking.

Altin contacted Peppercorn immediately, and found that she was awaiting his call, anxious and at first ecstatic to hear him tapping at the edges of her mind. Disappointment followed. She'd been hoping that he was going to direct her to send teleporters to Earth. Finally. But he did not. He told her what he needed.

"Guildmaster Meste will have it waiting when you get

here," promised Peppercorn, trying to find some hope in the fact that at least Altin and Orli were still trying with Red Fire. "Please hurry. It's going terribly down there."

"I saw," he relayed back to her. "Orli and I are on our way."

A moment later the two of them arrived in a *Citadel* teleportation chamber in the TGS offices. The last time Orli had been there was during the tour of *Citadel*, the first time she'd ever seen it before. They stepped out into the torch-lit space of the office proper, and it looked exactly the same, a low-ceilinged room with nothing to decorate it but empty desks that still hadn't been assigned permanent occupants. Waiting near the exit stood Guildmaster Cypher Meste and the diminutive enchanter Peppercorn. Both women looked haggard and worry worn.

The guildmaster diviner strode right up to Altin the moment he stepped into view and reached out her hand for his. He gave it to her immediately, palm up. Without precursor or warning, she turned it over and stuck him with a needle, hard and quick, drawing a long thread line down the back of his hand nearly to his wrist. She spoke only four words in doing it. When she finished, Altin knew the spell as thoroughly as if he'd been casting it every day for a year.

"You'll forget that by dinnertime," she said as she looked up at him. "That's the best I can do with no warning. If I'd had twenty minutes, you could have had it for a week. If we had three hours, you could have learned it properly yourself."

"Dinnertime will be enough," Orli said, taking Altin's hand from the guildmaster. "Altin, we have to go."

He knew that she was right. They all did.

"Mercy's favor," Peppercorn said into the hiss of air where Altin and Orli had been. "Mercy's favor on us all."

Chapter 45

Altin set the tower down directly on the surface of Red Fire's world. And true to apparently everything about this system and this bloody span of time, Red Fire the planet was just as red as the last planet Altin had explored, and just as red as the sun. It was also huge, titanic as rocky planets go, a great windswept rust ball with enormous mountains like rusty spines rising up all around, a land of rusty saw blades lying beneath a rusty sky filled with rusty clouds backlit by a bloated, rusty sun.

The tower settled heavily onto the ground of that alien world, sent straight from Prosperion to this place where, by comparison, the gray stone of that now distant planet seemed bright plumage. The tower thrust itself up amongst the jagged landscape like a rude gesture to Red Fire's oppressive monochrome, the singular monolith of otherness. In the next instant Altin cast the anti-magic spell on Orli's space suit. "Taking down the Polar Piton's shield now," he said right after. He spoke urgently, his breath quick. "This must be fast, before he finds me again."

"Wait. I'm still trying to get a reading for the Higgs

prism," Orli said. "It's not showing anything. It's showing no gravity at all. We should be floating if that was true. Which it can't be." She fiddled with the dials on the gravity prism for a moment more, growing anxious and hating every moment Altin stood there without the anti-magic spell on his suit. "It should be reading something."

"One of my students mentioned once that gravity might be an incidental element of the shield. Perhaps that is affecting your machine."

"It might be. I don't know."

"Well we are about to find out. What happens if the gravity is as you feared before, very high?"

"We get flattened."

"Can we test it? Maybe I can teleport something out there."

"Like what? It would have to be something sort of vertical, like us." She looked frantic. Her voice trembled as she spoke. "We don't have time. He's going to find you."

Altin cast about the room, looking for a surrogate to test the gravity. He spotted the little palm trees on the table nearby. "Here, this is vertical."

"It's too light, it will just blow over. And it's made of glass. Altin, quit messing around. He'll find you."

Altin teleported the decanter away, beyond the tower and the Polar Piton's shield, setting it in view on the ground outside the window. The little palm fronds on its stopper began to spin. They spun so fast they became a blur. Surprisingly, it didn't blow over. Had there been more time, Altin might have marveled at that. He did have time to notice, however, that it didn't break. It neither crumbled nor got pulled flat. That would have to be good enough.

"Well," he said, "it's not being ruined out there. So let's roll the dice, shall we?"

She sighed, the sound of it a tinny rasp in the speakers

inside Altin's helmet. "Take it down. Please hurry."

Altin reached out into the protective shielding he'd become so used to casting around buildings that he brought into space and, with a grimace, dismissed the spell.

A scouring wind blasted through the tower's windows the instant the magic shield was gone, nearly hurricane force. Books and parchments and bits of everything began whirling about, the wind circling and collecting violence in the round walls of the room. He immediately felt a tremendous weight upon him, he became that weight, had to fight to remain standing with all his might. His legs trembled and his spine felt as if it might compress. He felt a wrenching pain in his back where it pulled, and his abdominal muscles mashed together as his body began to fold, the very structure of his bones suddenly inadequate. He tried to push up against it, to fight it, but could not for long. For a moment he thought it might actually be an attack from Red Fire, but he saw Orli was folding too.

Her fingers feverishly worked the controls of the contraption she held, and just as Altin was forced to his hands and knees, the pressure was gone.

"Shit," gasped Orli, breathing as hard as if she'd run a sprint. "Five g's. That was close." He could barely hear her over the roaring of the wind.

"I should say so," Altin agreed. He stood and tried rubbing his aching back, but the boxy unit on the back of his spacesuit made it impossible.

"Get that spell on your suit," Orli demanded. "Now."

The great slam of Red Fire's recognition struck him the moment she said it, and once again Altin went down to his knees, the interior force greater than mashing gravity. He clutched at his head, grasping for his ears reflexively despite their being buried inside the bulky helmet.

Orli was at his side once more, the click of her face

plate against his, her mouth and eyes wide. "Cast the spell," she yelled, so loud it made the speakers crack. "Cast the fucking anti-magic."

Die, came the fury of Red Fire, a death weight of incalculable mass. *Die.*

Altin fought with all his will to focus long enough to cast the anti-magic spell. His hands shook with the palsy of his weakness and fear, but he placed it on the control panel of his suit and, finally, barely, enchanted it.

Red Fire was gone again.

"Tidalwrath's teeth," he exclaimed breathlessly, looking up into Orli's worried face. Bits of debris bounced off her visor. He could hear other bits ticking against his own when they struck. "I'm not sure I'll manage even a minute fighting down here, not this close to the source. That was worse than before."

She was already tugging him up to his feet. "Can you still go?"

"Yes," he said. "I'm okay."

Orli watched him for a moment, expectant in her posture and attitude. He looked back at her, shifting his weight to compensate for the gusting wind. He realized she was waiting for the teleportation spell that would take them out. He realized it because he'd thought about casting one.

"We have to take the stairs," he said. He reached out for her hand and together they made their way down the stairs, moving as quickly as the bulky suits would allow. The descent was interminable and Altin cursed himself for not having thought to just bring the top portion of the tower. Experiments in space made opportunities for the strangest oversights.

Soon enough, however, they were outside in the full force of the wind. Altin walked to where the little palm tree decanter was, leaned down and looked at it, searching for cracks or signs of fatigue. It seemed fine, though. Its fronds whirling furiously, but otherwise looking as it always had.

"So where is it?" Orli asked.

"Over there," he said, pointing beyond the decanter to a huge formation of dark red stone that was roughly eight hundred paces away. He started off immediately, once more pulling her along. The buffeting force of the wind had them staggering like drunks as they clambered over and around the rocks and boulders of the hostile landscape. Altin couldn't help the instinct that had him shielding his eyes with his hand against the blowing dust and grit as they made their way toward the dark tumble of piled rocks, a great mound of them, enormous stones that seemed to have collapsed together, like a fallen temple from some ancient time, though scoured clean of any remnant grandeur by the merciless sandblasting wind.

They got to it and quickly found some relief inside from the violent atmosphere. They moved deeper into the formation, carefully weaving through a veritable maze of giant, tilting stones, climbing over some, under others, and squeezing through narrow places carefully. In the process of doing so, Orli discovered, quite by accident and certainly to her surprise, that there were lichens there. It was a small patch growing on a rock, like cracked gray skin, and just the one spot of it, but there it was just the same. She took only enough time to lean close and turn on the suit's video feed to record it as she passed, her botanist's instincts coming naturally. "Well, there's the life it needs," she said. "At least some of it."

"Here," Altin said from up ahead, "down there."

Orli came up behind him and saw that he was looking down into a pit.

"I didn't think to bring any rope," he said, kneeling down to look inside. "I can't see very far down, and I doubt even an elf could climb the sides. Definitely not us in these suits."

Orli clicked on her suit's spotlight and shined it down into the hole. She could see the bottom. "About sixty feet," she said.

Altin was fiddling with the suit controls on his left sleeve. "How did you turn the light on?"

She reached over and turned it on for him.

He added his light to hers, and they studied the bottom of the hole again. He looked back up, directly at her, blasting his light right into her face. He quickly turned away when he saw her face contort. "Sorry." He felt so uncomfortable and out of place. Partly because he was in the suit, but mainly because being cut off from his magic left him helpless, unable to do anything for either of them now. "Somehow we need to find another way in."

"Did Blue Fire show you another way in?"

"No. This was it."

"Then we can use the prism. I'm not good with these because I never had any reason to use one before. They're all automatic on the ship. But I think I can figure it out."

Altin watched her face for a moment, then nodded. "What do you need me to do?"

"Come here," she said. "Get right up here and hug me as tight as you can. Don't let go."

"Gladly," he said, trying to sound chipper. It only sort of worked.

He scooted up to her and wrapped her in a hug as best he could.

"Turn off your light," she said, squinting again. "And don't pull anything loose back there." She gave him a very serious look at that, before adding, "And don't cover the jet ports."

He found the button she had pressed on his sleeve and turned off the helmet light. "What jet ports?"

"The little holes at the bottom, both sides and in the middle back. You should be able to feel the lip of them. They stick out a little bit."

"I'll try." He looked left and right, saw the jet nozzles and repositioned his arms around her, gripping the corners of the suit's blocky dorsal pack carefully and slightly lower than he had before. "That better?"

"Yes, except now I can't see. Get sideways a little bit so I can see my controls."

He scooted around so that he was hugging her at an awkward angle from the side, his right arm around the back of her neck and shoulders, his left across her chest. She lifted the gravity filtering device up to where she could see it, tugging it up by the short tether with which she'd tied it to her waist and contemplating its controls.

"Okay, on three, we're going to try a little test. Just a gentle little hop with your toes. More like standing up on your tiptoes than jumping, actually. Got it?"

He nodded.

"One, two, three."

They both lifted themselves up onto their toes, she with a little more force than he. They lifted into the air together, several inches off the ground and moving slightly sideways, then settled gently back down.

"Okay, I think that will do," she said. "I'll take a little more off while we're falling, so we don't pick up speed."

Altin began to realize what she was going to do. He laughed.

"What's so funny?" She squinted up at him through her helmet's glass.

"You're doing magic," he replied. "This spell is called Falling Leaves."

She smiled, but only until she blinked. "We can laugh later. Let's go. On three, we jump up and over the edge. I'll try to keep us from getting too wonky on the way down with my attitude jets, but don't expect much. We're kind of a mess like this."

"I trust you," he said, watching her through her visor. Even standing at the brink of death her beauty was radiant.

"On three. One, two, three."

They jumped over the edge, him clinging to her like the lichens had the rocks, and her tapping her backpack thrusters just enough to keep the two of them from rolling over sideways as they fell. They picked up a little speed, but she arrested it with a click of the Higgs prism dial. And then they were down.

Altin let her go and turned to where the pit became a tunnel, a low cave leading into darkness. He switched his suit's light back on. "It's really dark," he said.

"Altin, go. We have to hurry."

They moved into the cave and found that it headed very steadily down into the surface of the angry red world. For a time, it was fairly narrow, more like a crack than a cave, but eventually it started to widen until it provided more than enough room to move easily, in places, much more than enough.

They passed through wide tunnels and large open caverns, the surface of everything was pockmarked with tiny holes like those left behind by bad acne. There were no familiar formations, nothing like stalactites or stalagmites that might suggest there was water on this world, or at least that there had been at some time.

Onward they pressed, Altin leading them through twisting passages and down steep declining chutes. He moved through it all like a creature who'd lived there his entire life. But still he grew anxious and afraid. What Blue Fire had given him was recognition of the way, not a map. He had no gauge of distance. He had no way to predict how far they had to go. All of that pertained to his own ideas, human ideas of movement and time, things that had no corresponding part in the information he had gotten from Blue Fire, who had in turn taken it from Red Fire, from this world they were now sneaking down into. Altin only knew when they came to a place where they should turn, a place where they should climb, a place where they should jump. He even knew where not to go. But not how far.

They were nearing the forty-minute mark as they headed down, and both of them began to fret. Forty minutes with the orcs and demons pushing at the gate that was already all but lost before they left. Forty minutes with Red Fire's orbs draped all over Earth dissolving things, spreading disease. There wasn't going to be time. Both of them could feel it, but neither wanted to speak it aloud.

They moved faster, not quite running, but at a steady trot. Altin's breathing became loud over the speakers, but Orli didn't say anything. He wasn't a runner, and this was hard for him, not to mention that he had the heavy drill slung over his shoulder too. The work was made worse by the stiffening in the suit, its adjustments for the atmospheric pressure gradually bearing down on them. She knew he had no idea what the suit was doing in the same way that she knew she didn't know how much pressure it could take, or how much it would need to take. How far down could they go? How bad could it get? She knew nothing about this planet. She had no tools for measuring. The suit's alarm would sound if it got too bad. That's what she knew.

Red Fire seemed to sense that, or perhaps it was simply a quirk of fate, but they came upon a vast canyon then, so far across that their spotlights couldn't reach the other side. It was simply the end of forward progress, abrupt and absolute, as if it had been put there on purpose to block their way. There was back, and there was down.

Their spotlights revealed no more of the fissure's depth than it did about its width or the altitude of the ceiling somewhere high above.

"Well," she said as she looked up and then down for perhaps the tenth time, "did we make a wrong turn? Did we miss something?"

"No," he said. "This is it. We have to go down there."

"You're kidding me?" She leaned out over the edge and peered down to where the beam of her light simply faded to nothingness.

"No," he said. "I'm not kidding."

"Shit."

"I agree."

They both looked down. "So do we try the prism again?" she asked.

"We can't go back."

"No. We can't."

He moved up against her once more, prepared to hold on to her for the jump. Their eyes locked for a time, the bright sparks of spotlights reflecting in each. He didn't bother to turn it off this time, and she didn't ask. He felt her chest rise and fall with a sigh. He nodded, and then pulled himself tightly to her. "On three?"

"On three," she said. She pulled the prism up on its tether and set it to where it had been before, mitigating most of the planet's gravity. "One, two, three."

Once again they were falling. Altin clutched her so tightly that his arms began to tremble after a while. They started to tip over again and Orli tried to straighten them, but she let the gas flow too long and they tipped the other way. She tapped the control on the opposite side, trying to right them, but the jet hit Altin's arm so hard he lost his grip on that side of her suit back. The released energy swung him out from her like an opening door, his other hand gripping tightly and serving as a hinge.

He tried to hold on, to cling to her suit with that hinging hand, but he didn't have anything to grip firmly, only the corner of the suit. He couldn't risk grasping for something else because he didn't want to tear anything loose by groping wildly. So he broke free and started to drift away. They both knew that if he got beyond the range of the Higgs prism, he would plummet like a stone.

"Shit, shit, shit," Orli said as she tapped her jet controls trying to get closer to him. The jets weren't meant for flying, only for little thrusts to get across short spaces between ships or space station construction sites. If she hit the wrong one, or too much on one, she would take herself, and the Higgs prism, out of range.

Altin, however, remained calm. "Should I try my jets?" he asked. "Which ones are the controls?" He had crooked his arm to where he could look at the panel on his sleeve.

Orli might have laughed had she not been so terrified. "No!" she commanded. He'd only make it worse.

She turned two dials on her suit and a pair of jets fired for the barest instant each. She had to twist her hips to fix the angle some, but in moments she was drifting closer to him.

They reached for each other's hands and, still falling, finally caught one another. Soon they embraced each other again. It was Orli's turn to tremble now. "I told you not to cover the damn jets," she yelled. Fright was obvious in her eyes.

He sent a sheepish look back at her through his visor, that charming grin he had. "I know. My mistake. But look here, now I've got it right."

She wanted to throttle him, but she was glad that she hadn't lost him in such an awful way. She sent him a narrow-eyed "never do that to me again" look and allowed herself once more to breathe normally as they fell.

And they fell.

And fell.

And fell.

They fell for so long Orli wondered if perhaps they might fall out through the bottom of the world. They fell for fourteen minutes before the alarm went off.

It was a low, pulsing sound, and it came so suddenly it startled him. "What's that?" he asked. "It doesn't sound promising."

Her alarm went off next. "Shit."

"You seem to be saying that a lot."

"Yes, well, we're in it pretty deep now. Too deep. I don't know how much pressure these suits can take. They're made for space, not deep diving, or even for being too deep underground apparently." She called up the gauge in the helmet display. "We're going to run the power down really fast like this too. Where's the bottom of this fucking thing?"

She couldn't look down due to the way Altin was wrapped around her now, rather like a starfish on a rock, but he could see. He tilted his head as far as he could and directed the light down. Still nothing.

They fell for another six minutes.

"They're all going to be dead," she said after a while.

"We still have to try."

They found the bottom a few minutes after that. They came to rest as gently as the spell name Altin had given to the prism's effect implied, like leaves falling. The descent ended so gently and uneventfully it seemed the pinnacle of anticlimax after the near disaster high above.

Still, they were down.

Altin let go of Orli, who set the prism back to Earth normal again. He looked about them, shining his light around, turned full circle, with only the cliff face along which they had descended sending any of the light back.

The rest was utter darkness, as if they'd found themselves at the very core of nothingness.

"It should be here," he said.

"What should?"

"Something. I should see something. Over there somewhere." He pointed for a moment then switched off his light. "Turn that off," he said. "And dim these lights on our controls if you can."

She quickly obliged, and both of them peered into the darkness, only the sound of their breathing disturbing the absolute nature of the emptiness.

"There," he said after what felt a very long time. "Look."

"Where? I can't see where *there* is." It was true that they were completely in the dark.

He groped for her and found her shoulder, then turned her to face where he was looking. Then she saw it too. A tiny green light, like a pinhole in a black curtain, a glowing dust mote seen from a thousand steps away.

"Come on. That's him. It has to be," he said. They clicked their lights back on and soon were running toward the tiny spec of light as fast as the space suits would allow.

They covered the distance in no time and soon found a small opening, barely as high as Orli's knees and about three paces wide. "This is very similar to how it was before, on Blue Fire," Altin announced. "But will we fit?" He eyeballed the square block of her suit back in tandem with contemplating the narrowness of the entry.

"Lying flat, maybe," she said. "We won't be able to crawl."

"Won't be able to get out in a hurry either," he said. But even as he spoke, he was getting down onto the ground, preparing to slide in.

"Let me go first," she said, drawing her blaster from where it was strapped to her leg. "You can't do magic in that thing, remember?"

He cringed. He didn't want her going in first. But he knew that she was right. He was helpless if anything went wrong. It occurred to him that this was what life must be like living as a blank. So vulnerable. "Harpy spit," he swore. He couldn't stop the instinct that made him reach out and pull her back. "I can take that," he said, his eyes sliding to her gun.

"Oh, stop it," she said. "I'm bad enough with it as it is, and we've come too far for this right now." She yanked free of him and got down on her hands and knees, bent down and peered through the opening. "It's about ten feet to the other end. I don't see anything moving in there. And at least there's light."

She lay on her stomach and tried to crawl through, but the module on her back was too big. "Damn it. I'm like a pregnant camel in here." She flipped onto her side and tried to wriggle through, but couldn't get enough traction to move. "Push my feet," she said. "At least until I get far enough in to pull myself through with the lip on the other side."

Altin peered through the space into the area beyond. He didn't like this at all.

"Come on, Altin. Just do it."

He put his hands on the bottom of her boots, the chevron treads still filled with red grit and gravel from the surface far above. He gave a shove.

She pushed away from him with her legs and got her hands on the upper edge where the small opening gave way to the chamber beyond. The substance her fingers came in contact with was supple, spongy, like the rubber mats in the hand-to-hand combat rooms on the *Aspect*, but it held. She pulled herself through and quickly looked around, blaster ready as she verified that she was, in fact, alone.

She was.

"Come through," she said, holstering her weapon. "I'll pull you."

She reached back into the gap and, between the two of them, they managed to get Altin through as well. "We're definitely not going to be able to make a hasty retreat if it comes to it," he reiterated as she checked his suit for rips.

"There's no turning back at this point anyway," she said as she finished going over his suit carefully with her hands and eyes. "Now look and make sure nothing came loose on mine and that there aren't any tears anywhere."

He nodded that her point was accurate as he inspected her suit as well. "Nothing I can see," he said after a time. "Let's go."

Soon they were moving through tunnels again, although this time with no need of spotlights. The glow coming from the soft substance on the cave walls was everywhere. The small chamber they'd entered was covered floor to ceiling with it, a pale green luminescence that Altin said was exactly like the stuff he'd found on Blue Fire's world. They were definitely close.

"Be on the lookout for balls or tubes or barrels of this stuff," he warned. "She sent me a guide when I was there, a creature like a rolling log. It might be hard to spot since it looks exactly the same as the walls and everything. It will blend in. But look for motion of any kind."

"Are they dangerous?"

"I have no idea. I'm not even sure it was a creature."

Onward they ran, as fast as safety would allow, Altin's blind reliance on memories he could not actively draw upon guiding them. They ran through caves and caverns. They ran up gentle slopes. They used the prism twice more to accommodate long drops, though nothing of the magnitude of the last. On and on they went.

Finally they came to a long, narrow tunnel that was, in places, so low Altin had to stoop, though he never had to crawl. They squeezed through the tunnel's narrow places, ducked and leaned around several bends, until suddenly, around one sharp turn, Altin gasped.

"What?" Orli demanded as she came around the bend behind him. It became clear he need not answer it as she stepped beside him and muttered, "Oh, shit."

They'd emerged at the bottom of a tremendous chamber filled with red light. An entire cavern covered at every inch by projecting crystals, like broken fingers, each aglow like the warning lights of a billion ships' alarms, red beacons that seemed to radiate nothing but "Get Away!"

They both gaped, staring around them, slowly turning as they took in the awesome spectacle. It might have been beautiful had they not known what it was. Who it was, and what it represented to humanity and to Blue Fire.

Orli recovered first and patted her satchel filled with mining charges as she looked up into the seemingly endless vault above. "So, where's the heart? Let's do this."

"Gorgon's blood!" came what served as his reply. At first she thought he was still marveling at what he saw, but when she looked to him, she saw that he was pointing off to their right. "Look, here come the rolling things."

Orli drew her blaster and fired a few quick bursts at the nearest of six oblong creatures—if *creatures* were what they were. Even from twenty yards away she cut it easily in two, the bright beam of her laser halving it with the barest flicker of flame and a wet hiss of steam. Both halves came rolling on, however. Now there were five big ones, about waist high, thick as an oil drum and twice that wide, and two more smaller ones. She flipped her weapon to conventional rounds and sent two shots at one of the bigger ones. The flare of the discharge flashed white in the red chamber, and the concussive blasts echoed and amplified from everywhere around. The creature gave no indication that it had been struck, though Orli was confident that she hadn't missed, at least not with the first two rounds. And yet still it came, right along with the rest.

She emptied the clip blasting at it, certain she must have hit it several times, and probably the one behind it as well. But nothing changed, and on they came, rolling steadily forward in a strange and silent form of menace she'd never dreamed of before.

The chamber began to rumble, two tremors and then violent movement of the floor. The rough surface beneath them began to buck like a wild thing, and they were thrown to the ground by the turbulence. Orli staggered left, then right, tried to catch herself on a rock but missed, and then went down to her hands and knees. Altin was simply thrown straight up, flung a quarter span into the air, and then down he came, landing like a tossed sack of coal. He landed heavily, and worse, he landed on the drill. The bit nicked through his suit just below the knee, and with it a hiss of escaping air added itself to their list of problems more than disturbingly.

That was not the end of it, however, and they bounced around like beads of cold water in a very hot pan for what seemed an eternity. They both grunted and *oomphed* aloud as they bumped and tumbled around, wondering if it would ever stop. Orli tried to get hold of the Higgs prism, but it was impossible, the quake was too violent. She was left simply hoping that it would not be broken in the violence, fearing that being pinned to the undulating floor might get them snapped like dried twigs rather than just being tossed around. Better to be bounced than broken, she thought. The only real upside of the quaking floor was that it seemed to be affecting the rolling creatures too, which gave her and Altin a brief reprieve from their advance, assuming that was preferable.

Eventually the tremors stopped, and as they picked themselves up, they looked over to check on their presumed attackers, expecting them to be coming at them again, but rather than coming straight for them as before, the creatures were spreading out.

"Maybe I shouldn't shoot them?" Orli said.

"Maybe you should. At least they aren't coming at us now."

"Not yet. Now they're doing something that looks like a plan instead. We need the heart chamber fast, and I don't want to do that earthquake thing again."

Altin scanned a section of the cavern a few hundred paces from where he stood, climbing its walls with his eyes, seeking something familiar up there, something recognizable in the memory Blue Fire had given him. That seemed like where he was supposed to look. And then he saw it. "Look, up there. See where it turns orange by the bulge?"

She followed the line of his pointing and, after a moment, saw it too. She guessed it to be three hundred feet up.

"How are we supposed to get up there?"

"Can we use your prism? Make a jump?"

"Not accurately. These things really aren't meant for that. And I don't have any practice with it."

"Can we try?"

"Not together," she said after a moment's thought, and more than a little reluctantly. "But I might be able to do it alone."

"That's not an option."

"Altin, if that's it, I have to get up there. You're right about the prism. It's the only way."

"We'll do it together."

"We can't even fall together well. How are we going to fly three hundred feet jumbled together with dangling drills and blocked jets, and me not able to balance well even on my own? We'll have to be at zero g to do it, and I only have ...," she paused and checked the reading on her gas canisters. "I only have four minutes of jet thrust left. There's barely time enough to do it, much less for having to figure it out with you. If these suits weren't designed for flying one person, they damn sure weren't meant for two."

"You can use the gas from my suit if we use up all of yours."

"Altin!"

"I'm not letting you go up there alone. Besides, you said if we get separated from the prism, the planet's gravity could kill us."

"It can."

"So, we have to stay together."

Orli looked him straight in the face, eyes narrow, waiting. She didn't say anything.

He tried to match the intensity of her gaze, but hers was unwavering. He tried anyway, to wait her out. But she was still as stone.

"I'm not letting you go alone," he said finally.

"Then everyone dies."

"Orli." It was insistent, but pleading.

The glowing creatures were creeping forward, holding a formation that would not allow bullets to penetrate one and hit another. But they were cautious now. At least it seemed that Orli's bullets had had some kind of effect, even if nothing obvious. Unfortunately she'd emptied the clip, and she didn't have another one.

She looked from Altin to the approaching objects rolling slowly near. "Altin." She spoke his name just as fervently as he had hers as she looked back at him. She didn't blink. He didn't blink. They stared at each other some more, almost hostile in their way.

A single tear ran down his cheek. She could see it glinting in the orange light. She knew he recognized the truth of what she'd said, knew he'd seen what she had seen too. It was their only hope.

She lifted the drill strap over his helmet, pulled it off his shoulder and slung it over hers.

"I'll hold him off as long as I can," he said.

"I know."

He reached up to hit the catch that released his helmet seal, but she stopped him.

"Wait," she said. "Let me adjust the pressure. At least some to even it out." She looked up into his eyes. "Altin, this is really going to hurt."

"I know."

A few moments later she nodded. "Lie down," she said. "It will be easier once the prism is out of range. And you won't black out. Go home before you suffocate. You're not going to get much air."

"I'm not going home," he said once they had him laid out. "Not until I see that you are safe." He hit the latch on the helmet. It hissed as air escaped.

Immediately he could feel the burn of strange gasses in his lungs and the helmet was only open just a crack. Drawing breath was a huge labor as well, the pressure of being so far down pressing upon him instantly. Orli saw it in the way his face blanched, and she took his arm and adjusted the oxygen flow to its highest output. With the tear in his suit, the pressure was even lower than it could have been.

"Altin, get home. I will be all right. I have my amulet. I'll come back to you, I swear."

"I'm not leaving until I see," he gasped.

"Don't do this, Altin. Don't make this all for nothing. You fight as long as you can. Just like Ocelot said. You fight. You get me as much time as you can, and then you go home. Don't make me grow old alone. You go home, Altin. Swear that you will."

"Orli ... please."

"No, you fucking swear it, Altin."

Tears ran down both of their faces. But he agreed. He was already running out of time. He could feel it. "I swear."

"Please," she begged. "I will be okay. Have faith in me."

"I do." He gritted his teeth, steeling himself. His chest was on fire. His eyes ached. He tried to nod, but the effort seemed like too much. He started to choke on the mix of air; it was like coughing with a mammoth sitting on his chest. "Go," he rasped.

She smiled down at him, poured love from her eyes into him. "I love you." She turned quickly then and looked up at the wall, spotting the orange light high above. She spun the Higgs prism dial around to zero, and pushed off. Altin watched her soar away.

It terrified him. He tilted his head up and looked to where the rolling creatures still approached, but then the prism moved too far off and his head slammed back to the cavern floor with violence, rolling the helmet completely off.

The pull of powerful gravity stuck him to the ground like a brick of lead. He tried to look up but he could not. The pressure was intense, as if the mammoth had now brought its friends to sit on him as well. The sting in his eyes intensified, and his sinuses felt full. He thought his ears would burst.

He'd feared that some of the creatures would be going after her. He wondered if somehow they would know what she intended to do. He tried once more to look, but it was futile. He had to prevent them from chasing her, from climbing up the wall. He didn't need to see them with his eyes now anyway. His magic would work now that the suit was open like it was. It would work, but he also knew what else it would do.

A quick seeing spell showed him where the creatures were. Sure enough, several of them were rolling rapidly back toward the bright light on that far wall, and quickly too, one of them already trundling up the wall like some sticky, impossible snowball rolling up a cliff. The others were getting close as well, three of them. But not for long.

With a thought, Altin conjured a fireball as big as a house and sent it at the one already moving up toward Orli's goal. The flaming missile struck it with an explosive flash that Altin could see reflected and refracted by crystals everywhere. The flash was followed by a splat, which was accompanied by the crackle of flames and the hiss of escaping steam. He'd found his mark, and he was glad.

He sent three more fireballs into the remembered places of others that had gone after her, cast in rapid succession, *whoosh, whoosh, whoosh*. Again the flare of the strikes and the sound of fire and steam.

He finished the others near him similarly, burning them into puddles of nothingness, but even as he did so, the ground began to shake. The violence of the floor's movements bent and twisted him, for he could not bounce anymore. He was stuck to the ground like a barnacle to a boat, and he suffered every wave of Red Fire's anger, the undulating cavern floor painfully arching his back as he rode out the storm. In that same instant, as the quake once more began, there came upon his mind the full might of Red Fire as well. Red Fire had found him there.

Die, was the only thought that filled him. *Die, die, die.* Over and over again. Were the hatred in those thoughts to have possessed physicality, the whole of space could hardly contain it. It was the absolute refinement of hostility, the purest form of anger possible, and it swelled in Altin's every thought like a bladder into which magma poured. It ran searing red inside of him, and Altin could not gulp down mana fast enough to cool the fires. It swelled and swelled and swelled, and though he could, somewhere in the tiniest recesses of his mind, still conjure the idea that he might somehow fight back, it was not enough to give him strength to do anything. So he gulped at the mana, scooped into the motionless mist of that familiar pink sea like a man drowning, sucking it in like life's last breath as the unfathomable fury of Red Fire crushed him beneath all that hate. While the pressure crushed him. While the gravity crushed him.

He felt himself smothering. He felt himself ebbing away. Leaking out the things that were in him like the hiss of air coming from the rent in his spacesuit, from the oxygen pump spewing uselessly at his neck. Red Fire would stamp his imprint into him like a footprint on a bug.

He fought to see through the torrent of hate-filled redness that Red Fire pushed into his brain. His vision subsumed by the fire of it just as the red rolling things burned with Altin's fire. He blinked and struggled to rise against the impossible grapple of gravity.

He opened his eyes and willed himself to see. A red haze had come upon everything.

He saw the flicker of a white jet from Orli's spacesuit high above, sailing away from him, just a pulse of it and its soft sound. It looked like a feather, a white plume at the tip of a goddess' wing. It was the gentle breath of goodness in the awful place of hate and torment.

He gulped in more mana as he saw Orli disappear into the mouth of the orange light. He gulped and gulped and gulped and tried to hold on to what was left of him. His body was leaking horribly. Failing under the press of so many fronts. He choked on blood that poured into his mouth, that ran down the back of his throat. He could hear the bubbling in his own breath even as he felt his lungs burn with the fluid pouring in.

He gulped at the mana and the blood, gulped for oxygen. There was none. He couldn't see her anymore. Orli was gone. Or his vision was gone. Or both.

Orli Love home.

It was a whisper. Far away. Blue Fire in his mind.

Orli Love home. A plea.

He couldn't leave her.

Home. Home.

He had promised her he would.

Fire filled him. He knew he was drowning now. On his own blood. He choked up a gout of it that wouldn't clear his lips for the pressure and the gravity, so he choked on it again.

Orli Love home. Blue Fire was desperate.

He tried to pull more mana to fight, but he could barely reach it. Even the mist was vanishing. Just a puff left, a diminishing cloud fading into the vacuum.

He'd promised her. He had to have faith.

With the last wisp of mana, he cast himself home.

Chapter 46

Most of the cowardly humans had filed back through the gate, hiding behind the weakness of the golden queen's magical walls. But they would not hold for long. The demons poured around the palace like black blood, and they leapt and battered at its walls. The city walls had fallen easily. And now the palace would as well. The humans had even brought back the flying crystal sphere, but to no avail. Humans in a bubble, a water drop, its falling rain of broken stones all but meaningless. Stupid magic that would mark their graves when it finally fell from the sky.

Only the golden queen and her most ferocious guardians remained outside the gates, the last to fall back, the sharp barb of a scorpion running for its hole. The wicked elf was with her, of course, and a handful of horsemen, long deprived of their mounts. There also had appeared beside her an infernal wizard who turned everything to stone, and completing her deadly entourage were three of the sky god's humans in their ogre-sized armor suits. This group closed together, side by side, as the last human soldiers made their way through the gates. They bought time for the retreat, falling back step by step as the might of Warlord and his army squeezed them against those last remaining walls, the blood of her people running like pus from the festering wound their race had become.

The song of Warlord's battle with the golden queen would be sung forever, for on and on it had gone for nearly the entire day. And still they fought now. The human's left arm hung limply at times, evidence of a crushing swipe of Warlord's axe that had caved in her armor there. She still had use of it, but Gromf had seen it dangle more often than not. She would not last long, now that the slaves that healed her had just run back through the gates. Warlord would finally finish her, if he was quick and got her before she too ran and hid.

Gromf had long since stopped hoping that God would make short work of her. He'd briefly wondered if perhaps God could not, for it seemed that he had his opportunities, but Gromf realized that God needed Warlord to have the respect of the All Clans. It would not do for Warlord to ask God to help kill the golden queen.

But God also did not kill the elf. And the elf made Warlord's fight difficult. And Gromf was having an impossible time killing it as well. He could not understand God.

Even now, as Gromf loosed another wave of ice lances, the elf avoided them. Gromf sent ten of them, each thick as logs and three paces long. He sent them all in a scatter, drawing on the mana given him by the God Stones in his hands. He sent those ten and then ten more after, right behind, staggered in such a way that the elf might not so easily vanish to avoid them all. He waited a breath and then sent another wave even after those. But the elf sensed it somehow, it seemed to know, and it vanished and was gone anyway.

It ran at Gromf then, hurling those foul knives it used. Gromf could not dodge them in time, but God slapped the knives away. Again. As he had at least twenty other times this hour. God tried to slap the elf away again, as he had done outside the city walls once early in the day, but the elf vanished before the blow came upon it. Only once since that first time had God even touched the awful thing. It seemed nearly impervious to God's wrath, and even when struck, it took no injuries. How could that be?

God shouted demonic obscenities at Gromf constantly. "Kill the elf," God thundered down at him, his rage growing as the battle had progressed. "Kill it. That is what I made you for."

But Gromf could not kill the awful thing. It vanished when it should stand and fight. It could not be crushed. He could not burn it with his fire. The elf would not die.

And so they fought. Gromf sending his fire and his ice. Keeping the elf away from Warlord, but unable to finish it.

And the humans killed everything. These last were an awesome lot. The golden queen's fury seemed to spill into them and give them strength. The lances of her warriors bit like demon's teeth in their hands, the magic cast upon them flashing in strange unheard-of ways. Orcs and demons died in piles, the effluence of all that blood and gore oozing and sloshing with every step.

The humans of the new god sprayed their nasty death spray everywhere, the light of those short fires from their arms shone, and then holes opened in orc faces and demon carapaces, and more gore came forth. The magicians on the walls were helping protect them now, and the ice lances Gromf and his companions sent melted in the fires of that defense.

Two more of the human warriors went down, as there was not enough magic to protect them from crossbow fire. They were trying to get through the gate, but two demons had got in between.

Now they were cut off.

Warlord struck the golden queen with a swing of such force that she flew back against one of the palace's two massive gates. The clank of her armor against it resounded like a gong. Thousands of orcs shouted all at once, cheering Warlord on.

The spitting fire from one of the sky god's humans ripped into Warlord's armor then, the *tink, tink, tink* of the impact marking the path of holes that drew a line up his breastplate. He staggered back a step with the impact of each of them, driven back out of reach, unable to strike the killing blow on the golden queen.

The sound of a thousand humans, perhaps far more, rose up then to cheer her. She was back on her feet then, and once more squared off for the fight. She did not charge back at Warlord, though. She knew better now.

Gromf sent ice lances into the group of them, but the horsemen batted them away with the flats of their blades. The stupid human horsemen. Gromf hated them. He sent a long spear of ice at the magician that remained, a soft target he should be. That one stood at the far left of their formation and had no sword. He would not bat it away. But he saw it coming, Gromf watched his dark eyes widen as he realized what was on its way. The ice lance flew straight for his heart.

It shattered against solid stone. The infernal human kept turning himself to stone. Could none of these last puny weaklings die? Gromf shouted his rage even as the human became flesh again and set himself to fending off one of the demons blocking the gate.

The elf had retrieved its knives, Gromf knew, and he had to guard Warlord's back. He washed the area behind his mighty leader with a narrow band of flames, hoping to flush out the sneaking elf.

Sure enough, the elf appeared once more, its black

leather armor smoking after the fire passed.

It flung another dagger at Gromf, lightning fast, then it vanished again. Gromf knew it was coming at him now. Like it always did.

God batted away the knife just as Gromf put up a wall of flame all around himself, a thick one, and one he blasted out in an expanding ring.

He heard the shouts and agonies of his clansmen as they were consumed in the fire. But he saw the elf caught in it too, saw it appear and glare across it at him before leaping into the air like a cougar up into a tree.

It came down after the fire had passed beneath it and vanished just as God's arm slammed down, meant to crush it finally. A crater appeared and cobblestones exploded all around where the elf had been.

Gromf looked to where the knife had landed after God knocked it away. He knew the elf would get it again, for it only had a few knives left after fighting all day.

He saw the knife vanish, and he cast fire on the spot. He sent an ice lance right behind, so quickly cast that it was hardly more than a knife itself.

The elf appeared. Caught the frozen shaft and hurled it back at Gromf.

Gromf ducked, but the elf's reclaimed knife was also on its way.

Gromf rolled to avoid it.

Another knife came. He could not get up in time to escape this one.

God slapped it away.

The golden queen cut Warlord's chest plate open, the blade magically sharp and the blow aided by the rents the spitting-fire weapons of the new humans had made. But rather than dive back from her blow, Warlord stepped into it, letting his armor be cleaved clean through, opening a gash in his flesh that exposed the bones of three ribs. The wound gaped open, and the armor plating fell away, dangling from its straps like a wind charm. Warlord swung his axe down, a wide slanting arc that would split her from crown to crotch, but she managed to get her sword up in time to divert the blow, if only enough to redirect it some. It cut clean through her leg instead, mid-thigh, and she fell immediately, gushing blood in a glorious spray.

Three of her horsemen immediately leapt in front of Warlord's next swing and knocked the killing blow away. The humans of the new god sprayed their short fire at Warlord's exposed chest, but Gromf threw a thick sheet of ice in front of him, just in time.

The elf ran at Gromf, snatching up the short shard of ice again.

God slapped the elf away, finally making contact again with a swipe that sent it flying far off into the still-growing mass of demons crowding in from behind. Whether it survived or not, it would not get back in time. Gromf knew that at last victory was at hand.

Only God noticed that the crystal sphere had gone.

Chapter 47

"Colonel Pewter, I see you are still alive," came the call from Director Nakamura, though the colonel was too busy to respond immediately.

"Yeah," he finally grunted when he could spare the breath to speak—and as he was sending a backhanded swipe into the joint of a demon's leg. The demon buckled and fell forward, nearly knocking the colonel's mech into the gate. If he fell, he'd block it for everyone—assuming the rest of them got a chance to get inside anyway.

"It appears your daughter may have had some success with the Hostile world," said the director. "All the orbs have stopped moving. It's like someone pulled the plug."

"Well none of these assholes have stopped moving, Director," the colonel managed through clenched teeth. He sent a spray of bullets into a cluster of the demon's eyes as it drooped on its broken leg. He was down to nine hundred rounds. "If you've decided to finally pull your head out of your ass, it might not be too late for whoever is left down here."

He heard a loud clang behind him, and he saw the War Queen bouncing off the Palace gates in his rearview video feed, a blow from that big bastard she'd been fighting since the colonel and his men found her. He'd tried to kill the hulking orc several times, but the roaring warrior had a lot of comrades watching out for him, which had made it impossible to take him out.

The Queen slid down to the ground behind him, and the great brute lunged at her again. The colonel swung his gun around and sent a quick blast at it, knowing full well that the goddamn giant with the huge arm was going to block the bullets, just as it had last time.

But it didn't. It was dealing with the Queen's assassin again. There was almost a rhythm to how this battle went.

Without the giant's intervention, the bullets struck true, seven of them opening up a serrated line across the orc leader's massive breastplate. The colonel would have finished the brute off, but the demon he'd been fighting hadn't had the courtesy to die. It smacked him hard with a long sweeping swing of one great leg, which slammed him against the wall at least as hard as the Queen had hit the gate—and had it not been for that wall, he would have flown at least another hundred feet away.

"Colonel, we need to know where the magicians are," the director said. "We can't send help without them."

"They're on *Citadel*," he said, too busy to see the hope in that right then. He punched through the dent he'd made in the demon's face and jack-hammered out its brain.

"We need to get word to them. I'm assembling the Marines as promised."

"Damn it," breathed the colonel as the demon's death spasm nearly knocked him down again. It fell over and slid on the broken stilts of its legs, wedging the colonel's mech against the wall. "I'm kind of busy right now."

The director actually looked anxious then, guilty even, not that the colonel had the time to look down at the monitor and see it. "Colonel, I want to help. But my hands are tied without the Prosperions."

Colonel Pewter's voice was strained, both in trying to bite back a snide remark about why he'd waited this long to send help and in trying to yank himself free before some demon came up behind him and ripped him in half. He achieved both, though barely, and swung his gun around to spray four orcs rushing at him with glowing spears. They erupted into dark sheets of blood.

"Oh, shit," came Corporal Chang's voice over the all com, and the colonel turned just in time to see him lunging forward trying to protect the Queen. That mass of green muscles with the double-sided axe had just cleaved her leg in two. The corporal tried to hose down the big brute with his Gatling gun, but a thick sheet of ice appeared before him, turning to snow as the bullets struck, the spray of lead hitting so fast and violently that it filled the area all around them with bits of ice that fell like a hail storm had briefly settled in.

"Colonel Pewter," insisted the director. "The magicians. Let us help. *Help* us help."

The colonel's mind fought desperately to think. He was exhausted. He shot three more orcs, and cut the legs out of a demon sneaking in from above, climbing over the demon he'd just killed. What could he possibly do? Wave and shout at *Citadel* above? Shoot at them?

"I don't have any way to speak to them, Director. Maybe you should have come sooner."

It was the director's turn to swear.

"Where is Orli? Why can't she tell them? Is Meade dead?"

"We don't know. I haven't heard from either of them."

"Well, did you tell Asad to look for her, to scan for her tablet somewhere?"

"Yes. Still no word."

"Shit." Then it hit him. He switched back to all com. "Levi, are you still on the wall?"

"Yes, sir," said the commander. "I'm east of you now, I think. I got turned around in the mob pushing through the gate."

"Levi, find a magician. Any magician. You have to get word to *Citadel*. Tell them to send the teleporters. The director is finally going to help."

"It's about goddamn time."

"Levi, now. Before it's too late."

"On it, sir."

The colonel switched back to the director, who immediately asked if it was done.

"I don't know, Director. We'll just have to see. But if this city goes down, if these people all die, you better hope there's no such place as hell."

"I think my room is booked and paid for, Colonel. I'll order the fleet to resume fire, and we'll send air support back in for now."

"You do that, sir," said the colonel, not bothering to hide the contempt beneath the words. His ammo counter flashed at him, the reading: ninety-two.

Chapter 48

Kettle found Altin by the moans echoing dully out of the dark corner of Calico Castle's cavernous dining hall. At first she thought it was a ghost, so lost was she in the absent mood that had settled upon her as she set the long table again, set it as she always did at this time of day, preparing it for a meal that was never eaten there anymore, a custom she simply could not let go. If she stopped doing it, if she stopped assuming that Altin would come and eat, it felt like the world would stop too.

And so the first low sounds coming from the shadows gave her a fright as she stared into the gloom at the silhouetted suit of armor there, a rusting old thing that had been glorious one day long ago perhaps, but that had remained unassaulted by even her dust cloth since her third year in Tytamon's employ.

The moan came again, a few more times, before the flutter of her heart turned from fright to alarm. She recognized that sound.

She ran as fast as her stout frame could manage, her skirts hoisted above her fleshy pink knees. When she saw the strange shape of his spacesuit, she once more recoiled, thinking something supernatural might have come, but there could be no mistaking that face, that sweet, beautiful face of the boy she'd raised since he was eleven. A face now completely covered with blood.

She fell to her knees beside him and shrieked for Nipper to come. She cradled his head in her lap as his blood poured from his mouth in a river that pooled upon her white apron.

"Altin, sweet boy, wake up. Altin speak ta me!" She shrieked for Nipper again.

One of the heavy doors swung open a crack as Nipper came in. "Ya don't ha' ta scream, woman, I ain't deaf yet." Pernie squeezed under his arm even as he was pushing open the door. She ran to where Kettle was, knowing well what the pitch of Kettle's voice foretold.

"Tell Gimmel ta hitch a team," Kettle shouted. "Altin is here, and he's bleedin' from everywhere. We got ta get him ta Leekant fast."

Pernie knelt beside her and looked down into Altin's face. She'd never seen that much blood coming from someone's face before, at least no one that she loved.

"What happened to him?" she asked.

"I ha' no idea, girl. Now run and fetch me some clean rags from the linen, and a kettle a' hot water from the fire. Go and do it now."

"I can fix him," she said, scooting forward and reaching out to touch his face.

"Don't ya dare," Kettle snapped. "Don't ya cast one thing. Ya got no idea what all that magic is about. Yer a wee lass, and ain't no doctor yet."

"I don't want to be a doctor. But Master Grimswoller says I can heal."

"Pernie, ya needs ta keep that magic in yer head now. You'll do as I told ya, child!"

"But I can." She reached out and touched Altin's face. Both hands, his head held between them. She pressed her palms against his ears, holding him softly as she tried to think healthful thoughts. She knew how to find the mana now. They'd taught her quite a lot. She didn't know any healing spells, though. At least not human ones. She only knew how to un-wilt a daffodil. But how much different could it be? It was just health after all. So she cast it, the innocence of childhood folding her love for him into it like a prayer.

Altin coughed again, violently, before Kettle could stop her. The hot spray of blood he sent forth freckled them both.

"Pernie," Kettle shouted as she began to reach for the child's hands. But she stopped, knowing it was too late, fearing it might only make it worse to disturb magic underway. She didn't know which was more dangerous anymore, being a magician or being a blank.

Pernie let go of Altin a moment later, pulling her little hands off his face, oblivious to the sticky blood soaking them so thoroughly. "I think that helps," she said, smiling up at Kettle. "See."

Altin sat up and coughed out more blood. Kettle watched in horror thinking that Pernie must have ruptured one of his lungs. Perhaps both. He coughed and gagged and drew in ragged breaths. He was a mess, a slimy crimson ooze. But he was alive.

His first word came as if released from a bursting bubble, fast and wet, "Orli?" He looked around, and seemed to see Kettle and Pernie for the first time. He blinked and, in trying to wipe whatever it was away with his hands, smeared more blood into his eyes.

He reached for his robes but realized he was still wearing the space suit. Suddenly he scrabbled back out of the way, getting out of the space behind the ancient armor suit. "Don't go in there. Stay away from the armor." His eyes were aflutter then as he tried to clear them of all that blood. It ran in red tears down his face. He looked the part of some gruesome carnival clown in makeup that was a mask of melting horror and leaking death.

He stared into the space behind the armor, glared into it, the intensity of his blood-soaked expression enough to silence even Pernie's voice. He tried to cast a seeing spell, but he started coughing so violently he couldn't get it off.

"Please," Altin said, wheezing, gasping through the fit that wracked him. He nearly blacked out and had to flop over on his side. "Please," he said, weakly, still trying to catch his breath. It was barely a whisper. "Please, please, please." He kept saying it, over and over, staring into that place, watching it with a wounded ferocity as he lay panting, waiting for his vision to return. Every so often he would mutter the name of some god or another. He would curse them or praise them alternately.

He tried to cast a seeing spell again, but he simply didn't have the strength. So he stared, glared even, as if he were trying to burn a hole straight through all that dark space between them with the raw ferocity of his need to know. His need to have her back.

Kettle and Pernie backed away from the armor, backed away even from him. There was something terrifying in his eyes, something threatening the worst of all possible things, something so unspeakable, so unbearable, neither dared to ask. They stared with him, sharing the pall of his awakening dread, the growing thing that filled the room like rumors of a plague.

And then Orli came staggering out of nowhere. In a suit just like the one Altin wore. She appeared in a rush of air, a hot one, stumbling the moment she arrived. She took one running step forward and clanged off the armor suit, buckling it and sending it falling noisily toward Pernie where she stood. The child scrambled out of the way even as Orli staggered back, hit the wall and stumbled two steps forward where she tripped over Altin and went sprawling to the floor, her helmet bouncing out of her hand and sent skittering across the flagstones into the dark places near the farthest end of the room. She lay there motionless for a time, her suit smoking heavily, as Altin leapt for her, finding the strength to half dive, half crawl to where she lay, her name a desperate hope upon his lips.

"Shit," she said even as his cries rang out. She'd landed hard against the stone floor and knocked the air from her lungs. She gasped a few times more, before she fumbled to right herself. He was already there, rolling her over and helping her sit up.

She shook her head to clear it, and looked instantly relieved. "You're alive!"

"*You're* alive!" he rejoiced. "Thank the gods, you are alive." He sobered instantly. "But is it done?"

"The charges went off, if that's what you mean," she replied. "I waited until it blew."

"So is it dead?"

"I don't know. I only had time to drill one hole, and not even very deep. Red Fire must have known what we were doing because he started shaking everything. The Higgs prism kept me mostly out of trouble, but the damn wall was moving so bad I couldn't set the drill. So once I realized trying was pointless, I jammed a charge into the hole I'd made, and then just hung the bag with the rest of them on it. I set the timer for fifteen seconds and jumped. When I'd floated far enough away, I got my helmet off and the amulet ready, but I wanted to make sure the charge went off. The second I saw the fire blast in the heart chamber, I left. And, well, here I am. But that's it. After the flash, I just don't know. All I know for sure is: that was pretty damn close." She held up the stub of the fast-cast amulet, the chain still dangling from her gloved hand.

Smoke rose in lazy lines from the glove, drifting toward the ceiling, the strange Earth material obviously singed. "I guess now we wait and see. Or you can go look with a spell."

Altin tried again to cast a seeing spell, but he could not. He started coughing once more. "Ugh," he said. "I'm worthless now."

"Want I should heal you some more?" Pernie asked. Orli got up and ran for her helmet where it had rolled into a corner near the room's farthest wall.

Altin watched her go, saw that she seemed to be perfectly fine as she strove to pull something out of the helmet, and he turned back to Pernie. "Heal?" he asked, with perhaps more than a little horror in the expression that he wore. He was afraid he already knew the answer too.

"Yes," she said, nodding honestly up at him, her small face radiant with pride. "It was I what brought you back. Kettle said I shouldn't, but I did anyway because I knew I could even if I didn't know the spell. At least not exactly, I know the flower healing spell, but it worked, didn't it? I just made it for you. I can do it again too, you'll see." She moved toward him, reaching out her steady little hands.

Kettle's own hands darted out and snatched her back. "That'll be enough a' that sorta thing from the likes a' you, child," she said. "Ya done a fine thing, I'll grant ya, but that's plenty fer today, I'd say. Master Altin will be needin' seen ta by a trained professional from here."

Pernie looked as if she were ready to argue, but Altin stayed her with an upraised hand. "She's right, Pernie. But you've done a wonderful thing. I will be forever in your debt."

"Well, I was just going to—" she began, but she stopped when Orli's yelling turned all eyes to the far end of the room. Orli had extracted a small object Pernie didn't recognize from the helmet and now held it to her ear.

"Just send them, goddamn it. It's fucking dead. We killed it."

The three Prosperions stood staring, transfixed by the urgency in Orli's tone.

"I don't want to know why! They've already waited long enough."

Altin thought she was going to lose her mind. She was absolutely furious, but then, just as suddenly as the one-sided conversation had begun, Orli's tone changed, softening considerably.

"My father?" Another pause. "Okay. Good. Thank God. So you'll send them if they show up?"

More breathless waiting on the part of Altin, Kettle and Pernie.

"Okay," Orli said at last, her voice one of absolute relief. "We'll tell them. Pewter out." She looked up and saw them all staring at her, two faces filled with bewilderment and one with rising hope.

"Well?" said Altin, having partially figured out what was going on.

"The director said they'll come. The orbs have all gone motionless. He says they're turning gray. Nothing is moving, so it worked! It really worked. And he's going to send the Marines. But we have to get word to *Citadel*. We have to send the teleporters."

Altin's first thought was to teleport the two of them straight to the space fortress, but he knew immediately that could be the death of them. He was too weak. He glanced sideways at Pernie. For the barest flicker of time, he considered letting her try to heal him a little more, but he put that idea away even faster than he had set aside the inclination to teleport to *Citadel*.

"How long before they are ready to go?" he asked, buying himself time to think. "Aren't most of them deployed around Earth?"

"Yes, but they're gathering in localized areas now. Ten minutes tops and there will be plenty of them ready to go, but we have to send the mages, so they can figure out where they need to be. Which means we need to go now."

"Go where?" asked Pernie.

"Hush, child," snapped Kettle, her eyes wide and frightened.

"I can't do it," Altin said. "Not yet." He looked again to Pernie. His heart pounding loudly in his chest and in his ears. It was so risky. She would have no idea what she was doing. Fear and love had guided her before, instinct, animal power. But she'd be thinking now. That would be ruin. Wouldn't it? He didn't know much about healing magic, though he imagined it worked like all the rest.

"How much power do you need to talk to Peppercorn?" Orli asked.

Peppercorn, of course! He had enough strength for that. He knew as she said it that he must be more compromised than he'd thought. Even the obvious eluded him.

A moment later, Peppercorn confirmed that she and the *Citadel* mages were already on their way to Earth. A wizard on the wall had just contacted them and told them the news, and the spell had already commenced down in the concert hall.

"So now we wait," Orli said, once Altin announced that *Citadel* was underway. "I can keep us up to date through this." She lifted the helmet's earpiece and showed it to him in the palm of her hand. "It's not as convenient as my tablet, but it will do until you get your strength back."

Altin couldn't bear the thought of waiting the rest of this fight out. He turned to face Pernie squarely. She saw it and knew what that look meant.

"Altin, no," Kettle gasped.

"She'll be fine," he told her. To the child, "Only just a bit. No more than unwilting a daffodil. Do you hear?" He'd read the spell she'd used. He'd tried to cast it long ago when the guilds were first testing him.

"Master Altin," insisted Kettle, stepping forward and catching Pernie from behind, gripping her by the shoulders again and hauling her to a stop. "I won't let her do it. She's my ward, an' I say she won't. Kill yerself if'n ya must, but this child won't be doin' it fer ya, an' carryin' the guilt fer it all her life. No sir, not while I'm standin' here ta stop it."

"It's my castle," he said, straightening and staring the older woman down. "So she's my ward too. And I think there are few people in this world who are less inclined to guilt over something like that than Pernie is. Isn't that right?" He looked to Pernie for a reply, but most of that had gone over her head, and what hadn't had already dissolved in eagerness, anything like caution lost in the giddy joy that possessed her when she discovered she had a real chance of being useful to him.

"Altin, I forbid it." Kettle pulled Pernie in close to her body, right up against the bloody apron, and crossed her strong hands over the child's chest protectively. "I said no."

"Stand aside, Kettle. It must be done. Lives are at stake." He stepped forward and knelt down before Pernie, looked her straight in the eye. "No more than the flower, all right? Don't try to make it bigger just because it's me. You must have discipline."

"I won't," she said. A sculptor shaping confidence could not have found a better model than Pernie was right then.

Kettle started to speak, "Altin, I—"

"Kettle!" he roared. "There are things at stake larger than the guilt of a girl. Be silent!" The volume and severity of it startled her, and her eyes went wide. She'd never imagined such a thing from him before. But she was silenced by it.

Altin looked back to Pernie, his expression soft and gentle again. He shut his eyes. "Go on, then," he instructed her. "Just a little bit."

Pernie glanced over her shoulder and shot Kettle a little smirk of victory, even stepping out of her protective grasp. She put her tiny hands on Altin's blood-smeared face again and closed her eyes too. With remarkable discipline, she reached into the vast and churning whorl of mana, and as deftly as she might have snipped off a raven's wing or a frog's leg with her little knife, she plucked out a slender strand of mana and poked it into Altin as tenderly as if she were threading a needle. She then began pushing growthful thoughts into him as she chanted the words of the spell. There was no reason why it had to be a flower, she knew, for there was nothing in the words that seemed to be about flowers at all. In fact, she thought most of the strange words taught by Master Grimswoller and the other teachers at school were silly anyway. She simply knew that flowers grew. That they knew health from lethargy. Vigor from decay. So she filled him with it. Just that tiny bit. Just as he'd asked. Just the small thread she'd gathered and fed into him so carefully, pushing it in and feeding it as gently as if she were blowing across a hot spoonful of stew. And, after a time, she knew not how long, it was done. Enough to heal a flower, just as she had promised. She released the spell.

When she was finished, she opened her eyes, wondering if it had worked. It seemed like it had. And he was smiling back at her.

"You're a genius," he said to her, his green eyes wide, the whites white now and nearly aglow. He hugged her, a long, strong hug that mashed the sharp corners of the spacesuit against her ribs, pushed into her skin painfully. But she didn't care. Then he did something he'd never done before. He kissed her. One warm kiss upon her little cheek.

Then he stood and spun round, facing Orli. "She's done it!" he proclaimed. "It's enough to get us there. Let's go fetch Taot. We have to help them hold out until they come."

"Help who?" Pernie asked eagerly. "And who is coming?" But they were already gone, Altin and Orli vanished with a single rush of air, leaving her behind, again. Which really didn't seem fair. Not now. Not after she'd proven herself to him. She had magic. She should be with him in case he needed her. And yet here she was, alone with Kettle, like always. It definitely wasn't fair.

And Pernie knew exactly whose fault it was.

Chapter 49

Taot spun and rolled and blasted fire to melt away the ice lances being flung up at him, his attention fully on keeping himself and his two riders alive. His first instinct, wanting to swoop down and lend his fiery breath to the defense of the gates, proved too dangerous right away. The battle at the gate was pinched down to the area just outside the palace walls, a tiny knot of Prosperions stuck in the role of cork, whose demise seemed to be inevitable at this point, as a pair of demons had got in behind them and impeded their final retreat. Altin didn't want to think who it was that might be down there fighting in the gate, so close and yet trapped outside, although he feared he already knew.

Whoever they were, the handful of human combatants were embattled on all sides by the piercing thrust of pointed demon limbs, the snapping grab of pincers and mandibles, and the mashing, bashing blows of so many oddly concocted variants of blunt weaponry, perverse designs that only deranged gods could have seen fit to arm any creature with. And then there were the orcs in all their numbers and with all their assorted weaponry as well and, of course, their spells.

The walls around the palace were swamped with gnashing tides of enemies whose great numbers pressed upon one another in such a way that they often turned against each other for want of an enemy to fight. And even with that self-consumption, the numbers of the enemy grew. More and more demons continued to flow into the city, causing the horde around the Palace to spread like a black stain expanding in a ruined cloth. For those amongst the ranks of the deadly host that were not bent on destroying their fellows, most were happy for the chance to take shots at anything flying by. And a low-flying dragon with two human riders was a particularly savory target for the orcs. And so it was that Taot and his human friends discovered upon arrival that they had more than enough to do in simply keeping themselves alive, much less swooping down and coming to the aid of the Queen. They were, in a way, the target of every enemy that was not directly engaged with the monarch and her valiant but very small band.

And if the projectiles being hurled up from the ground weren't trouble enough, the treacherous skies were made more so by the blinding-bright stripes of laser fire coming down from above. It descended from orbit at unpredictable angles, appearing suddenly like plummet-lines of burning death as the starships fired with brutal accuracy and cut hissing troughs through the seething demon sea, great canals carved into the enemy ranks with banks of rent bodies that writhed and hissed and squirted foul fluids into the air like fountains, spurts and spouts that splashed into the flow of gore oozing through the city in steaming streams and pooling into lakes of wretched hideousness. But even those seared swaths filled in with new enemies nearly as soon as the laser beams had passed, the press of the enemy, the supply of its assailants seemingly without end.

The laser fire was the most dangerous for the dragon near the Palace wall, so Altin guided him away, directing Taot to take them back toward the rear of the enemy mass, the place where the incoming mobs crashed against those who crowded one upon the next in hopes of something to kill, some trying so desperately, so eagerly, to find something to bite, stab or mangle that they would simply crawl up and over the rest of the lot and continue toward the Palace anyway.

For a moment, Altin considered getting to work with Orli and the dragon fighting along that line, even though doing so would represent but a drop in the ocean in terms of overall effectiveness, but after only a few moments flying over that colliding line at the rear of the enemy, he realized it was almost as dangerous to be flying back there as it was near the Palace walls. Not so much because of projectile danger from the orcs, for most of them were forward and trying to get through the gates, but instead because of the fleet aircraft flying all around.

Several dozen fighters flew back and forth across the ranks. They streaked by at incredible speeds and strafed the attackers with bullets, burned them with lasers and blasted into them brutally with missile fire.

At first they hadn't seen the fighters, for such was the nature of their speed. But as Taot was banking and prepared to dive in for the trio's first attack, one such fighter came shooting down from above. The heat of its passing nearly blistered their skin, and, making things worse, Taot got caught in its passing jet stream, which nearly twisted the poor dragon into a knot. Fortunately for his riders, he was adroit enough to spin with the whirling winds, escaping the air currents in a graceful pair of barrel rolls that just managed to keep Altin and Orli in their seats.

Barely had he righted himself, however, when the

fighter's missiles struck the ground below. The explosion was tremendous, and hot blasts of air churned upward at them, the heat brought upon a column of smoke and flame and a powerful concussive wind that buffeted the dragon yet again. It hit him so hard it drove him straight up, nearly twenty paces all at once, cramming his riders down upon his backbone as he rose with such violence that their bodies compacted, their spines compressing as they absorbed the force of the sudden rise. Taot managed to bank out of the worst of it, for the fighter's passing did mark a straight line, but even moving off that path, the air currents the fighter's pass set in motion, the chaotic random whirl, were too dangerous and impossible to navigate—not to mention what damage might come from inhaling the smoke of chemicals made on distant Earth.

And there was plenty of that. Huge clouds of smoke filled the air in greater and greater volume, choking and foul. Some of it smelled dark and woody, but some of it did not. What wasn't from burning timber and the possessions of dispossessed or dead citizens came from noxious things the dragon had never smelled before, acrid, artificial and alien. Taot did not need to know what it was he smelled to know it was not healthy for him to breathe. And the smoke that did not come from any of those other things was worse in its own way, for some of it was foul and yellow, odious plumes of dense, greasy smoke that curled all around them, reeking, oily, heavy with the nauseating stench of burning flesh and hair. That smoke was the most disturbing, if not for the dragon, certainly for the humans riding on his back.

In addition to the fighters attacking the rear of the crowding enemy, still other aircraft flew out over the plains. They flew sorties tracing the length of the demon line stretching into the city from beyond its broken walls, the steady stream of it constant as demons came from the blood-soaked fields like a flow of black lava, filling the smoking scar that marked where the main body of the host had trashed and ransacked their way toward the Palace gates. These bombers added their own criss-cross of laser fire, bullets and missiles to be dodged, and farther out, their bombs went off like kegs of captured thunder being opened beyond all those broken farms. Tons of them, tactical nukes going off in breathtaking eruptions that unfurled into the sky, great gray mushrooms of smoke, umbrellas of churning ash sliding up from the ground along neat narrow columns as if some angry god, an artist god, was sculpting cumulous clouds in the very likeness of his wrath. All about them the ground shook and concentric rings of rushing air smashed bodies and dismembered demons totally. At the edges of the blast waves, remnant limbs and hollowed-out carapaces blew like tumbleweeds across the field. It might have been a vision from the lowest depths of hell, though it served the cause of good.

All of this went on in the skies above and around Crown City, and though Altin had little familiarity with the combat capabilities of planet Earth, he knew within moments after having teleported the three of them into the sky above Prosperion that continued flight in the battle zone would be deadly for them all. The aircraft shot and bombed endlessly, pruning and carving away at the enemy, streaking in and out so fast that Altin could not keep track of them. Even Taot, veteran of the skies that he was, could not keep track. By the time even that great hunter heard them coming, they were already long gone. There would be no way to dodge them if they stayed. The lasers, though visible, moved far too fast, and the spitfire bullets could not be seen at all. Only the hiss of bullets cutting through the air announcing those projectiles had passed, and it was only luck that preserved them when the third fighter in less than a minute came whipping by. It didn't take human or dragon very long to realize that they needed someplace safe to land.

Unfortunately, in an ironic sort of way, the Palace walls were fully defended, jammed tight with men and women who stood shoulder-to-shoulder hurling spells and projectiles all around, flinging them down with fury upon the constant wash of the ravenous enemy, the shouts and epithets of their last hopes following each new weapon, each new spell they threw, a chorus of desperation rising into the air to mingle with all that smoke.

The long, banking turn that took them out of the path of the latest fighter brought them soaring toward a part of the city where the fighting had already passed by, enabling them to drop low enough to avoid collisions and crossfire, and yet not requiring that they fly above the thickest mobs of the enemy. They flew in toward where the temples were. As they approached, they could see why everyone was at the Palace now: the temples were, all but one, completely destroyed. Bashed in as if a temple-hating giant had come along and kicked in all the pumpkins in a patch. Most were entirely unrecognizable, reduced to rubble, and even the Temple of Anvilwrath was little more than a heap of ruined stone. The ten square city blocks upon which it sat, rising once in tiered majesty, were now transformed to a ruined, marginally geometric mound of broken stairs that led up to a jumble of felled marble stumps. And stumps were all that remained of the mighty columns that Altin had once thought an impregnable barrier. The priests might as well have relied on a few stalks of wheat to keep them safe. The temple wasn't even contested anymore, the bastion of its divine strength no more, no longer defended, no longer even sought after as the demons had all moved on to the Palace and the final victory. The orcs hadn't even bothered looting it.

Only the Temple of Mercy remained standing, somehow preserved in its place across the great temple square, occupying its own modest rise, gleaming white still, staring out at the ruin of Anvilwrath, and the city, alone now and seeming somehow sadly justified.

"What do we do?" Orli asked, leaning forward to speak in Altin's ear, her voice high over the wind and her arms wrapped tightly around his waist, if awkwardly due to the bulky spacesuits that they wore. "We can't stay up here."

Altin meant to land near the Temple of Mercy, but as they approached, they saw that two smaller demons were eating bodies in the streets nearby. He pointed. "We can't land there."

She shook her head when she saw them. "Not yet, but maybe we can take them out."

It was his turn to shake his head. "There's no point. Nowhere is going to be safe. Not without your people coming down in those battle suits to clear the streets, one by one. What's taking them so long, anyway? Are they here? Surely it's been enough time. We can land near them if we can find the staging area."

"I can't ask them again," Orli said, even as her hand reflexively reached for the com controls on her spacesuit's sleeve. Her hand looked small as it hovered over the control panel, her delicate fingers seeming too fine for buttons designed for gloved fingers three times as thick. "They are too busy to keep checking in every three minutes."

"Well, how long has it been since Peppercorn went back to Earth with *Citadel*?"

"It's been twelve minutes since I asked," she said. "Ensign Nguyen said they should be coming right away. Fly over that way, toward the river and we can see."

Another fighter shot by, not unlike the one Altin had teleported deep below Fort Minot. He wondered if perhaps the pilot might be the same man, though he knew it couldn't be. He hoped that man was still alive. He hoped everyone would still be alive. At least, everyone that was left.

Taot carried them out over the city's northern wall as directed by the magician's thoughts, soaring low enough to be out of the direct flight path of most of the fleet fighters—at least they hoped—but high enough to be out of reach of leaping demons, for there were still a few in the bloodstained fields, devouring what remained of the dead and eating the choice morsels of wandering livestock. There wouldn't be much cleanup for the victors, whichever side that was. Not much to bury, if the winning side saw value in such things.

They flew along the south bank of the Sansun River, looking for signs of the incoming Marines, projecting with their imaginations what they hoped to see, though neither knew how the men would arrive. Or where. They swept upstream for two full measures, but nothing, no sign of fleet landing craft. No gleaming march of incoming Marines. They swung back again. Where could they possibly be?

They flew out over the ruins of Little Earth, but there were no fleet ships there. Orli cursed, and Altin sighed, and they flew back toward the river again. That's when Orli shouted, pointing and leaning out over Taot's wing.

"There," she cried, her outstretched arm directing Altin's eye to a place about a measure and a half back toward Crown, a place where a fleet transport ship had just landed in a fallow field. Except it hadn't landed there, at least not precisely. It had simply appeared. "They're here! They're finally here!"

They flew toward it, and as they did two more transports arrived, lined up neatly next to the first. By the time the dragon was flying directly over them, there were four more.

Taot swung back around, and they watched, soaring in a circle above the field, as the line of transports grew longer, left and right, and the cargo doors were flung open from each in turn. Out poured the gleaming battle machines of mechanized Marines, fifty to a ship, pouring out like mercury, shimmering even beneath the clouded sky.

"Thank the gods," Altin gasped as he watched the Marines running out and forming up into fire teams and then into platoons. A second row of fleet ships started forming behind the first, another twenty of them side by side. More came. They appeared in different places across the plain. Some in fields, some on the great avenue that led into the city gates.

They came and came and came, and for a time Altin could not believe so many warriors existed on Earth. But still they came, and continued to come, even when the first wave of them moved off, running together in a shining wave of pounding metal feet. They ran in perfect formation and came quickly to a wide place where demons had broken through the northern wall. The demons devouring the dead near the break turned at the sound of the Earth people's approach, saw them coming and howled with delight. Something new to kill, new humans in metal shells to crack open and eat like mussels and clams. They leapt up from their grisly meals and ran at the newcomers, roaring with deadly glee.

Not one demon got close. The combined spray of that many bullets ripped them to shreds so quickly that all Altin could see from his place upon his dragon was a black dust around the demons for a moment and then the lot of them burst into flames, their bodies blasted into goopy shapeless heaps and the dark armor, broken like so many dropped ceramic tiles, burning with low flames that were blue around the edges and yellow where they danced like tongues probing for the sky.

The Marines pounded into the city without even stopping, charging through the carnage they'd just made, splitting up by platoons, by fire teams, working in formations, all the while missiles firing, spraying demon guts everywhere. The sound of the collected Gatling guns seemed to rattle off the very clouds, and soon the black scar that a solid third of Crown City had become filled with the quicksilver flood of all those battle-suited warriors from Earth, the movement of the incoming like an injection of liquid silver flowing toward the city's disease-ridden heart.

Another wave of Marines came in from the south end of the city, and the blasts of their missile fire and the horizontal lines of their lasers filled the scene with distant light. Altin and Orli could not help but fly toward the line of the encounter like insects to a new flame. They soared above and watched as the wave of technological brutality crashed upon the back of the demonic horde in an armored tidal wave.

The demons at the rear of the invading host, those most recently through the gate who had rushed in only to discover they had to fight their way in just to get to fight, stopped when they heard the Marines at their backs. They stopped climbing up the backs of their fellows, stopped killing their companions and eating them out of frustrated rage, and turned and roared their jubilant war noise. Now they had an enemy to kill and rend, just as their comrades thought they'd had at the north wall. And so their teeth were blasted in. Their mandibles blown off. Their horns and antlers and assorted spines, all brutalized. Bullets by the thousands pounded into eye sockets and down throats. Jointed limbs were burst apart like old trees in the wind of Earth's ferocity. The demons staggered and stumbled, tilted and toppled, tangled amongst themselves, bounced off and gored one another. They floundered and foundered, and great collisions of stilted monstrosities were viciously carved apart. They fell together like so many toothpick piers and pillars made of rotten hay, tinder-tender things blown away by the veritable monsoon of bullets and ballistic missile blasts.

The dying creatures blew strands of their yellow pus blood into the air, sometimes so high Taot had to tilt and bank to avoid being splashed with that fetid spray. It flew up at them everywhere, great fountains of it as if from a field of geysers shooting ochre gore. Both Altin and Orli shouted with what felt like righteous ecstasy. The carnage was sublime.

And still more and more Marines poured into the city, and by the thousands they blasted their way into the blackness, the phalanxes of their unity cutting through the demonic mass like a great plasma torch of war. They cut and cut, spreading the wedge of their brutality like wildfire, steadily pushing and driving toward the Palace gates, filling the streets with rivers of flowing demon ichor.

The starships above continued to strafe the Palace walls. The air was heavy with the humidity of all the burning flesh, the acridity of molten demon armor and thousands upon thousands of burning orcs. The bombers and fighters continued to mow down the new demons as they came through the gate that was somewhere out in the prairie, keeping them pruned back.

The shouts of the Prosperions rose higher and higher as the onslaught of the Marines became apparent to them. They saw the orc shamans turning and trying to fight, but they had no time to summon even a small bit of magic then. Such was the number and the ferocity of the suited Marines that most of the enraged orcish magicians had barely uttered a sound before bits of flying lead broke through their faces and pushed bits of brain out through the backs of their heads. A few set ice walls in place, hoping to hold the Earth people at bay, but the lasers from the starships melted most of them instantly away. What clumps of ice remained were turned to vapor by those upon the ground, by the lasers lancing from mech chests and by the fireballs the Queen's mages cast from their places on the battlements.

And so it went. The influx of the Earthmen had finally come. An enemy without magic set upon the magic-resistant demons and the magic-wielding army of the orcs like the very soul of irony. While the formation and initial push of the Earth forces seemed to take forever to get set and under control, the purging of the city went fairly fast once it was underway. In less than an hour after the last ship was teleported from Earth to Prosperion, the demons were nearly all gone, down to the last few thousand and all but a handful of orcs, a last stand of them formed up near the gate where the Queen had gone down, the last little patch of pitched battle for the Prosperions, in a place too narrow, too delicate to attack with brute force and bombing runs. But even there in that place beneath the gates, it was obvious how it had to end.

Chapter 50

God roared his outrage as the red lights began streaking down from the sky again. He raised his great long arm up in a gesture of fury, and his curses for the new god filled the air with such violence lightning crackled from the clouds and it began to rain for a while. The rain fell into the holes that the new god's red lights burned and made them hiss and steam even louder than before. But eventually God's curses gave way and the sound no longer shook the rain from the heavens.

But still Gromf wondered at what he had seen. He'd thought God had vanquished the new god, but now the new god's children were once more sending their red lights, their spears of straight lightning, of fire made from blood and cast from somewhere far away.

This made Gromf uneasy, and it took his concentration away from the fight. He only lost his thoughts for a second, barely a blink, but when God stopped roaring, when the rain ceased, he glanced back to see what had happened to make it so.

That is when the elf stepped into him from nowhere, appeared in the absence of Gromf's defensive fire, showed itself in the timing of its own device. It slipped the long tooth of its dagger between Gromf's ribs. He felt it like heat sliding into his lung. He turned from looking upon God to look into the elf's eyes, green like pine needles and just as emotionless. The elf was a war creature, like Warlord. It was a thing of death. There was no shame in dying on its blade, though there was remorse, regret for the things that Gromf would not see.

Gromf looked away from the elf then, content to die if it was God's will that it be so. He had fought with the creature for a long time, enough to let Warlord strike down the golden queen. He'd seen her fall. She could not survive such a wound, not in this place where her cowardly healers had run off, not in the middle of this glorious war. She would bleed out and die right there at the gate of her great fortress, slain by the greatest of the orcs. He'd seen that much. He could be content, even if God saw fit to let him die now too. His blood would mix with the golden queen's and feed the weeds that would one day grow in this place, sown at the moment of humanity's downfall.

He just wished God hadn't made the clouds cry. Even as the elf withdrew his long knife and let Gromf fall to the ground, Gromf watched the towering figure of God, his great and glorious reach pressed heavenward, and Gromf felt some bit of fear. He supposed it would not matter now that he was dead; his fear was for the greatness of God and Warlord.

God roared and mashed into the skies even as Gromf's vision began to dim. He heard sounds like running thunder and saw strange shapes shooting by in the air above, black shadows like birds flying, but far too fast, their passage marked belatedly by the thunder that they made. They spat the red fire at God as they came on. They sprayed him with the fire spray that punched holes in steel. They flew by and went away and came back and spit their foul weapons at God again and again.

God swatted at them but could not hit them all, and then a streak of smoke drew a line in the air from one of the passing dark things, these birds with impossible speed, and some long, slender object struck him, some arrow-like thing of the new god with a little fire burning behind it as it flew in. The smoke line crossed the space, fire erupted and then God's reach was lost, falling out of the clouds like a broken spear, falling down to crash in a long line across the orcish host.

It fell so close to Gromf that the impact rolled him away from the dancing feet of the elf, away from the sounds of the orcs the elf was killing so expertly.

Gromf rolled over on the wave of the impact and lay staring skyward again. The dark birds of the new god still streaked across the sky. Another of them painted a band of smoke against the clouds, and the gleaming tip of its fire-feathered arrow flew into God's roaring mouth. God's head exploded and rained down in a hail of gravel. Some of it fell upon Gromf where he lay. Feebly he tried to reach out and take a piece, to touch it, to see what God was made of. But he could not touch such a thing, so he pulled back his hand. His last act would not be sacrilege.

He fought to stay awake. He fought for consciousness. He wanted to see God regrow his head, perhaps two this time. He waited for God to send forth another arm, to grow it like a root, an upthrust root sprouting instantly into the sky, even longer and more twisted than the first. He waited for God to drag the new god down from the sky and strangle him.

But God stood motionless instead. He stood on his many-joined legs and teetered there. He teetered and teetered and absorbed blast after blast from the weapons of the new god's children as they flew by. He teetered and spewed out the gravel rain. He could not even roar his outrage now that his head was gone. He swayed for what seemed all of time, leaning to and fro in glorious defiance, until finally, bested it seemed, he fell like any mortal might have. At first he staggered, stumbled, crushing orcs beneath his feet, but then he pitched forward into the Palace wall, crashing into it like a falling tree. He had not even the last gasp of greatness in breaking it with his fall. The wall held strong, and instead, God slid down it ingloriously, crumpling against it and coming to rest a ruin of himself, his great body bent backwards and twisted oddly against the Palace gates. Gromf could not keep watching, and so he looked away.

He saw a dragon flying by. A bad sign. An omen.

He recognized the frightful cry of Warlord then, wondered if Warlord had seen the dragon too. He wondered if Warlord believed in such a thing. He wondered that he did. He wished he had Kazuk-Hal-Mandik here to ask.

He lay there listening. Unable to move. His breath came in wet rasps. He fought to stay awake. He wanted to die hearing the sound of Warlord crying victory. At least that to send him on his way. He kept forgetting to listen. He forgot to see sometimes. But always he came back with a start, fought to hear.

The battle went on. Warlord pushing to get in. The skies filled with smoke. The ground thundered physically beneath Gromf's back, tremors that began to grow. Gromf thought the vibrations must be Warlord filling with the spirit of God, God who gave himself, his strength, to Warlord who now shook all of Kurr with his might.

But then the children of the new god came. All of them.

He rolled his head to the side and saw them coming in a great metal wave. Their heavy arms of steel raised together, pointing accusingly, spitting their short fire and punching holes in everything. The demons roared and fell all around him. Orcs howled and fell all around him too.

They fell for a long time.

Gromf listened for the sound of Warlord calling victory anyway. He clung to consciousness, waiting and hoping.

For a time, Warlord's fury did grow. Gromf heard it dimly, increasingly muffled as the bodies of demons piled up. Blood began to pool around him, rising high enough to fill his ears. He fought for the strength to raise his head. Managed it even. Only to hear Warlord's voice break, his strength crack as if with some horrible blow. Warlord let go a long raspy shout, indignity and outrage. The sound came in staccato thumps, the notes pulsing with the rhythm of one of those human weapons ringing its metal ring, its unseen projectiles slamming into Warlord's lungs, piercing his flesh and rending his triumph to nothingness. Warlord cried out once for God. At God. And then he fell silent. Other orcs cried out his name. "*Warlord!*" they shouted in unison, sounding like younglings in Gromf's sodden ears. "*Warlord, no!*" they cried. He heard the courage leave them just as he felt it leave himself.

His head fell back into the rising ooze. He thought dimly of the human who had drowned in the water of the artificial pond, could see the human's face and hands pressed against the transparent cover of his strange armor, his mouth carping for air before he died. Then Gromf carped for air too. He carped and gasped, tried to raise his head again as his mouth filled with gore. He tried, but he could not. And then, at last, the light left his eyes. He fell back and worried no more. Discipline had abandoned him, left him with worthless God Stones, drowning in the mire.

Chapter 51

After the initial joy of victory, the time of sorrow was long. The cleanup process after such barbarism and brutality was exhausting and heartbreaking both. Two worlds laboring to remove the carnage, two worlds mourning for what was, between them, well over a million deaths. The losses were staggering and seas could have been filled with the tears that flowed from the bereaved like blood from inconsolable wounds.

The names of all who had been lost were written upon monuments on both planets, every single name, every single man, woman and child, all the Joneses, Moraleses and Xiongs of Earth mingling with the Sawblats, Hotsands and Steepleworths from Prosperion, two monuments precisely the same, sprawling across capitals in recognition and declaration of mutual apology. The cost of learning trust had been grotesque. Unspeakable. Beyond recovery for millions more. Mothers so broken there was no hope for them even in newfound interplanetary peace. The cost was simply too high for rejoicing, even for relief. Suicide alone added over ten thousand names.

But in time, four months perhaps, something that started to look like normalcy began to show itself again.

In places, anyway. Not much, not in large ways, but sometimes, in glimmers. In laughter rising on a breeze here and there, like new shoots in springtime, as if human spirits began once more to grow, to hope, to give signs that life, as always, goes on. The scars would remain forever on the trunks of those trees, but the forest would rise around the remains and, someday, would be whole again. Someday.

One of the first official recognitions of this on Prosperion was the dedication of the Fire Fountain on the plains beyond Crown City, the first ceremony since the defeat of the orcs and demons, and one that marked the full recovery of Her Majesty, who, like so many others, had spent long weeks in the care of healers.

She limped out to the front of the stage, a wide platform ten spans in the air, upon a scaffold covered with the crimson banners of the kingdom. With the Fire Fountain's concrete walls at her back, a great gray block nearly four hundred paces on a side, she looked out over the crowd and smiled. She raised a hand and waved to them, the bright morning light gleaming spectacularly from her golden armor, giving her the aspect of a risen sun.

"People of Kurr," she said, her voice enhanced by the illusionist sitting at the far end of the high stage, chanting quietly. "And people of planet Earth. I stand before you in great awe, humbled by the scale of your courage and the scope of your strength. In all the times of strife and war that this world has known, none have seen the magnitude of the conflict you have just come through. No time in history has known such calamitous barbarity, such unchecked and ravenous evil, evil that spanned worlds. Evil that spanned a galaxy. And yet you, all of you, from Earth and Prosperion alike, stood before that great evil and did not flinch or falter. You stared straight into its eyes. You leaned into it, your hearts as your weapons, your will sharper even than your blades, and you defied it. You defied it and you knew victory.

"You knew that victory at great cost. You lost friends and family. You lost ships and homes. But you did not lose yourself. That held through it all as you held to right and truth and dignity. And, in doing so, in holding to faith in yourselves and your fellow humanity, to all of our humanity, you triumphed. We triumphed. And so here we stand today, united, united as humans in a vast galaxy filled with hope and menace, with opportunity and danger, a great vast future for us to challenge and explore. We stand united by common cause and mutual need. By respect. By humility. By love. And by the mutual debt of blood."

She turned then and looked behind her at the people seated along the back of the stage, and inclined her head to the dignitaries assembled there. "We are all so bound," she said. She had a smile for the new leader of the Northern Trade Alliance, Director Bahri, a wizened older man whose dark, sad eyes still reflected the apologies and shame he carried on behalf of his predecessor and perhaps his entire world. He'd spent a long time in private council with the Queen. She was sure he'd do his best to make amends, despite his refusal to hand over the deposed Director Nakamura that he might meet his fate at the edge of her headsman's axe. Still, she could smile at him as he sat amongst the many world leaders from Earth and numerous officers of the fleet, the lot of them mixed among the notables from Prosperion, the dukes and duchesses of Kurr, the marquis and marchionesses, earls, barons and a few minor lords. The assemblage represented a collection of power upon two planets the likes of which had never been gathered before. A first in the known universe for either world. Most of the gathering smiled back at her, warmed by and welcoming her words.

JOHN DAULTON

She turned once more to face the crowd. "I stand before you now to acknowledge that friendship formally. To declare the unwavering promise of this kingdom to fight alongside planet Earth whenever she may call, to aid her with my own steel if I must, my own magic and my own blood if needs be. That is what friends do. We must all pledge it. Promise to aid and protect. We must promise to work together through all things. Including working through ourselves and our human failings. We must never again let grievances escalate to war. The cost is too great, the opportunity to eradicate our species too high. And so we must protect one another, with arms and with diplomacy. We will repel all enemies together in war, but we will resolve all differences in words and in peace. This is my promise. This is the promise we must all speak, for it is the only way.

"And as I look out over this place, this battlefield where so many of us have known misery and loss, I see the faces of my people shining up at me. And I ask them, I ask you all, who here will swear upon their lives the promise of friendship that spans the stars? Who will stand for honor and peace in this great and vast universe with me? Will you join me? Say it now with your words and forever after with your deeds. Long live the alliance of—and more importantly, the friendship between—Earth and Prosperion!" She drew the broadsword from her back and thrust it skyward at the bright sun, where the light struck it and flared like a great spark sent by Mercy herself to relight the flame of hope. "Long live the alliance! Long live friendship!"

The sound of well over a hundred thousand voices rose as one, all in echo of the Queen. *Long live the alliance! Long live friendship!* Swords and spears and even small children were hoisted on high, the chants of the people raucous and wild. The War Queen saw blasters raised up as well, Earth weapons pressed into the air as fleet people joined in. "Long live the alliance," they cried. "Long live friendship."

The Queen turned back and saw that the Earth folks behind her had risen as well, and they came forward to stand beside her, her own nobles following their lead, all but the Marchioness of South Mark, who sat glaring at the Earl of Vorvington who had joined them as well, and, in that way, she glared at them all. For a full five minutes the crowd chanted and cheered, and the words became the general cry of glory and the release of pent-up anxiety. Soon hats were flying and hugs abounded. Strangers shook hands with aliens who were now friends. The Queen could hardly stop the tears that burned in her eyes.

She turned to the director during the storm of sound and leaned near his ear. "My people will never deceive you, Director. I will never deceive you, just as we never have." He smiled, and once again she could see the fleeting shame in his eyes. She touched his arm. "He did what he thought he had to do, as did Captain Asad and the rest. Egregious errors on their parts, but that is the past and cannot be undone. Punishments have been handed out where crimes were committed, and there is little more to be done. Such is the unsatisfying flavor of justice sometimes. You and I are friends. We move forward from today."

He nodded. "Yes, all is past. You are a rare woman to allow it. But yes, we are forever friends."

"Good. Then as my first official act of friendship, let us get this Fire Fountain dedicated and get to the food. I haven't had a good meal since they put my leg back on. I'm sure I need the sustenance or I'll be forever with this limp."

He smiled. "Yes, and I could use something to divert me from guilty thoughts. Being out here ... seeing what I saw when I first arrived. This is such a dearly won place."

She patted him on the arm. "You must not dwell on it today. At least today."

"I will do my best, Your Majesty."

Eventually the crowd simmered down, and the Queen could get on with the dedication ceremony.

"As you all know, inside this vast concrete box that our Earth friends have built for us, lays an open demon gate. To date, we have no known means of closing such a thing, though our diviners are working on it night and day, and of course, so is our heroic Galactic Mage." The crowd began cheering and shouting Altin's name, a great chorus of *Sir Altin, Sir Altin, huzzah!* Over and over they chanted it, and Her Majesty let it go for quite some time, sparing a glance over her shoulder at him as he sat blushing amongst the other notables. She winked and beamed proudly at him, then turned back and raised her hand, bringing them to mostly quiet again. "Together they will seek a way to close that foul portal forever. However, until such time as that means is found, and as a way of symbolizing our trust and our mutual dependence upon our sister world, planet Earth, the fleet has agreed to install and forever operate this Fire Fountain with us." She turned to another illusionist sitting beside the one amplifying her words and nodded. "Behold," said the Queen, pointing into the sky. "This is what goes on inside this plain gray box."

In the air above the crowd appeared an enormous illusion, providing a view of the interior of the Fire Fountain. There were several piles of something dark and smoldering laying about on what was otherwise a plain concrete floor. The walls were plain as well, very tall, but unadorned for the most part, no attention to aesthetics wrought in. Only the long, narrow strips of clear glass that ran the length of each wall broke the monotony of those mighty walls, narrow strips, barely six Earth inches wide, though several Earth feet thick. Only those windows and, of course, the guns and cameras that hung about the ceiling high above.

The guns were monstrous, nine-foot-long Gatling canons with seven barrels each, all of which fired rounds nearly as thick as a man's wrist. There was a gun turret in each corner and one mounted at even intervals all around the high ceiling, placed with enough frequency to have one to cover every twenty-foot square below. While few of the Prosperions assembled knew precisely what they were, there was a deadly aspect to their alien construction that few failed to recognize. They might not know specifically what those things were, but most could fathom what would be the end result of standing in front of one. And the Earth people in the audience knew exactly what they were, and to the last of them they began to grin appreciatively. There was a lot of firepower in that massive concrete box.

Just as the crowd managed to take it all in and marvel at both its size and even at its conspicuously bare and bland design, which for some seemed something of an anticlimax, a huge black demon appeared. It simply popped into view standing on the ground, its seven long limbs already clawing for something to kill. The illusionist conveyed the sound inside as well as the view, and the moment it appeared, the air filled with its roars just as three of the guns went off. The flash of their barrels and the thunder of their fire carried over the crowd and out across the plains as a spray of supersonic bullets pulverized the beast below. The demon twisted and raged and lashed at nothing, gore oozing from holes that opened in its body faster than could be accounted for, until it finally broke into pieces, flames ignited in its joints and steam hissing from the cracks in what remained of its hard armor shell.

Then new fire came. The whole of the scene consumed

by it. The Prosperions knew what this new inferno was. It was the activation of some powerful enchantment Her Majesty had arranged. And for a long time there was nothing to see in the illusion but a bright yellow box of flames hovering above them all, fire raging violently and looking as if it had been locked up in a cube of glass high above the crowd.

When the flames died away, there was once again nothing in the room but a smoldering pile of something black upon the floor.

The crowd cheered as one, and their noise filled the air again, just as another demon appeared in the box, followed immediately by two more. Their fates were the same as the one before.

The crowd cheered and shouted even louder, joining their noise with the raging ruckus of the demons as they died and the glorious roar of the Gatling guns. The demons writhed in agony and with every contortion the people purged themselves of more and more pent-up rage. It was an orgy of bloodlust and revenge. The people purged and purged as they watched ten more demons die.

Finally the Queen motioned that the illusionist should cut the image off. She raised her hands for quiet, but still had to wait some time for the crowd noise to subside.

"This," she said when at last she could be heard, "this is the place where we will always be reminded of our fragility. Our vulnerability. This is where we can come and see what is at stake for us all. This is why our worlds need one another. This is the memorial to our fallen, but also the monument to remind us that we live in a new universe. We can, in our sorrow-filled memories, come here and also recognize our strength.

"A page has turned upon us, and we find ourselves faced with a new reality. Our very achievements, all the things we have learned, discovered and revealed by our magic ...," she paused and turned, pointing to the director and his nearby officers, "all the things we have learned, discovered and revealed by our science ...," she faced back out into the crowd, "these things we have unlocked with our hard work over centuries and millennia, and these things now dictate our need for one another. And it is here, at Fire Fountain, where any who doubt can come and look and understand. Let none of us forget."

She called for a moment of silence then, a time of prayer and mindful thoughts for all those who were gone. She did not lead them in it, nor did she call for a priest. She simply asked that they do it, that they call up the faces of those who had sacrificed and could not be saved. And remember them.

When it was done, she raised her head and proclaimed that it was time for the feast. And there, revealed by the release of the hiding enchantments put upon it, was spread upon the field behind the crowd a feast so enormous no other in history was its match. There were tables and chairs for everyone, and more notable for the historians than the simple scale of the feast was the fact that there were no special places for the nobles or the dignitaries from Earth to sit. The Queen waited until the crowd had seen it too. She gauged it by the growing waves of whispers and muttered wondering. She smiled. "Today we feast as friends and equals," she declared. "Now let us eat!"

The crowd roared and many of them ran for the food as if they'd not eaten in all these long months since the war was won.

Her Majesty turned back to face those assembled on the stage. "My hope is that you will all mingle amongst the people and make acquaintances with them. There are none of us holding titles today that do not owe their privilege to those people down there. The blood of the farmer and the housewife paid for our privilege. Today we give that sacrifice its due."

"Your incompetence bought them their sacrifice," snapped the marchioness, her voice a raspy whisper. "Don't think to lecture us anymore this afternoon. We sit through this from you because it is what must be done, but you brought this upon them. You make me sick, standing there in your gleaming armor still today. Arrogant woman. You should be in that prison on Earth with that idiot director they deposed!"

Before the Queen could respond, the marchioness motioned for her teleporter to take her away, leaving the Earl of Vorvington staring wide-mouthed in the space where she'd so recently stood. He looked up at Her Majesty with his red jowls reddening all the more, as guilty in appearance as if he'd said it too.

"Let it go, Vorvington," said the Queen. "All will settle in time." She flashed a somewhat embarrassed look at the new director, which he acknowledged with a crooked left side of his mouth. He'd seen plenty of that same sort of thing himself back on Earth, and there would be arguments among his fleet officers, hard feelings and resentment for a long time to come. She shook it off, however, looking to Altin instead. "Sir Altin, if Miss Pewter can spare your attention long enough, would you be so kind as to take the rest of us to the feast?"

He glanced down at Orli, who smiled and giggled as she nodded that of course it would be okay.

"It would be my honor, Your Majesty." A few moments later the lot of them were engulfed in an adoring crowd.

Chapter 52

Several hours after the feast at the Fire Fountain began, Orli and Altin sat together, legs dangling over the ledge that marked the entrance to Taot's cave. The feast was still raging out on the prairie far away, measures and miles from them. The people were happy, allowed themselves joy and drunkenness, which most often turned to tears. But they were trying to move on. So were the two young lovers, which was why they were here.

They'd been out on that ledge for some time. The Queen had not only graciously allowed them to go, but when she'd heard where they were going, she insisted that Altin take Taot a full mammoth haunch right off the cook fire and give it to him with her full compliments and gratitude. The dragon hadn't been much for the gratitude, but he'd been delighted at getting an effortless meal of that size. In fact he'd been sleeping it off ever since. In the silence that had fallen after all the bones were crunched and the tissues chewed and chomped, the two of them had come out upon the ledge and sat together staring up into the stars. For a while they chatted about the banquet and the Queen's speech. They talked about plans, about Kettle, about lost Tytamon. But for a long time after, they sat in silence, each swept off in their own thoughts, their own memories, and the night was long upon them when Orli finally spoke again.

"The Queen said it's been a hard-won happy ending for everyone in that last toast she made." Her gaze fell from the sky as she said it, dropping in the turn of a breath to where it came to rest, staring down into the darkness below. The valley floor was barely visible even with Luria nearly three quarters full, a pale pink arc hanging low in the eastern sky, featureless as a forgotten memory. "Is it really happy, though? For everyone?"

Altin nodded, running his finger absently over the back of her hand, enjoying the cool satin of her skin. "I suppose it is. Or will be. Although I'm not sure when I will feel it all the way. The work on the battlefield in the days after your people came will haunt me forever. I'll never forget those faces, those bodies all gnawed upon." He shuddered and forgot for a time to stroke her hand. After a while he started up again, finally looking to her. "But yes, I suppose we will be happy again. If we don't allow it, then what were we fighting for?"

"It's not going to be happy for us all," she said. "Some of us will never be. One of us anyway." She pressed her lips inward, her sad eyes resigned.

This startled him, and he turned to her with fright dawning like frost commencing upon his heart. "What do you mean? What are you saying?"

She could see the rise of terror in his eyes, the frantic look beginning, the fear of losing her somehow. Again. She could read it as plainly in his moonlit face as if he'd worn a sign. She smiled and stroked his cheek with the curl of her fingers. "Not us," she said. "We'll be happy. I am happy now. But I'm sad for Blue Fire because she's out there all alone. Alone and violated. It's not fair."

"He never made it, though," Altin pointed out. "He

didn't get to her. He was still tunneling when he died."

"Does it matter?"

He looked away. "No. I don't suppose it does."

"I wish there was something we could do for her."

He nodded. He let go of her hand. Felt guilty for it. That he could be happy, that he got to have Orli in his life. It was true Blue Fire had nothing now. She was silent all the time. She had no joy in the victory. Nothing to celebrate. Only memories of fear added to that long-abiding loss she'd known for millenniums beyond count.

Altin scooted back far enough to lean against the rock face, only his calves and ankles dangling out into the open space above the valley far below. She reached out and absently ran her fingers through the soft hair on his shins, her gaze still directed down into the valley as his returned to the sky.

Luria hung in the darkness as a wide crescent smile, and he thought that at least she was happy all the way. Altin gazed upon her bright face for a long time, thought about how much had come to pass since that first time he'd gone there, his first time standing upon another celestial sphere, a world that was not his own. He remembered the first time he'd seen that red, rocky place, how alive he'd felt staring back at Prosperion.

And then there had been Red Fire. Another red place. This time angry and violent. Two ends of a long trail. He let go a long sigh as he thought through it all. All his new friends, all the ones he had lost.

Orli heard the breath leaving him and looked back at him. She smiled, her eyes sparkling as Luria's pink light caught them just right. She scooted back against the cliff face beside him, snuggling up close for warmth in the chill of the night. "I'm sorry," she said. "I didn't mean to spoil the mood."

"It's all right," he said, putting his arm around her and

drawing her tightly against him. She always smelled so wonderful. "It's going to be a while before we stop doing things like that."

"It is," she agreed. She looked out across the end of the valley, far to the west between the pair of mountain peaks where the sun had lost itself behind the mountain range several hours ago. A lone star hung there now, dangling between two spires like a brilliant jewel lying in the cleavage of the world. She watched it for a while, and then, suddenly, she started, nearly jumping to her feet as she turned to face Altin again. Breathless, she asked, "Is that Hope?"

Her urgency startled him, the energy that radiated suddenly in her words. He frowned and asked, "Is what hope?"

"That," she said pointing back toward the star. "That star. Is that the Hope star?"

He leaned forward, looking around her, then nodded. "Yes, that is Hope." The star of Hope, named for a mourning woman of Prosperion myth. The eternal lover waiting in the sky for a lost sailor only the gods knew was never going to return.

"It's a blue star," Orli said.

He nodded. "Yes. It is." He didn't know what else to say. She seemed all aflutter now, like a flock of birds had taken flight in her.

"Altin, it's a blue star. Like Yellow Fire was. Like the original Blue Fire. Blue Fire's lover."

"Okay," he said, smiling but still completely lost.

"Think about it. How did her husband die?"

Altin blinked a few times, trying to catch her intent, but could only answer the question without insight. "You said the sun blew up."

"No, not blew up, it flared. Solar cycles. It blasted the world he lived in."

Altin nodded. He'd understood it well enough when she explained it to him before.

"Don't you see it? We killed Red Fire in the heart chamber."

Altin continued to nod, but he still wasn't seeing what she saw.

"We blew up his heart. But not the life. Or at least, I don't think the life. It's all still there. In the living things."

"Yes, but, Orli, what are you on about?"

"Altin, it's the exact opposite from Blue Fire's mate." Altin's blank look forced her explanation on at increasing speed. "They need both to live. Don't you get it? To kill Blue Fire, we were going to destroy all the life on her world. She needs the living things, remember? That's why she was 'defending' Andalia. She thought the Andalians were killing the essential life. It was a prospective nest for her. The life came first. Life provides life; it's the life energy for them, for her species. Life is the spark ... or something like it, and the heart chamber is the soul. It must be. And if it is, that means we can bring him back!"

"Bring who back?"

"Blue Fire's husband. Yellow Fire."

He looked completely perplexed, his eyes narrowed, his head moving marginally side to side. "What are you talking about?"

"We can go get his heart."

Altin's eyes narrowed even more, but his mouth fell open, and by the look of him, she might as well have just told him the sky was made of foxtails and that Queen Karroll was an orc.

Her own expression shaped impatience and more than a little frustration too. She knew that she was talking too fast, that she was skipping parts that needed to be filled in, but in her urgency, her elation at this epiphany, she could hardly contain herself. She pulled in a long, slow breath to calm herself, and began again. "All right. Look, do you remember when we were in Blue Fire's great cavern getting the Liquefying Stones for the *Citadel* mages? Remember what you told me about the heart chamber? How she had that cluster of dark green stones in the middle of it? The core of the heart chamber, you said. She told you it was the father's gift. It was some kind of something special. Remember?"

He nodded. He remembered it quite clearly.

"Well, Red Fire had one too. It wasn't blue, it was orange, but otherwise it was just like you said it would be, a concentrated batch of different crystals, a patch that was clearly a different type of stone. The father's gift. Or maybe it was the mother's gift in this case. I don't know. But what if that part is still alive? What if it's dormant or something? Plants do it all the time, geophytes with storage organs like bulbs and tubers. The precedent is totally there."

He shook his head a little then. He didn't speak what he was thinking, but he thought it anyway. They weren't talking about a dormant plant. They weren't talking about plants at all. And more importantly, Yellow Fire had been dead for thousands and thousands of years. Maybe even millions. They didn't really know how long it had been, but however long, it was longer than any flower bulb was going to stay alive.

She could see what he was thinking simply by the way he moved his head, by the way he lowered his eyes briefly when she'd finished saying what she'd said. She saw and knew precisely what was going through his mind. "And don't think it's a matter of time either. These creatures are made of stone after all. They live for millions and millions of years. Far longer than any of the organisms on their surfaces do. Who knows how long a perennating organ for one of them might last? What if we could transplant that? What if we could go to his world and find that part, that piece of him? What if that *is* him? What if that's his mind and soul, and all the rest is ... like skin or some other body part?"

Altin watched the light of her enthusiasm grow. Her eyes were wide and glistening with it, her hands moving frantically as she spoke. He wanted to share in that enthusiasm, but it didn't really make enough sense for him to get caught up in her energy. "What if it's not?" he said. "What likelihood is there that it is? You're making wild assumptions here. What has ever happened to suggest that this is how they, how Hostiles, work?"

"It's not about likelihoods and suggestions, Altin. It's about hope. Don't you see? It's so obvious. Just ask her. Ask her if it's true."

Altin looked down at his thick silver ring and touched it, turning it on his finger slowly. The pulsing light from under it painted his finger green and part of his hand to match. "She doesn't like to talk to me anymore," he said. "I make her sad."

"Well she can deal with it for this. Just ask her. She's probably already heard us anyway, so go on and try."

"I don't know. I think you're shooting at pretty high-flying fowl with this."

"Just do it. Please. Don't make me beg."

"Fine." He drew in a long breath of the chill night air and sent the idea as best he could to Blue Fire. He asked the question through images, asked if she thought it might be true, if she thought perhaps there was a chance that the essence of her mate might still be there, waiting in silence like some lonely iris bulb, an ancient thing lying in a lifeless cave on a dead moon, orbiting a dead planet, orbiting a moody blue sun.

Unlike the Blue Fire he'd come to know before the war was won, the creature she'd become since did not send forth waves of anger or remorse. She didn't send forth much of anything. It was as if her strength had been taken away. Sharing thoughts with her was akin to watching a bird that's flown into a pane of glass and now lies on the ground, not quite lifeless, the forces that animate it still working, but the thing that it was, the vibrant thing, now somehow gone.

He tried to show her the image of a human heart, the essence of it beating in his chest. He did likewise with the mind, conjuring in his mind the images he'd seen on Doctor Singh's monitors, the drawings in Doctor Leopold's offices. He linked those ideas to what he understood of being. Of life in its essence. Of souls. He contrasted that with images of body, of arms and legs and toes. He connected that to things of the world, to trees and grass and creatures roaming there. Things of blood and tissue. Of hair and hooves and, well, and meat. One part was physicality, one part was essence, spirit. One was animating, the other animated. He tried to convey the essence of *me* and then *you* to her, all wrapped around those two ideas, the shape of what it was to be someone rather than something. He shaped it as best he could, reiterated it, made it feel the way a question feels, adding it to the idea of that lonely bulb, in turn attached to the image of the father's gift in her own heart chamber. He asked, and then he waited.

He waited for a long time, the silence in his mind as uncomfortable as had been the endless hum of her misery before Red Fire died. So it went for several minutes, him staring blankly out of his eyes, listening to his own thoughts for echoes of another's with tension in his body, expectant and on edge as if he expected twigs to snap somewhere in the dark woods of a nightmare. He'd just about given up when finally a thought came. It was as close to a *maybe* as she could communicate. She didn't know.

He sent the whole pack of images again, wanting to be sure she'd at least understood the question properly. Wanting to make sure that feeble response was what he thought it was, neither confirmation nor denial. She had. And it was.

"She doesn't know," he said at last. "I don't think they think about themselves in that way. Souls and selves are things for priests and philosophers, bulbs and bodies for botanists and people of biology, doctors and the like. None of that is really the kind of thing they have concepts for. At least that is the impression that I got."

"Ask her if she thinks it's possible."

"She already said she didn't know. She didn't say it wasn't true. She just didn't say it was."

"It is. I just know it is."

"But you don't. And we don't even know if life has anything to do with it. For that matter, we don't even know if there is anything alive up there anymore. It might all be dead by now, what little there was. The life that was there might have become bound to him somehow."

"Well, it would only take you two seconds to find out," she countered, her chest swelling defiantly. "You could look up there like you always do, with a seeing spell."

"But there wasn't anything alive when we were there. I didn't see a single thing."

"I did. You can go and see if the lichens are still there."

He didn't recall any lichen, but he wasn't going to argue the point. "Even if I saw them, how would I know they are alive? You're the botanist, not me."

"I will tell you. Just go look. Then come back and do that illusion like you did when you were showing the Queen the armies on the plains. The spell the *Citadel* mages do all the time in the concert hall."

"Well, I never saw them. So at least tell me where to

look." He was trying not to let exasperation become apparent in his voice. There was no point in this.

"We were in the big jumble of rocks, not all that far from the first pit we jumped in. If you can get me close to that, I'll show you where they were."

He could tell she wasn't going to relent, so it would be easier to oblige. Besides, he didn't want to say no to her anyway. Not today. Not on a night like this. "Fine," he said. "Let me go look."

He closed his eyes and pushed himself into the mana, shaped the taut line that ran across the vast distances between his world and that from which Red Fire had once made his angry presence known. He found the place where they'd first had to learn to fall together, Orli operating the Higgs prism and the jets for both of them. He opened that vision up in his mind, saw the place, a narrow, natural corridor of broken stone, dark but lit well enough by the diffuse red light of the planet's ever-present rusty atmosphere. He ran his vision up and down, looking for something that looked like the lichens he knew from Prosperion. There was a patch on one rock, a whitish flaky place, that might pass for that sort of thing.

He tethered the spell to that location, bound the view of it to a thread of mana and pulled back into his own mind again. He wound that thread around a globe of nothingness that he fashioned with a thought, like covering a ball with string. He wrapped it tightly around until it was a semi-solid thing. He opened it to the vision he had left upon the surface of dead Red Fire's world, and then spoke the last word of the spell.

When he opened his eyes, Orli's face was set aglow, her pale features washed in the red light of the illusion that hung above them and a single pace off the edge of the cliff. "Well, there it is," he said. "That's where we jumped. There's something on that rock on the right that might be your lichen, though it doesn't look like it's doing well."

She peered into the luminous sphere before her, leaning forward to study what was depicted in it. "Can you make it bigger?" she asked. "Like a close-up right on that?"

He resisted the urge to grumble. He reset the image again, much closer to the flaky patch on the rock, staring right down at it from what might be only a hand's width away.

She clapped her hands. "You see," she said. "It is still alive! I told you. Life didn't die with Red Fire. Which means there really is a chance Yellow Fire can be saved."

"I think that might be a very large leap from one to the other," he said. He wanted to hope with her, but he could not. It was too farfetched. His expression flattened as he shook his head. "While I would love to believe it possible, I still think that the odds are so small they're going to slip right through the net."

"So what? I mean, what would it cost us to find out? What would it cost us to try? We could go to the Fruitfall system, find his world, find his heart and then transplant it. It really could be just lying there waiting for us. For her. There's no risk. If I'm right, he might come back to her. How happy would she be if it were true? How happy could her ending be, like the rest of us, those of us who made it, get to have? And if I'm wrong, then nothing happens. Everything is the same. Blue Fire lives out her awful eternity all alone and miserable, for all of time, long after you and I live our happy lives and die. Just her alone. Forever in endless, nagging, horrible misery."

Altin's shoulders rose and fell with the currents of his exasperation. He didn't try to hide it this time. Orli really was laying it on thick.

"Don't sigh at me," she said. "You know it's true. Nothing changes if I'm wrong. But what if I'm right? Doesn't she deserve a chance at happiness, just like we get? Isn't it only fair to try? Isn't it only honorable after what she's done, and what she's sacrificed? Humans aren't the only race that matters, Altin. She fought with us. This is the right thing to do."

He couldn't help but nod at that. It wouldn't be difficult, he supposed. They'd have to find the planet of course, but they'd done that sort of thing before, and they did know where Fruitfall was. But from there, well, then they'd have to ... just do whatever they had to do. They'd have to figure it out. Make it up. Invent. It wasn't like he hadn't been doing that all his life. And Orli knew much more about this sort of thing than he did. Perhaps it was possible. Except there was one other thing. A huge problem. The thought struck him like a noxious odor that's just blown through an open window. It turned the corners of his mouth down, brought them back to reality from where they'd been slowly rising as he thought through the hopeful possibilities. "What if we do it," he said, "and it works, but it doesn't work the way we want it to?"

"In what way?"

"Well, suppose it does bring him back to life, but the *him* it brings back is Red Fire? What then? While I totally agree with you that Blue Fire deserves a chance to be happy, I think that what we don't know is dangerous. Suppose there is something in the arrangement of all those crystals in Red Fire's cavernous insides. Imagine some sort of mechanism in all of that. What if once you place Yellow Fire's father's gift in it—or any father's gift in it—it works exactly the way it was designed to work, the way it worked before? Think of a blacksmith's forge for example. It is of little consequence who pumps the bellows, but simply that someone does. As long as they are pumped, the coals will be hot. How do we know that is not how it is with Hostile worlds? We could simply be bringing Red

Fire back to life after so much effort was spent to get rid of him. And while I know that is less hopeful, I should think that it is at least as likely, if not more so, than hoping we can bring Blue Fire's long-lost husband so easily back to life."

Orli seemed to deflate at all of that, the sails of her enthusiasm drooping as Altin's logic blocked the wind. "Well, we could still try," she said, but there was not much heart in it. "We killed him once, you know." That was true, but she didn't seem to mean it, and he could tell he'd spoiled it for her. He saw it in her face and felt the fool. Why? Why had he taken it from her, snuffed the radiance of hope? What was wrong with him?

He stared off into the night for a time, confronted by the star of Hope and irritated with himself.

Eventually, his head began to move, the barest of motions, nodding as his thoughts settle themselves in place. "You're right," he said. "We could still try. And as you keep saying, there is hope, and perhaps more than a modest chance."

She looked up, studied him, searching his face to see if he really believed that in his mind, for it seemed to her as if he'd said it with his heart. She knew how he was. How he'd do anything for her. But he was right, and his points were painfully true. But she did want to hope, and she wanted to help poor Blue Fire more than anything. Her mouth twitched a little from side to side, then she queried him to see. "Do you really think so? Do you really suddenly think it's possible?"

There was something in the way she said it that gave him pause, and he saw the scrutinizing angles of her eyes. "Why shouldn't I?"

"Because I don't want to get her hopes up if you really do think it's dumb and dangerous."

"It's not dumb. But it is dangerous. And we'll have to

get permission from the leaders of both worlds before we do. We need to make sure we do it right."

"They'll never approve it," she said. "You know they won't. Which means we can't tell them. We can't even suggest it to them. If they think it's remotely possible, they'll do something horrible. I know they will."

He straightened and locked eyes with her. "Orli, I want to help. I will help. But we are not going to put both worlds at risk again for this without running it by the Queen and the fleet. Not without preparing them for what might happen if Red Fire does suddenly come back. Imagine all those orbs coming back to life with him, all those dead things drifting between the planets around your sun? They're not gone, you know, not the hundreds of thousands of little ones. Not all of them anyway. Roberto said the clean-up is going to take years. Which means until that is done, it is dangerous and requires that we tell the leaders of both our worlds. We must have them in agreement. And perhaps with their agreement, we can also secure their help. Anything less would be reckless. It's not ideal, but it's true."

"They'll never approve it. There's no way."

"I know." He looked down, unable to watch the futility, the open sorrow that came upon her perfect face.

She slumped back down against the cliff and stared vacantly at her knees. After a while of mulling over what had been said, she finally spoke again. "And it's not my world. Not anymore."

He hid the smile that came upon his face. She sounded petulant, which he knew would lead to her return to normalcy. "Of course not. That is the greatest joy of my life."

She crossed her arms and huffed, refusing to look at him, but he could see she was coming around just as he knew she would. They sat in silence once again, but after a time, her expression softened and she just looked sad. "I only wish she could be happy," she said after a time. "It's not fair."

He watched her, ached for her, ached for Blue Fire too. He knew Orli's heart was in the right place, that she cared and wanted to do the right thing. This was the part of her that had become the botanist, the part of her that had fought and survived a terrible disease, stayed strong to keep others alive no matter what. It was what made her so heroic in his eyes, even as she pouted against the cliff.

He watched her for a long time. He would watch her for eternity if he could.

"Orli," he said after perhaps an hour had passed. He climbed to his feet. "There's something I have to tell you." He reached down for her with both hands. She gazed up and took them, curiosity obvious in her expression as he pulled her up.

"What is it?"

"I spoke to your father," he began. "And he agrees with me."

"About what?"

"About how you are the most amazing woman I have ever known. About how kind and clever and passionate you are. About how there is nothing that could make me happier than to spend my life with you. He's given his permission," he said. He paused, then knelt down before her, one knee firmly in the dirt. He clung to her hands and stared up at her, his green eyes bright beneath the light of the smiling moon. "Orli, marry me. I want to spend my life with you. I know you are thinking of the happiness of others right now, of Blue Fire's, but I'm not. Not now. Now I am thinking of myself. I'm thinking of my own happiness." He paused again, his lips pressing together for a moment, as if he'd suddenly realized something extra, something even he hadn't expected before he'd begun.

"Orli, before we go off doing, well, what I have a feeling we're going to do, before we spend more time seeing to the happiness of everyone else in the galaxy, I want this for me. I want you. I need you. So, will you marry me?"

Pink Luria sparkled in the tears that filled her eyes, her bosom swelling and her whole body animated by the sudden flare of inner radiance. "Of course I will marry you. Of course! Of course!" She nearly leapt with glee, bouncing joyously on the balls of her feet, every cell that made her charged instantly with so much energy. "I've been waiting forever, hoping you would ask. I've waited and waited." She pulled him to his feet, stared up into his gleaming green eyes, glistening with joy as hers were, and poured forth all the love in her heart, all the gratitude, the wonder, the admiration, even the fear that somehow he'd been lost to her more than once over the last two and a half years. She sent it all forth, let it gush into him in the moments of that precious gaze. "I love you so much. Yes, of course, I will marry you."

They kissed, and for a long time after, they held each other, savoring the warmth and rapture of the moment. They did so for so long that eventually Taot came awake, scenting the pheromones blowing heavily upon the breeze that blew into his lair. He recognized them immediately and filled Altin's mind with ravenously carnal images as he had so often done before, an unabashed appreciation and visualization of what he knew to be the natural eventuality. Normally such vivid physicality embarrassed Altin into blotchy shades of red that blushed from cheek to jaw. But this time, Altin did not fend the images off at all. He welcomed them, sent them back to the dragon, reflected intact, in agreement with Taot's assessment and with what sufficed as a nod between them. He let the dragon know that he had in fact finally chosen himself a mate and that he was happy. With that news imparted, he then forcefully, if affectionately, shoved the dragon out of his head. With the dragon's lustful thoughts gone, Altin was left with just his own.

He and Orli remained pressed together for a long time afterward, perhaps two hours or more, though time had no measure for them in that moment so sublime. Orli just leaned against him and listened to his heart, savoring the purest happiness she could remember in all her life as she stared out into the stars beyond his embrace. It was funny how long she'd been waiting for him to ask her, how long she'd known he would, expected and anticipated, and yet, somehow he'd managed to surprise her too. She was so happy it nearly hurt. They both were.

They might have remained there for another two hours to come had not a thought struck her about what he'd said while he'd proposed. It struck her like a shot. She tipped away from him a little and looked into his beautiful, amazing face. "Hey," she said. "You said that there was something you had a feeling we are going to do, about us seeing to the happiness of everyone else in the galaxy. Does that mean what I think it means? That you'll help me get Yellow Fire back for her?"

He smiled. "Yes," he said. "For her. And for you. Anything for you."

Chapter 53

Her Majesty was outraged when she got the news that her Galactic Mage intended to be married on another world. "Impossible," she proclaimed, looking as if she might hurl her scepter at any moment across the open spaces of the throne room. "I forbid it! It must be here. There is no other possibility."

This of course, opened up a huge argument about propriety and the customs of the land, which were at the heart of the decision for the couple to be married somewhere else. Altin and Orli simply would not wait two years, and there were no such "archaic restrictions" on planet Earth. They even suggested that Her Majesty might take this opportunity to set such tradition aside, but that was equally unthinkable. The scandal that would arise should Her Majesty sanction such a hastily arranged marriage would undermine the respect not only of the monarchy, which existed almost entirely for the preservation of social structures—of which two-year engagements were but a small part—but of the social structures themselves. It was rather a long and uncomfortable lecture they had to listen to, and it may or may not have been true, but true or not, neither Altin nor Orli cared. They simply refused to wait any longer than a month at most. They insisted that it was so, and they would absolutely not be moved. "Not by any force known on any world that we have found." Those were Altin's very words.

Which, of course, put her Majesty in a precarious place. She could hardly imprison them for insolence, though she threatened them with it twice in the course of making her arguments. But what other options did she have? "I shall have you both in jail," she shouted at them at one point, "and you as well." This last was directed at Orli's father, apparently on account of his having sired her. "And you'll be lucky if it's not the headsman's axe for the lot. Such is the crime of theft in these lands, and you are stealing this opportunity from me and from my people. Your wedding is bigger than just the two of you, you know."

Fortunately for everyone, she relented on that, and eventually agreed to a compromise, a solution that came from the tactical mind of Colonel Pewter, who did nothing but wish his daughter happiness. His solution: they were to be married on a fleet ship to avoid controversy on Kurr. It could be done in orbit above Prosperion, so as not to be very far from her kingdom, but upon the deck of a ship, making it the territory of planet Earth, a place free from the laws and customs of Kurr. The reception, of course, would be at the Palace. As would be the rehearsal dinner the night before.

It was eventually agreed, and it was on that first grand occasion that they were all given quite a surprise. Director Bahri had just given a fine speech to a rousing round of applause, when there came the *thud-thudding* of the herald's staff echoing into the dining hall from the vicinity of its wide double doors. This sounded at the same time a messenger came sprinting along the shadowy edges of the room and around the back of the dais upon which the planetary rulers and the bridal party sat. Tiptoeing up behind Her Majesty, the man whispered into her ear just as the herald's announcement rang out for all to hear.

"Seawind of the White Meadow, Speaker of the High Seat and emissary of String," called the herald. He looked frightened as he spoke the words, his face gone pale and the normal solidity of his voice hollowed by the incredulity that had gone to work inside of him.

Standing beside him was a lean figure, an elf, whose gaunt face was dominated by eyes green as seaweed and with hair to match. His skin was green as well, though pale, almost gray, and he wore a suit of scale mail armor that looked like a cascade of pressed birch leaves, though it made no rustle when he moved.

A hush fell across the room, total awe in every face but the Queen's and those of the fleet officers for whom the magnitude of the event, of this arrival, was lost.

The elf glanced briefly around the room, then bowed, a supple movement like the bending of a willow switch. He looked to Her Majesty for permission to approach.

She stood, remarkable in itself, and motioned him forward with her hand. "Approach, Seawind, and call me friend."

The elf walked, nearly gliding, between the tables and came to stand before Her Majesty. "I call you friend in the name of the High Seat and the people you call elves."

"I call you friend in the name of Kurr and the people you call *dra'hana'akai*."

"Then friends we remain."

"Friends we remain," the Queen repeated. She looked to her left, where the marchioness sat. The barest movement of her head indicated that the marchioness should give up her seat immediately. In that rare moment, the angular face of the woman did not so much as blanch. She rose and made to move the earl down a chair. The ripple of rank would have the guildmaster diviner without a seat had the elf called

Seawind allowed it to go on.

"I haven't time to share in your repast," he said. "For I have much to do to prepare. I come only to petition your permission to remain in your lands for the span of two days."

"And to what extreme movement of fate do we owe the surprise and timing of this visit, friend Seawind?"

He looked from her to where Altin and Orli sat at Her Majesty's right hand. "Tidalwrath's banishment nears its end. He will retake his place in the heavens and once more reign upon the seas."

The Queen smiled patiently and nodded. The rickety old Grand Maul had been on about that when they dragged his feeble form out from under the rubble of his temple seven days after the war was won. "Yes," she said. "The priests of Anvilwrath have mentioned that to me."

"Then you know he will avenge the death of his brother."

She managed to hide the impatience that would have sounded in a sigh behind a broad smile, forcing it into the first wind of laughter instead.

"Friend Seawind, I'm sure you know that I am not as inclined to prophesies as many others are. And even if I were, the priests of Mercy have promised me that the sea god holds us no ill will. So while I appreciate your taking the time to let us know, in truth, I've had about all the religious conversations I care to have for at least the next hundred years. Besides, this is a wedding party we're having. Sir Altin and this lovely child of Earth are to be married on the morrow. This is a time of celebration. Let us put off the dire forecasts for at least today."

He bowed, a short thing. "As you require. I ask again only for two days' liberty in your lands."

"And what will you do in those two days, friend Seawind?"

"I come for the bodyguard. It is time for the exchange, as

the treaty requires."

The Queen's brow wrinkled at that, and she followed Seawind's gaze to where it settled beyond her chair, to where she knew the royal assassin to be standing guard, invisible as always during events like these.

"It is that time too?" she asked. She looked more than a little irritated at having not been notified of such a thing in advance. The look she shot her Guildmaster Diviner was a dire one. "Who knew these were such eventful times?"

"They are," confirmed the elf.

"Then you have chosen one of us as the new protector?"

"Yes. We believe the *dra'hana'akai* assassin has been revealed."

"Who is it?"

"I will come for her tomorrow when it is certain."

"Well, that's frightfully vague, friend Seawind. We've many wizards and many warriors, you know. Perhaps you can tell me a little more, that I might make sure *she* is ready for you when you come." She emphasized the gender, glad for at least that much insight, as she pried for more details.

"Tomorrow the last sign will appear and the time will be right. Then we will go."

"Oh, how hasty you elves are for such long-lived people," she said, laughing it off in her most monarchial way. "But, yes, of course. Two days as you like. But not another word of this sort tonight. And please, do consider joining us as we celebrate the coming nuptials."

He bowed again. "I must beg your leave, friend Karroll. I have much to do."

One corner of her mouth twitched, but she forced the other side to join it, and pushed the two together into a smile. "Very well. Off with you then. My people will supply you with anything you should need." She sent a glance like an arrowshot to the messenger still standing open-mouthed behind her chair. His silent bow proved that he would see her orders were obeyed.

Seawind inclined his head and backed out of the room as was proper in this place. When the door closed behind his departure, near pandemonium broke out inside. Most of the Prosperions present looked as if they'd just seen a ghost, and the rest of them looked as if they might be ill. The air filled with the noise of so much speculation and murmuring.

Orli turned to Altin asking the question that was on the faces of nearly every officer and official from planet Earth. "What was that all about?"

"I only barely know," was his unsatisfying reply. "Tytamon would have been the one to ask. He was the only one alive when that agreement was made. The rest is in the notes and scribbling of the ancients, who likely had to guess at the particulars of the treaty themselves."

"You mean it isn't written down somewhere?"

"No. It was an agreement signed in blood by the reigning kings of Kurr and the High Seat of String. The parchment was burned as part of the binding ritual."

"Oh," she said. "Well, even still, that's very exciting. Look at us; we're to be married at the height of some ancient prophecy. And here people used to say I was boring."

"No, you're still boring," said Roberto, Orli's man of honor, as he leaned around from his place at Orli's right hand. He'd been listening all along. "But I have to tell you, you've gotten a lot more interesting over the last few days."

They both laughed, though Altin couldn't quite muster the merriment to join in. He knew enough of the elves to be well sobered by the appearance of Seawind. Such an arrival had not happened in well over two hundred years. His expression grew stony as he tried to recall the details of that distant happening.

Orli saw it, saw the absent look as he contemplated it, and she elbowed him soundly in the ribs. "Hey, none of that serious crap on the eve of my wedding, you hear me? Unless there's some shit storm going to hit right now and ruin everything, something immediate and horrible that I need to know about, I want nothing but smiles, happiness and fun. I mean it!"

He looked at her, his eyebrows raised, while Roberto laughed. "Welcome to the rest of your life, pal," said Roberto with a signature sideways smirk. "She's only going to get worse over time, I can tell you that. Although I guess the upside of life here on Prosperion will be that she can actually get a broom that flies."

Orli's eyes narrowed, and she shot her friend a scathing look, though one with more than a hint of laughter in it too. But she turned right back and resumed the main thrust of the point she was trying to make with her soon-to-be husband. "I'm serious. Your people seem to have this stuff going on all the time. It's one weird prophetic event after another around here, so if we don't need to sweat this one right now, let's not. No serious faces. I want us all to be happy, even if just for two damn days."

Altin grinned at her exuberance even as he agreed with what she'd said. He thought about the endless stacks of prophesies that had wrapped themselves around the history of Kurr. Some had wrapped themselves around Altin and Orli too. Those were the ones that could be wrapped. Because they could be made to fit. All the others were discarded. And there were heaps and heaps of them. All forgotten now. Tossed onto the burn pile of things nobody thinks about after "the one true" prophecy comes along. At least for a while. Then that one unravels too, unmaking itself in time as history pokes holes in it in the same way the winds rearrange cloud shapes or a rising sun changes the figures one imagines can be seen in peeling paint above a bed. When that happens, all prophesies have the chance for life again.

He supposed that an occurrence like the collision of

several worlds and the peoples, the beings, that occupied them was more than enough to stir things up for a while, more than enough to give all the priests and oracles a thousand visions to find in their tea leaves and the patterns of thrown bones. He supposed in a way it would have been more surprising if an elf *hadn't* shown up than it was that one had. Had this whole galactic tempest of the last two years gone on without their notice, that should have seemed strange indeed. So he smiled, and shook his head. "No," he said at least. "Nothing terrible is coming. At least not that I know of. And if the elf knows of anything, his request suggests we've got at least two days, so I think in that you are in luck."

"Good. Then you're in luck too. So eat up. You're going to need your strength tomorrow night." Her grin was wicked as her eyes narrowed with the pleasant threat.

He grinned and made a show of cramming a whole dinner roll into his mouth.

Chapter 54

Orli stood before the full-length mirror in her room at Calico Castle. Altin had taken the time to clear out a floor of Calico Castle's tall central tower for her to claim as her own. He'd been reluctant to do so for himself, saying it still didn't seem right, but she convinced him that the time had come, and soon, they would share the topmost floor together, with this one beneath to serve as hers alone. It was furnished in much the style of the great ladies of Prosperion, but with Kettle's help and some from grumbling Pernie, Orli had made it more like something she could consider home, a perfect blend of opulence and practicality.

There was not, however, the least practical thing about her wedding gown, and even now, less than an hour before the wedding ceremony was to begin, the royal dressmaker, Perfuvius Needlesprig III, was still making tucks and touches, and generally preening at the gown like a nervous artist before his first gallery show.

"Every illusionist on Kurr will be getting this," he said. "They'll be showing this in courts and courtyards everywhere. I think that the whole of the continent shall see a full day's loss of productivity. Many are already calling for the occasion to be made a permanent holiday."

Orli simply beamed as she looked into the mirror, watching him working with his deft hands, his fingers moving over the surfaces of her gown like a pianist's over white ivory keys. She could see Kettle standing behind, the woman's ruddy face blotchier than usual for all the fits of laughter and tears, the moods upon her so vast and undulating Orli hardly knew what to do. And Pernie sat back there too, her little face glum and brooding, bored most likely by the monotony of the whole event, but surely also put out by having been shooed away by Perfuvius, who had twice made reference to her "grubby little hands" and how they must not be staining Orli's pristine gown.

It was a happy time, and Orli checked the timer ticking down on her tablet, which she'd leaned up against the mirror on a dressing table near the wall, unwilling to trust her reading of the large enchanted hourglass sitting beside it. What if she read that thing wrong? What if the magic didn't work somehow, and she was late? What if a million other things. So to reduce that one bit of stress, she'd brought the tablet and set it up, just in case. Between the two chronometers, she had a strange pairing of alien timekeeping to keep her calm. Which wasn't really working anyway.

Perfuvius tugged down on her skirts and settled them with a swipe of his hand, then he turned her away from the mirror and looked her up and down directly with his practiced eyes.

"Your face is the face of Mercy herself," he said, "and your skin is as flawless as new-fallen snow. Sir Altin should count himself lucky if he doesn't swoon and fall right out of the ship before he can say 'I do.'"

Orli smiled. "Thank you, Master Needlesprig. You are very sweet."

He turned to his small audience and presented her to

them: "Is she not the most beautiful creature to ever set foot upon Prosperion?"

Kettle clapped and cried and tilted her head from side to side, her cheeks aching from smiling for so long. Pernie, still seated on the bed, made a face and poked at Orli's regular clothes, the plain trousers and the blouse she'd been wearing earlier in the day.

"What's the matter child?" asked the royal dressmaker to that face. "Do you not recognize genius when you see it? This gown is a cloud brought down from the heavens for our sweet Orli to ride upon."

Pernie muttered something awkward under her breath, but Perfuvius had already moved on, his capacity for paying attention to a child long past. He glanced over at the hourglass, unable to make any sense from the time ticking down in alien numbers on the tablet nearby.

"Oh my, we've got to get your shoes." He spun to face Kettle. "The shoes, woman! Where have you put the shoes?"

"I had 'em brung upstairs, all the boxes in ta' the master's suite," she said. "I'll run and fetch 'em now."

"Be quick about it," he snapped. "We dare not be late."

"Oh, they won't be startin' a thing without this sweet girl," said Kettle to that. "But I'll get 'em quick all the same." She hoisted her skirts well over her stout ankles and nearly sprinted up the stairs.

Master Perfuvius glared at the hourglass as if it were speaking the most horrible profanities. He gasped aloud a few times, then flipped an exasperated expression at Orli when five more seconds passed and still Kettle had not returned. "What can she possibly be doing up there all this time?" he gasped. He called loudly toward the stairs up which Kettle had run only moments before. "Woman, the shoes, I say. Where are the wedding shoes?"

In answer, Kettle's voice came down that same narrow

passage anxiously. "Which ones?" she shouted. "Which ones? I canna carry 'em all! Ya sent a spider's worth!" She seemed all aflutter, as if making a selection incorrectly might jeopardize the universe, and leaving a pair behind akin to neglect of the most heinous kind.

"By the gods," huffed Perfuvius. "Must I do everything!" He stormed off after her, insisting, "They're marked, woman, they're marked. We eliminated the others yesterday."

Orli watched him go, her own smile nearly as wide and permanent as Kettle's had been since before the sun was up. This truly was the happiest day of her life. She looked at herself again in the mirror. The dress fit so perfectly, it set her figure off to all its best effects in every conceivable way. Her hair, like it had been at the ball that seemed so long ago now, was once again a gleaming pile of white gold upon her head, glittering combs and supporting enchantments holding everything in place. Altin would be surprised indeed. No more tomboy in hunting pants, at least not tonight.

Her eyes went absently to where her regular clothes lay as she had the thought, and she saw Pernie still wearing a pout as she absently prodded at them.

"What's the matter, Pernie?" she asked, turning and going to sit beside the child on the bed. "You look like something's bothering you."

"It's not," Pernie said, though it came too flat and too rapidly to be believed.

"Well, you don't seem very happy. Aren't you happy for us?"

"No." That came out abruptly, and then Pernie turned away. She scooted off the bed and moved across the room to Orli's new great chest, where she began to flip its heavy brass latches up and down, making as much noise as possible with them and clearly intent on blocking out anything Orli might have to say.

"Why not?" Orli pressed anyway. "You know I love Altin very much. And he loves me. We're going to be together forever and live here all the time." Orli went to her again, moving around her so she could face her again. She crouched down so she could look Pernie directly in the eyes. "That means you and I can be friends forever now too. You can teach me all sorts of new things about Prosperion, just like you helped me learn the language all through the summer last year. Doesn't that sound like fun?"

"No," Pernie said. She flipped open the chest and looked inside, hiding her face from Orli's earnest eyes. She made a point of pulling out bits of clothing, tossing them aside and wrecking all the careful folds.

"Pernie," Orli said then. "Please, tell me what's wrong. You can be honest with me. That's what friends do."

Pernie stared reverently down into the chest, never looking up at Orli squatting beside her there. Something about her aspect had changed. "So what are you gonna do with this?" she asked.

Orli looked into the great chest, following the child's gaze to where her blaster lay. Her pale brow furrowed beneath the majestic coiffeur Perfuvius had made. "Nothing if I can help it," she said. She watched Pernie staring at the weapon and shook her head some. "Is that what this is all about? My gun?"

Pernie looked at her then and smiled. "You won't need it anymore," she said. "Not with Sir Altin to keep you safe. You could give it to me. Then we could be friends."

Orli was still frowning. "I don't think that would be a very good idea. How about when you get older? Then we can see about getting you one. Roberto can show you how to use it so you don't hurt anyone."

"He's already showed me how," she said.

"Well, still, I don't think you need to have a weapon like that just now. It's pretty dangerous for a little girl."

Pernie made a face at that. "No it's not. Master Altin said I can keep Master Spadebreaker's pick and it can cut through anything. Roberto said this can't cut through lots of stuff."

Orli heard Perfuvius and Kettle at the top of the stairs. She stood and shook her head. "No," she said. "Not until you are older. But you can have it when you turn eighteen, how's that?"

"Miss Pewter," called the master dressmaker, sounding as if he were finally coming back down the stairs. "Let's hurry now. It's almost time to go."

Orli turned toward his voice as Pernie pulled the weapon out of the chest. Orli heard the click of the safety and spun back in time to see Pernie glaring up at her with the darkest look in her narrowed eyes. And then the child fired, point-blank at Orli's heart.

Chapter 55

A slender hand pushed the blaster away, green-fleshed and barely a blur, appearing just in time to direct the weapon down and away from Orli's tender bosom. The bright red line of the laser vanished through the gauzy skirts of her wedding gown instead, passing through them so closely that she could feel the heat against her thigh. She'd barely gasped, barely had time to realize what Pernie had done, and then it was over. The shot was fired and Seawind was standing there with his hand still on the gun.

Pernie blinked up at him, bewildered by his arrival, but her first instinct was to pull the gun away. She yanked at it with all her strength, several long tugs, her jaw set and her expression indicating that she was intent on having another shot. Though, perhaps not, for the child had nothing to say.

The elf caught the girl's gaze in his own when at length she stopped pulling at the gun, and for a time the two of them simply stared into one another's eyes, Pernie's blue ones as fearless and studious as were his forest greens.

Shadesbreath appeared beside her as this went on, manifesting silently at her right hand like a wraith from the grave. "Let go," he said as he gripped her wrist gently in his gray-green hand. He could have opened her fingers with the press of his fingers there. She swung her gaze around to see who it was, her eyes flung wide upon recognizing him. He glanced at the weapon, a negligible movement of his head, then looked up to his elven companion with a nod. He repeated the soft command. "Let go."

She opened her hand mechanically, and watched the gun rise as Seawind lifted it away. Seawind nodded to Shadesbreath. "It is done."

"It is," the royal assassin confirmed.

"I will take her."

"I will tell the Queen and fetch the pet."

Seawind and Pernie vanished as Kettle and the royal dressmaker came into the room. Kettle saw them go and began to scream. "Pernie! Pernie!" she cried as she rushed forward into the empty space, but it was already far too late. She stared blankly at where the girl had been, her eyes wide, her mouth wider. But there was nothing she could do. She spun on the assassin standing there instead. "What's that monster done with mah baby girl?" She squared up to the leather-clad figure and looked as if she might grab him by the throat. "Where is that wee child gone, ya filthy murderer? Ya got no right ta take her, so ya can go right now an' get her back. I'm givin' ya three seconds an' then yer gonna get it good. And don't think ya won't neither, 'cause I done fer worse than the likes a' you."

Shadesbreath looked into the florid face of Kettle whose whole body was swelling up like a fighting rooster, and whose eyes looked as if they might begin to steam. His own eyes narrowed, as if he were thinking, as if he had to search for the right words to say. Apparently he found them, for he simply replied, "I understand separation will grieve you. But it is as it must be." With that he vanished, leaving Kettle to gape into the air before her as she sputtered and spewed, repeating his parting words over and over again.

"It must be? It *must* be?"

Orli could only stare with her, still stunned by having nearly being shot and just as wide-eyed and stupefied as Kettle was.

Perfuvius Needlesprig III glanced back and forth between them for a moment, but all he could think to say was, "By the gods, Miss Pewter, what have you done to my dress!"

The End

For more information about the author, his
other novels and his works in progress, please visit
DaultonBooks.com.

If you would like to be notified when
new releases are made available, sign up for the
Daulton Books newsletter.

Made in the USA
Charleston, SC
14 June 2013